Seven Aprils

ByEileen Charbonneau

LSI Print 978-0-2286-0651-2

http://bwlpublishing.ca

Dedication

To my sister: anotherTess, from another time, who also leads with her courage

Book 1

April 1860

Chapter One

Ashokan-on-Hudson Township, New York

Tess stood in the icy waters of the creek. She lifted her skirts higher, enjoying the feel of the breeze on her legs. The dawn light dappling through the maples' leaves was just enough to warm her face as she looked skyward. She lived for these quiet moments of her "spring airing", as her father called it when he was in a good mood and brought out his fancy talk. "Laban, Andrew! The birds have graced our skies with their return. Little sister is looking wan! Clean your rifles, my progeny, fruit of my loins! I believe her spring airing excursion into the wilderness is in order!"

What he meant is that they were low on meat. And she was due for her "airing" because she was the best shot.

Their mother had died before the birds' return five years before, when Tess was just budding into her womanhood. The month of April had been hard on her ever since. But that was heart sickness, without a cure that Tess could divine. Her father's fancy talk had won him her ma's hand, but it did not keep her alive.

Suddenly, an unearthly scream, like a tortured woman's, came from beyond the dense thicket and the stone wall, the lands of the Ashokan widow. She knew that scream, she had heard it around their cabin all her life. Old Pitch. Something big went down, something bigger than Old Pitch, its vibrations scattering the birds from the maples, the birches. The scream again. And the scent of first blood.

Tess thought of going back to the campsite to fetch Laban and Andrew, but her heart's pounding said there was no time for anything except grabbing her rifle from the bank of the creek.

She threaded her way through the low brush. The bluestone wall demarcation of the widow's lands faced her. But it was cattle-low here and easy to scale, once Tess had kilted up her skirts and tied them around her waist.

It was a different world beyond the low stone wall. More of a garden, set up to look like the wild woods, but with paths carved through. And flowers, not struggling through the scrub and skunk cabbage, but planted, lining the paths. Tracks of the cat dug deep in the earth, then disappeared. Old Pitch had taken to the trees.

Tess rounded the first bend. There, under the limb of an old oak, a fallen horse still protected his rider, wedged there in the curve of the animal's gracefully rounded withers. Both man and horse panted, wild-eyed.

Prowling silently before them was the biggest panther Tess had ever seen. Old Pitch. All her life her father and brothers had tried to frighten her with stories of the cat that carried off wild pigs, fawns and naughty little girls. But her mother told her he was God's creature, not the Devil's, the last of his kind, and the screams were his way of pining for his hunted-out kin.

So much glistening black in the dawn light—the cat's pelt, the horse's glistening mane, the man's hair and boots. Old Pitch had attacked once already, bringing them down, clawing through the man's face, the horse's neck, both gleaming with blood. Once the panther sprang again, it would be too late for her to get a clear shot, Tess thought.

Old Pitch stopped his pacing. He crouched down. Tess stood, raised her Springfield to her shoulder, hoping the wind was going the right way and he didn't pick up on her scent. The cat's hind quarters shifted while he pressed his paws into the ground. Then, those powerful back legs propelled him through the air.

Tess exhaled, fired.

The panther went down, claws extended. A gasp came from the man. The horse went into action, pounding Old Pitch with its head. The panther opened his mouth, but only a wheeze of his unearthly scream came out before his body finally stilled.

Wary of the horse's powerful head, Tess approached, grabbed hold of the skin behind the cat's neck with both hands, and dragged the heavy body back.

Returning, even scented with her kill, the horse allowed her to kneel close, as if he knew only she could help his master now. Fresh red stains seeped through the man's light colored breeches, joining those at his shoulder and face. Yes, the panther had had one more swipe at him.

Long fingers unclenched, reached out. "My hand," the downed rider said.

The eye that was not closed over with a bloody gash was as green as the budding oak leaves above them. Maude the tinker woman would have called his a changeling's eyes, they were that wondrous strange. He looked younger than her brothers, but maybe only seemed so because his face was clean-shaven.

She took his offered hand. It was strong, but without calluses.

"Now. Your foot, please," the calm voice continued. "Place it in the pit of my arm."

She put her bare foot there.

"Now pull. Hard."

She pulled. His yell was almost as short as the pop of his arm.

"Perfect," he said evenly, though he was blinking his brow's sweat and blood from his one seeing eye. "Thank you."

He rose to his knees, hovering over his animal. "Easy, Moutamin," he crooned, as if the horse was a sick child.

The horse's nose sniffed at his waistcoat. The man gave out a hollow, sad laugh. "Here then, you great baby," he said, his hand groping until he found cubes of maple sugar candy. He felt along the blasts made by his horse's pained snorts. The horse's tongue received the sugar candy like a tame dog.

The man kept stroking his horse's beautiful curved neck, as he found his saddlebag, finally pulling out a pistol.

Of course, Tess realized. It was the only way. There was no hope for the animal, who began to thrash. The man's hand shook now, the movement going up the weapon's barrel, making it flash silver in the dappled sunlight.

"Best keep talking. I'll do it," Tess offered.

He shook his head. His good eye blinked twice, chasing the rivulets of blood down his cheek. She thought he was going to refuse. But he released the firearm.

"Most kind of you," he whispered.

"Well. He's a right fine horse."

"Yes."

As Tess warmed the pistol's muzzle in her skirts, the horse rooted again at the man's coat. "None remains," Moutamin's master said, patting that fine curved neck. "But the sap's running again," he continued brightly, "It is late this year. Soon you'll have new grass and maple sugar to your heart's content. Soon."

He looked away. Tess jammed the barrel in the horse's ear, and fired.

It was a powerful firearm, and kicked back. The horse jumped, shuddered, then stilled. Tess wished she'd worn her apron. She would have covered the head with it. But why spare him? Blamed ignorant the man was, not to sense the panther traveling through the woods, to ride straight into Old Pitch's ambush. Let him cover the blasted head himself, with his tight woven gentleman's coat. Now two fine animals were dead and this no-sense man was—

A strangled sound interrupted her thoughts.

Tess had seen the sheen of tears locked in her brothers' eyes when they'd buried Mama, but she had never before seen a man's face soaked wet with them.

"Thank you," he whispered gruffly.

He rose to his feet, touching his hand to his brow. Then his knees buckled and he slid back to the ground, as motionless as the panther.

Tess felt fear grip her insides. She knelt, loosened his scarf, which was the rich color of currents. Her fingers combed the hair back off his forehead, careful to avoid the bleeding gash, which had missed the eye, but sliced through his brow. Wet hair. Cold, damp forehead. Like her mother's, when Tess couldn't think of anything else to do for her. She didn't know how to help him now, either. She rocked back on her heels, wiping her mouth with the back of her hand, fighting her fear, her instinct to flee back over the wall.

He covered her work roughened hand with his fine-boned one.

"Are you still here?"

"I'm here."

"I could barely see you before. I suppose the other eye is swollen over now, is it?"

"Yes. That's all. That's all it is."

"I am deeply in your debt, Diana," he whispered.

"My name ain't Diana."

"Of course it is. Wild Diana of the woods."

He grinned full now, like he was drunk.

In the distance, men's voices called out. "Ryder!" and "Where the devil are you?"

Tess slipped her hand out from under his. "You be all right, hear?"

She left him, dragging the panther's weight behind the chokecherry bush, and watched.

Two men found Ryder. They were dressed like him, like rich men, with high hats.

"What in the name of God happened here, man?" one of them demanded as they raised him to his elbows. "Oh, Ryder, your poor horse."

"Where did she go?" she heard him whisper.

"She? Who?"

One helped him to stand. The other laughed, though he looked around nervously.

"What, another mistress? One with claws instead of a jealous husband this time? Oh, my friend, will you never learn how deadly the women are?"

Ryder tried to shove them away, but the bigger one tackled, then put him over his shoulder. As they walked, his companion slapped their friend's face.

"Ryder! Don't you faint dead away on us now! We're not going to explain this to your poor mother, that is your obligation!"

Both kept talking as they strode, their bright ribbons of language sailing above the carnage, making light of it all. How far did they have to go, Tess wondered as they disappeared beyond the hemlock branches. Did they know what to do for him?

She heard footfalls coming from the other direction. Her brothers approached. Andrew had her boots tied over his shoulder. Laban whacked the side of her head.

"Didn't we tell you stay out of the widow's game land?" he demanded.

Tess steadied her stance. "My kill. No gentleman without the sense to track it proper is going to steal this animal from me!"

They backed away. "Damnation," they both said at once, eying her bloody skirts.

"Come away," Andrew urged.

"I need to skin the cat."

Laban looked to the wall. "Not here," he warned.

* * *

At their campsite, Tess worked her knife quickly as Laban and Andrew threw their belongings together, muttering.

"Damned girl."

"Woman. Old enough to bring ruination on us all. Old enough to hang. Dangerous woman."

"How we going to explain—"

"We're not explaining! Not to Pa, not to anybody. Who else is going to patch us up after scrapes? Remedy us? She may be a murderess, but she's good at the keeping of us. And she's kin."

Hard at her task, Tess almost smiled. Her brothers were afraid, she realized. Because of the blood and her powder-burned hand. Did they think she had shot the man, not the horse? Well, she probably could, if one provoked her bad enough.

But not that man.

Chapter Two

Mr. Strong the storekeeper sat in the cabin's front yard, in their best chair, a rolled up chapter of *David Copperfield* in one fist, a crockery cup of burnt coffee in the other, looking displeased. Her father barreled through the doorway.

"Ah, in good time. The angel of our abode has arrived," he called out, "returned after her excursion!"

Their father was in high-handed deal making voice. She was glad that she'd stashed the panther's pelt high in the beech tree. Tess glanced behind her. As usual when Strong came visiting, she was abandoned by her brothers. She grabbed the folds of her skirt.

"Not expecting a guest." she said. I'll clean up."

Inside the cabin, Tess stepped out of the stained brown serge dress and into her best green merino before donning her full apron. She surveyed the damage her father had done to the place in her absence. From outside, the sound of the shopkeeper's complaints kept her company as she scrubbed down the trestle table in the main room.

"There's a pretty greeting—grunts like a wild Indian, and bloodied like she's been taking scalps!"

"The boys must have had some luck hunting and persuaded her to butcher the deer, is all," her father claimed. "Now, how many educated women would be at your bidding after a hunt?"

"She'll scare away my customers. Tall as a man. Never smiles. How am I to know she's got a tooth in her mouth at all? I'm wasting my time and money!"

Tess heard her father's calculated pause, before a manufactured tenderness went into his dickering. "Ah, never mind, then. She is a jewel with whom I cannot part."

"And I'll not part with my best cook stove and four pigs besides, no matter how fast she does sums and can cipher!"

"Now, now, let's not let hunger despoil our judgments," her father soothed. "Allow the girl to wallop you up your best breakfast since the last Mrs. Strong." His voice rose "You hear?" he shouted back into the cabin. "Eggs and a big slab of ham!"

"I hear," Tess called back, reaching for the skillet.

What was her father bargaining for? Expecting her to walk the eight miles to Mr. Strong's crossroads store to work his account book? How often? Was that to be the cost of the storekeeper's stingy gifts of the cut-away chapters of *David Copperfield*? She was to be hired out in return for a book, a stove and four pigs? Where were her brothers? Did they know about this? Of course they did. That's why they'd treated her decent on her 'spring airing' this year, why they'd abandoned her. And why they weren't clamoring to be fed now.

Tess sighed hard as she worked. She did not like that man Strong, or the way he looked at her. His store smelled of rats' leavings. She remembered hiding in her mother's skirts, when she was 5 or 6 years old, as he branded a servant in the face with a hot iron. The shopkeeper could keep his presents. She didn't care what happened after David Copperfield's silly wife and baby died on him.

Tess loaded the plates before she called them to table, then tried to slip out behind her father. But he took a firm hold on her apron's waistband.

"Won't you join this sumptuous repast, dear daughter?"

"Ain't fit," she murmured, refusing to join him in the higher form of speech they both knew from Mama and her books. She wiped her smudged chin with the back of her hand.

"Another asset, Mr. Strong—attention to personal grooming as well as restoring our dwelling to tidy beyond reproach, as you can see!"

He'd soon have her scrubbing down Strong's store daily in their bargain, Tess thought. Her father reached up and yanked the calico kerchief from her head. Her waist-length braid tumbled over her shoulder. "There," he proclaimed. "Now tell me if that's not a glorious harbinger of womanly treasures?"

Silence among them, then. Tess felt her senses ignite, wary.

Mr. Strong returned to plowing through her fried potatoes.

Her father kept his hold on her apron's tie. "Well?" he demanded.

Slowly, their guest's gaze followed her rope of hair to where her apron strained against her breasts.

"Send her over for a week's worth of meals before I decide," he proposed.

Her father pushed her out of the storekeeper's reach. "And who will take her then? No. Wedded, all legal, then bedded. I ain't budging on that."

Tess felt a pounding at her temples. "Wedded?"

Her father avoided looking at her. "Well, what do you think his presents and my hard bargaining were about, girl? Don't you know courting?"

Something in her expression made both old men roar with laughter. A heavy, cruel sound. Tess felt her legs ache for wanting to run. But she refilled their plates, ignoring the section of Mr. Dickens's book that the shopkeeper placed within her reach.

* * *

After they'd eaten, a card game began between her father and the shopkeeper. That was enough to bring her brothers out of hiding.

"Missed a good hunt out Bullet Hole Road way, boys," Strong informed them. "Bounty would compare favorably to a few scrawny pelts you might have had your sister skin."

"What bounty, Mr. Strong?" Laban asked.

"Soul catching, boys! Our grand and glorious civic duty!"

"Aw, our ma would never allow us to—" Andrew began.

"You ruled by women? Even dead ones?"

"Promises, Mr. Strong," her father said quietly. "Promises made as their mother lay dying."

"Before they reached their majority, then! Don't you know you're men now Laban, Andrew? And you like the sport of a hunt, don't you?"

"Yes, sir."

"We do, sir."

"Well, you don't know the thrill that's to be got when you have hunted with a most irritated Southern squire looking to haul pickaninnies back to the plantation! Could have used your skills, out there, boys. This batch slipped through the Big Woods, I'm thinking. Maybe headed up the Hudson under steam power, being served ices and sugar candy by the damned Republicans. All no thanks to you two!"

"Now don't blame my boys for what abolitionists have wrought!"

"And why should I not? There are even rumors about your neck of the woods, being linked to the Waterford's farm. On a trail. And they're damned Quakers."

"What are you saying, sir?"

"Only that the Fugitive Slave Act is in force. Allowing, nay obligating us to assist in the apprehension of stolen property of our Southern brethren, despite recent goings-on in Washington! Those damned troublemakers like Asa and sister Sarah Waterford would have all black runaways invade our northland to take our work and marry our women!"

"Well, we cannot have that, of course," her father obliged.

"Not when you have got a perfectly good offer to keep your own girl close and also have the honor of becoming the next Mrs. Strong, eh?"

"A new cook stove? Not one all made of salvaged parts?"

"And we can bag up our gritty linens and send them over?" Laban entered the return of bride price negotiations. Her brothers were looking to be rid of her too, then. Not as a live-out servant, but for life. Through the waves of her own panic, Tess silently wished the latest escaped slave folks Godspeed. She left a full bottle of whiskey in the men's easy reach. Then she slipped out the back scullery door.

* * *

Tess climbed into the beech tree. She found her treasure safe, hanging from a stout branch in its homespun sack. She held it and leaned back on the strong limb. Maybe she'd spent too much time in her books and in the wild, not enough among people. She should have known what both old men were up to. Where was her sense?

Tess brought the panther's pelt out of the linsey-woolsey bag. She'd skinned it early enough, before it had time to set up and smell of death. She felt its musk wildness seep in through her skin, rush her blood faster. Value. It had value, though she knew it belonged to the owner of the land beyond the wall. The widow's land, the widow's panther. Not hers. Her mother had taught her better than to steal. Tess resolved to make it good, to pay back the widow, some day, somehow.

12

Now, did she have the sand to use that pelt to disobey her father—breaking one commandment to fund breaking another?

Well, she was a law breaker already, every time she lit the blue lamp for fugitives traveling through the Big Woods. Maybe what she was now contemplating was following a higher law, as her mother and their talks with Quaker neighbors Asa and Sarah used to ponder out together. She loved those quiet times with her mother and the Waterfords, mostly listening and eating Sarah's corn cakes.

Tess promised God to think harder on her transgressions later. For now, she needed to be calm and crafty and vigilant, like the panther was before it sprang.

*　*　*

Tess climbed down from her refuge and walked back home, carrying the heavy pelt. Inside the cabin her father and brothers were all snoring deeply. So was the storekeeper, still in their most comfortable chair. They'd found the whiskey just fine, and emptied the bottle of it. Tess quietly rolled her mama's books and a tin of matches within the panther skin, put on her long deerskin coat, and headed out.

She was beyond the barn when she thought of her mother's blue signal lamp she and the Quakers had agreed upon. What if her father or one of her brothers found its hiding spot? What if they left it out in the night, and a fugitive trusted them? A northward-bound wanderer might think her homestead safe. She had to get it out of there. Even if it meant doubling back.

Tess turned, risked running, though it made more noise. Balancing the heavy pelt on her shoulder was a trial that threw her natural gait off balance. So did her thoughts. It wouldn't be stealing, Tess told herself. The blue lamp belonged to Mama, who'd brought it into the marriage from her homeland in Connecticut, a place of learned scholars, a place that Pa talked about to impress others.

Well, the lamp now needed passing in a female to female line, like Mama's love of stories and her usefulness with the mending and the medicine plants. It belonged to Tess. It was due her.

She slowed as she approached the barn. No need. It was quiet. She slipped in the milk house door.

There it was, hidden behind the slop bucket, in its own framed wedge of the wall. Tess set down the pelt. She lit the lamp carefully, keeping the flame low. It would get her through the densest of the forest on this moonless night. It would guide her to the cattle drivers' road.

She turned. The smell reached her first. Sour. Pork fat. Whiskey.

"And where are you going all bundled so tight, Miss?"

Mr. Strong leaned his arm across the opened doorway, blocking her way into the night, the stars. The storekeeper's shirt was unbuttoned, and his braces dangled loose, hitting the side of his leg, impatient.

Chapter Three

Tess forced her voice low, and calm. "I seek a stray pig sir, as I heard the grunting."

"How have you never seen fit to grant me a smile?" he asked, coming closer.

"If you'll let me pass—"

"Not without another look at the goods." He pushed her back against the barn wall, holding her at the jaw, exposing her neck. The blue lantern swung in her tightened grip. His large square hand yanked her braid from its careful winding about her head, then he forced her mouth open. He did this to other women, Tess realized suddenly. His wives, his servants, his caught slave women.

The sourness of his breath intensified as he smiled slowly. "Good teeth. Young, full of health. You'll flash those teeth for the customers, display just enough of that hair to loosen their purses." His powerful hands shifted to her breasts. "And you'll push these up high with a good pull of corset strings when you're mine."

Maintaining his hold, he pinched her nipples hard, causing shooting pains that clouded her sight. Tess bit her lip to keep from crying out, as she felt his hardness rise between her skirts.

"It's me you heard, Miss, not any pig grunting. You got more shine than your mother's pretty hair, no matter how hidden out he keeps you in these woods. I'll wager you can even talk proper, with the right inducement. There's 'won't' not 'can't' in your eyes on that. Such as you will take on airs with a fancy wedding, unless we start like this."

Tess's heart hammered hard, but her voice surprised her in its calmness. "You'd best release me sir, for I have no wish to harm you."

He let out a blast of laughter. "Harm me is it, you silly cunt?"

Tess stabbed her knee into his groin. When he cried out, stumbling backward, she whacked him hard with her mother's lantern. Its blue glass broke, splashing paraffin oil on his shirt before the flame ignited.

He screamed, waving his arms, making it worse.

Tess grabbed his braces as the flames caught his beard. She hauled him to the pig's trough and dunked him once. Again. He kept screaming.

A light lit the window of her brothers' sleeping loft. Tess stumbled backward, then turned and ran.

She heard the shopkeeper's screams all the way down the mountain trail to the drover's road.

* * *

Tess headed the way the fugitive slaves went, following the North Star into the misting night. Stay low to the ground, she thought at the mist, don't blot out the stars. Her tears were already doing that. She smelled her own burnt flesh, but preferred it to the stink of the shopkeeper's hands, mouth, beard.

Stop crying. Look for the star. She knew its name, Polaris, from Mama, who Pa once loved for her good manners and book-learned education and speech. So Andrew told her, though Tess had only memories of Mama hiding her lessons and her books, along with her acts of kindness to the runaways. And her father had once beaten her mother bloody for using her educated speech as she spoke with the fiddler at the Harvest Frolic. That was just before the winter that killed her. Tess chided herself. *Stop thinking about such things, just keep tramping.*

16

She heard hoof beats and tinkling wagon bells and hoped the darkness hid her long enough to disappear among the standing pine along the drover's road. But she lost hope when the reins pulled the wagon to a stop. Next she heard the cock of the muzzle-loaded gun.

"Stand where ye be, stinkin' night crawler, for yer within me sights!"

Tess felt the burden of her pack weight nailing her deeper in the mossy ground.

"There, then. It's wisdom rules ye. Now turn with all slowness, shape shifter."

As Tess followed the voice's instructions, she was rewarded by the wide grin that split Maude O'Neil's weathered face in half.

"Glory be to God, is it Lucy Monroe's sapling wandering the road in the dead of the night?"

"It is, Ma'am, and not meaning any mischief, if you'd think to lower your fine gun and pass me by."

The woman cocked her head. "And miss a story in its very brewin'?" She snorted. "Not likely. Come aboard, young one."

* * *

Tess didn't realize how hungry she was until she smelled the tinker woman's stew on the boil.

"You must dip this brown bread in it, lass, on which I'm placing the last of Mrs. Dykeman's butter. I bartered a fine handkerchief for it. It's good I know that lady's preference for the wee blue flowers woven on me handkerchiefs, aye? Being she churns the best butter in the valley and can get hard currency for it."

Tess loved Maude O'Neil's dancing talk, but now felt in awe when it was directed towards her alone. She ate, there at the camp they'd set up in a part of the woods where

Tess had never been. She tried to hide the tender burns in her palms. She tried to remember the manners of taking small bites and smiling between them when with company. Soon, she was comfortable enough to notice that the tinker woman's lack of a full set of teeth did not hinder the way she enjoyed her meal.

"So, then, darlin' girl. You had enough of those brutes with whom ye live. You be striking out on yer own at last."

"At last?"

"Oh, have I not eyed ye, since yer mam passed, bowing under the burdens the menfolk have made upon ye? She's a shy one, but bright-minded, Lucy's youngest is, I'm thinking, and will have enough of their good-for-nothing laziness by and by."

"Some have it worse."

"And others are dead, my girl, swiped from God's earth by a drunkard who did not know his own whiskey-soaked strength."

Was it true what some said about Maud O'Neil? That she could see folk's thoughts? Tess ventured a direct look into the woman's light eyes, but saw only kind attention before Maude spoke again.

"So, now. I've had the grand pleasure of providing ye transport from the Big Woods."

Tess looked around the campsite. "We're clear of the Big Woods, Ma'am?"

"We are. And now will you tell me what induced ye to strike out on your own?"

She should protect Maude O'Neil, who'd been so kind to her, Tess thought. She reached for her pack, wincing at the pain it caused in her hand. "I'd best go, Ma'am, and should not have stayed so long."

"Go? Why?"

Tess felt nailed to the woman's direct look. "They'll be after me, as I did some harm to Mr. Strong."

"The shopkeeper Strong?"

"Yes. The lamp broke. I didn't mean for it, I was only trying to keep him away from me, you see."

"Yer mam's blue lamp lit him up?"

"That one, yes."

"Dead?"

"Not when I left him, but—"

"Herself looking after you, praise be to Brigid and all the saints. Hands!" Maude demanded.

Tess held them out, turning palms up.

"Ach, not too bad, but some blistering. Ye tried to put the old reprobate out."

"I did put him out, though I had to dunk him twice."

They began laughing together then, until the tears came, unbidden.

"Talk, girl," the tinker woman demanded.

"It must be sinful to laugh over what I did."

"You did? What was it he did, in the dark, in the dead of night?"

"He thinks to marry, and wanted his husband rights beforehand. I was trying to get away from him, you see?"

"And that's a right thing. A holy thing, my lamb."

Maude O'Neil patted her cheek. "I'll put on a tea to boil whilst I dress those hands with what's left of the butter."

Tess wiped her eyes with the back of her wrists. "Ma'am, they'll be after me."

"Not tonight. But yer right. Strong, he'll be seeking his revenge, that one. Ye be in want of means and a plan, my girl."

"A plan?"

"A renegade female has almost as little chance as the runaway slaves. Folks would feel obligated to return ye to yer father and brothers. And those would be the upstanding ones. Others would do much worse to a Big Woods girl out on her own. No, ye'll be needing to disappear as Lucy Monroe's youngest and become what I took ye for, I'm thinking."

"What did you take me for, Ma'am?"

"A shapeshifter, laddio."

* * *

Maude O'Neil's deceased husband's wedding finery was a gift, the tinker woman insisted as she spun Tess around.

"There now. How do the bands underneath feel?"

"Strange."

"No more strange than a lady's corset. Did ye never try on your mam's?"

"I did. It made me stand taller, which Pa didn't like, so he sold it away."

Maude snorted. "He would. Well, let the bands do the same, and ye'll appear a barrel-chested young man, as was my Hugh in his well-worn, but respectable suit of clothes. Now I will let out these swallow-tail seams to bring it more up-to-the-times fashionable."

Tess stood still as Maude worked her quick stitches. And listened.

"Keep yer story as close to yer own as possible, for you be yer own treasured brother of yerself now—a quiet, respectful kind of man, who would show kindness even to the likes of me," Maude advised. "Keep straight in the back always, my lad. Fill out where yer padded with your good strong bones, and walk like you owned God's earth and all her creatures. That's how the men walk it, poor blighted creatures that they be."

Last to go in the transformation was her braid. Her hair. The only part of Tess that she knew was beautiful. But its mix of browns, its lustrous brightness had helped get her into this fix, so she was well rid of it, she told herself when tears threatened. Maude cut it carefully, tying off each end with ribbons.

"Keep it safe," the tinker woman advised. "It will fetch a decent price at the wigmaker if ye are down to yer last pennies. And look at it now and then, remembering who it belongs to, yer dear sister Tess, who is in hiding, and safe."

Tess traded her mother's copy of *Robinson Crusoe* for Maude's best carpetbag as they worked out the last details of her new identity: a patched-together scholar looking to make his way in the world after a fire from which he'd salvaged only the panther skin and his books.

* * *

They climbed back into Maude's wagon and continued to travel north, with the river. Tess's first test came inside a rough tavern in the town of Clermont, where she stood spitless among grizzled tradesmen, unable to even try out her man's voice at first. How had she thought she could follow Maude's instructions, expectations?

"Come now, young squire!" the tavern keeper demanded. "What have you got to trade?"

Tess opened the carpetbag and drew forth the panther's skin. All hooting, even the slurping of cider and beer silenced.

"Looks still ready to spring, that one does."

"Who bagged it?"

"I did," Tess told the truth and watched their eyes change.

"Our scholar hunts down dangerous prey! A round of drinks on the house in your honor, sir! Why, that's as fine a pelt as ever I saw. Would you take ten in script for it?"

A patron with a yellow vest stepped forward. "He's trying to cheat you, young man. "I'll offer twenty-five in hard currency."

Another whose neckwear glistened like a red jewel in the fire's light stood. "Exactly what I have been seeking for the front hall of my patron's country house— a little wildness to offset the French Chateau grace. I believe I can do better by our brave hunter."

21

Her silence seemed to signify hesitation, Tess supposed later, for a bidding war resounded off the tavern walls. The panther skin finally fetched her one hundred and twelve dollars, more money than she'd ever seen in her life.

"There, then. There's yer start, my man," Maude approved, welcoming her back to her wagon. "Now, to the dockside. Let the mighty Hudson open up yer world of possibility."

* * *

Tess found her new name when a sloop man shouted "Boy! You got enough muscle to help us load these bales?"

"I expect I do," she tried her voice and swagger together as she jumped down from Maude's wagon.

The man fell back and pulled his hat off his head.

"Oh, I beg your pardon, young sir. I thought you were of the rough and tumble kind, as you were riding with the tinker woman."

Sir? How did she become a squire in the tavern, a sir here? Behind her, Maude snorted. "Think ye to be the only one can fetch a traveling companion of the finer sort? Mr. Boyde thought you were calling him by name, is what! And the young scholar's republican enough to help ye get yer bales under sail. Why not offer him a stop or two of his scenic river excursion in return?"

Tess looked down at the first bale waiting on the dock. It was addressed to Mrs. Cole of Ashokan. The widow.

The sloop man noticed her hesitation. "That's fresh from the free-labor cotton mill," he announced. "If you're willing to heft it right to the widow lady's door, Mr. Boyde, I'll do better than free passage. I'll share with you her delivery fee. You look a sight better than the rabble dock rats I'd have to trust at the Ashokan pier."

Ashokan. The Widow Cole. The sloop was traveling south. Back down south, with the tide.

Tess looked up at the tinker woman's wagon. "The blessings of God, his mother and all the saints be on ye,

22

Mr. Thomas Boyde." Maud completed Tess' baptism as a man.

* * *

The widow's spread was high on a bluff overlooking both the town and the river. So near and yet so far from the Big Woods to the east. All of its structures, large and small, reminded Tess of ancient edifices in Mama's book about the Greeks and Romans and the fine things they made and did. Had she always wanted to be seeing such structures as in that book, Tess wondered. Is that why she didn't even have enough good sense to be afraid?

At the top of the terrace, she set down the package, removed her hat and wiped her forehead with her sleeve. A tall iron fence surrounded the property, made down below in the foundry, no doubt. A small boy looked down at her from the porch of the gatehouse, where he was juggling brightly colored balls of wool.

"Morning!" he called out. "Watch this!"

He closed his eyes tightly then tossed the spheres of colorful yarn up over his shoulder. One eye peeked at her. "Did they all land in the basket?" he asked.

Tess replaced her hat and grinned. "All but one. Amazing."

"That's me, the Amazing Jeff Lovell, at your service, sir!" he said, bowing before he climbed down the porch steps.

"I'm Tom Boyde, with a delivery for Mrs. Cole."

Once he'd lifted the latch and opened the gate, the little boy looked her up and down, stopping his gaze at her hands.

"You hurt?"

"Burns. Almost healed."

"Where's your cart?"

"No cart."

"You carried that package? All the way up here? With burned hands?"

"It's not so heavy."

"Or you're very strong!"

She smiled. "Your own strength will come with the years."

He cocked his head. "That's what Dr. Cole says."

"Dr. Cole?"

"Ryder Cole, the widow's son. Mama says we have to call him doctor, being he is a surgeon and physician both now, lately back from schooling in France. You're not from around here, are you?"

"No."

"That's why you're not laughing."

"Why would I laugh?"

"Some folks do. They think there's not much to Ryder Cole. That even his own mother won't trust the foundry to him. He's abed. Restless there, and short with me sometimes. Mama says I must forgive him, because he misses his horse. Brought down by a panther, imagine! Come on, then, Mr. Boyde."

Tess followed the small boy. "Is he badly hurt?" she ventured.

"'He'll get better if he behaves himself,' is what my mama says. She's housekeeper of Belle Haven, my mama."

They walked a graceful path lined with sycamore that led to a three-story structure painted a golden yellow and gleaming with the tallest windows Tess had ever seen. She kept pace, trying not to stare, as the boy continued his story of the day she knew well.

"Dr. Cole, he says a woman helped him, that she shot dead both panther and horse, which was a mercy, as his horse was beyond repair. Diana he calls that woman, after that Roman goddess who lived in the wild. You know that one, sir?"

"I've heard tell," Tess said, remembering her mother's stories of the old time Greeks and Romans. So that's what he was about.

"Now Dr. Cole's friends," the boy continued, "the one who brought him home, they said he'll be seeing mermaids swimming up the river next. Mrs. Cole, she sent those friends packing soon enough. She says they're too wild for him in his recovery. Soft steps here, sir, we're under his windows," Jeff warned, tossing his curly head toward the second story. "That's the way. You walk real quiet Mr. Boyde, even burdened. Now, you can make your delivery to my mother, round the side. Here we are then, scullery door, where… oh, pardon, Ma'am," he said quickly, noticing a figure standing between linens blowing in the spring breeze.

Tess instinctively straightened at the sight of the beautiful woman dressed in jewel-toned green and wrapped in a shawl of many swirling colors.

The woman laughed in a way that sounded like sleigh bells. "Keeping good guard at the gate as usual, Mr. Lovell?" she asked.

"As usual, Mrs. Cole. And here's Mr. Boyde with a delivery from the river."

The splendid woman assessed the package quickly. "On washday, perfect! Perhaps the new shirts might be pummeled to a softness that keeps my precious bane down in his bed a while longer! Ask your mother for a mug of cider to refresh Mr. Boyde."

"May I fetch the refreshment to you as well, Ma'am?"

"If you promise not to balance it on your nose, young sir!"

She laughed again, putting a puzzling ache in Tess's heart. This was the Widow Cole. Not ancient. Not shrouded in black, but as vibrant as this new spring.

With the boy disappearing inside the house, that wide smile was for Tess alone. Tom, she reminded herself, trying to make the bandaged heels of her hand disappear inside her coat sleeves. The lady was merely finding an awkward young male amusing.

"You are a well-dressed deliveryman, Mr. Boyde."

"Only a sloop passenger, happy to be of service, Mrs. Cole."

"A passenger with Ashokan as your destination? How fortunate for us."

"I am hoping there might be a use for me here," Tess spoke the thought as she had it. It was followed quickly by a second, silent thought—that she deserved to be locked away in a madhouse.

Chapter Four

The Widow of Ashokan placed her emptied cider mug on the tray between them. "Are you a reading man, Mr. Boyde?"

"I am, Ma'am. Not the learning sort. For pleasure only."

"Exactly the kind I am seeking! My recovering son will take as his only sustenance medical and scientific treatises. Now, those of that description cause his already considerable ill-humor to deepen towards unbearable, as he is not nearly well enough to begin his practice at his dispensary. Perhaps you might guide me on something to offer him of a more imaginative nature?"

"Well. I do have a book here, Mrs. Cole," Tess said, reaching into one of the many pockets of her refashioned coat, "a story that takes me clean out of myself every time I read it." She hesitated only a moment before offering the lady one of her mother's books.

The widow took it with care.

"Mr. Poe? The poet who died so tragically? *The Murders in the Rue Morgue*," she pronounced the title, frowning slightly. "I'm afraid this might be a little macabre."

"Oh, but it's a wonderful figuring of how the deed was done, Ma'am!"

"And I see it has been treasured for many years, sir. Forgive me my hasty assessment."

Tess returned the woman's smile. She'd feel better about the high price the panther pelt had drawn if this woman took one of her favorite books.

Tess wondered if her time sipping cider with the Widow of Ashokan gave her the courage to rent a room at the boarding house on Chestnut Street, where she told the landlady she was from Connecticut, which she was, through her mother. Then she tried mightily to get used to being served meals along with the other boarders, without jumping up to serve and to clear dishes.

Around the table, talk was not of a burned shopkeeper out in the Big Woods, but centered on the towns prosperity, the foundry's new orders from Washington City, extra business for the bookbinder and the carriage maker. There were rumors of war with the southern states. She listened with wonder at the polite way political arguments ran, with even a raised voice meriting an apology to the ladies.

On her third morning as a townsperson, Tess spied the sign posted inside the window of Ashokan's Main Street bookbinder, Ezra Krebs, stating a need for an accounts keeper. She walked on to the riverside, finding a deserted bend near the Catholic church to practice throwing her shoulders back and her hand out before she lost her nerve.

"So pleased to make your acquaintance, Mr. Krebs." No. What had Maude reminded her of about men? They were direct with each other. That was too many words. Leave the "so" off. "Pleased to make your acquaintance," she repeated over and over.

She thrust her hands into her pockets, but kept the phrase going as she circled blocks of tightly spaced factory workers' lodgings, clustered near their church. Then she returned to the main street, launched into the shop, and knocked her leg into the corner of the proprietor's desk with a too loud, "How do?"

Only his bemused expression kept her from bolting. "I do fine, young sir, most mornings. Might I be of assistance?"

"T-Tom Boyde," she stammered. "That's my name, Mr. Krebs…you are Mr. Krebs?"

"The very same. Pleased to make your acquaintance, Mr. Boyde."

She breathed out her frustration. "I'd hoped for the job, the one on the sign, sir."

Mr. Krebs's spectacles slipped to edge of his nose as he looked down at her hands.

"Would they not take you at the foundry, Mr. Boyde?"

"The foundry? I did not go there, as I have never worked with metal, sir."

"Off the farm, are you?"

"That's so," she admitted.

"I like hard-working farm boys, but I already employ a couple of them, out back at the presses."

"I can do sums, Mr. Krebs. And I have a clear hand." Those were the attributes her father seemed keen to sell her off for. Did they have no value here?

"Your education, sir?"

"Education?"

"How many years of schooling have you?"

"Oh, my whole life, until my mother died. She was well-versed."

"No formal schooling at all?"

"No, sir."

"Perhaps you might help a craftsman with latches and the like, at the foundry," he suggested now, "if they think you too slight a fellow for the heavier work."

He was dismissing her. Kindly, but without so much as a trial. "Will you not give me a chance to fill your needs, Mr. Krebs?"

"Well." The careworn man smiled for the first time as he took up a small parcel from the shelf behind him. "Suppose you transfer and check the sums on this shipment of inks with my order in the account book."

She returned his smile. "Gladly."

Was he beginning to see her differently, or was he only amused? Tess took her place at the desk with its inkwell. To her relief, the proprietor was summoned to the room behind the bookbinder's public space, so that she could concentrate on her task and take in the finely bound volumes around her. She had never seen so many books all in one space.

Just as she'd uncovered a mistake, the bell above the door sounded. Tess carefully wiped the pen before lifting her head. The Widow of Ashokan came forward, in a hat graced by both feathers and a little knot of jet ribbons, her wide smile one of recognition.

"Why, Mr. Boyde, how fortunate! I was just making inquiries as to your whereabouts."

"Mine, Mrs. Cole?" Tess barely breathed out.

"Yes. To return your treasured volume and inquire about more recommendations. Ah, Mr. Krebs," she greeted the returning proprietor with a gloved hand that held the window's sign, "how very discerning of you to engage our new resident! I was about to suggest that you seek our learned Thomas out."

"Our—? But, my dear lady—"

"You were overcharged by fourteen cents on this shipment, Mr. Krebs," Tess offered, "which I will note both on the invoice and in your account book, if that will suit, sir."

* * *

With her placement at the bookbinder, Tess became a true town person, she figured. The town of Ashokan was enjoying a shared prosperity that did not extend to the Big Woods. The Widow Cole even funded a free school for the foundry workers' children, in a fine brick building, close enough that the children could join their fathers for dinner out of the packed pails that both brought to the hills. But the foundry cast a pall of smoke about Ashokan too, night and day. From the Big Woods the glowing buildings looked grand, like a fairy kingdom lost in the mists. But Tess had trouble keeping her room free of the black soot that clung to the windowsill, and sometimes her eyes stung and her throat felt raw as she was doing accounts.

The two pressmen working behind the shop soon took her into their easy company. David Flanders and Joe Hartness were from neighboring farms south of Ashokan, sending most of their wages home.

As the season changed Tess found, to her astonishment, that while she was never considered a beautiful woman, as a man, eyes lingered on her with appreciation. Town girls invited her to family dinners and dances over the harvest and winter months. She was further grateful to her lanky, bashful shop mates then. She provided introductions in order to get the sharp-eyed females off her scent. She never had cause to regret the introductions, for Davy and Joe were well-raised boys, kind and respectful to the ladies. They began to replace Laban and Andrew in her heart.

* * *

Tess was minding the front office while Mr. Krebs was downriver in New York City on that raw day in February. She heard an anguished scream from the back room.

"Tom!" Davy cried out after it. "We need you!"

She saw the ink streak across her vest front as the pen skittered to the floorboards.

Beyond the pocket doors that separated the shop from the pressroom, it took a moment for her to register what she was seeing: Joe's arm, caught in the platen machine. Cold, hard metal at the end of his wrist, where his hand should be. His face was a mask of agony. Davy stood beside him, eyes darting about the shop.

"A lever, need a lever," Tess spoke her thought.

"Broomstick?"

"No. Metal. The poker. At the fireplace," she directed. She looked at Joe, who nodded, his face so taut in its suffering.

Together, she and Davy wedged it into the small space between the plates, then put all their weight on the end. It was not enough. They tried again. Again. Joe groaned. *Do not panic*, she told her accelerating heart. *Think.*

"More help," she said.

"I'll go," Davy offered, bolting for the door.

"I felt it budge," Joe gasped out. "One more man should do it, Tom. Wish I could oblige." He bit down on his lip hard. She saw the veins in his neck.

Tess felt tears forming. "Yes, you're the strongest of us."

She came closer, began stroking his hair through her fingers. A woman's gesture, she knew even as she did it. But it eased the suffering in Joe's eyes, so she didn't care.

"I'm glad for your company, Tom," he said.

Davy returned with the man Tess had successfully avoided since she'd come to Ashokan. Dr. Ryder Cole.

"I hear you require some assistance, Mr. Hartness," he said as he manned the space beside her. As they went to work, she saw him in snatches—a flash of his deep red waistcoat, the clench of his jaw as they leaned on the makeshift lever together. With a metallic groan, the plate finally lifted.

Tess swallowed hard at what she saw. The crushed hand's fingers bent at splayed angles. Two had split open and looked like meat in a butcher shop. A hacking noise came from Davy before he backed away and bolted out the rear door toward the outhouse.

"Might you support your companion's arm?" Ryder Cole's hand both showed her how and blocked Joe's own sightline to his injury.

"What's wrong with Davy?" Joe asked.

"He will return," Dr. Cole answered, opening a box of gauzy material and working a quick, tight swaddling around the injured hand. "There. Now, sir, do you think you can walk to my dispensary?"

"Sure," Joe answered. Before his second step his knees gave way. "I guess not," he amended.

"Quite all right. I am sure we can manage you."

Tess linked her hands with Ryder Cole's, supporting her friend between them.

The doctor's voice continued its serious but affable tone as they headed across the street.

Doctor Cole's dispensary was not full of the fearful looking things Tess imagined were in such places. It was like a well-furnished parlor with many cabinets.

The doctor convinced Joe to take a little whiskey and lie across a high-set armless sofa. He showed Tess where to find clean cloths and a bottle of lavender water. Then the doctor gently placed the injured arm in a flat wooden trench with straps and went to work.

Each time Joe yelled, the doctor apologized, and counted aloud the bones left to treat.

"Are you ready to resume, Mr. Hartness?" he asked, and waited for Joe's nod of?

assent. Then he went back to work.

Tess soothed Joe's brow with a lavender-scented cloth. Finally, after the work was completed on the last bone, the doctor sent Tess into one of the cabinets where she found a stack of neatly folded blankets. She covered Joe with one, as Dr. Cole brought his tools and the bloodied trencher to a dry sink.

Joe's eyes began to droop, then close. Tess felt the doctor's touch at her shoulder.

"Mr. Boyde, is it not? Tom?"

She turned. Those sparked green eyes. The gloss of his dense black hair. She darted glances at his shoulder, his hands. "Yes, sir."

"At long last we meet. My mother speaks highly of you, even though you resisted all her invitations to visit us at Christmas."

Tess searched for the door. "Will Joe be all right again? Will he get the use of his hand back, do you think, sir?"

"That is hard to say. There were multiple fractures of the metacarpus and phalanges, one compound."

"Compound?"

"The bone that broke through the skin of the third phalange—finger. That's a compound fracture. I was able to set them all, thanks to your care and your friend's tolerant nature. The press missed his thumb, which is fortunate, too. Much will be up to him."

"How is that, sir?"

"If he can be as patient in his recovery as he was with that weight on him, if he can count on your continued care, I would say his chances are good."

Tess looked straight at him for the first time. The still red, panther-made scar over his right eye bent the brow downward. She saw kindness. Interest, too. And no recognition. "What should I do, doctor?"

He smiled. "Exactly as you have been doing. Helping him to stay calm, still, hopeful in his recovery. You have a tranquil manner, and a strong stomach. Those are important components of a gift for healing, I think. Are you wedded to the scent of books fresh off the press, Mr. Boyde? Have you ever considered medical service?"

Tess felt her cheeks burning with embarrassment. Was she wrong about the kindness? Was he mocking her?

"I am not educated, sir."

He frowned. "Now, on that point, my mother disagrees heartily, ever since she enlisted your assistance in expanding my own horizons. Remember? When you recommended Mr. Poe's mysterious murders? A subversive choice to pull me away from my studies and experiments. Which worked. That man Poe had a mind like a steel trap enclosing that fevered imagination."

"You enjoyed the stories, then?"

"Very much. And the other diversionary tales my mother has acquired for me by way of your recommendation. But perhaps I will not have a chance at interesting you in our newly forming association without enlisting your fellow workmates as well."

"What association is that, sir?

"Our town's Republican club. You are a Republican, I trust? For Lincoln and the preservation of the Union? Come now, Tom, we are in trying times and must all take a stand. For our country and against the great stain of slavery."

"Well, yes, I suppose I am a … republican."

He frowned. "There is no 'supposing', Tom! As the foundry workers will be exempt from military service, we are mustering up a militia among the other of our town's young men. A patching up militia, to be ready, should hostilities come and our union is threatened. Our first meeting is Wednesday. Oh, are you and your comrades musical at all? Play an instrument?"

"Why, no, sir."

The whimsical look the scar gave him intensified. "No matter! I am sure such things can be taught, and the confounded instruments can be made tuneful."

"Sir, I don't understand what music has to do with healing."

"Oh, did I not say that part? Well, the great powers that be in Washington have not provided for the wounded, and only grudgingly stated that the army's musicians might be stretcher bearers and attend the wounded. So I have devised that our unit will be skilled in medicine first, and music second. Now, where is your missing musketeer?"

Tess walked to one of the room's front windows and spotted Davy. "He's out on the porch, sir."

"Good. The two of you can settle your friend in his own bed. And tell him I will visit him tomorrow. Oh, if he'll have me, of course. Now, I am overdue for dinner,

which my mother will have served over my skull if she
finds me here."

She'd done it, Tess realized, watching him stride past
his medical dispensary. Fooled the only person in Ashokan
who had seen her as a woman. Even impressed him, though
she wasn't sure how. Was being a man who treated hurting
folks the way Tess Barton did naturally make her worthy of
his interest? She only had her sense and feeling for those
suffering. And something else: a burning curiosity about
how to fix a bone thrusting out of skin.

Book 2

April 1861

Chapter Five

On the Hudson River Railroad

Tess's heart raced as she tried mightily to conceal the fact that this was her first train ride. The shoreline of the Hudson River sped by, out there, in the dark. She could see its waves reflected off the moon's glow, and in the lights cast by the sloops and occasional steamships. The arched car with its wide windows and swinging overhead lantern was not like being on a wagon, even on the smoothest dirt of a corduroy road. They were clicking and clacking along iron rails, at breakneck speed, and it was like being rocked in a giant cradle. She wished she had her pen and paper handy, she would write it all down in a letter to her sister self.

"Aw, help me out here, will you, Tom?" Joe pleaded. "Button's loose, it's too dark in here, and my hand's still sore. We got to be presentable for the ladies of New York town. Listen, I'll trade you six peanuts and half a carrot for your services, how would that be?"

Tess frowned. "That'd be as grand as a tour of the continent. Give it over."

Her friend and now fellow soldier laid his uniform's blue kersey overcoat in her arms. As she adjusted her stitches to the rhythm of the train, Davy nudged her shoulder.

"Your sister as smart-mouthed as you?"

"Every bit."

"Huh. Your bad influence is the why of it."

Joe's voice turned sly. "Wish she'd come to bid you good-bye. Rather her be sewing my buttons."

Tess felt sudden, overwhelming sadness. "So would I."

She missed being that sister whom she was leaving so far behind. How did she ever think she could do this, even in the company of her new friends?

"Sorry, Tom," Joe said. "Don't mean disrespect toward the lady."

"I know." She hoped they would drop the subject.

"Tom?"

She pricked her finger. "What now?"

"Your sister—she mad about you signing up?"

Who should she ask that question to? The coiled braid in the secret pocket over her heart? "I'm not sure."

"It's only just for the ninety days, President Lincoln says. Only to keep the capital city safe from them hot heads from South Carolina."

"Three cars back—the Massachusetts boys are calling us Minute Men," Davy added. "on account of us joining up with them—just like in the Revolution!"

"Write to her about that, Tom," Joe advised. "Wouldn't want to miss out on our chance at glory, before the politicians start their compromising again."

"I'll do that."

"She can't be as peeved as the doc's ma. She plum cut him off, Davy heard."

"Private Flanders listens to town gossip with half his ears and all his imagination. My mother is merely distressed by the haste of our call-up."

"Begging your pardon, Doc—Captain Cole," Joe Hartness apologized.

Dr. Cole, tinged with cigar smoke from the parlor car where he was lounging with the other officers, stood by their seat. "Your sister is distressed, Tom?" he asked gently, the way he always talked to her.

"Yes, sir," she whispered.

"What is her name?"

"Tess. Theresa, sir."

"Your elder or younger?"

"My twin. She came into the world before me. Elder. Elder twin."

"Ah. Twins. A strong, unique bond. Would you like me to compose a letter to her, explaining the circumstances by which—"

"No, sir. But I thank you for the offer."

"Well. I hope she will come around to the idea."

"I do too, sir."

"Good. Now, to sleep. Save your night vision for guard duty, not preening yourselves for the cheering ladies on the streets of New York."

He enjoyed ordering them about in these small ways, Tess realized, as he made his way back to the officers' car. But he was not a seasoned army man. He did not lord his wealth or education over them, either. And he did not pay much attention to the separation that was supposed to exist between officers and enlisted soldiers. He was a puzzle to her.

Tess felt Joe's slowed breathing, then his head eased onto her shoulder. After a snort, it shot back upright.

"Oh, sorry, Tom."

It's all right."

"Truly?"

"Sure. You can use my shoulder 'till I embroider you a pillow, brave soldier,'" she imitated Sarah Prentice's wiles as she had bid bade them goodbye at the station.

Davy guffawed.

"*Awww!* Miss Prentice likes Tom best, they all do!" Joe insisted, whacking her shoulder before he burrowed in, yawning.

* * *

Camp Brewster, north of Washington, D.C.

Tess climbed the small hill where Ryder Cole and his guest were surveying the camp. The sea of hospital tents spread out over rolling swamp and pastureland. Tess wished they'd left more trees over the campground. She smelled rain in the air. Would it flood? The bearded man in the brown suit was about forty and might have been lame, as he was leaning on a wooden cane. But his eyes brimmed with intelligence. Tess hoped he was another doctor, come to ease their workload.

"This is Private Boyde, sir. Tom, Mr. Frederick Law Olmsted is the Executive Secretary of the Sanitary Commission. He asked to meet you."

"Me, sir?" she breathed, her fear igniting.

Ryder smiled. "Yes, as you are an individual largely responsible for his high opinion of the condition of our camp."

"You mean the other camps are worse off?" Tess asked, her astonishment overcoming her pleasure hearing her captain's praise.

Mr. Olmsted nodded. "Son, I'm concluding a ten-day inspection. Seventy regiments, crippled with scurvy and dysentery." He looked to Captain Cole. "Sixty-nine regiments, I should say, sir. This one seems to have learned the lessons of the war in the Crimea."

"Mine were second-hand lessons," Ryder said.

"Of course. You are too young to have experienced those horrors. But you were a good student of your French doctors who went through that conflict, Captain."

"Our latrine pits and garbage burial are only a part of our relative health, sir."

"Oh?"

"Once they found out that Tom here could make their rations palatable, our company began eating together. The other companies discovered cooks of their own and followed suit. I believe that achieved camaraderie as well as better health for our entire regiment."

Tess thought her fellow soldiers would perish for want of knowing how to boil water before she'd risked revealing her knowledge of open-fire cooking. But she was glad of the result. Ryder was right, eating together had achieved more unity than their company music sessions afforded.

They must have been the most tone deaf band in the Army of the Potomac, as they lacked the knowing of how to carry a tune in a bucket. But Ryder was right. Musicians were the ones detailed as stretcher carriers, and so theirs were as close as the army got to a medical battery. Their doctor captain was busy training them in care of the wounded, not marching tunes.

"Once appetites returned," Ryder continued, explaining to the inspector, "our Tom went hunting up beards and hair, so we got rid of outbreaks of lice, too."

Olmsted laughed, stroking his long brown beard protectively, as if she'd hack into him with her scissors next.

His sharp eyes scrutinized her face closer. Many had before, of course. But not for this long. Once a man accepted another man, Tess found that his gift was not to look too closely again. It was the opposite gift from the one they bestowed on women who interested them. None before Mr. Olmsted had this much cunning she thought, as he continued to scrutinize her form and features. Tess began to feel warm.

"I understand you volunteered along with your captain, Private Boyde."

"That's true, sir."

He turned those sharp eyes to Ryder Cole. "Were you present at this man's swearing in, Captain?"

"I was beside him, Mr. Olmsted."

"And did you check the contents of his shoes after he swore he was "over eighteen years of age?"

So. Tess breathed easier. Olmstead's concern was with her youth, not her sex. Many boys had stuffed a paper in their boot scrawled with the number eighteen, so that they would not be lying when they swore they were "over eighteen."

"How long have you known this lad?" Olmstead asked Ryder sternly.

Her captain crossed his arms. "Tom Boyde is a worthy citizen of my home town, sir, a fellow member of our Republican Club, and a great favorite of my own mother. I would not think to doubt his word."

Tess stared at Ryder Cole. He turned his head just far enough out of Fredrick Olmsted's sightline to give her a slow, private wink.

"I beg your pardon. You are quite right to be piqued, sir," Mr. Olmsted said. "It's only that such awful days are coming, I fear, with trials that beardless boys should not have to endure." He shook his head. "Well, it is not I who should be questioning your judgment, gentlemen. I, who need all the help in my own endeavors that I can muster."

"Help, Mr. Olmsted?" Tess asked. "How can we help a government official?"

"The Sanitary Commission is a civilian organization, private, treading very lightly upon the Surgeon General's pleasure. I invite you, Doctor Cole, and your sensible assistant into the city—to express the means of your successful encampment, and explain the dangers and shortcomings. We need you to talk with our representatives. Battle is coming. We will not be ready to handle casualties. But at least the government men can be forewarned, and the Sanitary Commission thereby gain future credibility."

"Will the two of us talking in this way to the lawmakers help our soldiers, sir?" Tess asked.

Mr. Olmstead's eyes softened. "Well, stranger things have happened in Washington, Private Boyde."

* * *

"Mr. Olmsted called me your assistant," Tess said quietly as she poured steaming water into the dry sink in the medical tent.

Ryder handed her the instrument he'd used to poke under the bandage of Private Blake's axe injury. The spring breeze blew through the open tent, larger than the ones they slept in, and set on a raised portion of the camp grounds. Their present patients were suffering from accidents, dysentery, and typhoid fever. Tess liked the way Dr. Cole's eyes were always checking them, their breathing and comfort, even when he was engaged in another task or speaking with her.

"I have recommended you for a raise in rank, Tom. Use the tongs, not your fingers. There, just so. Now, I don't want you taking your new rank and moving on. I need you here, in our very unmusical Company D, enhancing my reputation. So I raised your medical standing as well."

She laid out the cloth to receive his cleaned tools. "Where would I go? We signed up together, sir."

"You and Hartness and Flanders, you mean. Three musketeers. All for one, one for all?"

"Yes, sir. And you."

"D'Artagnan, am I? The baffle-headed nobleman that the three are always rescuing?"

"You read that story, too? Wasn't it exciting?"

He grumbled at her attempt at distracting him. "At the town's farewell dance, did you three promise my mother to look after me?"

Tess tried to hide her smile. "Well, that lady's a mite fond of you, sir."

"You slide around my question like a Quaker hiding runaway slaves, Corporal."

"Has my new rank been approved as fast as that, sir?"

"I am trying it on."

"You probably shouldn't do that. Military seems touchy about such things. Dr. Cole, I been only trying to help. With the cooking, the cleaning, the clipping of the beards. Not for any fussing over what I done."

She watched the quirk of his eyebrow disappear into his curls. "What are you afraid of?"

"Sir?"

"Your use of English grammar slips when you are afraid."

Tess felt her cheeks flame. "I never pretended to learning." He knew that much about her. She was living such a big lie that she'd followed Maud O'Neil's instructions to be scrupulously honest about everything else.

Ryder frowned. "Now I have embarrassed you. Not my intent, I assure you. Tom, I do not care how you have acquired your education, you are as bright-minded as the devil!"

"I am?" What sounded like a compliment also called up the devil's name. What did that mean? The how of men talking to each other sometimes baffled her.

Her superior sighed hard. "What is it you fear, man?"

"They wouldn't force me away from Company D because I know how to treat lice, would they, Dr. Cole?"

He shook his head with a snort, reminding her, suddenly, of his fine Arabian. He had not replaced his horse, as she'd expected. Another puzzlement. He sobered. "No one desires you away. I was teasing you. I am embarrassed, Tom, don't you see? About you feeling tied to me, to a promise you might have made to my mother."

"The lady didn't hold a firearm on me, sir."

"She has much stronger weapons in her arsenal."

Tess thought of Olivia Cole, whom this man resembled so closely it was hard to remember he'd been fathered by the one whose miniature portrait Olivia Cole had showed her at the dance—the sea captain with the blue vest, wild hair and laughing eyes.

"Your sister should join this unholy alliance with my mother and your comrades in arms," he said now, finishing their task, and pulling down his starched while sleeves.

"My sister?"

"Yes. Have you posted her any letters?"

"No."

"Why not?" Those eyes iced suddenly. "Have you plans of returning home soon to make things right with her? Have I been wasting my time training you? Are you going to leave the service once our ninety day enlistment is up?"

"No, sir! I mean to stick it out until the hostilities are over, just like we all planned out together."

The tension in his shoulders eased. "Well, then. You must tell your sister this. Think how she must feel of your abandonment after all she has done to preserve us!"

"She's done?"

"In teaching you to sew and cook and that kind way you have with the sick." He pulled his coat on. "Forgive me, Tom, but I see these things as her gifts."

"They are. They are her gifts, sir."

"Then why not let her know you are well and safe down here?"

"I think she knows, sir."

"Think she knows? Are you relying on the bond of your joint twin births to communicate without words?"

"No, sir, not exactly. I do write her. Every night."

"But you do not post these letters? Why?"

Tess scanned the instruments, the back wall of the hospital tent, the doctor's medicine bottles, neatly categorized on shelves made from empty ration boxes. Ryder Cole's eyes stayed as steady as the ones that held the panther's gaze. His mother's eyes. Fierce, demanding.

"I don't know where to post them to!" Tess finally blurted out the truth.

He went stock still. "What has happened?"

"She... Tess, that is. She ran away."

"Tom, sit down."

She looked to the tent's open sides for escape.

"That is an order. Sit."

She did, on a high stool, staring at the scrubbed-clean table, fighting tears. No amount of the soldiers' teasing about her quirks of modesty as they undressed freely around her could provoke tears, only this man's kindness.

He paced, his hands clasped behind his back.

"Why did you not tell me this before now?"

Tess groaned. What could she do to stop his questions? She heard him sit, reach into his vest pocket, draw out his silver flask with the swirling pattern of his initials etched into its side in the Spenserian hand her mother had taught her.

"Here. Drink," he said softly, but with steely sureness. "One swallow, there's the good fellow."

Tess obeyed. The whiskey burned her throat.

"Now. Tell me. Why did your sister run away?"

Tess kept her eyes on the doctor's vest pocket, where he was returning the flask. "They wanted her to marry. A cruel man, an old man, against her will. She didn't mean for..what happened. She had to run!"

"What happened?"

"There was a fire, an accident. He got burned."

"So were you. That young chatterbox Jeff Lovell, our housekeeper's son, he told me of your burns. You helped your sister!"

"Well, yes. Afterward, Tess, she ran away. She had to, sir."

He blinked. Once. Twice, before recovering his voice. "And you left her?"

"She left me! W-with word that she was well," she continued, tripping over the words, losing command of the lower pitch of her voice, "and in hiding. But not the where of her."

Ryder Cole drew out his whiskey again and sent a short swig down his own throat. "Think," he commanded. "Think about where she might have gone, who might have taken her in. She is a woman, Tom, even if she is your remarkable sister. She could not have gotten too far. Think. Among your neighbors, your friends back home."

Tess shook her head in misery. "They would find her, they'd find her and bring her back and… the Waterfords. *Maybe I could send letters to the Waterfords*," she realized.

"Who are the Waterfords?"

"Quakers. Asa and his sister Sarah."

"Of course you have Quaker friends. They taught you how to slide around direct questioning as well, I suppose. Great railroad conductors, I understand, these Quakers. Of certain traveling-by-night cargo?"

Tess remained silent. She didn't trust him that much.

Chapter Six

Pennslvania Avenue, Washington, D.C.

Tess had always dreamed of the city of Washington as being close to heaven, or at least Mount Olympus. She knew better now. Even from the small tearoom's window, it seemed she was watching the rabble of the world and its barnyards pass along dusty, unpaved Pennsylvania Avenue.

"Tom! Have you finished reading?" Captain Cole called her attention back to the writing paper.

"Sorry, sir. Yes, I have."

"Well? What do you think?"

She considered her words carefully. "You got everything covered, sir. And it's real polite in addressing the 'esteemed members of congress.' But it's angry at the same time, about all the shortcomings."

"Are my points made in a clear manner?"

"Mostly. Except for a couple of sentences I get lost in. But that's from my own ignorance, I suspect."

"Nonsense! Which sentences?" he demanded.

"Well, there's this one—"

Ryder Cole leaned so close that Tess smelled the small smear of ink that stained his brow. He grunted softly. "Heavy with phrases, quite right," he decided. "Two shorter sentences would have much better effect. I will try again."

"Captain, maybe you oughtn't to be asking me."

"Mother's orders," he brushed her objection away impatiently. "Now, where else?"

Outside the teahouse window, a fiddler began *The Eighth of January*.

Tess pointed to another paragraph. "The part about the transport of medical supplies reads to me, well, ah.. jumbled. And maybe a tad demanding in tone."

"Jumbled? Demanding? How? Oh, hang it all, read it aloud!"

After listening to her run out of breath on his packed together sentences, Tess watched Ryder Cole's hand quicken to the rousing music as he pared and strengthened his document. The fiddler was joined by a tin whistle, then a fife. The trio played on, staunchly patriotic for *Liberty*, then laced with sentiment for *My Old Kentucky Home*.

As dusk settled over the city, the small band blanketed the filth and noise with the beauty of their music. Then they were gone.

Their fingers touched as Ryder Cole took the sander from her hand. Tess blinked. "Allow me, sir," she said, sprinkling the grains over his final document.

Ryder leaned back, gazed out the window. "They were quite good, were they not?"

"The musicians you mean, sir?"

"Yes, the musicians. I am not all that single-minded. I know the sound of good music. Wish I could recruit them. We are miserable as a band, are we not?"

"Yes, sir."

He laughed. "We should seek out an amusement, perhaps a dance, when our task is accomplished. Perhaps we might find those fellows again, and cajole them to knock some knowledge into our own hapless crew."

"I don't dance much, Captain."

"Oh? My mother found you a most considerate partner at the town dance that preceded our departure."

"I stepped on her toes plenty. So she was being kind."

"My mother is not kind. She has a demanding, iron will that does daily battle with her more sanguine, womanly temperament."

"You misjudge the lady, sir. She was most good to me from our first meeting, when seeking to ease your own recovery, I would remind you, respectfully."

"Why, Tom, defending my mother has your speech heightened and your color quite raised. I must write to her about what a champion she has!" He gave out another short laugh and took on a brief resemblance to his father's portrait.

Then she saw distress in his eyes, but did not guess its cause until he spoke again. "We will find your sister. If I have to turn the state of Connecticut and its borderlands of eastern New York upside down and shake her out! Then, along with my mother, you will have two perfumed paper correspondents, and be the envy of every man in the company. How would that be?"

Caught. She was caught again, in this small space, in the warmth of this man's eyes. Then her woman's loneliness got the better of her.

"Would you consider dropping Tess a line now and then, sir?"

"Why, Tom, there's nothing that would please me more. And let me assure you that my intentions will be ruled by the highest esteem for her honor and maidenly virtue."

She frowned. "Tess ain't needing any of that, Captain. She just needs to know you're looking out for me."

A brow shot into his yanked down forelock of hair. "Oh? And am I, Tom?"

"I'm not complaining, thus far."

He laughed longer this time —a sound as sweet to her, Tess realized, as that fiddler playing *Cripple Creek*. "So I notice. As you stand for hours in the broiling sun or drenching rain, waiting for shelter or rations. As you sit by sick farm boys fighting off diseases they have never known. And break up city thugs fighting among themselves instead of saving it for the rebels. We have had some harsh shocks and hard knocks, Tom Boyde, even if I will write to your sister about cheering crowds and thrilling train rides."

"You can tell her everything. Honest, Captain. She won't respect you if you don't."

"And will you, Tom? Tell her everything?"

"Oh yes, sir. She'd castigate me something fierce if I didn't."

"And she would know if you were hiding more unsavory elements, would she not? Due to your extraordinary twin bond?"

"Oh you can be certain sure of that, sir."

"Remarkable. Transcending even the great divides of sex."

"We're all of us human, sir."

He pushed his chair back as if he were on the one in his office at home, the one on wheeled castors that almost kept up with his energy. "You have allowed me to participate in a remarkable scientific study. I am most grateful."

Tess felt her insides churn. What was she doing? Where was her sense?

"I envy you, Tom."

"There's no need for that, Captain."

He reached across the table, squeezed her shoulder. Tess didn't let any but Davy and Joe do that, before now. She didn't pull away, though she was angry with him, angry that he saw everything in the light of his scientific inquiry. His letters to Tess would be another part of his study. Still, she couldn't keep up the pretense of being the reserved medical assistant to this man, her superior. This was dangerous, but she couldn't discourage any touch from him. Had that horse of his witched her into taking over the job of looking after this over-educated and under common-sensed man?

What a fix she was in now.

"Listen," Ryder implored, maybe sensing the blackness that had come over her spirit, but not its cause. "Your twin would not change her mind and marry anyone without consulting you, would she?"

Tess sighed. "No, sir."

"Oh, buck up, Tom! There's time for you to do your brotherly duty on her behalf and see her settled! She is hardly on the shelf yet, though she's reached all of... you are both over eighteen, are you not?"

"Yes, sir."

"How much over?"

"Twenty, Captain Cole," she said, feeling the hardness around her mouth. "We are twenty."

"All of twenty!" Ryder exclaimed now. "And didn't Mr. Olmsted take you for a drummer boy? If she has got the female version of your youthful looks, she'll pass as a fresh-blooming seventeen for years yet. Much better to marry her off later, after this war is over and we can all settle ourselves in the business of life, don't you agree? Much better than an unsuitable match now, when you cannot look after whatever blackguard takes her away from you. There. That notion appeals to you?"

"Yes, sir," she admitted. How damned overbearing men were.

"Good. Settled. Now, let's deliver this paper and make our declarations to the commission, then see if the ladies of Washington have a ball ongoing for two considerate dance partners, shall we?"

"That'd be right fine," she said, wishing to be back in her skirts. She wouldn't step on her partners' toes were she in skirts, she felt sure.

Ryder Cole blinked slowly. "What did you say?"

"Say, sir?"

"'Right fine.' You said 'right fine.'" he answered his own question softly, going somewhere back behind his brilliant green eyes. Tess wanted to look away, but could not. She knew better than to feel for this man. There were many barriers between them, besides the fact that he wouldn't give her a second glance as a woman—plain, ill-bred and without hoops or crinoline. Without even the braid of hair she kept in a deep inside pocket of her tunic. And now she knew another reason his eyes would never linger in appreciation—she was already on the shelf, too old.

"Is your sister good with horses, Tom?" he asked softly. "As good as you are?"

"Oh, better."

He grinned. "What? At everything, then?"

She lifted her head higher. "So she tells me, sir."

Her superior gave out a long sigh. "Well, in lieu of enlisting her, I'd best get you raised in rank faster, to cease all these bothersome 'sirs' between us."

* * *

Watching him before the Washington men, Tess wished Ryder had kept more of his side whiskers, but he'd wanted to set an example for the men when she was hacking off hair and beads. Now Captain Cole had only his panther scar to show some hard experience as he stood in the echoing room before the members of the Sanitary Commission and a few members of the United States Congress. Too young and too arrogant, despite the changes they'd made in his document.

The document was clear, impassioned, and they'd honed out some of the demanding tone. The gentlemen listened as Ryder spoke the words well, without the whips and cracks of her uneducated mountain speech. Though they'd grown up close to each other, she was Big Woods, he was River. And he'd been to Columbia College, in New York City, then across the wide Atlantic.

Tess had been taught to resent rich landowners. But now that she knew Ryder, she began to see his self-assurance as an impediment, much as her own lack of schooling was. Ryder Cole thought he had power over things, from finding Tom Boyde's sister to the Medical Corps's conduct of the war. Tess needed to be there when he learned differently. This might be one of those times.

Suddenly, she was asked to stand before the old men. Ryder's eyes told her there was no way out of it. She approached, her footfalls echoing.

She wanted desperately not to disgrace Ryder. And she thought she'd done all right at first. Until she answered the question about the women.

Her inquisitor, a well-fed man in a jacquard vest, roared out his response. "Invite the female nurses into hospital and camp?" he repeated her suggestion. "Private Boyde, surely you do not think we should indulge these women's requests to be of service? Such sights as you and the good doctor have witnessed are hardly fit for the eyes of the ladies."

Tess spoke quietly. "Ladies have seen plenty of the toils, sickness, and sufferings of life, sir. And Captain Cole told me it was a lady, Florence Nightingale, who convinced the English government to do what you folks are trying to convince the federals to do—keep standards of health for the soldiers. It appears to me that good women are standing by, and I believe it would be cruel to keep them from serving in the way they so fervently desire."

Ryder Cole passed his graceful fingers over his eyes. But how could she answer differently?

* * *

Once they were dismissed and on the steps of the white stone building, Ryder's discontent crested its banks.

"You could have informed me you had your own program to foster, Private!"

"I was only just trying to answer the questions."

"They were bent on distracting us from getting what we need for the men! They wished us to appear spendthrift and radical. And you tumbled right into their trap!"

"Trap? I thought we wanted the same things."

"This is Washington, Tom!"

"It's a stupid ignorant mistake, not allowing the women to serve."

"You may be right, but—"

"May be? After you praising everything I done, every blessed part of it women-taught? From mending to wrestling up a meal? After you telling me about Miss Nightingale and her service in the Crimea?"

"It was the timing, not the cause. We need the Sanitary Commission established first. Damnation!"

"Why? To provide this here city with another government institution? Another place to siphon off money instead of getting fighting men what they need?"

A hot choking gust of air brought the putrid smell of the nearby canal to their nostrils. Ryder Cole smiled slowly. "Well, yes. There is that risk. Maybe you do know Washington," he conceded.

Tess felt a hard clap at her back. "Gentlemen, gentlemen, your service has been rendered in splendid fashion. Do not be disheartened, I pray you! Now, is it not time to cease your deliberation and seek out some diversion?"

Tess turned to see the congressman who'd most mocked the women volunteers who wanted to serve as nurses for the army. He smelled of hard liquor and cigars. Two assistants, reed thin men with small eyes, flanked him.

Her captain put on his affable smile. "We were of the same mind and are off to see if there might be a dance in progress that—"

"Dance? Dance? How very quaint! How delightfully provincial!" The man's laugh was echoed on cue by his associates. "Allow me to show you men of action the way to Madame Lanier's establishment—the more direct path to some horizontal refreshment!"

Chapter Seven

She needed to get out of here, Tess thought for what had to be the fiftieth time. Where was Ryder? There, in the adjoining parlor, smoking cigars with the Washington men, accepting his grateful nation's thanks with yet another toast. Ignoring her. Maybe still angry about her speaking up for the ladies who wanted to become battlefield nurses. Captain Cole had left her in this plum colored room with a gaggle of women in their under clothes. Her head began to ache.

"You don't have to be all buttoned up proper here," the woman draped across her lap assured her. "In fact, it means you're not having a good time."

Tess's eyes smarted from the stench of cigars. But that was the least of her problems "Oh, I'm having a fine time, Miss."

"Arabella," the whore reminded her, "not 'Miss.'"

The girl was about her own age, Tess imagined. And not well. There was a yellow cast to her skin that the paint and powder could not disguise. Jaundice.

Arabella slipped off her delicate shoes. Her silk stockinged feet disappeared into the folds of a dressing gown adorned with peacocks and branches of flowering fruit tree

"And what is the source of your fine time, Private Boyde?"

"Well." Tess swallowed, looking to the larger room beyond where a doe-eyed man in a velvet vest plunked out a tune. "The piano player's the best I ever heard."

The eyebrow arched. "Oh?" Arabella smiled delicately. "Of course. I understand. You wait right here, darlin'," she murmured, squeezing Tess's arm before moving on.

Oh Lord, what had she done now?

Arabella had a short conversation with their hostess. That glorious owner of the establishment stood among surrounding men in the piano room. Madame Lanier was the most imposing of the women and the only one of them fully dressed. Her gown was purple velvet and black lace. To Tess's astonishment, she drifted up, lifted her skirts in that peculiar way hooped women did, and sat close on the gold brocade sofa.

"I hear you enjoy my music, Private Boyde?"

"I do, Ma'am." She smelled like peaches, under all the flowers and spice.

"Dear Mr. Rolf, our piano player, he is not of the usual … persuasion of a man in his position. He has a wife and two small children, you see."

"That right?"

"*Ah, oui.* So. *Quel dommage, n'est ce pas*? His passion is for them only, and for our pianoforte. I value that he does not place his hands where they do not belong, yes? For this I pay him well enough to keep well his lady, his babies."

Madame Lanier's eyebrows slanted. They were having some kind of conversation, and it was Tess's turn. She cleared her throat, then spoke slowly, at the risk of the beautiful woman thinking her a fool. "His pursuits ought to keep both days and nights full and happy, then."

Madame Lanier smiled broadly. Tess could see little cracks in the paint that made her face look like it was all one tone of creamy flesh.

"You understand, then? *Très bien*! Yes, I envy Mr. Rolf his contentment in domestic bliss. And he is a gifted composer of the popular song."

"Those are his tunes? They're fine."

"Indeed. You are a musician too?"

"Oh no, Ma'am. I'm learning about fixing up sick and damaged people, to make myself useful and independent when I get back home."

"Ah, a noble pursuit!" Madame Lanier smiled companionably, ignoring what Tess started to feel, the jealous eyes of other men in the room. She was taking too much of their hostess's time. And her not even an officer. But Madame Lanier continued talking, reminding Tess of Olivia Cole. "And you like medical service under the tutelage of the captain doctor?"

Tess glanced over the woman's head and into the big parlor that was growing more dense with smoke. One of the politicians clapped Ryder on the shoulder before another roar of laughter. What were they talking about? Was he drunk? Would she have to get them both back to camp across the river?

"Do not worry. No harm will come to him in my house," the woman said so softly Tess wondered if she'd only imagined it. "So!" she said, louder. "You are pursuing your heart's desire, Private Boyde, as our Mr. Rolf is, yes?"

Tess looked at her own hands. "I suppose in a manner of speaking I am. Was. See, I didn't expect it to pull me into a war. And down here into the Southland, among the federal government folks and …well, in the company of such as you, Ma'am."

Tess hoped her bafflement about her own predicament did not sound like disapproval, for who was she to be looking down her nose at the way another woman made her way in a world that men had made?

"Would you care to dance?" Madame Lanier asked suddenly.

"There ain't room—"

"We shall make room. Come, my brave Private Boyde."

It was for all the world like dancing with Olivia Cole, an awkward start smoothed by the patient smile of her partner. Still, her second thought of the Widow of Ashokan in a place like this was making Tess color to the roots of her hair. Maybe Tess was blushing for the widow's son too, for he certainly wasn't on his own behalf.

Tess lost track of the room's descending quiet, the woman's kindness so relieved her. She bowed when the dance was done. Madame Lanier smiled, showing teeth that were so white Tess wondered if they were painted too.

"There. That was all I needed to know."

"Know, Ma'am?"

She opened her China fan and made a deep curtsey to command the attention of all around them. "Private Boyde, as I have heard you were the fearless champion of the ladies' nursing cause, I lay claim to you myself tonight, sir," she declared.

Tess scanned the room, past the faces of shocked and disgruntled politicians. Where was Ryder? The smoky parlor was emptying. Men were coupled with bare-shouldered women on their arms. There. Ryder's was Arabella, the jaundiced one.

Oh, hang him then, he was on his own. Tess was weary with looking after him. Madame Lanier waited for her response, the swells of her breasts poised, on display to all above her violet gown. Tess asked God what to do now, though she doubted God would take any notice of her here, praying from a fancy Pennsylvania Avenue whorehouse. Escape. Escape behind her army rank.

"I don't believe I…have the means, Madame Lanier. I need to send my pay home to my sister, you see."

She felt her captain's hand at her shoulder. "Our night has been paid for, Tom, by grateful fellow advocates of our cause. Now, don't insult the givers, or the gracious beauties who dispense our gift. I trust I will not have to make that an order."

He said the last sentence quietly, but not quietly enough, as the barrel-chested Congressman who'd brought them there had another fit of laughter.

Tess, in that moment, hated them all. Captain Cole saw it. But his mouth twisted with annoyance even as his eyes sparked their remorse. "Oh, the Hell, Tom, stop fussing over a simple indulgence. Go with Madame Lanier. I will be just next door."

That fact fired her anger hotter.

The politician stood between them. "Captain Cole, you country boys with your quaint and loyal ways are worth the price of twenty evenings here!" he claimed.

As Mr. Rolf began a soft version of *I Dream of Jeannie with the Light Brown Hair*, Tess turned from them both and offered her arm to Madame Lanier.

Chapter Eight

So many scents, Tess thought, scanning the veneered woods of the bureau and wardrobe, the brass of the bed's headboard. The dressing table with its mahogany mirror reflected glass bottles shaped like seashells and diamonds. Tess wanted to touch them, lift their glass stoppers, find the source of each of those scents. *Dangerous thoughts. Look away.*

Was the room next door like this one? Was Ryder noticing mirrors and furniture and glass bottles glowing under candlelight? Tess doubted it. *Stop thinking about him.* He wasn't thinking about her. Some fellow musketeer. She would have done far better to stay at camp, rolling bandages with Davy and Joe.

The triple hung bay windows had an iron balcony beyond them. Maybe she could escape that way, if there was a trellis or a tree within reach. Now was the time to get away, as Madame Lanier had left her alone while she saw to the "evening's last details." Tess allowed herself a quick lift of the stopper of the most beautiful of the bottles. Lilac. She breathed deeply of spring.

She walked to the deep green velvet and their gauzy inner curtains, cleared them aside to look out at the lamp lights that tracked their way up Pennsylvania Avenue to the president's house. And yes, there. A means of escape, a hardy crabapple tree.

"Let us cocoon ourselves, shall we?"

Tess turned. Madame Lanier stood in one of the room's three doorways. Dress and hoops gone, she was still imposing in her silk dressing gown. Tess felt more trapped inside her uniform than when the boys first teased her for not joining them at the swimming hole.

"Would you loosen my corset strings, love?"

Tess swallowed. "Sure."

Madame Lanier's dressing gown sang as it slid off her shoulders and to the ground. Tess released the back tie that held in the cinch at Madame Lanier's waist. She watched the ties slip through their grommets as she waited the space of a few of the woman's deep breaths. "Is that all right?"

"Perfect."

Tess secured the ties in the new position.

"You have done that many times before, _cheri_," Madame Lanier said. "Now. Would you not like to do the same?"

"Ma'am?"

"Shed your uniform for one night? Remember who you are underneath those handsome shades of blue?" The woman eased Tess down before the dressing table with a gentle press at her shoulders. "They suit you, the blues. Did you wear the color in your other life?"

Tess took in a careful breath. "Wore mostly homespun, back then. Browns from walnut casings, yellows from onion skins. A little green cloth from sage." She was babbling. The truth, of course, and in detail. "I do admire the shade of blue. Made a mix of milk and blue pokeberry for my sleeping place in the loft once. Never got to paint it, though."

"Why not?"

"My pa said I was putting on airs. Said plain board's good enough for the menfolk of the family, and it was good enough...for—for..."

"For you?"

"Yes, Ma'am, for me."

What was she doing, talking like a magpie to this woman, and almost giving herself clean away besides? She heard Ryder Cole's laugh from the room beside Madame Lanier's. Her head hurt. If they discovered her a woman, would the army think he knew all along? Would they blame him?

"You are a chemist, Private Boyde, with the making of your paints! Perhaps you'd like to investigate my beauty concoctions?" Madame Lanier gave out a short, throaty laugh. "Purely in the interest of scientific study, of course?"

"I'd like that fine, Ma'am," Tess said, turning her attention to the lace-covered table.

"Good. Sit."

She reached over Tess's shoulder and picked up a brush with an ivory handle as fine as those on Doctor Cole's French-made surgical instruments. "We will do only what you like tonight, I promise."

"Thank you," Tess whispered, hearing the relieved crack in her voice's low tone.

"Your hair has a lovely natural curl. May I?"

"Uh… all right."

The hostess began her task. Tess tried to lose herself in the cut glass bottles leaking their scents, but the deep massage of her scalp was too wonderful not to revel in. Her mother had brushed her hair like this, so long ago. She closed her eyes, remembering.

"You have never seen yourself as beautiful, have you?"

Her eyes opened. Tess stared at the reflection of a stranger. Slicked down, always-pulled-behind-the-ears strands were now soft waves framing a round, flushed face, a nose off-kilter since Laban let the handle on the pump up too fast when she was eight and broke it.

"Beautiful?" Her laugh sounded like dry leaves before a storm. "What would the point of that be, Ma'am?"

Madame Lanier's brows slanted in amusement. "Well, it's been the point of my own existence for as long as I remember."

"Oh. 'Course. Beg pardon, Ma'am."

The light, throaty laugh came again. It was true. This woman was not going to force her to do anything. She was not full of meanness like the few predatory men that Ryder, Joe and Davy shielded her from at camp. Maybe Ryder was right, maybe everything would be all right if she could just relax in this strange, gaudy place.

Madame Lanier laid down her brush. She swiped three fingers full of a substance that looked like butter from the lilac-scented jewel bottle. She brought it to Tess's temple and began kneading it in, counterbalancing the throbbing there.

"Better?" she whispered.

"Yes."

The skilled hands anchored her jaw now, and continued the gentle massage of her cheekbone, sliding across the bridge of her imperfect nose. The massage continued around her ear, down her throat. Is this how Madame Lanier started with the men? Those jealous men who were angry at the lady's choice of partner-of-the-evening? It's a wonder this woman didn't live in a castle with those men at her feet, Tess thought.

"Can you see it yet?" Madame Lanier asked softly.

Tess stared at their reflections. "See, Ma'am?"

She kissed Tess's cheek. "That every woman with the fire of purpose is beautiful."

"Woman?"

"And I see your purpose as well as I see the affection you carry for your captain." She frowned. "As if you haven't got enough burdens, my darling girl."

Suddenly, the weight of the day crashed down, turning the bottles blurry as Tess struggled to take in gulps of air. The woman's long, strong fingers unbuttoned, then lifted off coat, vest and blouse until she found Tess's own corset: plain boned muslin, tied towards a different purpose. She loosened the strings.

"Breathe easy now. I will not add to your burdens. You're safe here. You'll always be safe here, do you understand?"

Tess looked up at the woman's reflection. "Will I?" she whispered

"Yes. Now, let's get that uniform tucked away for a few hours, shall we? Then how about a few of my night-off girls and I help you into some silks and finery?"

Soon Tess had what she'd always wanted, though she'd never known it before that moment—seven sisters dousing her in lilac water, powdering her shoulders, pulling her waist tight under corset ties. They graced her neck with amethysts, found ear bobs, painted her lips and cheeks. She shyly pulled her braid from its secret pocket for them to marvel at. Then they combed her shorn hair back and pinned the cascading fall to it, even planting silk flowers where they attached it.

As her transformation continued, they told her about picnics along the Potomac on their days off, and going to the theater where goddesses on a gold chariot were pulled by a great mechanical lion with real smoke coming out of his nostrils. Encouraged, Tess told them about her mountains back home, and how cool they kept the evening breezes even at this summer time of year, and the white birch trees with mushrooms growing in their shade—mushrooms big enough to fry up like a steak.

When the girl in the cinnamon colored dressing gown asked about Ryder and his scar, Tess even told them about the first time she'd laid eyes on her captain, his doomed horse and the panther. When she got to the panther's death throes, the girl let out a shriek, followed by mad giggles from others to hush up.

The door to the adjoining room swung open.

Tess felt Madame Lanier's hand take her shoulder in an iron grip. She looked up into the mirror and caught sight of Ryder Cole standing in the door frame. His eyes darted around for an instant, then landed square on her face.

"Diana?"

It was her turn to shriek.

Chapter Nine

Madame Lanier shoved Tess's head, face first, back down on her arms.

"Captain, you do not belong here," she said.

The menace in her voice did not stop his barefooted approach. Tess had gotten enough of a look to know that though stripped down to his one piece, his trousers were still on him. And his voice had its usual soft comfort for the distressed.

"Is this young woman ill? Perhaps I can—"

"There is nothing for what ails her in your bag, Captain. She has recently... lost her brother."

Tess felt the approach of his familiar lye soap and leather scent. And another scent she knew too well—strong drink.

"Was he a soldier?"

Tess managed a sniff and nod from her lowered head.

"I am very sorry."

She felt his gentle touch at her shoulder, his handkerchief placed in her hand. "Please. Miss"

Tess let out a wail so loud he uttered a succinct curse and stepped back.

"You are wearing out your welcome, Captain," Madame Lanier reprimanded. "Please return to your evening's delights."

"But...where is Tom?"

"Private Boyde has graciously relinquished this room to this lady in her distress, sir. Kindly follow his example."

"Oh. Oh, yes, of course." He stumbled back another step.

He was a different kind of drunk than her menfolk, Tess decided. He seemed slower, more dense-minded, but sweeter than his sober self. Tess heard the creaking of the floorboards beneath the thin woven carpeting. Hesitation. A halt in his retreat. "If you are sure I cannot be of some assistance. Perhaps some laudanum?"

"No. But thank you, doctor. Go along now. Guide him toward his destination, Arabella."

Another shrieking sound made Tess's heart stop. This time it was a warning whistle from the street. The cinnamon gowned girl rushed forward and reported back from her perch at the window. "Raid."

"God's Diggers!" Madame Lanier groused. "That's what I get for entertaining rival factions on the hill."

The grand bedroom soon filled with half-clad government officials from the smaller chambers. Mr. Rolf and women in their dressing gowns suited them up quickly. Tess felt herself planted behind the bed's brass head.

The piano player was a small man but had mighty arms. He hoisted up the jib windows with such force that they almost disappeared into the floor above. Madame Lanier directed the exodus through them to her balcony. Politicians kept disappearing through the windows. The odd procession stopped when the congressman who had purchased their night's revels and Ryder Cole were still within the room.

Madame Lanier grabbed the congressman's coat lapels. "Your people did this!" she accused.

Arabella rushed into the room with missing parts of Ryder Cole's uniform.

The congressman raised his hands. "My dear lady—"

"Make sure Damon's Salon is hit with an inspection within the week to keep us even, Congressman, if you'd ever like to enter my parlor again!"

She stuffed him out the window without ceremony.

Behind her, Arabella kissed Ryder's cheek and murmured something at his ear. He glanced around, looking confused.

"But—I cannot go without Tom. Where is Tom?"

Madame Lanier sighed hard. "Perhaps Private Boyde heard the alarm down at the necessary. Meet him back at your campground, yes?"

"I will do no such thing. Tom would not leave me and I—"

"Mr. Rolf?" Madame Lanier summoned. Those mighty arms tackled Ryder.

"Yes, ma'am. This way, Captain," he said, lifting him over his shoulder and ducking through the window. Ryder's head came up and slammed into the frame. Tess pressed her hand to her mouth, but smiled when she heard his indignant protests resume on the balcony.

She left her hiding spot as the women of Madame Lanier's house engaged in a fit of frenzied housekeeping. Silks, feathers, and even a braided whip were tossed into the large trunk at the foot of the brass bed. Tess spotted Ryder's boots among the debris.

"Those are his. My captain's."

No one seemed to hear her.

She fetched the boots and climbed through the window to the balcony.

Ryder Cole was on the street below, leaning on a lamppost, looking lost. He glanced up. His eyes locking on hers. She dropped his boots and ran inside the house without looking back.

Tess entered the bedroom just as Arabella jammed her own uniform in Madame Lanier's trunk.

"I have to go."

"Not yet…Diana," Madame Lanier said, draping a fringed, black silk shawl over Tess's head and around her shoulders just as the door opened with a bang.

"Gentlemen," Madame Lanier announced in her most welcoming tone to the uniformed men, "how thoughtful of you to pay your respects to my visiting niece upon the tragic loss of her brother. I hope you will make your time here brief in respect for our loss."

Once the inspection was over, Tess left Madame Lanier's from the tradesmen's side door with ferry fare in her pocket and directions back to camp. She expected she could get in before the first bugle call, and hoped Joe and Davy had cleaned up the dispensary so they might start catching up with their caseload.

She almost tripped over Ryder Cole's booted foot. He was propped in a townhouse doorway, snoring softly. She'd never heard him snore before, but then he didn't usually sleep with a tenacious grip on his silver spirits flask either.

"Captain." She shoved his shoulder. "Captain Cole."

One bloodshot eye opened. "I am watching for you, Tom. I know you're still in there." The eyelid descended again.

"We need to get back now, sir."

"Not without Tom. I will not leave without Tom."

"I'm here now, sir. Let's go."

He blinked once, twice. "Tom."

"Yes, sir."

"You are well then?"

"Yes, sir."

"And your sister?"

"My sister, sir?"

"Theresa. Tess. Is she well?"

"Captain?"

"It was she, was it not? Your sister is not boarding with Quakers, is she, Tom? She's right here in Washington. She killed a panther once, but now she's a whore."

Her blood iced, but she managed a smile. "I think you're confused, sir."

"Am I?"

He tried to sit higher, but his whole upper body swayed and his head fell unto his hand. "Oh, God, what am I saying? In the candles' light, that girl, the one who lost her brother. Did you see her?"

The truth. "I did sir."

"And she was not—? Of course not. I humbly ask your forgiveness."

"You have it, sir."

"Good. Good, then. Let's return to camp."

His knees shook as he used them to slide his back up the wall.

"Tom," he called.

"Yes, sir?"

"Am I standing?"

"Not quite, sir."

"Pressure. I believe it has to do with the pressure of my blood, not being sufficient—

"You're falling-down drunk, sir."

"Yes, well, I know that. I was attempting to analyze the physical nature of the condition."

Tess sighed hard. He breathed science, this man, even when drunk. And heavy-lidded and red-rimmed, his eyes were still beautiful.

"I am a terrible example to you and the boys. And I am about to compound my transgression by heaving up my supper, if you'll kindly hold my hat?"

Tess led him to the gutter where the rich foods he'd indulged in went back to the earth. He coughed twice before heaving again. This time the profusion was tinted red. Wines, it was the color of the red wines he'd been drinking, Tess told herself. Not blood. It was not blood. Ryder knelt higher, rested back upon his knees, then fumbled in his pockets.

"Might you spare me a handkerchief?" he asked in a small, pained voice.

He found Tess's offering after two failed reaches for it and blotted his mouth. It was his own, Tess realized too late. Olivia Cole had sent Ryder two dozen handkerchiefs embroidered with his initials, by personal post.

"Why…this is mine," he said, staring.

"Yes, sir," was all Tess could think to say.

"She used it. The one who lost her brother. To wipe off some of her face paint, see?" He glanced up. "And you missed a spot yourself, Tom. There. At your chin. Lip paint, I should think. So. We are a couple of miserable sinners, then?"

Tess had sinned with him a few times in her dreams, both day and night ones, so she couldn't help grinning.

"Yes, sir," she agreed, handing him back his hat. "But I think you're doing restitution enough for the two of us."

* * *

They reached the Potomac River crossing as the birds were heralding the coming day. The bearded ferryman wore a line of worry on a strong face that went with his muscled arms. "Best high tail it, soldiers. This was not the night to go over the wall."

Ryder sniffed his indignation, though the way his face went even greener gave his recent indulgences away. "We are not over the wall, sir. We are a doctor and assistant, on leave for official medical business and returning to camp in plenty of time to perform our duties."

"Oh? Please excuse me then. You need to be ready, and near front lines? Best take a couple of my horses. They're over by my spring house on the other side, see? I rent them out to such as you needs to get in quick. I won't charge you a thing except your good handling of my mounts, and I'll come and pick them up myself, how would that be, after the march?"

"March?" Ryder Cole demanded. "What march?"

"Why the one down south, doctor, ain't you heard? Seems like the Federals are looking to get this war started proper and take Richmond."

* * *

When they reached the spring house, Ryder ran his hand through his hair. "I cannot ride this horse, Tom," he said. "Perhaps there is a carriage for hire—"

"Look here, sir. I doubt you've got any more food in your belly to come up, and I'll be right alongside you."

"You misunderstand. I promised not to ride another horse until I have saved three lives—in memory of my fallen Moutamin. It was the least I could do after causing the death of the best mount I have ever—"

"The panther went after you and your horse, sir."

"The panther and my own arrogance."

"That may be. But we need to get to the march, Captain, where you'll catch up to your three lives, I'm sure."

He raked his hand again through that shining black hair still smelling of Arabella, then planted his hat on his head. "You do not understand. I made a sacred vow—"

"What about your doctor's vow? You going to let one blamed fool act cause another?"

"You don't have to venture your opinion in a way that leaves me—"

"Being a mule-headed no-account to your animal and your name both?"

"My name?"

"Well, it's Ryder, ain't it?"

He frowned. "My name does not signify how I seat a horse. It is a family name, from my maternal great-grand—"

"Ryder Cole, seat yourself on this horse, now!" Tess yelled, exasperated.

"Well." He sniffed before mounting the brown mare who was not nearly as beautiful as his prized Arabian, "if you put it in that way."

By the time they reached camp, Tess noticed a high color had returned to her captain's face, with all vestiges of both his nightly delights and his early morning misery replaced by his more familiar fired heart of purpose.

Chapter Ten

On the march toward Manassas, Virginia

The heat was much worse than Tess ever remembered back home. A dense fog of dust stirred up by the wagons and tramping soldiers made sighting ahead difficult and accidents frequent on the way to Centreville.

Ryder had named their horses Morning and After for the cure they'd provided his flagging spirit. He resolved to buy them from the ferryman. They'd gone through briar patches and open fields and had remained steady through delays and blocked roads. How could she complain more than her poor, sold-into-service mare, Tess thought as she swept her sleeve across her brow.

"The land is level here," Ryder called to her. "Let's try to cut away and get further on."

Morning kept an attentive eye out for her stable mate who was carrying Captain Cole as they detoured into an open field. Perhaps the mares didn't trust their new masters yet, Tess surmised, but they trusted each other. Ryder dismounted in the wake of distant artillery fire.

Two infantrymen appeared over the ridge. Except for their uniforms, they looked like boys, lost on the way home from school, Tess thought. Time slowed in the rippling haze of heat. One of the pair fell down. His companion knelt over him, there in the parched field.

Ryder advanced, joined the soldiers.

"He'll be all right," the kneeling soldier said, looking up. "Might you spare some water, sir? He went and drank my canteen dry, just like when we was kids."

"Where are you coming from?" Tess heard the doctor ask gently as she joined them.

"We're part of Colonel Richardson's force, in retreat from Blackburn Ford, sir. Our regiment got lost, near as I can figure. Went slam into Beauregard's army, fresh as you please, raring and ready. Them Southern boys can take this heat, can't they?"

Ryder closed the lids over the eyes of the downed man, then felt the pulse of the kneeling one.

"Nothin' wrong with me, sir," he insisted, "it's my brother got shot."

"You are suffering from sunstroke."

The boy's eyes darted between Tess and Ryder Cole. "Naw. Listen, Captain, your regiment got a doctor you can spare to look at—?"

"I am a doctor. Tom is my assistant. Water, Tom," he commanded before returning his attention to their patient. "Your brother is dead."

The boy shook his head, as if bothered by a fly. "But I promised Mama to look after him."

"There was nothing you could do. You must tell her that."

The soldier stood, weaved. Ryder took his arm, then held Tess's opened canteen to his mouth. "Slowly. Drink slowly," he instructed.

Tess saw a steely cast to Ryder's changeling eyes. "Mount up, Tom," he said curtly, pointing to the road with his chin. "Signal that ambulance wagon to take on this man." Then, more quietly, "And tell them to send a stretcher from their dead wagon."

"Yes, sir." She tried to sound as capable and experienced as he did. But she turned quickly so he couldn't see the lie of it in her eyes.

They had just seen their first battle casualty.

* * *

74

When they finally found their regiment by the woeful sound of Davy Flanders trying to play *Boatman Dance* on his fife, the men's cheering startled them both. Ryder dismounted Morning. Tess slipped off After, following suit, joining the march again within Company D.

Except for their encounter with the brothers of Col. Richardson's company, it didn't seem they were heading toward a battle. The regiment meandered, was given halting orders often because of the heat. They picked fresh, bursting blackberries along the road.

Around the campfire at night, the men sang, played cards, read their bibles. Tess wrote letters for the illiterate. Letters that included bequests and farewells. She wrote her own letter to the sister with her name, and also the reply, carefully addressed back. She enclosed both within a message for Asa Waterford. She wondered if the kind Quaker and his sister would go along with her scheme.

Later that night, she was glad to have the familiarity of seeing to the needs of the captain's horses.

Ryder Cole joined her at the creek, dropping a brush box at her feet.

"On loan from Lieutenant Calmenson," he explained. "I will purchase grooming equipment for our new companions at the first opportunity."

Tess thought he would leave the box to her and return to his fellow officers. But he removed his coat, rolled up his sleeves, then reached for a hoof pick. As she tended her mount After, Tess wondered if Ryder had groomed his Moutamin himself. Was that why there seemed an almost brotherly connection between the two? He spoke softly and made clicking sounds to Morning before he lifted each hoof. The mare responded beautifully to his attentions. Her stablemate allowed Tess's care without complaint, too. When her captain was preparing the body brushes with a curry comb Tess spoke up.

"I can't afford to buy After from you, sir, so if you'd want to return her—"

"And separate these perfectly matched two? I think not. They surprised me in their performance today."

He handed her the first brush, then began to tend Morning briskly with the second. "I have been too spoiled by the look of finer bred horses to appreciate such as these." He gave Morning a long stroke with the brush that made the horse nod in delight. "You sit a horse well, Tom," Ryder said quietly.

Tess hid her face against After's withers. "I'm fond of all animals, sir."

He smiled. "Animals, women, men. I am most fortunate to have you in my company. You were of good service today." He touched her shoulder lightly. "You need not be ashamed of your feelings for that young soldier. As long as those feelings do not get in the way of our duties."

"Yes, sir."

Tess dipped the brush in the water bucket, shook it out, and tended After's sparse and tangled mane. If she lay the mane carefully, her mount's appearance would improve.

"Tom?" Her captain's voice had lost what little authority it had exerted.

"Yes, sir?"

"Our excursion into the Capitol city. The…night time extension of it. I hope you know it is not my usual practice to frequent houses with the reputation of Madame Lanier's."

Let him squirm. "If you say so, sir."

"No, not if I say so! I am sure the gossips of Ashokan, even those among our home company, have delighted in proclaiming otherwise, and my younger years have certainly not been blameless, but—Tom, what I'm saying is, my habits are different now. I am a man of twenty-five years. Educated by both teachers and hard experience. Reformed. Steady. What I mean is—damnation, now I sound the perfect prig, do I not?"

"No sir. You sound, as you say, imperfect, but well-intentioned mainly."

"That's it, exactly! And now, as long as you hold me in that much esteem, I wish to tell you that I have completed a letter to your sister."

Tess felt the color rise to her cheeks.

"To make her acquaintance. To assure her of your good health. To express my interest in studying the complexities of your unique bond. I shall send it to the Quakers you spoke of, and—"

That arrogance needs nipping, Tess thought. "No. I will take it. All letters will travel through me."

"Oh? Yes. As you say." He looked toward the trickle of creek flow in the distance and cleared his throat. Then his attention returned to their horses. "What do you think of the farrier's work of rasping the rim of these hooves?" he asked.

Tess wasn't thinking of hooves. She was hoping the Waterfords could find it in their hearts to ferry about this strange correspondence.

* * *

Early on Sunday, the twenty-first day of June, the battle began. *Why did the sides go to war on the Lord's Day?* Tess wondered, although such thoughts were frivolous and unpractical. And they did little to distract her from the bursting shells and rattle of artillery in the distance, around the muddy creek they called Bull Run.

Tess liked having the doctor, Joe Hartness, and Davy Flanders in plain sight as they prepared the stone church to become a field hospital. They removed seats and covered the floor with blankets, hauled buckets of water from wells, and brought in hay from nearby fields for bedding. The destructive sounds approached closer as they worked, as Ryder Cole laid out his instruments and medicines.

"I sure wish I knew the way it was going," Joe Hartness said to Tess and Davy as they tromped out into the open field to fetch hay bedding. "It don't seem right, us not being in the thick of pushing those rebels back after the way they took down Richardson's men."

"Somebody's got to look after the wounded," Tess reminded him.

"Sure. And I'd be grateful myself, Tom, if it was your face I saw if'n I went down. But I'm not as suited to… well, the choring, the cleaning up as you are. We're in uniform. We're soldiers."

"Summer soldiers," Davy groused. "Untested. We ain't even been issued weapons."

"You signed on with Captain Cole," Tess reminded them, "trained by him for the work required. This work. There's tedious parts to every job."

"Tom, I'd much sooner be cleaning and oiling a rifle than—"

"Get your back into that haying, Private," Tess ordered.

Joe narrowed his eyes. "Well now, will you listen to the new corporal flaunting—"

They heard a crack. Joe's head jerked suddenly to one side. He looked as if he was trying to remember the rest of his thought, before he fell, staining the summer wheat red.

"Take cover!" Tess yelled as another shot came, then another. Three. Three snipers. What were they doing here, so far from the battlefield?

She grabbed the shoulder of Joe Hartness's vest and dragged him into the wheat field's protection with her.

"We are unarmed!" she shouted.

A silence of a few more seconds. Then, three cracks again, in rapid succession.

They were fast loaders.

Davy Flanders let out a garbled blasphemy.

"Davy? You hit?" Tess called.

"Just my boot heel."

Another round of three shots fired in rapid succession. In the seconds they took to reload, Tess crawled closer, reached Joe's hand, to feel the strong, pounding pulse at his wrist.

"That you, Tom?"

"Yes. Stay down."

"I'm sorry for saying that about your rank, was my own envy speaking."

"Hush up, now. Lie still."

"I require your forgiveness, considering our chances—"

"I said hush!"

Tess tried to think like the doctor would. Head wound, its bleeding profuse. *Damnation. Where are the shooters? Stay calm. Find them.* Tess dug a clump of parched Virginia soil and pitched it, drawing their next volley of three. There. The trees.

The hooves of a lone horse sounded, left the road, approached. Tess rose to her elbows to see a young federal officer riding toward them. His eyes reflected the sky, his long hair was as gold as the wheat around them. He and his fine horse seemed to have sprung up from the beautiful land itself.

Tess knelt, holding her palm secure against Joe's wound's flow. "Snipers, sir!" she called out a warning.

The officer brought his mount to a precise halt. Close enough for Tess to see he was a captain. He reached deftly into his saddlebag.

"Where?" he demanded.

"Two in the south field's poplar, one east, in the oak."

"Ah. Yes." He pulled off his buckskin glove, drew his revolver, aimed. He fired off four shots in rapid succession from his repeater. Two bodies fell from the poplar. The remaining one slumped, arms dangling, from the oak.

Tess blinked, swallowed, turned to the horseman. "Good shooting, sir."

He grinned, showing even teeth. "Fine spotting, Corporal."

He reached into his coat, unfurled a billowy white handkerchief placed it in Tess's hand. His own was hot from the discharge of his firearm. Then he rode for the trees.

Davy joined her, unsteady on his unheeled boot, and looking dazed.

"We have to help Joe," she told him, which seemed to bring his eyes back into focus.

"He'll be all right, won't he Tom?"

Joe groaned, answering for himself. The golden captain's handkerchief was large enough to tie around his head. The white reddened, but the blood flow was decreasing.

The captain returned, dropping three rebel rifles at their feet.

"All dead," he announced, with a nod back at the trees. "Can you get your wounded in?"

Tess nodded. "Yes, sir."

"Good. Fighting's moving this way, best return to the church. Rebel shells are landing in the road back to Washington. An awful tangle. Time to lead the tourists home, as their show is over. I do not believe we will be marching on to take Richmond today."

He touched the rim of his slouch hat, decorated with a fancy plume.

"Thank you, sir," Tess breathed out. "Sir?"

"Yes?"

"Who shall I say came to our aid, sir?"

He grinned again. Seductively this time, as if he knew she was a woman. "Last in his class at West Point, Corporal. You may tell any who asks that."

Chapter Eleven

"Tom."

"Sir?"

"I will finish here. Go. Find Hartness and Flanders. Rest. An order."

Ryder Cole could barely speak, his own fatigue so wore on him. She wouldn't add to it with a protest, something else to fight, when they'd been fighting Death all day on the sorry, drenched retreat toward Washington. So she left him cleaning a few remaining instruments with the precious little fresh water they had left. His fine hands were swollen like a workman's.

She'd lost count of how many men she, Joe and Davy had held down after they'd run out of ether, while Ryder Cole had sawed through flesh, muscle, and bone to release a limb. No one was meant to endure what the injured and dying had, or to see what she and her comrades had seen. None except maybe Mr. Lincoln and Mr. Davis, if they had the power to stop it. But Tess was afraid that they didn't have the power, and she didn't know who did. She wanted to tell someone these things, ask someone with more learning the questions that were eating her like a gut-wound.

When she reached the tent's opening, she looked back. In his small circle of lamp light, Ryder Cole's shoulders shook. She couldn't leave him this way, because he was her friend and she loved him, no matter how complicated it had made her life.

"Ryder?" she whispered, calling him his Christian name for the first time. Sending it out through the darkness sounded so intimate, so forbidden.

His back stiffened. He turned only a slice of his face toward her, listening.

"You earned that seat on your horse this day, sir. Don't be fretting on that account no more. Uh—any more," she corrected herself quickly.

He allowed her to see the rest of his face then. A thin trickle of blood flowed from where he'd bit down on his lip in his effort to contain his emotion.

Men were foolish that way, Tess decided, preferring another wound over the release of salty, healing tears. She didn't think Ryder Cole was like the rest. Hadn't he showed her the full measure of his grief when he'd lost his horse to the panther and her bullet? And they had been strangers then. She walked to him, shaking her head. "We've seen more than enough hurt. Don't hurt yourself," she whispered.

A tenderness entered his bright eyes, reminding her that, for all his wealth and travel, learning and experience, he was young, like her, and as untested by war. He gave her the gift of his slow, shaky smile. When the effort made him wince, she instinctively touched her thumb to his lip, pressed the small wound.

His nostrils flared, the muscles in his neck corded. "Go to bed, Tom."

She stepped back. Tom. She was Tom. He couldn't show a man the tears he'd shown the woman who'd shot his horse for him. And her touch, she feared, had prompted another feeling. But even in his distress, he was not taking it out on her.

Oh Lord, what was she doing to this man?

There was no room for her to sleep anywhere among the sea of wounded outside the tent. She couldn't find Davy or Joe, who'd been dismissed hours earlier, after the wounded man from an Ohio regiment ripped off Joe's bandage during surgery. Tess hoped Davy had helped Joe find a dry spot.

The rain turned to a fine mist. She began shivering. Where were any of the hometown boys from Company D? They'd make a place for her, they always did.

Ryder Cole had ordered her to bed, instead of off duty. That man would never be a proper officer. Well, isn't that why she'd followed him? They were both something temporary, for the good of the union—he a soldier, she a man and a soldier. She was there because she wanted hands like his, knowing, healing hands. Though today he had been more of a butcher. Still, his kindness had never left him, and his steady voice acted the morphine's part when it ran out.

She pictured him there inside the tent of the most severely wounded, watching over them. No, not the most severely wounded. Those fellows were put outside and made as comfortable as possible, to wait for death. The ones the doctor sat watch over were the ones he still had hope for.

An hour's rest she'd take, if she could only find some shelter. Then she'd go back on duty. Maybe Ryder would allow her to relieve him then. Doctor, she must think of him as Doctor, or Captain. Not Ryder anymore. And no more touching.

The field was full of strangers groaning. There. Under the oak, just out of the furthest campfire's light, a small space between two sleeping soldiers.

"What's the matter, boy?" one of them called out softly

"Sorry to disturb—"

"Hey, you're the doc's man, ain't you? The doc who don't mind treating those outside his own regiment?"

"Yes."

"Good team. Off duty now, are you?"

"Yes."

"You going to sleep standing up, or you want to lie between Rodgers and me?"

"If you wouldn't mind."

"Hell, no. Settle in."

"Thank you."

Tess collapsed gratefully between the men.

She thought of the woods around Ryder's place, full of game animals and beauty. She remembered the lake, and the cool fresh scent of the water at dawn, to put herself to sleep amid the carnage.

It worked. When she opened her eyes she saw the sun dappling through the leaves of the oak. As late as that? She sat up.

The kind soldier was still asleep, as was his comrade Rogers on her other side.

"Jesus, Tom." The lanky form of Davy Flanders stood above her.

He reached for the shoulder of her coat, took hold, and yanked her over the sleeping men so hard she tripped over Rogers.

"Easy, Davy!" she chided with a soft laugh.

"What you whispering about?"

"Well, these fellows were mighty peaceful nighttime companions. I wouldn't want to disturb them."

"You quit that kind of talk! Ain't respectful."

He signaled to the Negro men walking beside a wagon. "Two more here," he called, pointing to her sleeping companions.

"They're dead?" she whispered.

"'Course they're dead. This is where all the dead got laid out last night. What are you staring at, Tom? Don't we know what dead looks like?"

"He talked to me. He made room—"

She'd kept herself steady though all the suffering. Why was she shaking now?

She felt Davy's hand on her arm. "Maybe…maybe someone else spoke. A joke, like. Getting you to talk with a corpse. Was dark, wasn't it?"

"Yes. Yes, it was dark."

"Don't think about it no more. You'll make yourself crazy."

The shakes were leaving. "How's Joe?"

"Even his mighty headache left him. Likes the new bandage, but wants blood on it, to show any ladies. Don't worry about him none. It's me gone lame for the want of a boot heel."

Tess looked up into her friend's open, honest face. "Thanks, Davy. Thanks for coming for me."

"Aw, it's your damned coffee we missed. And the doc's way too prickly in the morning without you beside him."

Chapter Twelve

Washington D.C.

Back in the capital city, there was enough going on in commandeering private homes for hospital space and trying to make their patients comfortable that Tess didn't see Dr. Cole for hours at a time. But she cleared a small room for him at the home turned hospital on N Street: a dressing room with a window, a quiet place, close to his surgery. It contained a servant's rope bed he almost never slept in. Tess found him sleeping twice between surgeries though, his head in his hand or resting on the table with bloodied instruments. He was forgetting even the things he'd learned from his French teachers.

Tess sent Joe in to shake him, so he wouldn't have to wake under her touch.

When Frederick Olmstead, the Surgeon General visited, he pulled her aside.

"Corporal Boyde, the situation here in Washington is abominable. We were not ready for so many casualties. I have pointed out this regiment, this company as a model in sanitation procedure, in humane treatment of the wounded. But it is now headed by a doctor who begins to look worse than the soldiers under his care."

"We're short staffed, sir."

"I know that."

"We need nurses, Mr. Olmstead. We need the ladies."

"That is self-evident as well. And I am working diligently toward that end, be assured. But I have held Captain

Cole up as a model doctor. Tom, he is no longer in the heat of battle. There are surgeons and physicians here to relieve him."

"Order him time away from here, sir."

"Order? I'm not his superior."

"He trusts you. He admires you. Please. Order it."

Two hours later she caught the chipped crockery cup that slipped from Ryder's fingers before it landed in his lap. Its steaming contents splashed her hand, burning her knuckles. Her gasp woke him.

"Tom?"

"Coffee ain't working any more, Captain."

"Working?"

"To keep you awake."

"I have been relieved. For three days. Olmstead brought a major down on me." He blinked. "Your skin, it will blister. Let me find a salve, dress it. God, Tom. I cannot move."

"You're pure spent, Captain."

"Spent, is it?" There. That bemused look she loved.

"Sir, please take your leave. To your room."

"Room?"

"You remember, I found you one. Placed your gear there."

"Good of you, Tom."

She frowned.

He ran his hand through his hair deeply, at the scalp, a gesture she'd seen often over the past days. It succeeded in lengthening his sentences. "I am burning my best assistant. I believe that is a violation of the Hippocratic Oath. Yes, time to go before I accomplish even greater damage. It isn't far, Tom?" he asked quietly. "This room?"

She smiled. "No sir. Follow me."

Still, on the way there, he was called to the bedside of two soldiers, and consulted with a doctor who Tess was not able to wave away.

By the time they reached the room, he sank down on the small cot, its thin feather mattress the only acknowledgment of his rank.

Tess didn't want to touch him, but if she didn't he was going to sleep in his foul-smelling, bloodied uniform. So she pretended he was one of her brothers after a drunken spree, yanked off his coat and began his undressing.

He didn't wear a scratchy woolen one piece, but a long shirt, wonderfully soft, with a label assuring the wearer that its cotton weave was produced in a Catskill mill by free workers with cotton that was not the product of slave labor. Was it from the package she had delivered to his mother that first day in Ashokan? This man was Republican to his underwear, Tess thought with a fond smile.

He stayed in that vague, blinking half sleep, as she got him down to bare skin, free to enjoy the woman's feelings the look of his lean, angular body caused in her. Pale, beautiful skin, marred only by a whitened scar under his heart. What had caused that, she wondered as she found another shirt in his bag. As she put it over his head, he breathed deeply of its lavender scent.

"I have not written to my mother in days."

"You can do that when you wake, sir."

"Have you heard from Tess?"

She smiled. "I have. Our Quaker friends are helping her make her way in the world, though in hiding."

"Well, that is splendid news."

Maybe he was awake enough to pull down his trousers himself. When she rose from the bed, he grabbed her wrist.

"Tom. I am ashamed to tell you something."

"Sleep now, Captain. Tell me when you wake."

"Now," he insisted. "I need to tell you the truth. You will understand?"

"Understand what, Captain?"

"About the place where I feel a need to go, while on this imposed leave."

"Where is that, sir?"

"Madame Lanier's."

Tess smiled. "Might I come with you?"

He blinked. "Well. Yes. We'll both go. And I will not breathe a word of the place to your sister, if you will keep my mother unenlightened."

* * *

At Madame Lanier's big bedroom dressing table, Tess reached for the purple bottle. She wondered if it would smell like lavender, that scent his mother had sprinkled among Ryder Cole's shirts. It did not. It was heavy with an exotic fragrance she could not identify. If she tried a lighter, frosted glass atomizer, would she find a scent that suited her, that would spray away the smell of death and dying? There, that was it. Her mother's scent. Lilac. Tess dipped the stopped and placed the scent where the girls did, behind each ear, across her wrists, between her breasts.

She didn't tell her captain why she'd wanted to return to Madame Lanier's house. There was the depth of the zinc lined bathtubs, and the kindness, and the allure of those bottles. And the chance to free the breasts she'd thought annoying encumbrances since she was fifteen.

The peacock feather she placed among her long, added-on tresses tickled her bare back deliciously. Still, the pleasure of it, of her bath and the giggling fuss the girls made did not distract her from thinking about Ryder in the next room.

Why shouldn't he enjoy the pleasures of the flesh? It was the same kind of good time she was having here—choosing a scent, putting the rouge on her cheeks, the rice powder to even out her complexion and make it glow in the candle light. The same kind of pleasure, because she was imagining he was kissing her, sliding those tender hands between her legs where, even now, she was feeling wet with yearning. This was just as wrong as what he was doing with Arabella, wasn't it?

"Now you've done it."

Tess looked up, past the startled, guilty reflection of her own face to that of Madame Lanier.

"He wants you."

"Me?"

"You. His 'Diana.' The girl who threw his boots down to him off the balcony. The one who lost her brother to the war. And he's as nervous as a cat after what happened last time."

"What happened, Ma'am?"

"He couldn't rise to the occasion of his visit. Do you take my meaning, backwoods girl?"

"Yes," Tess whispered, wondering what had happened to Madame Lanier's French accent and refined ways.

"Arabella fawned over him like I tell my girls to do when that happens. He didn't take it well at first. Doctors think they know every damned thing! So he concocted that he was too busy thinking about how you, that would be Tom, his corporal, was faring. As if 'thinking' has much to do with anything that goes on in men's nether reaches! So Arabella says, sure, that must be it, so he calms some, and lets her start on him again. Then he hears you and my shrieking hyenas and meets your female version as the damned raid turns the place upside down!"

Tess nodded, remembering. "Arabella was whispering in his ear as he took to the window."

Madame Lanier grunted. "Telling him that he could have her for free when he came calling again. That's stand-ard procedure after a raid, mind, but my Arabella, she makes it sound nice and personal. But now, tonight, he doesn't want any but his bereaved Diana. I know these over-educated, thick-skulled ones. You're the cause of his misery. And now he wants you as the cure, Corporal Boyde."

Tess stared at her hands. Demure, calm, placed in her lap, below the corset's pretty blue trim. And red where his spilled coffee burned them. The skin of her knuckles hadn't blistered. It was only a little pink and peeling, could be covered with rice powder.

Tess breathed deeply. "Well. It's only right. I got him into this confusion he has about himself. I'd best try to get him out. Can you help me, ma'am? With the particulars? Like how to check on his nether reaches?"

The woman sighed deeply. "Oh, my dear. I don't know."

"Please, Ma'am. I love him. And I'm fairly bursting with the yearning for him myself."

The beautiful woman frowned. Tess saw the lines of it even through her smoothing face paint.

"Broken in, are you?"

Tess shifted her sight to between Madame Lanier's eyes. "Oh, yes, Ma'am. I'm broke to the saddle," she said. And waited.

"All right," Madame Lanier finally agreed. "I'll help you."

Tess's smile was so shaky she hid it behind her hand. And it emerged with a sound that was something between a laugh and cry.

"And knock him off that pedestal. He's no world-renowned lover of women. That peach-faced boy probably writes home to his mama weekly!"

"Daily," Tess admitted. "He's kind too, Madame Lanier. If you could see him on the field, in the hospital."

"Well, he'd better be, with my new girl. Or I'll cut his heart out."

"Thank you, ma'am. And I'm truly sorry for the trouble Ryder and me have caused you."

The woman shook her head. "Oh save your sentiment for your lover, little one. You summer soldiers are a sorry bunch, but you're more entertaining than the politicians at least."

"Madame Lanier?"

"What is it now?"

"You're not a French lady, are you?"

"No, I'm not. I'm as backwoods as you are, I suspect. Missouri. But I worked my way down the Mississippi to New Orleans, where I picked up a thing or two to sell here in Washington. And that's our secret now, ain't it?"

"Yes, ma'am."

Chapter Thirteen

Dark. Giving Ryder time, space, to change his mind, slip away, get out. But he stayed, standing just beyond the doorway of the darkened bedroom, thinking of Tom's hesitant, across-the-ranks friendship, and that innocent, healing touch after Bull Run. And what his body had done to him in its wake. Stop. Stop thinking on it. If Tom had even understood what his touch had done, he'd already forgiven it. Ryder was sure of that, at least.

He envied the straightforward way Tom Boyde saw the world. Ryder wanted to help those sensitive hands become as skilled as his own. Would he have to abandon him to others, who might turn his talent into butchery? Yes, he'd have to, if he couldn't resolve this, here, in the dark. His gut clenched. But he had to find out, and now. Find out what? Ryder Cole considered himself an educated man, but he could not name this terrible thing that might be true about himself.

He tried to concentrate on the lilac perfume, on finding the girl in the darkness. The shrouded girl, who smelled of spring. She would not even talk, Madame Lanier had warned him. He didn't care. He'd agree to any conditions to buy her services on this moonless night.

His eyes adjusted enough make out a vague outline, sitting up against the bolster of a mahogany four poster, like his own bed at home. Madame Lanier's bed, in the best room of her house. The bed where she entertained her most important clients—senators, congressmen, ambassadors. Had she found out the fortune he was heir to? Is that why she'd agreed? Crafty women, women who lived by their wits, were good at finding out such things. And he was in a nest of such women. He should be more careful about guarding the way into his mother's fortune.

He stepped forward. His hand took hold of the post. No, it was not like his bed. He felt plain reeding, not the medallions and carved sheaves of wheat of his bed at home. Still, he clung to the bedpost as if it was the link to his past, his home, himself. The girl had not moved. Perhaps they would stay at their stations all night.

No. He'd come this far. Unlock. Unlock something, his grip, his voice.

Her scent intensified.

He'd forgotten to put in the order for more calomel for the second floor of the ward, for the men who were getting sick with—

A rustle of sheets. A hand covered his. Strong. More like tanned leather than a woman's hand. He finally loosened his grip on the bedpost.

He kissed into the girl's palm. She gasped. He felt the bones beneath her skin startle. A soft sigh escaped her, along with the scent of mint leaves and a little port wine, more pleasant than the whiskey scent of his own breathing. Her fingers stroked his face, a face he'd shaved as smooth as a bridegroom's. To please her. To thank her for taking him on. Did it please her?

He caught the scent of her skin beneath the lilac, a little salty. Skin. This was no bride gowned in soft white, but a naked whore, her ripe body filling the darkness, robbing him of breath. Could she sense it? Would she laugh? No, not laughter, but a soft, pleasant sound, like a whicker of a loved horse.

He could breathe again. The fingers manipulated his cravat free, and opened his shirt. Her mouth planted feathery kisses along his tense jaw. This was not the other one, Arabella, chattering, laughing in his ear, while he was too drunk, too worried about Tom. He'd made a good choice. This one, this silent huntress.

Only through the prism of his injuries did he remember the day he'd lost Moutamin to the panther. But the wild-wood woman he could barely see was at the center of it, fierce, protective, understanding his grief. Now he'd captured Diana at last, and she was all his for this night. The delight of it surged through him, making him hard. She found it, that delight, with her clever whore's hands.

She continued making him as naked as she was, swiftly, expertly, knowing all the buttons and closures of his uniform. She must have done this before, for many soldiers, he thought, shocked. Why? This was good. He needed experienced hands. And Madame Lanier's was a clean house. There would be no debilitating venereal disease to come of this night. How many men this girl had had before him didn't matter. That's what he was paying her for, her skill. His imagination about his virgin huntress would do the rest.

Strong hands, not strangers to work, kneaded his shoulders. He was her work tonight, and he didn't envy her the job of him. She knelt higher, offering her breasts. Wonderful, glorious. His thumbs stroked her nipples. Her gasp delighted him. Made him feel more bold, powerful. Women could not hide that, could they, that intensity of female scent? That hardening bead feel? Or was she cold? Or afraid?

"I will not hurt you," he heard his own gruff whisper. Stupid. Stupid notion. She would laugh at him, he'd ruined everything.

But she didn't laugh. She shook her head like a colt. Then she kissed him shyly, like a girl, not a lush whore. Yes. This was right, so right, his hands at her flared hips, pulling her closer. His tongue traced her lips, plunged inside, tasted. Woodland, yes, she tasted of woodland, of camp fires.

Hunger, desperate hunger, now penetrated his being. He ate, he devoured. Her fingers fisted in his hair, yanked his head back, breaking their connection. She was strong; his scalp ached.

"Forgive me," he said, panting, shocked, ashamed. But terribly, gloriously happy. Oh God, were all these strange circumstances what it took to give clear evidence of his manhood? He'd never felt more alive, aching, craving entrance. She was beautiful, she had to be beautiful. Hadn't he seen her, grieving for her brother, and on the balcony throwing him his boots? His first look was through a dull mirror's reflection, the second at a distance, and in the drunken haze of a damned fool, his rational part reminded him. But before that, she'd pulled his dislocated arm and shot his horse. He had seen her close then, had he not? No, not her. But what was the harm, putting the two women together? He was paying enough to have two all night long.

Easy. Easy now. Little shudders in the girl's breathing came as he placed her beneath him, deep in the featherbed. His fingers landed light touches at her taut, muscled belly, making her giggle. A good sound. Ryder felt the blood pounding at his temple. And at that other place, beyond hard, bursting with need.

She gripped his shoulder. Why? Had she changed her mind? Would she push him away? It's what he deserved, after all, for hauling himself and his band into the hell of this dawning war. No. Her grip eased.

"Diana," he whispered.

She responded with that sweet whickering.

"Tell me when."

She based one hand against his chest, while the other took hold of his erection. She stroked it, as she bestowed gentle, maiden's kisses at his cheek. Who was this woman, so full of contradiction? The air itself seemed to pulse in the charged stillness between them.

He sprang then, taking her wrist, locking it above her head as he kissed her shoulder, then along the soft mounds of her breasts. Her surprised reaction was high pitched, lovely, making him feel powerful and charming, as if he were giving her a gift, not paying for her intoxicating body's services. He explored lower. His hand parted her legs. She opened them with a sigh.

He delved. She gasped, sweet against his ear. Deeper. Her secret space muscled in around his fingers. Hot, wet, slick.

"Now?" he barely managed to ask.

The colt nod came again, her soft braided mane against his shoulder, evoking a protective tenderness in him he did not know he possessed, never mind should be giving to this hired girl. He imagined he could see her eyes. Nut brown, with sparks of amber. Glistening. He lowered himself between her thighs.

Something prevented full entrance. Something that made everything, suddenly, not right. Not right unless she was Diana, the Virgin. *Stop. Get out.* But she had his shoulders in that strong grip, and was writhing with her own need under him.

"Now," she whispered. A guttural sound, her first word was as desperate as he felt. Or did he imagine that, because his own compulsion was so great? He plunged through. Through what? *Hymen, you idiot. A membrane. The word is hymen.*

The knowledge of what he was doing, the scent of her blood spilling didn't stop him, for she was still sinuous, licking his earlobe, drawing him deeper into her with those intense, pulsing squeezes. So he took her buttocks between his hands, brought her higher, plunging deeper, until he felt their hipbones touch. He emptied himself inside her.

He collapsed into the hollow between her breasts after, hoping against hope that he would die, and never have to think through the consequences of the night he regained his precious manhood.

"Thank you," he whispered against the beat in her throat. Her arms wrapped around him. She kissed into his scalp as if he were not the thief of her maidenhead.

He shifted himself up against the bolster, and placed her gently under his heart.

"You're angry." Her first sentence, laced with fear.

"No, not angry." Think. Say the right thing. Say anything to keep her from bolting. "That is, not with you. Listen to me now. Stay here, a moment. Promise you will wait for my return."

She nodded, nuzzling into his chest, stifling tears, breaking his heart.

"Good girl. Do not cry. There's my girl, sweet girl. Stay. I will not be long. Stay."

Madame Lanier fisted her hands at her hips, annoyed with him for asking Mr. Rolf to pull her out of the company of two loutish major generals, raising their glasses to her gracious beauty. Ryder was only a captain, after all, standing before her in a downstairs ante-room, his clothes hastily yanked on, his feet bare.

"What are you complaining about?" she demanded in a furious whisper. "I know plenty of men would pay extra for 'bursting cherries' they call—"

"That is disgusting and unmanly. I would call them out."

"You'd be a dead man many times over, Captain Cole."

"Good God, why did you not tell me?"

"I did not know."

"What?"

"Listen. I took her in. Not as one of my girls. She was helping out around the place. Like a little sister she was playing dress up that night you happened in on—"

"Little sister? Oh, God. How old is she?"

"Oh, she's old enough to know better, don't go fretting on that account! Save me from you damned principled Yankees! Well, perhaps she lied because she fancied you, and knew I would not have allowed it otherwise. You were…what did she say? Kind. About her brother. It is a compliment, is it not, that she fancied you?"

"Yes. I suppose it is."

"So, what is eating you about it, Captain?"

"Madame Lanier, I do not know what to do now."

"I'd say you have done enough."

"I have not. I need to look after her. That's it, yes. She's mine. You'll keep her for me, won't you? As she was before, a companion to your girls? Were she passed around, why, she could get diseased—"

"I run a clean house, sir!"

"Venereal diseases travel both ways. Your clients can go elsewhere, and acquire one of them as easily as the poorest of my men. If she were ever infected, I would never forgive myself. So. Now that I have played a role in her ruination, I should like to do whatever necessary to keep her. Do…do you suppose she will allow that?"

The whorehouse madam sighed. "Why don't you go back upstairs and ask her? I've got customers with simpler needs looking for me."

Chapter Fourteen

I am scented with him now, Tess thought. She slipped the chemise over her head and changed the sheets. Afterward, she was not able, somehow, to release the bloodied linens from her arms. She breathed deeply into them. And wept.

Her father had forbidden her to ride astride on the day she'd turned fifteen. Claimed it would ruin her for a man. Tess didn't know what that meant, and Maud O'Neil hadn't been through with her wagon in months, so she'd asked the only other female she trusted, Miss Waterford, when she came into the Big Woods looking for her botanicals. The Quaker woman gently told her about what virginity was and what lying with a man would do. Her father said riding astride once her flow started would do it too, and make her husband think she was a whore. But Tess loved riding too much to stop. So she thought she had ruined herself already.

But Ryder had known, even before the blood. Because he was a doctor, was that how he knew? No pain came with the bleeding. Having him inside her was the furthest thing from painful. Why had she bled?

The clock on Madame Lanier's staircase landing struck one. Tess heard low grumbling. The shift change. She had to wait, because he'd made her promise to, after he talked to her all soft, like she was one of his mares. She knew the sacredness of giving her word, but she wanted to run away. She'd made things worse, when she was trying to help him. Stop it, stop crying, even in a chemise and lilac scented, it was unmanly. And she couldn't do anything unmanly except…well, what she'd just done.

Tess could not bring herself to regret the time, to regret the places his fingers, his mouth, his deep dives had taken her. It was a failing that would keep her outside heaven, she was sure, this lack of remorse. But she owed him assurance that he was still a woman's man.

What had made him angry, once it was done? He hadn't ruined her. Loving him would never make her feel ruined, just as riding horses hadn't. Maybe there were no understanding men, even when you lived as a companion beside them. But she loved this one. Worse, now. Well, she was Tom too, and Tom still had his friendship. Ryder wouldn't take his anger out on Tom. Never. Because her captain was almost too kind for this world. Stop that. Dangerous thought, especially in wartime.

The tears finally stopped flowing. She wiped her cheeks with the backs of her hands. Crying helps you feel better, her mother always said. And it had.

No one came into the room. Had Ryder paid for more time here, or was she about to be shoved out? Tess daubed lilac water behind her ear.

She hoped Madame Lanier was not too angry. Would that experienced woman still explain how to keep a baby from starting out of what they'd done this night? Tess needed to know that, or she'd get into an even worse fix. She leaned against the bolster and brought her hand inside the opening of her chemise. She rested her middle three fingers on the spot where he had first held, kissed her breasts. That was one thing she did understand now—how women put up with having too many babies. It was a big price to pay for this fleeting glory whose echoes still coursed through her. But the glory. The glory was like lying under a star studded sky, and the taste of the clearest spring, and an orange in your shoe on Christmas morning all put together, Tess decided.

A soft knock. She shoved the stained linens under the bed. His scent—sandalwood, leather, metal, and what, edging it—fear? Or was that part of her own scent on him? Footfalls. He stumbled into, then drew up one of Madame Lanier's fancy painted chairs. Tess could make out its gold highlights. Ryder sat on it, then reached out into the darkness. Tess sensed that healing hand. She'd seen him offer it to patients a hundred times. Now it was hers, so she took it.

More silence. Then, finally, he whispered in an almost strangled voice. "Listen. Miss. Might I hold you? Nothing more, I promise."

Tess lifted the covers. He was mostly dressed, but she felt his cold feet slide along her calf. The raging storm inside him had left, she thought. His hold on her was gentle. His sleeves were rolled up and he wore no vest or coat. He tucked her head under his chin. His hand slipped out of hers and held her jaw gently.

His questions began. "Are you well?"

She nodded slowly. Had he sensed, smelled her tears?

"Good. My given name is Ryder. Might I know yours?"

She shook her head.

"As you wish. Might I continue to call you Diana, then?"

She nodded.

"Diana. I would not have asked this night of you had I known you were a virgin. Do you understand that?"

Tess shook her head. It produced a long, tolerant sigh from him. Did he think her slow-minded? She was not slow-minded. Ryder Cole connected himself to peculiar notions, that's all.

"Your brother," he said now, changing tack, confusing her, "the one who died on the night we…uh, met. Was he your last living relative? Are you alone in the world, Diana?"

She nodded again, hoping he didn't realize she was answering only the last of his questions. Tess didn't care how many living relatives she had, she was still alone in the world.

"Well, then. I should like to keep you."

She was too stunned to move. He took her stillness for something else.

"I know it was painful for you, tonight. And I was awkward, clumsy. But it will get better between us, I think, if you will give me a chance to prove myself more worthy of your favors, your kind attentions. I will pay for your lodging here. I will supply all your needs, and things that give you pleasure as well, if you will reserve yourself for me, be mine alone."

Tess felt the hand holding her face grow cold. She caught it before it slipped away, kissed into the palm, then directed his fingers over the contours of her smile before she had him feel her nod.

"Yes? You are sure?"

She nodded again, vigorously, making him laugh. Making him laugh! What power that was. He breathed deeply at her temple, then behind her ear where she'd placed the lilac water. His voice went low and gruff. "Someday I hope to coax you out in the sun."

She yanked herself to the edge of the bed.

Ryder groped, found her hands, held them. "I do not understand this shyness. But I will never force you into my sight, I will never force you in any way, Diana, I swear it. God help me, for I am no saint, but I am not that kind of man. You have given me this privilege that belonged to another. Were your brother alive he would rightly slice my life out for what went on between us tonight. I know they are not right, or fair, or proper of me, these conditions. But you must agree to be mine alone. I cannot share you, Diana. I'd rather lose you now than share you."

His alone. She would always be that, Tess thought, stunned and fearful of it. She didn't want for the comforts he'd promised as payment. She earned thirteen dollars a month in the army of the United States of America and sent most of it to the Waterfords to keep for her. Did a private whore make that much? It didn't matter. She was not anybody's whore, even this spoiled, rich man who wanted one all to himself.

He took her face in that gentle, giving hold again, honoring one of the peculiar demands she'd put on their—what did Madame Lanier call it? Liaison.

"Are we in agreement?"

Tess nodded.

"Well, then." His voice sounded very young. "Good." He gave out a short, helpless laugh. "I—have been a little confused lately, and, well, you have provided me with more than you will ever know, and for this I am forever in your debt, sweet girl."

He kissed her forehead like she'd seen doting brothers do, but leaving the small swipe of his tongue to mark her something else—his lover. It banished the last edge of her annoyance. She knew exactly what she'd provided, he wasn't all that hard to figure.

"I will leave you to your continued recovery, then," he said,

She would never recover from the feel of him beside her like this. Tess found and then touched his bowed head, there in the darkness. He halted his retreat. She threaded her fingers through the waves of his hair.

"Diana, don't," he breathed out. "God, your touch. You must not do these things." Schoolmaster again. But with a crack in his resolve. Where was its point of origin? The soft cotton of his shirt sifted open beneath her fingers. He groaned. Yes, there. How she loved undressing him. Tess led his hand inside the open ties of her shift, reveled in the catches in his breathing. She'd never before thought of the soft parts of her as powerful.

"Diana, I have taken your virginity. Made you hurt, bleed. Are you sure this is your desire?"

Buttons, of his blue wool trousers, released under her fingers. He was hard there, against her hand. Was she doing that, truly? She licked the salty muscled flesh of his chest.

A sharp intake of breath. Then, his arguments again. "Madame Lanier says that I… That you, uh, should—" But even as he made excuses for her, he drew down the sleeves of her shift.

Her breasts rose with her breathing. Her mouth was wet with wanting him to do what he was doing, kissing her deep, deeper. The pleasant bursting, and she went drowsy and senseless, barely hearing his triumphant snort.

"Hey, now," he called, "Where are you going?"

Here, she was most exactly here, coming alive again as he taunted her earlobe with soft swipes of his tongue. She tried to push him away, as she did when her horse did that. But he was not her horse, and the swipes grew stronger, more insistent. And then that beautiful voice again.

"Astounding," he whispered, "so beautiful, this curve of your shoulder. And the place…here, where the inner part of your arm is so very—" He stopped. "Bless my soul," he said suddenly, startled. "If I am your first lover, how the devil do you manage to unfasten my clothes entirely in this pitch dark?"

Tess grunted her annoyance, and tried to smother further questions under kisses. Was she kissing him properly? She coursed her callused, soldier's fingers through his scalp, making deep, hungry sounds well up from him. Like something wilder than what he was in the daylight. Is that how all men were in their need?

"Better, it will be better this time, I promise," he breathed out like a gruff, fervent prayer as he took her down under his lithe body. Tess welcomed his searing heat between her thighs.

* * *

Afterward, Tess turned up the lamp enough to watch him sleep. She ran her finger along his strong, clean jawline. He'd shaved for a whore. And was full of promises. It was part of being rich, she supposed, and a failing, but one

105

she could forgive. Besides, men don't keep promises they make to whores, Madame Lanier had warned her. Even the men who brought presents and shaved.

They'd finished together this time, something he called an "apogee," before he tried "apex," then "pinnacle," the word she finally understood. He'd laughed sweetly when she placed soft kisses at his temple. The Ryder Cole Tom Boyde knew almost never laughed. Now he sighed deeply and shifted to his back under the sheet, the thin, summer weave blanket, sleeping like a soldier, ready to be awakened. But he slept well. Perhaps even dreamless, for his eyelids did not twitch. The marks of the aftermath of their first war engagement were finally easing. Did she dare think that their time together in this bed had helped?

That was what Tess feared he'd sense in her, their common soldier's bond. She feared it even as his fingers traced her face in the dark. The thin, tinny chime of Madame Lanier's clock sounded again. Two o'clock. A tap at the door. Tess brought the lamp with her and opened it.

Madame Lanier took the lamp, surveying Ryder Cole with a rueful shake of her blonde curls. She turned down the wick.

"Don't move him yet. Please," Tess said softly.

"Sweetling, he's got this room fully paid up, whenever you two need it, even if Richmond's not taken before Christmas. I'll not disturb him. But I'm bound to look after you now. We need to figure out the times you'll be available to him. You'd best not add carrying his brat in your belly to your apprentice surgeon duties, yes?"

* * *

Tess brushed his coat as the clock finished its longest chiming. He opened his eyes.

"Tom?"

"Yes, sir."

"What hour is it?"

"Twelve, Captain."

106

He looked confused by the light streaming through the heavy wooden slats of the Venetian blinds.

"Twelve?"

"Noon," she tried to help.

"Noon? How did I sleep past that damned off-key bugle's call? Wait. We are not at camp."

Tess turned back to her task, smiling. "Not hardly sir. Or at the hospital. We're on leave until tomorrow, remember?"

"On leave. Quite right." She heard him climbing out of bed and donning the clothes she'd set out on the fancy chair. "Have you been here all night, Tom?"

"Yes, sir."

"With whom? Arabella? Is she yours now?"

"Ain't none of them ours, Captain."

"Do not get obtuse on me! You know very well that I mean."

"I enjoy all the ladies' company." She tried to make it sound stern, castigating, as if he was invading her privacy. Which he was.

He touched her arm with his knuckle. "I beg your pardon. I am envious, I think."

"Envious?"

"They enjoy your company too, Tom, in case you have not noticed." He finished his dressing. "Nothing but giggles and excited whispers when you are around them." He sniffed the air. "And now they have made you coffee."

"There's some for you as well." She poured from the chipped pot with painted pictures of the old French King's palace full of looking glasses. She put the cup in her captain's hands, careful not to let her fingers touch his.

"Tom, my… lady. Have you been in her company? Does she talk to you?"

Calm. Stay calm. Tess commanded her suddenly jangled nerves. Tell the truth, whenever you can. "She does sir, yes."

"Is she—?" Tess feared he would hear her heart breaking. Was he about to ask Tom Boyde if his lover was beautiful? Was that all men cared about?

Ryder stared hard into her eyes. "Do you like her, Tom?" he asked quietly.

"Yes, captain," she said. "I like her fine."

"She's very shy."

"Yes, sir."

"Tom, I intend to visit as long as she welcomes me. She will be careful not to conceive a child and I will not allow a venereal infection to pass between us. Meaning of course, that we will not share intimacies with others. I am not certain that I made all of this clear. Will you make sure she understands, Tom?"

"I will, sir."

"Excellent. I am in your debt again." Tess saw discomfort enter his eyes. "You do not think much of me in this, do you?"

Tess frowned, thinking hard. "Sir. We're at war. You and this lady, you're in special circumstances. That's how I see it, sir."

"That's it. That's it exactly! Tom, how have I existed without you at my side, making the world clear?"

"You teasing me, Captain Cole?" she asked, a flame of annoyance.

His eyes became the eyes of the spring leaves on the day they'd met. "Not at all," he assured her. "I am in complete earnest."

He shoved her shoulder so hard she hit the door frame. "Come on then, we have much to do, and now only half the day to do it." He stopped. "Oh, I should leave her a note. I'm afraid I am not versed in the etiquette of this kind of—" He hesitated, wincing. "You would not know if my girl's literate, would you, Tom?"

Tess frowned. "She can read, sir."

"Well, how am I to know? I am not nearly the favorite you are. She barely speaks to me."

Chapter Fifteen

Outside Washington, D.C.

Another piece of worn crockery shattered at a distance the members of the medical corps had paced off as two hundred yards.

Joe sent out another of his whooping laughs of wonder.

"Leave some targets for the rest of us, Tom," Davy complained.

Tess grinned, switched the repeater to her left hand, and fired again, this time at the mudware remnants. They flew into the air.

Ryder shook his head. "Who taught you that kind of shooting?" he demanded. "Not your inestimable sister."

The smile left her face, along with the fun of the target practice. "Tess and I learned together. And it was hunger taught us. We had us a hardscrabble life, sir."

The look on his face gentled. "And that is why you send most of your pay to her. And seek bettering your lives in learning a trade while at war."

"For us both."

"An extraordinary bond."

"No, sir. It's real ordinary."

Davy shrugged. "Aw, just give me my turn."

Ryder gave out a short snort. "We might relax our rule to change shooters after two misses before Tom depletes our supply of targets. Now," he turned to Davy, "with one hand only, Private Flanders. Aim at the gray bottle next to the… ah…devastation that your comrade has wrought."

"Captain, if I could only have my Springfield—"

"You will not have time for your Springfield if we're pinned down with medical supplies, perhaps holding a wound closed and a man's life in your hands. Now, aim!"

Davy did.

"And fire," Ryder instructed.

Davy pulled the trigger. The bottle exploded.

"Damnation," both Davy and Joe breathed out in wonder.

Ryder smiled. "There, now. You are getting its feel. Ease back the hammer and fire again. At the cobalt bottle this time."

Davy stared at the smoking gun barrel. "I'll never get used to that, sir. It firing nigh onto forever."

Ryder exhaled. "Not forever. Six shots. Count them. Always know how many are left in the chamber."

He was a good teacher, Tess thought, glad to be watching again, and not the center of their attention. It allowed her to cheer the boys. And it allowed her to admire Ryder Cole with a woman's eyes.

He'd unhooked the right side brim of his Kossuth hat so it better shaded his eyes from the sun that glistened off the gold acorns. He'd lost both of his captain's ostrich plumes on the field at Manassas, but the hat was still handsome.

For their target shooting, Ryder had removed his coat and rolled up his shirtsleeves as he did in surgery. Tess had seen him that way many times, of course. But without his full apron, and without the blood to distract her, she now took pleasure from the way his vest harnessed his tautly muscled chest. He'd paid a washerwoman to iron a sharp crease down his trousers.

Tess could imagine everything under his clothes now, too.

She thought of their night, of the salty taste of fear on his cool skin. Even inside his mouth had been cold. She'd pressed her body to his coolness, making him gasp, laugh. Then that part of him grew hard, harder, against her thigh. Her bound breasts tingled now, remembering. She felt a wetness between her legs and a longing, deep longing, to be Diana, and in that bed with him again.

Joe left her side to join Ryder and Davy. "Beg your pardon, Captain," he said. "Why are we playing a rich man's game with your fancy firearms?"

Ryder frowned. "I am attempting to train you in self-preservation!"

"With Starr repeaters?"

"They are excellent weapons, with a range—"

"But only officers and the cavalrymen are allowed pistols."

Ryder sniffed. "These are not pistols. They are revolvers."

"And the army ain't going to issue revolvers to the likes of us, sir," Joe insisted.

"The army is not doing the issuing. I am."

"We can't take these, sir."

"Why not?" He waited, his eyes probing theirs. "Well? What's the matter with you three?"

Tess watched her comrades look down at their boots. "Good of you to think of us, sir," Davy finally said.

"It's not at all good. You are the worst musicians but best field hospital staff in the army. What is this all about?" Ryder demanded.

Davy stepped forward. "Joe and me, we ain't suited to the hospital work, Dr. Cole. Not like Tom is. And it was mighty irritating to be shot at that way, sir, in the wheat field, without a thing we could do about it. And that wheat field called attention to what we are missing."

"Missing?"

"Fighting, sir. Fighting hard against the rebels."

"To end the war, then go home," Joe agreed.

"And you believe that you are all that stand between stalemate and surrender?" Ryder asked sharply.

Joe twisted his hat between his hands. "No, sir. But we're volunteers. And our ninety days service to President Lincoln and to you is done, sir."

Tess watched Joe's words hit Ryder. "You wish to leave the service?" he asked quietly.

"No, sir. We're in this fight, same as you. And folks ain't talking about being home for Christmas, not after Bull Run."

Tess saw the pain enter Ryder's eyes. He nudged a piece of shot up crockery with his boot heel, then continued more slowly. "You wish to be reassigned, then?"

A silence. Davy Flanders gave Tess a quick glance. "We were thinking on that, yes. Not that we're sure yet, mind. But we figure it would hardly be fair to you, to take these fine revolvers without us telling you that, Dr. Cole."

"They are not a bribe."

"Sir?"

Ryder looked toward the glass bottles in the distance and the shimmering heat rising off them. He exhaled, a small, exasperated sound. "I must seem very willful, insisting you take these weapons, as well as come out here, be trained in their use. It is a failing. One that I do not often even see in myself, yet am diligent to correct, when I do. I did not realize how dangerous it would be for us," he continued. "I foolishly thought I could keep you safe. I cannot."

Ryder removed his hat and pulled his hand through his glistening black hair as his stance cocked a little to the right. Tess remembered the panther's lunge at his thigh and wondered if that leg was bothering him. "Well. These Starr revolvers should help, wherever in the field you are."

He stood very straight again, tucked his Kossuth under his arm, then made a small bow. Tess was sure an officer shouldn't do that toward his own men, but she was proud just the same, and would never tell on him.

He spoke in his most formal voice. "I thank you, gentleman, for your ninety days' service. It has been a great pleasure having you under my command. Now, as you can practice with your firearms yourselves, I will head back into the city." He replaced his hat, lifted his coat from the flat rock. Then he walked over the small crest of the hill.

Tess glared at her comrades. They kicked up dirt.

"Aw, Tom, we didn't mean, well, to hurt the doc's feelings. Talk to him, will you? Explain," Davy urged.

"Explain what? That you want to go screaming into battle but don't want to hear the screams on the operating table? That you want to make blood pour but not clean it up?"

"It ain't like that! I already took a shot myself, didn't I?" Joe protested, touching the reddened scar on his forehead.

"And he's trying to keep you from taking another shot. He can't help it that he's rich. Money don't mean the same to him as it does to us. He values our lives! And this is how you repay him? Desertion?"

She picked up Ryder's weapon and holster from the flat rock. He'd remembered his coat, but he'd left his own Starr repeater. Dear God, she'd never make a soldier out of that man, she thought, stung with exasperation as she caught up to him.

Ryder Cole did not look at her. Tess pretended to stumble in order to fall back behind his stride.

"Forgot your Starr, sir," she said quietly.

"Shit," he said, even more quietly.

She saw their horses waiting under a tulip poplar. "Morning and After ought to rest a little longer before we head back to hospital, don't you think, Captain?"

"We?"

"Sure, we. Unless you don't want me along, sir."

"No, no," he said, with a distracted air. "You are welcome."

They walked in a silent, mismatched companionship. Tess scanned the trees. Though they were not near enemy territory, they were not in Ashokan, either. The capitol city was a stone's throw from Virginia, and surrounded by Southern sentiment. They couldn't both afford to be brooding within their own thoughts, not in blue uniforms. She hoped Ryder wouldn't brood long this time.

She was always happy in his presence, no matter what his mood. And Lord, how she loved the new feelings he had caused. Stop it. Stop thinking about that when she was Tom, and her captain was getting too far ahead of her with the strides of those long legs.

She'd caught up to him by the time they sighted the stand of poplar and the picketed horses.

"You are off duty until tomorrow, Tom."

"I'd just as soon get back, turn in early."

"I would too. Last night was recreation enough for the lady who suffers my company." He cast her a sly, side winding glance. "For your companion at Madame Lanier's, too?"

Tess felt herself blushing to the roots of her greased back hair.

He shoved her shoulder.

He was touching her again, she realized, now that Diana had eased his mind about the propriety of doing so. *Bless you, Diana.*

Tess wondered why he thought it a suffering to be under his mouth, his hands? Though both he and Madame Lanier claimed it should have hurt that first time, it had not. It was the furthest thing from hurt she could imagine, and imagine it she would, whenever she needed to, until they were in that big, splendid bed again. But not now. Now she was Tom. His corporal, his friend.

"I'm right sorry about the boys, sir."

Ryder sat under a tulip poplar at the water's edge. Both their horses drifted to his side. Morning nudged his hat off his head, then nuzzled at his vest for the carrot within. He'd bought a sack of them from the farmer whose field they were using as their firing ground.

He shrugged, then grinned up at his horse. "This was supposed to be for getting us back into Washington before dark, you ugly cuss," he protested.

He teased Morning the way he used to tease his Moutamin, though he had never called his treasured Arabian ugly, Tess would bet on that. Her heart swelled as she watched them, realizing that Ryder and horses just plain took to each other, no matter what the breed or looks or station of either. She would rather have that quality than her superior skill with firearms.

Ryder snapped the carrot, tossing the other half to her. She placed it under After's champing teeth, then sat beside her captain in the shade.

He leaned his head against the tree's trunk and stared at the almost cloudless sky. A sudden, decimated look came into his eyes

"What will I tell their mothers, Tom?" he asked. "What will I tell their mothers when they die?"

She'd thought she'd known the whole of his concerns. She hadn't.

He closed his eyes.

"You can't do a blame thing about which of our company will or won't come through. You know that. They know that. Listen. We may get called out soon. That's what rumors are saying, at least. Davy and Joe will be better on the march, camping out. When they remember how tedious regular soldiering is most of the time, they might just think their hospital time was right refreshing."

Silence. Until she didn't think she could bear it.

"Do you think they will keep the Starrs, Tom?" he finally asked.

"I do, sir."

"That's good."

"Now, I like your pistols fine, captain," she said emphasizing the word 'pistols' to provoke him, "but, truth to tell, I'm better with a rifle."

"Is that so?" His face became more earnest. "I shall procure you the best one Mr. Colt, Starr, or Remington has to offer."

"I didn't say that to prompt an offer!"

"I know. And it does not matter if you run off to become a crack sharpshooter for the federal forces. I will not take it back."

"I ain't had thoughts of leaving my duties at your side, sir."

"Oh?"

She looked away. "The work suits me."

"It suits you to a fine degree, corporal." He frowned that other frown, the one he used when he really wanted to smile. "What is the next rank?"

"Sergeant, sir."

"Sergeant Boyde." His exuberance was back. "Yes, that sounds right."

"Aww, you're not going to put in again for my advancement, are you, sir?"

"And why not? That way you can wear a red sash on parade, and have a splendid sword with which to threaten the hospital's ladies with sublime authority."

"The ladies?"

"Yes. Our hospital will be the trial station for accepting the nursing care of dedicated female volunteers. I hope this pleases you, sharpshooter."

"Oh it does, sir! And why didn't you tell the boys that the ladies were joining us?"

"Will it make a difference as to their decision?"

"Oh, I should think so!"

He winced. "I don't know how to put this delicately, Tom. Our female nurses will not be handsome women."

"Sir?"

"That is one of the stipulations upon our volunteer women, you see. No nurses may be young or beautiful, only hardened matrons or old maids used to caring for brothers, fathers, as they will be around great suffering and, well, men."

It was Tess's turn to frown. "Don't know how to put this delicately, Captain, but the consideration of their physical beauty was not in my thoughts. The ladies will be doing the women's work that Joe and Davy don't care for. That might keep the boys attached while we're at hospital duty in Washington. That is what I'm thinking."

"Oh. Oh, I see. Yes, of course. We may not have lost them quite yet then!" The beaming look faded quickly, replaced by a scowl. "Well, you don't have to roll your eyes and give me that "you moron" look again! Let us mount these pampered nags and go home, shall we?"

Chapter Sixteen

February, 1862, Washington, D.C.

Viewing the unfinished Capitol dome and its scaffolding through her heavy black mourning veil gave it an ominous, wintry look. Tess tried to take a deep breath but the corset pressed about her ribs. Eyes watched her. Under the privacy of the veil, she was able to stare back. Female eyes did not stay on her long, maybe because she was a walking possibility for them, the wives, the sisters, the sweethearts of soldiers. Men's eyes remained longer. Even in respectable black, she was a woman alone, in a public place. Damn Ryder. What had he gotten her into this time?

There he was, fresh from his latest meeting with the Sanitary Commission, coming down the white steps, out of breath. Looking very young, despite their months at war. He was a resilient man. And now, a frightened one, Tess realized, his beautiful eyes searching for her. How strange, to be able to remain so steady during operations, then be afraid of seeing his lover for the first time in daylight.

He had taken care in his appearance. His uniform was better looking than even on the days President Lincoln visited the hospital: highly creased, its brasses shining, drawing the eyes of the women, even the ones strolling on higher ranked officers' arms. Ryder ignored them. That pleased her. He stopped. Their eyes met. He stood before her, pulling off his hat.

"Diana?" he whispered.

She nodded slowly.

"I was afraid you would not come."

She frowned, annoyed that he would think she'd not keep her word. And because she had thought of doing just that.

"May I sit?"

She touched the place beside her.

"Might I hold your hand?"

She offered it—gloved, palm up. He twined his fingers through hers gently, then settled their joined hands on his leg. Tess could feel his muscled strength beneath the wool of his trousers.

"Well. This is fine," he said to the cloudy sky, "This is quite fine."

It was a lot closer to ridiculous, Tess thought. The man who'd shared her bed for almost a year was behaving like a schoolboy. Her fingers twitched. He released them.

"I brought you some things." He reached into his coat's inside pocket to place a small leather case in her hands. "This, first." Dyed dark red, with a pattern of a Greek key tooled around its edges, it reminded Tess of some of the bound books in Mr. Krebs' store back home. The case had a clasp that opened with a touch of her finger. Inside was a small, neat stack of paper, and a handsome matching pencil lacquered in that same red.

Ryder took a deep breath. "This might prove useful, yes? In our communication?"

Tess closed the leather case, putting it in the deep pocket in her billowing skirt. She didn't want it. She didn't want anything except to be back at Madame Lanier's, in the dark, in his arms. Why had he insisted on this meeting? Why was he spoiling everything?

"Perhaps we should walk?"

She leapt to her feet too fast, forgetting the corset, the hoops, and became entangled in her skirts. He caught her arm. "Easy, love," he whispered, "there's my girl."

They strolled together, her arm cradled in the crook of his. Like the other couples, like an officer and his lady. Except she wasn't his lady. She was his whore, who didn't belong here, among respectable people, in the daylight.

"Diana, I have been thinking about your situation."

She didn't like the sound of that.

"I feel I have been remiss in not providing better toward your welfare, both at present and in your future."

She released her hold on him, but he caught her hand. "Stay," he commanded with quiet authority, bringing her captured fingers to the clean shaven plane of his face, inhaling. It was one of his gestures from deep in their nights together. She let his breath warm her hand through the silk of the glove.

"It is most good of you to come here, to walk with me. I should have said that first. It is a wonderful gift. I love seeing you in the light of day, even draped in your mourning. Please, let us begin again."

Tess nodded her assent. They continued walking.

"I would like you to remain in mourning, switched from a sister to a widow, and myself a cousin, your husband's commanding officer, perhaps? Under that pretense I might help you to settle yourself here in Washington. You need to get away from Madame Lanier's, Diana, before you will not have a choice. I have brought you down the wrong path."

She shook her head. The arrogance of this man. He had not brought her anywhere. She had left her father's cabin a free woman. She had been free ever since. It may well be that she was traveling, as he said, the wrong path. But it was hers, and she guarded it as fiercely as she guarded his back during operations and on the battlefield.

"You are not listening. I have made you so angry you are not listening to me anymore," he muttered.

Startled, Tess pulled away, stumbling backward. How had she allowed him to get this close? To read her so well? Or was she just as arrogant as he, thinking she could control such things? She gave up the illusion of control. Everything else dissolved with the surrender. Of their own will, her shoulders began to shake. She began to cry. Not quietly, but with great, loud sobs and hiccoughs.

Ryder cursed fiercely, grabbed her hand, and pulled her, tripping on skirts, off the strolling path and under a willow. He pulled her close.

"Take this damned drapery off. Let me see you," he growled.

She wailed louder, grinding her forehead into his chest.

"Diana, stop, you are breaking my heart!"

She smelled maple sugar candy, there at his pocket. The scent of home finally soothed her, allowed her to breathe more evenly. His grip at her forearms eased, released, shifted to a gentle embrace as he spoke. "Please. Dry your eyes and listen to me, will you do that?"

Tess fished around in her pocket. Madame Lanier had stuffed it with all kinds of things. She finally found a black-laced handkerchief.

"There, there's my girl," Ryder said, standing back. "A good blow to rid yourself of the sniffling, now."

She snarled low.

"Or… not," he conceded, waiting for her to compose herself in her own way. Patiently. Damn him.

"Diana," he summoned, "I have rented you a house. Near here. In a more…" he hesitated, "residential—part of the city. You may still visit with your friends at Madame Lanier's when it pleases you, of course. So long as you are discreet. I have told the landlady that you are a war widow, named Diana Henderson, and that I am your cousin and physician, so your reputation will not suffer for my visits, you see? And if anything should happen to me, Madame Lanier has instructions to—"

Tess stifled a small cry coming up the back of her throat.

"There is little chance of that, of course, as I am not a fighting man. And the whole city is buzzing with rumors of an end to the conflict these days. Do you hear them?"

She nodded slowly.

"If that is the case we will all be going home. Where is your home, Diana?"

She turned. He caught her waist.

"Listen, even if the war is ending, even if I am destined never to see you, I have done damage to your future. Damage I am now seeking to rectify. A year's rent is paid. Would you look at the place, consider this new arrangement at least, before you send me packing?"

* * *

The downstairs sitting room was bigger than the whole of her cabin at home. Together they climbed a set of spindled stairs that led to a bedroom with its own fireplace. Sunlight flooded in, illuminating wallpaper of delicate blue Sweet William. It smelled of the cinnamon cake the landlady had left on a small table against the window.

Tess turned around. Madame Lanier's bed stood against the wall. He'd bought Madame Lanier's mahogany four poster. Tess sank down on it, a haven of familiarity in all this strangeness. Ryder stood above her, his fingers grazing her cheek under the veil.

"Will the place do?" he asked quietly.

Tess raced through the complications to her already too dangerous life. She dug into her right pocket, hauled out the leather case, opened it, then wrote in carefully small letters on its first page.

Tom must come. Whenever he likes. Tom is my friend.

Ryder scanned the words, frowning. "It is good for you both that I am not the jealous type. First he stole my Arabella. If he ever sights you as the object of his affection, I will let my scalpel slip in the vicinity of his ribs.

Tess growled and scribbled again, presenting him with the cream-colored paper.

Do and you will lose us both.

He laughed. "I see. I will tell the landlady Mrs. Harris that Sergeant Boyde is your dear doting brother then, and apt to show up at your doorstep as unannounced as I." He

122

blanched suddenly. "Oh, what an idiot I am—even with you in full mourning to remind me of the loss of your actual brother. I am so sorry."

Tess bowed her head, ashamed, because Laban and Andrew were surely alive, well, and most likely scheming to steer clear of any army recruiters back home. She took her lover's hand and pressed a warm kiss in its palm, ending, as he'd taught her, with a flick of her tongue over the fleshy part. He tasted of leather, of ink, and the metal of his instruments. His hand had grown as familiar to her as her own.

"Shall I show you the dressing room?" he asked, suddenly breathless, "And the back stairs?"

He could have shown her hell as long as he would act on the delicious promise of that hunger in his eyes

One of the dressing room doors connected to the bedroom, the other to the back stairway. The small room contained a chest with fancy rosewood inlay along the drawer faces, and a wardrobe of a clean, high style, its brasses lacquered to look like gold. Too much space for her meager clothing, even with the mourning weeds added. There was no looking glass, and no windows. Tess stood still in the middle of the room.

"Close the doors," she whispered.

His face registered surprise at the sound of her voice. She undid the clasp at the back of her skirt and let it drop the floor, hoping the gesture would signal his thoughts toward desire. It did.

He did as she bid him, enveloping them in their familiar darkness. Tess listened for the click of both door latches. Then she flung off her veiled bonnet with a soft giggle.

"I love that sound." Ryder Cole's deep, melodious voice rose up. Her fingers reached for the strings of her petticoats, but found his already circling her waist.

"Is it a good time?" he asked softly at her ear. "For everything?"

His hands shifted to either side of her head for her reply. Tess nodded, grateful that her monthly regularity made figuring her safe times easy. But he'd visited her when she was not safe, too—holding her, talking, sometimes kissing her so deeply she wanted to take her chances. He'd always eased away first, laughing, not angry. Never angry. Would he be that kind of a husband? Always attentive, considerate, never angry?

"How splendid. Then allow me to find you, Diana," he urged, "under all your finery. Let me hunt you out."

He worked with deliberate slowness. One by one her petticoats, then her hoops collapsed to the floor. So did he, kneeling, his hands seeking in the dark.

"Ah, there's my girl," he said softly as his teeth caught a patch of bare skin beneath her corset. Caught, held. His tongue began stroking there, making her gasp. She leaned over him, her hands sliding though his jet hair, shining through the darkness. Her fingers fisted.

"Ow," he complained softly. "Unhand me you difficult, expensive, exquisite jewel of God's creation, so I might bed you properly.'

"No. Here," she demanded, in a different voice, one even she didn't recognize. Ryder sucked in a startled breath. She'd shocked him. Again. His recovered voice was gruff-edged, but still soft and respectful.

"All right, then. Here."

He brought her underneath him, nested in a raft of her discarded first layers, while he remained fully clothed. Not at all fair, she thought, tracing the face she knew so well in the dark and the light. He made a small grunt of displeasure when she found his collar.

"Oh, no," he insisted, taking her wrists and planting them above her head. "You will not have at me with those nimble fingers. Not until I am finished with you."

It was a game, a wonderful, artful, grown man game. An exquisite tease, his fingers peeling away her stockings, traveling higher, releasing, releasing. They danced along the curves of her body. His tongue collected juices from her mouth, then probed down her neck, around her breasts, then suckled there. He moved lower, ever tasting, teasing. When deep inside her, she went mindless, all sensation. And then languid, melting into his arms' hold, listening to his soft laughter full of a man's pride. Conquering pride. He kissed her cheek before leaving her completely bereft of his touch.

She heard him lean back against the bedroom door, blocking even the sliver of the day's dying light escaping under the threshold.

"Your turn," he said.

Tess thought it would be simple, undressing him, but this time it was not. With her heightened senses, she relished the feel of every button and clasp, every slip over a shoulder or elbow. She worked slowly, hoping to gift him with the same sweet agony of anticipation. Yes. This was a lovely, complex game, dressing down her man.

He laughed more freely than he did at Madame Lanier's. Tess did too. She wrapped her legs around him and he even seemed to go deeper when he was inside her. She saw red bursts behind her eyelids at the end, the color of her tooled leather case and pencil, the color of the wine dark sea he'd read to Tom from his book about another war, a long ago one between Greeks and Trojans.

"Thank you," he said, as he always said, when they finished. Then he held her against his heart and said something new. "Do not go this time. Please. This is your home."

It was tempting, so tempting, to drift off to sleep with him, there nested in their clothes on the dressing room floor. He'd been trying to outlast her after the completion of their joining for all the months they'd been meeting. No. He wasn't going to outlast her this time. She felt his even breathing already in the hollow between her breasts.

Couldn't she close her eyes? Just for a moment? She kissed his forehead, almost wishing to make Tom Boyde disappear in the mists of the Potomac River, so she could spend the rest of the war keeping house for this baneful man, as he'd planned for her. But she knew better, especially in these new circumstances. She had to get her bearing, figure so many things out. She had to get away from him. And how could she think of killing Tom Boyde? Who would keep his accounts, his supply lists? Who would assist at operations? Who would watch his back?

Tess eased Ryder out of her arms and felt around for her shift. She had to get to Madame Lanier's. Yes, there she could think straight, find advice. He'd called this place her home, had tried to seduce her with the beautiful blue wall papers.

Tess placed the rest of her clothes over her arm and opened the dressing room's door. It was dark outside, damn him. She turned, wondering if he would be all right there, on the floor, in a windowless room. That was her mistake.

He hobbled her with a grip at her ankle.

"I ordered a new featherbed tic," he said, kneeling, now capturing her waist between those strong hands. "There is not a light lit in the house. I'll close the shutters and bank the fire in the bedroom, how would that be?"

Her own fire was going in an opposite direction, she thought. And he knew it. He stood. She felt him advance. She retreated. Not fast enough. He lifted her into his arms, unleashing a sharp, delicious longing. She dropped her carefully gathered up skirts. And circled his neck, breathing in his scent. This was as close as she'd come to a human being since she'd had her mother's love: this casual affection from a rich man for his whore.

Tess suddenly thought that she would die of loneliness.

"Ryder!" she called out, as if he could help. He stopped, placed her on her feet. "Have I done something wrong? Diana?" he persisted, taking her head between his hands for an answer.

"No," she whispered, kissing that place below his ear where his jaw angled hard and fine.

"Well," he said. "I believe that is the first time you have said my name. I'm so pleased, though I thought I had shoved you into a coat hook!"

She smiled. There, it eased a little, that need to be loved whole. She could bear his affection now. She took his hand and led him to the bed.

Ryder stroked the slick inside places that only he knew, that burst like a rocket full of flowers instead of destruction. In return, she placed him inside her, squeezing until he moaned in his ragged pleasure, and had to surrender. The things they did helped her forget everything but his tenderness. His breathing began to even out again. "Get off me, now," she whispered, grateful that the practical voice had returned.

He dutifully responded to it.

In his arms and under the coverlet, she enjoyed mapping the strong planes of his face, the breadth of his chest. She searched for the scar, the one not like the ones from the panther. Older, deeper, not left to heal on its own, but sewn together. She tapped against it until he roused.

"*Mmmum?*" he murmured.

"What's this?" she whispered.

He sat up higher against the bolster. "A gift, curious girl. From the pistol of my first mistress's husband."

Her breath caught. She shook her head. *Take it back. Oh Ryder, don't tease me. Take it back.*

He only laughed. A hollow sound, bled of mirth.

"Shall I tell you about it?"

She nodded slowly.

"I was studying medicine in Paris. Studying the social life of that city even more, I am loathe to admit. I had the misfortune of falling into a desperate love for a beautiful woman."

Though there was not a shadow of affection in his voice, Tess felt a hot stain of jealousy rise up her throat.

"Madame wanted a dalliance," he continued, "and instead got an American boy who did not know the rules of such things. Who thought love conquered all. She complained about my blood on her bedroom's tapestries after her husband shot me and fled. I did not care about the pain, only that I had thrown away my honor and soul for her. I stumbled around the streets until I collapsed in the doorway of one of my instructors. He berated me without mercy for wasting his time should I die. So I dutifully recovered under his care."

Tess leaned over and kissed the scar.

"Do not do that!" he snapped.

She fled to her side of the bed.

She heard him exhale. "I sought to amuse you. My youthful indiscretion turned me back to my studies with a will. It made a good doctor of me, Diana. And I will never make that mistake again. Unless…" He took her head between his hands. "Your late husband is not a vengeful ghost, is he, Mrs. Henderson?"

She hoped the sob sounded like a snort, but he must have felt something, with those fine-boned hands.

"Stop," he insisted, his voice hard as flint. "Or laugh. But no tears. No tears for me, ever. Promise."

"Can't."

He brought her head against his chest. "Diana," he whispered, "what are we weaving here?"

Tess eased back beside him in the bed's downy comfort. She began to understand the way he cut women up, as neatly as he opened wounds in surgery. Cut them into Mother, Whore, Spinster, Sister, Nurse. That French woman had done some cutting herself, before her husband took a faulty aim at his heart.

Stop worrying about him, her practical voice reminded Tess as he slept soundly and she placed his neatly folded uniform on the dressing room's chair. *Ryder Cole got you into a terrible mess. Now he pulls you in further with this house, this bed, and his life's stories.* And Tom's army uniform was at Madame Lanier's.

Tess could think of no other choice but to dress and walk Washington streets after dark without a damned male escort. She only hoped that it was now so late that even the roustabouts were abed.

Chapter Seventeen

The next morning Tess stood before the cracked mirror yanking down her cropped hair to try and cover the bruise. McCrum woke from the patient's cot in the corner of Ryder's hospital office, beginning his day's litany.

"Tom, my dear boy! Are the slaves free yet?"

"No, sir, not yet," Tess answered.

"The war is still on, then?"

"Yes, sir."

"You ain't supposed to be 'sir'ing me, young one, not since you got your three stripes."

Tess sighed. "You are a civilian. They mustered you out of the service, Mr. McCrum."

"Hang that! On what account?"

"On account of your age, sir."

"But I'm not a day above two and sixty!"

"Your sister produced the church record of your christening date, remember?"

"I remember more than you'll ever know, you scamp!"

"Mr. McCrum. I'm only saying that my calling you by 'sir' is right and proper."

"And what's proper about fighting a war with the likes of you in the ranks?"

Tess blinked back a familiar fear. "Sir?"

"What's your battlefield experience?"

She smiled "Why, Bull Run, mainly, and a few skirmishes in Virginia. My regiment's been stationed here in Washington over the winter."

"Well, I am a veteran of the war with Mexico, and was with Andy Jackson at New Orleans on the eighth of January eighteen hundred and fifteen besides! What right have they to throw me out of this war?"

"McCrum!" Tess heard Ryder's voice thunder as he arrived on the ward. "Are you badgering my assistant again? While the thrice-cursed flies are returning to the surgery? While the damned boll weevils trot back to our larder?"

The rangy and grizzled McCrum stood as tall has his crippled stance would allow and saluted though, since his sister produced the proof that he bore all of eighty-three years, Ryder was no longer his commanding officer, but only the commander of the old man's volunteer efforts at the hospital.

This morning Ryder Cole hardly looked like anyone's officer, from his unshaven face to his creased, misbuttoned uniform. Tess had left his uniform neatly folded as he slept. What had happened since?

"And where in bloody blue blazes have those fastidious, infuriating women stacked my aprons this time?"

Tess grinned. Ryder made a practice of getting a full day's cussing out of his system in the hour before the nursing ladies joined McCrum in volunteering to descend upon the ward for the day. McCrum saluted smartly. "I will commence a search, and erratify the pesky varmints of the larder, directly following a visit to the necessary, Captain, sir," he announced, before taking his leave. Ryder closed the door of his office and backed Tess into a corner.

"Where in hell have you been?" he demanded.

"Starting up the coffee, sir. Shall I bring you a—"

"I mean where have you been all night?"

"Off duty, Captain," she warned.

"And brawling."

"What?"

"You heard me, brawling. Your hair doesn't cover the effects of the whack above your right eye."

"Brawling, then," Tess agreed, trying to keep the mounting anger from her voice.

"Let me get a proper look at it."

"It requires nothing, Captain."

"Suppose you let me be the judge of that. Sit."

She did, in his chair by the window. The lilac scent of his whore's nightdress fought with the sandalwood soap that his mother sent to them both. Tess concentrated on breathing slowly as he lifted her hair and examined the bruise.

"A glancing blow," he judged. "You almost got out of the way of it. Was your assailant drunk?"

"Yes, sir." *Thank God he was,* she thought, remembering.

"Were you?"

"No, sir."

"Truly? I am surprised you sustained any damage then."

Try not sustaining damage in ridiculous hoops and skirts yourself sometime, Ryder Cole, she thought fiercely at him.

"Damnation, Tom, I needed you last night. Diana has left me! In the middle of the night. I rented her a house to keep her safe, to protect her reputation, and she left me. I spent the hours until dawn looking for her, and for you to help me find her! Banged down Madame Lanier's door until she threw a pot at me."

"What did you do that for?"

"Are you listening? Diana took to the streets! You know it is not safe for a woman on the streets after dark!"

"She's all right, Ryder. And she ain't left you."

"She is? She hasn't? Tom, you have seen her?"

"I kept her safe."

"Then I was right in thinking that she sought you out? And you took that punch for her, did you? You did! That's why you look ready to slice me to pieces!" he said, the discovery sounding in his voice.

"What if I did? She's worth it."

"I... know that. She is well, then?"

"Well enough."

Ryder shoved her shoulder lightly. "And how does the other fellow fare this morning?"

"Worse. His friends had to fish him out of the canal."

Ryder shook his head and Tess saw the shadow of a smile. "Tom. Why did she go?"

Tess shrugged carefully, then pulled a scrap of the laundry paper from her inside coat pocket and tossed it on his desk.

"From her," she grunted, turning away, but catching Ryder's dash for it with her peripheral vision. He yanked open the note scrawled with imperfect block lettering that she labored hard to make different from Tom Boyde's and from his sister Tess's Spenserian hand.

Give Tom a key to the house.

No more secrets from him.

He understands how it is, with you and me.

Tess almost felt sorry for Ryder as he collapsed in his desk chair, the note dangling from his long fingers.

"How can you understand?" he whispered.

"Understand, sir?" she asked, feigning innocence of the note's contents.

"I do not understand my need for this woman myself. I am sick with it, Tom, with no desire to get well. I should know better."

Tess fought the urge to touch the top of his disheveled head of hair and tell him he was safe in their liaison. But she swallowed the inclination and growled.

"Why didn't you tell me of any of these plans of yours?" she demanded.

He frowned, looked at the floorboards, then paced a few steps. "I did not know if she would accept the house and our new arrangements," he finally began. "Diana, she's a good girl, even if she's shy towards peculiar. But she's my girl, you know?"

"No. What does that mean?"

"There, now. I knew you would take it in that way!"

"What way?"

"The way that makes me a hopeless degenerate. And, well, perhaps you are right."

"Ryder, back up. You didn't give me a chance to be wrong yet!"

A woman of their combined ages opened the door of the dispensary and filled its threshold like a thundercloud.

"Doctor Cole!" she proclaimed. "How is it the men in this ward have not had their linens properly turned down and made ready for their morning bathing?"

Ryder turned, smiling brightly. "Good morning, Nurse Truscutt," he said.

She surveyed them both in one quick sidelong lash of her eyes. "*Hmmph*," she judged, "A day off duty does not seem to have done either of you two much good!"

Book 3

April 1862

Chapter Eighteen

April 1, 1862, Washington, D.C.

Lieutenant Breene's rank was not voted in by stout Hudson River Valley volunteers, the way Ryder's was. It came by virtue of his being a border state congressman's son. Although constantly complaining about his own delicate health, which Tess attributed to too much pork and too little exertion of either mind or body, he was indifferent if not hostile to patients. Tess tried to steer clear of him during his inspections, always conducted with a gaggle of hangers-on in tow.

Nurse Truscutt was not so inclined. Not today. Without warning, she pulled open the officer's blouse and yanked back the collar of the shirt beneath.

"As I have suspected—'SC,' clearly marked. This item of clothing belongs to the Sanitary Commission, and is meant for patients' use only! And I smell my stewed peaches on your breath!"

Before Tess knew what was happening, the powerful woman yanked off his coat and misbuttoned vest. Breene lost his balance and sat at the foot of Private Pollan's cot. Nurse Truscutt then pulled off his shirt. As his astonished Washington friends looked on, she waved it like a flag above her head. The patients of the home's ballroom-turned-ward began cheering. Tess wanted to join them. Breene rose from the cot with a vengeful look.

"You stupid cow!"

As Tess came between them, he knocked the crockery bowl of wash water from her hands. He wound back again, pushing Tess aside and aiming his fist at the woman's face.

"Breene!" Ryder Cole shouted from his office dispensary's doorway. He was soon surrounded by visiting surgeons.

Slowly, Lieutenant Breene turned. Ryder descended like an avenging angel, the surgeons at his heels. "You are dismissed from this hospital, sir."

"You cannot. I am the inspector. My father—"

"I can and have. And if you raise your hand to one of our ladies at a subsequent posting in this city, you will find yourself court-martialed, were your father representing your home state, the czar of Russia, and the queen of England besides!" The tense silence between the men spread down the length of the ballroom's floor. The forgotten crockery bowl spun a wide circle until it came to rest at Ryder's boot.

"Do I make myself understood, sir?"

"You do," Breene answered.

"Good. Repair your coat to your shoulders and leave this hospital. With only what belongs to you."

Breene neither responded nor saluted in his retreat. His friends followed in silence.

Ryder eased his stance and retrieved the bowl from the floor.

"Are you well, Miss Truscutt?" he asked quietly.

"I am, Doctor." But she was shaking. He covered her hands with his own and held them. Her face, which Tess thought habitually sour, softened. Then "Truculent Truscutt", as even her fellow nurses called her behind her back, smiled.

"Would you be so good as to ask our Mr. McCrum to bring the mop?"

"Yes, Doctor."

"Thank you."

He released her hands, steady now, and ready to resume her work.

Ryder cleared his voice. "And you, Tom?" he asked.

"I'm well, sir."

"Good, then. If you have Private Pollan's information handy, I would like to show these doctors how the tincture of plantain leaf and exposure to sunlight you suggested seem to be helping his wound."

Ryder brought the field surgeons to Pollan's bedside as if the morning's spectacle had never occurred. The normal sounds of a working ward resumed. Tess's hand faltered as she found the notes Ryder had written concerning the patient. Private Pollan tugged at her sleeve as the doctors talked over him.

"I smell peaches stewing, Tom. You suppose that damned flim-flam officer left us any?" he asked.

"It's possible."

"Well, our captain's got Miss Truscutt and the ladies sweetened up enough for a helping all around, I'll wager. We deserve a celebration after this grand day we lost us our thieving inspector, don't we?"

* * *

Later in the day Tess and Ryder sat on the small wooden balcony outside Ryder's office. From their perch Tess spied the workmen packing up from their day's labor on the building that dominated the city. Tess imagined Lieutenant Inspector Breene was there now, complaining to his congressman father of his humiliation and dismissal.

"I hope your mama don't have any political aspirations for you, sir," she teased.

Ryder raised his head, smiled. "Why, Tom, can you not picture me twenty years hence, as Senator Cole, braces

136

barely reining in my belly, waving my walking stick as I make my point under the Capitol's new dome?"

She smiled down at his flat middle, blushing, and tried to cover it with a laugh. "Don't have that much imagination, no, sir."

"You refer to our altercation with Breene cutting my life in politics short?"

"His father is a powerful man."

"Well, I would rather have our difficult Miss Truscutt as my ally than all the congressmen's sons in Washington put together."

"I see bad things in his eyes. He can hurt you."

Ryder shrugged. "But she might help me someday."

"How?"

"Oh, you never can tell."

Tess sighed. "I see, sir."

"You see more than I'd like you to see."

"Such as?"

"That my devotion to our female nurses is less than altruistic."

"What does that mean?"

"Altruistic? Why, benevolent, philanthropic. Selfless."

"It's more complicated, you mean? On account of they're helping us keep the place and the men's spirits up? Maybe this hospital feels more like home to them, what with women around and the food better. There's even laughter, sometimes."

"As when women forcefully strip men of their ill-gotten gain?"

Tess snorted. "He did look plucked as a red hen!"

Ryder's face sobered again. "Yes, the women provide us with all that. But I was thinking of something more personal." He looked away. Tess was intrigued by the flush that visited his face.

"That being…?" she prompted.

"Hang it all, you know!"

"Know what, sir?"

"That I surmise that one of the ladies serving here is Diana."

"Captain?"

"I smell it on her. Oh, she tries mightily to get it out of her skin with her lilac scent. But this place seeps into your bones, as the battlefield does."

"Maybe the scent was from yourself."

"I thought so at first. And I wanted to believe it. Tom, Diana should not be here. She should know only beauty, in return for what I heedlessly took from her. For the pleasures that have comforted me." He swallowed as if there were something stuck in his throat. "Tom, is she Truscutt?"

"Truscutt? No!"

"But she is physically strong, my Diana is, and her hands are work-chaffed like Truscutt's. I realized this when I held those hands today. Diana's tall for a woman, like Nurse Truscutt is, and—"

"I said no!"

"Easy, Tom. Listen, I do not care, truly I don't, if Diana looks like an old horse or a little gray mouse. Perhaps… the girl who looks at me when she's scouring pots in the scullery, then?"

"They all look at you, Ryder Cole, ain't you noticed that much?"

"Why, no. Do they? Why?"

"Good Lord Almighty, will you quit plaguing me?"

"Just say I am right. My girl, she's one of them, she serves here?"

"No! Yes!"

He cocked his head. "What, both?"

"Yes!" Tess gasped at the purple spots that suddenly exploded before her eyes like artillery fire. What was wrong with her? *Breathe. Deep, strong. Think. Give him an answer.* She fixed her eyes on the flag over at the President's house, still flying in the gathering gloom. "She serves, yes. But you ain't seen her, not here."

"Why? Tom, how can I protect her if I would not even know her passing on the street? What if—Tom, we've been together often through the winter. What if a child should come of it?"

"There's no child, sir."

"I know she is careful, but nothing Madame Lanier teaches her is entirely without the risk of it. I cannot be casual about these things. Tom, listen, if something should happen to me—"

"Nothing will happen! Who else can keep these battle-axe women sweet?"

He took his final gulp of coffee. "It is not the one with the bent shoulders who delivers the fresh shirts on Tuesdays, is it?"

Tess straightened her spine, which made her captain throw back his head and laugh. She had to laugh too then, because he so rarely did and she wanted it to last longer.

A horse and rider suddenly appeared on the street corner below, catching Tess's eye by the smartness of his seat and, as he drew closer, the braiding on the saddle. As the horse slowed, Ryder watched him too as he came to a halt beneath them. Tess stood, gripping the balcony's railing. She felt Ryder's fingers at her back. Through her woolen coat, the blouse, the free-labor cotton of the shirt his mother had sent her, she felt his fear.

"Captain Ryder Cole?" the horseman called up.

Ryder leaned over the rail. "I am he."

The man saluted. "New orders, sir."

Joe Hartness was on guard duty below and waved. "I'll fetch them up to you, Doc," he offered affably, making the courier frown. "You need to sign for them, sir," he said.

Tess saw a flinch beside Ryder's right eye.

"As important as all that?" He turned to her. "Apparently, your powerful Washington forces work faster than I imagined, Tom," he said.

Tess took hold of his sleeve. He shook her off. "None of that, then," he said. "I would change nothing. This morning was too good a time."

Once the rider left, Company D gathered around Ryder. Tess tried to memorize the faces of her comrades, hopeful, expectant, there on the Washington street. They'd be on the march again, she was sure. In the open air, the fields, the countryside. She should be happy as they were, but dread circled her heart, because she knew that the humiliated Inspector Breede had something to do with this uprooting. And she now knew what the aftermath of battles looked like. *Memorize these faces*, she told herself.

"Where we going, Captain?" Joe Hartness asked.

Ryder lifted his head from his contemplation of the papers. "Down the Tennessee River with General Grant," he said.

Chapter Nineteen

April 6, 1862, Pittsburg Landing, Tennessee

In their panic at the sound of close gunfire, several of the writhing men reached for weapons they no longer had. Tess tried soothing them, reaching her free hand over theirs. But the chloroform from the operating table was catching her in its fumes, making her sick and dizzy. Another round of gunfire broke the last panes of glass, and shattered an oil lamp.

"Private Flanders, some light here if you please," Ryder called out without looking up from his work.

"Yes, sir," Davy called over the din as the spilled oil joined the room's stench. He rummaged for a candle, lit it, but handed it to Tess to hold over the operation. Ryder tied off the artery, then wiped his hands on an apron so blood-soaked his gesture only succeeded in smearing the stain.

"What's going on out there, Captain?" Joe asked as he mopped the plank floor. "Don't they know this cabin's the hospital?"

A fresh round of artillery answered.

"We will have to enlighten them further," Ryder said in that level voice he reserved for their worst circumstances. "Would you close this wound for me, Tom?" Tess had already threaded the needle in the darkness. She looked down at it, steady between her fingers. Yes, she could do this. After an amputation that had taken him a fraction of the time as the ones after Bull Run, he'd saved the man's knee and left enough skin to make her job easier and the soldier's recovery less painful.

If the wounded man survived this place, she thought, and the steamboat trip to hospital facilities at Evansville or Mound City. And infection, the slow, merciless way most died, even after all their best efforts. Tess realized she had learned to separate the segments of their patients' care over which they had no control. When had that happened?

"Any sign of the transport, Joe?" Ryder asked their comrade, now stationed at the crack in the door whose view led to the dockside.

"Not yet, Captain."

As her seamstress stitches wound through their patient's pale flesh, Tess wondered to whom those calm hands belonged. She heard Ryder quickly untying, then pulling his heavy apron off as he spoke. "The next three limb wounds require washing and dressing, Tom. Check for signs of concussion in the second man. Call for me if you discover anything that needs my attention."

"Where are you going, sir?"

A round of fire punctured a water bucket.

"Outside to mark the place better," Ryder answered quietly in the silence between rounds. Tess felt her gut clench as she watched him calmly rip the lining of red flannel out of an empty supply box. "It should not be you, sir. The patients need you."

Ryder smiled. "None of us will have needs if we can't get the armies to recognize a hospital zone. Join me when you are finished, with anything red you can find."

What isn't red? She wanted to ask him, but Ryder was already at the door.

"Flanders! Hold that man down! Sit on him if you have to!" he admonished as he crossed the threshold.

* * *

When her assigned work was complete, Tess found Ryder tying the red flannel strips to the pitching posts of the tents of wounded growing off the cabin. His hands shook so badly that the last of the cloth became entangled in his fingers. She'd seen his hands like that before, of course. When he'd bolt up from a nightmare, in the dark, in their bed. She had known what to do then. Hold him, kiss into his palms, listen to his fears. Afterward, take him into the deepest, warmest parts of her body with joy and love. She didn't know what to do now as his eyes darted up to meet hers, then looked away.

"It's the cold, sir," she tried to assure him as she untangled the flannel from his fingers, then took over the work.

"It is not the cold. It is nerves. I will be all right again, inside. When I have to. Don't tell on me, Tom."

"Tell what? That you can't work a decent a four-square knot? You weren't brought up a sailor, sir."

He quirked his brow. "And you were? Or was it your extraordinary sister who had an adventure in the Merchant Marine?"

"If she instructed me after, I was a poor student. Look at that sorry thing, will you?"

Her captain leaned back on the medicine chest that shielded them from fire and laughed. It acted on Tess better than an hour of uninterrupted sleep, something else they sorely needed.

The gunfire became more distant.

"Falling back. Reforming positions," Ryder judged from behind his closed lids.

"Ceasing fire for the day, maybe." Tess hoped saying it would make it so.

"That means another battlefield search for the wounded among all the dead. We have not room enough for them, Tom. Or enough supplies. The chloroform and morphine are gone."

Along with the acrid smell of the battle came something else. The scent of a coming spring rain.

"And we will be awash in mud if they do not send more transports," Ryder said.

Tess looked along the hazy stretch of river. "One's coming sir."

Ryder sat higher.

"It's the *RC Wood*," she read out the letters on the steamship's side. "Seems like General Grant hasn't forgotten us."

Chapter Twenty

The stretcher carriers took the wounded from the tents first, then went on to those inside the cabin. There was now enough room for Company D to gather around their captain. Ryder looked stunned as he read over the dispatch. "My God. It was worse than at Waterloo."

"That there in Tennessee, Captain?"

"No, Joe. It was another battle, in another war."

"What does the dispatch say, sir?" Tess asked.

Ryder's eyes met hers. "They estimate over ten thousand casualties on each side."

"That can't be," she whispered. The whole population of Ashokan was but two thousand souls. Ten towns' worth of men down? The images of all the dead, the wounded lying in the pelting night of rain flooded into her being, threatening to wash her soul away in its horror.

"Hey, now," Joe countered, "We won! Beauregard's in full retreat toward Mississippi."

"Two days of battle," Ryder said tonelessly. "Twenty thousand."

"Only ten, sir. Ten of ours, you said," Davy Flanders maintained.

"We're all Americans. We must count the casualties of both sides."

"No, we don't," Davy Flanders maintained.

Some of the other band members murmured agreement. Tess saw a flash of surprise in the dispatch officer's expression. Was it over such an open show of dissent?

"They're the enemy, Captain," Private Muller argued further. "Ain't it bad enough we got to treat the wounded the rebels left behind?"

Ryder's steel sure voice rose strong. "We are dedicated to the care and comfort of the wounded," he said, "the ones from our regiment, other states, and wounded Confederates. Without prejudice. These are the conditions under which Company D performs its duties. Do you take my meaning, gentlemen?"

Sometimes the Ashokan boys rolled their eyes when Ryder did his high-minded speechifying, but this time they looked surly.

Davy shoved Tess's shoulder. "We do, sir," she answered.

The smartly dressed officer who had brought Ryder his orders frowned. He was a captain, like Ryder, from an Ohio regiment. And another medical man, Tess surmised, from the MS on his buttons and green epaulettes. Like Ryder, except clean. She smelled replacement. So did the weary members of their medical band.

"Captain Cole, please continue reading, there's more in the dispatch. I am to relieve you, sir."

"Relieve me?"

"It's written here," the officer pointed out the place on the document.

"But this is my company."

"The members of your company remain with me. You and your staff sergeant are to board the *City of Memphis* bound for the hospital at Mound City."

"Why?" Ryder asked. The look of bewilderment on his face made Tess want to cry.

Joe Hartness ambled forward. "Ain't no whys in the army, Captain," he chided Ryder good-naturedly. "Button up now, sir. We'll be here. We'll do you proud till you and Tom get back to us."

The surly Company D of the Third New York Volunteers, against all Tess's expectations and their own bone-weariness, then gave a rousing cheer.

* * *

Ryder stared around the confines of the comfortable stateroom on the second deck of the *City of Memphis*. "Who did this to us? I cannot stay here," he said.

"Orders," Tess reminded him, folding his coat. "We're off duty until Mound City, sir. Orders from the Medical Director of the Army of the——"

"But the men we treated after the battle are on this ship. We could make a good six of them fairly comfortable in this room, could we not, Tom?"

Tess grinned. "I dare say we could, yes, sir."

Ryder swung open the door and started down the hallway. He almost ran into a young bespectacled officer.

"Captain Cole, Sergeant Boyde?"

"Yes?"

"I'm Anderson, sir. Lieutenant Anderson. The Sanitary Commission would like me to gather some information from you about your experience at Shiloh."

"As long as you do not interfere with our work."

"Work? But I was told—"

Ryder grunted. "Tom, have you got my bag?"

"I do, sir."

"And fresh bandages and dressings?"

"Done, sir."

As they continued down the ship's deck, their new companion took out his small pad and stub of pencil.

"Soldier!" Ryder called to a stretcher-bearer, "Where are you going with that man?"

"Topside, Captain," the bearer informed him.

Ryder looked into the eyes of the patient. "Does the light hurt?" he asked the head-swaddled man gently.

"It does, sir."

"Into my stateroom if you please—4B. And keep the blinds on the window pulled."

"But Captain, this here's a Johnny Reb."

"Carry your prisoner to where I have directed you. I will bear responsibility."

"Yes, sir."

Tess heard a low whistle, then scribbling from Lieutenant Anderson. Ryder detoured two more injured men to their stateroom before they moved on.

Lieutenant Anderson cleared his throat. "I am to ask what wounds proved fatal at Shiloh, Captain Cole."

"Mostly those shot through the head and abdomen, at first. Then they began succumbing to other injuries made worse by our lack of supplies, and their lack of nourishment."

"What did you do to provide?"

"Tom?" Ryder released the question to her as he swooped down on another stretcher, checking a man's pulse.

"We slaughtered a bull, sir," Tess offered, "and then rendered a soup from it."

Ryder looked up, smiled. "Tom's a wonder at the open campfire hearth and the soups," he said before gesturing ahead. "Look, that must be the operating room."

From its confines a tall woman in calico and a Shaker style bonnet appeared before them.

"Who are you?" she demanded.

Ryder stood, swayed with the motion of the ship, then righted his stance. "Captain Ryder Cole. Third New York Volunteers."

Something changed in her eyes. "Dr. Cole, who held down the cabin at Shiloh Church?"

"The same, Madame. My assistant surgeon, Sergeant Boyde, stands beside you. And our Sanitary Commission scribe, Lieutenant. Anderson." Ryder crossed his arms. "And under whose authority are you?" he asked.

The woman's eyes flashed their fury. "I have received my authority from the Lord God Almighty. Have you anything that ranks higher than that?"

She waited, relishing his stunned silence, Tess thought, before she jabbed her finger into Ryder's chest. "Second deck, stateroom 4B is your assignment," she commanded. "To your bed, under express orders of the general." Her eyes swooped over him like a hawk's now, "If you find any suffering because of poor care aboard this ship, you may have your scribe write a scathing indictment to the Sanitary Commission, who will have me shot. Do we have an agreement, Captain Cole of the Third New York Volunteers?"

"We do, Madam."

"Good." She eyed Tess and Anderson. "Get him out of here. And have a care to rest yourselves. We will need you two for stretcher duty when we disembark."

The door to the operating room closed resolutely.

"Who was that?" Ryder asked Anderson.

The lieutenant grinned. "Mary Ann Bickerdyke, late of Galesburg, Illinois, Captain. "They call her the 'Mother Bickerdyke.'"

Ryder snorted. "Nurse Truscutt of the West."

"Sir?"

"Tom, we must introduce these ladies, who were undoubtedly separated-at-birth sisters. When we do so, the war will come to its conclusion."

* * *

As they watched the last soldier transported off the dock, Mrs. Bickerdyke cast Tess a too-knowing glance. Presenting herself as Tom Boyde was more difficult with older women, who looked at her harder than the doting younger ones. Mother Bickerdyke was also, like Tess, a woman in a man's war. Maybe she would not choose to look too closely.

Once the last patient was securely landed, Ryder leaned against the ship's railing. Mother Bickerdyke left Tess's side and approached him, frowning.

"You did not follow my orders, Captain."

"I slept," he protested.

149

"Not in the bed assigned to you."

"It was occupied. But I slept."

"Badly."

"Well enough."

He and Tess had barely found space on the floor at the bed's feet. Ryder's hand had casually draped over Tess's shoulder as they lent each other warmth. That's how Mrs. Bickerdyke had seen them as she paused in the open doorway with her lantern. She'd shaken her head and moved on. Perhaps that's what she was suspicious about, Tess thought with a jolt—their almost intimate closeness. Did she think them more than comrades? That was ridiculous. That was stupid. That was…true. Tess felt her face go crimson as Ryder tried to pass the calicoed woman.

"Madam, if you will grant me leave—"

"See your mother, young man."

"My mother?"

"She is my second floor matron at the general hospital here in Mound City. More good-looking than I generally accept in my nurses, but she has a decent hand with the washcloth. And even-tempered. A shame you didn't inherit that from her, Doctor. Come. I will take you there."

Tess watched Ryder struggle mightily to suppress an oath more colorful than the ones he spouted prior to the hospital invasion of females in Washington. Then he politely offered the woman his arm.

Chapter Twenty-one

Mound City, Tennessee

Tess looked out over the dance floor of Mound City's Community House. No one would be seeking her out as a partner, the way the girls in Ashokan did. She wasn't even officially invited to this ball, as it was for officers. But both Ryder and Olivia Cole had exerted influence. The city presented the gathering in appreciation of the medical assistance given to both sides, but the families invited were carefully selected Union sympathizers.

The tune ended. Tess tried mightily to appreciate the musicians, who were powerful experts at their fiddles, bull fiddles, banjos and knuckle-bones. All manner of polkas, schottisches, waltzes and gallops sang through their fingers, the steps called out by an ancient man with merry eyes. She wondered if he and the fine musicians were slaves or freeman.

Ryder's arm was still occupied with his dance partner's as he approached, nodding to her and his mother before he delivered the blue-gowned girl back to her chaperone. She let out a skitter of laughter before the next one who sported his name on her dance card took her turn.

"He's barely tolerating them," Olivia Cole said at Tess's ear.

"You think, Ma'am?"

"I am his mother, Tom. I know. Are they all spies for the Southern cause or is it as I thought? Is he over-fond of this woman he's keeping in Washington?"

Tess heard herself sputtering like a boiled over kettle. The Widow of Ashokan frowned. "You do not have to spare me, my dear. Or lecture me about a woman's natural delicacy. I did not find the strength to rebuild my family fortune and raise a recalcitrant child from my natural delicacy!"

"Was he always a handful?"

"Was he? Why, when my dreadful bane was but a lad of twelve—" She stopped abruptly. "No. You will not do this, you young scoundrel. We will remain on the subject of this woman of his in Washington City! Her name?"

"He calls her Diana."

"Why, that is the name of the girl who shot the panther. You remember. Before you came to us, Tom."

"I believe he took it upon himself to name them both."

"Of course. His presumption!"

"And the lady's reluctance to name herself."

"Truly? Is this secrecy a part of their liaison, Tom?"

"I'm afraid so."

"But you know her? This Washington woman?"

"I do."

"How?"

Tess felt herself coloring. "Through a mutual acquaintance, Ma'am."

Mrs. Cole's frown deepened. "Is she a fortune hunter?"

"Oh, no. She doesn't even desire what he's provided."

"What does she desire?"

The dance ended. Tess looked for him over the heads of the hoop-skirted women. Ryder had dragged her to this ball for the duty Tess now realized she was fulfilling very badly: keeping his mother clear of his secrets.

"Tom," she persisted now, "what does this woman want of my son?"

"I don't know if I can rightly say, Mrs. Cole."

Tess studied the floorboards of the community hall. Hickory, she thought, from the grain. The caller tapped for attention with his bow and the musicians stuck up a fine, rousing reel this time. Had Ryder escaped his sea of beauties? Why wasn't he relieving her of mother duty?

"He is not only paying for this woman's services, but showering her with gifts, perhaps with affection."

Is that what he felt for Diana, Tess wondered, watching the swirling skirts. Was it affection?

"Tom. Please give me your full attention, for at any moment—" Olivia Cole's voice cracked. "No more time. Here comes the French one!"

"French one?" Tess whispered, her heart pounding. The music stopped and the dancers clapped their appreciation.

A circle of female voices interrupted the flow of talk and the fiddlers retuning of their instruments. One voice, coming from the figure they surrounded, was lower in pitch. It made the others grow silent, almost reverent.

"The clever English chemists may have created this new color they call mauve, but it took Monsieur Worth of Paris to form it into such a confection, yes?"

Ryder was across the hall, helping the young knuckle-bones player replace a paper flower garland back to the rafter. The woman's laugh, throaty and sensual, made him go stock still. The circle of women below them opened. The way to him was clear. "And," the deeply accented voice continued as she walked toward Ryder, "if I stand beside the brave hero doctor of the Battle at Shiloh, regard how well my mauve gown compliments his Yankee blue!" He stepped down from the short ladder. The woman's oval shaped skirts of that strange color skimmed Ryder's legs. He remained motionless. They were almost the same height. Her wheat-colored hair was studded with dark jewels. Her perfect, ivory complexion set off her wide mouth, which now parted slightly, twitched. Large, dark eyes held Ryder's startled gaze for what seemed like an eternity. Slowly, Ryder smiled. Tess was too far away from him to see if its delight reached his changeling eyes. The woman returned his smile with a dazzling one of her own, stretching that mouth over perfect teeth. She offered him her hand with a deep curtsey.

A hush, then a rustle of skirts, made the circle around them wider. Did she hear Ryder growl before a ringletted matron rushed between them?

"Madame d'Youville, may I present—"

"Ah, but Captain Cole and I are hardly strangers!"

The crowd gasped together in delight. Intrigue. Something to turn their thoughts from the injured crowding the hospital just a short walk away. Ryder bowed, kissing the black gloved hand, his back blocking their sight of his face. Mrs. Cole pulled Tess close and spoke very quickly.

"Her husband is now deceased. She followed me here, Tom, I never welcomed her! She came bearing gifts for our wounded, tokens of esteem to honor her 'dear boy grown into full manhood since we parted.'"

"No thanks to her!" burst out of Tess before she had time to think properly.

"Why, Tom, he has told you of Madame d'Youville?"

"He has, Ma'am." Don't ask how, Tess prayed silently, for he did not tell Tom, but Diana of his French lover.

"Men!" his mother's exasperation won over further curiosity. "I had to yank the full story out of him after the panther attack. I saw the scar that harpy's husband caused my very foolish son to bear."

The band stuck up their next tune. The local maids were claimed by other partners as Ryder rounded the floor with his former lover in an airy waltz. Madame D'Youville's rosy skirts kept sweeping past his legs, much closer than country custom allowed, sending up shocked gasps. The music signaled a partner change, but she was not sharing him. Those painted lips almost touched his ear as she whispered, then flicked out her tongue. They left the line and walked out through the opened doors and under the half-moon's light.

Beside Tess, Mrs. Cole's voice dropped to a disconsolate whisper. "The bullet hit the spot that, if touched in the slightest way, could always bring a laugh from him as a baby, as a boy. Now, he has no feeling there. She did that. She drove the laughter out of him." Olivia Cole covered her mouth with a shaking hand. "Oh dear, now you are going to berate me too, for having too much delicacy to serve the wounded!"

Tess reached into her dress coat's pocket and handed Olivia Cole her folded handkerchief, glad for the distraction from her own screaming thoughts. Mrs. Cole pressed the handkerchief to closed eyes. "What shall I do about Madame d'Youville, Tom?"

Tess's hand tightened around her sergeant's sword hilt. She growled low. *Talk*, she told herself. *Say what you want to be true.* "He does not care for the lady, Mrs. Cole. And his card's full enough as it is."

Olivia Cole's fingers curled around Tess's hand, squeezed. "But she is so beautiful." Yes. The kind of beauty that steals all the air from the room.

"He's a man now. Who knows better. He will tell her to cast her net elsewhere." Tess felt even more covetous than the silly girls and their mothers throwing out their lines for a rich Yankee doctor on a Tennessee dance floor. But her wishful thoughts achieved their purpose. They caused his mother to smile.

"How did you acquire so much good sense before you have even got your full share of man's whiskers, Thomas Boyde? Wait. Do not tell me. Ryder says you ascribe all your fine attributes to the tutelage of your mysterious twin sister. Whatever the source, I am firm in the belief that you are quite perfect in his eyes." Tess heard her teeth grinding as she tried to smile. Perfect? Sensible? Why, she didn't have any sense at all or she'd never have wound herself in all the knots she was caught in now. She was jealous enough of her own self. She didn't need some French hussy thrown into the mix, that was for damned sure.

"Do not leave him, Tom," Olivia Cole said softly. "I am sure he tries your celebrated patience. But he is my hope, my future. He must not lose you. You are his Polaris." The widow of Ashokan's hands felt right, there between her own.

"We're in the wartime army, Mrs. Cole. We don't have those kind of choices."

"And they have already separated you both from the Third New York. Why? He has been too much a force in Washington, I fear."

"Ma'am?"

"Tom. Enemies question our family's character."

"What enemies?"

Mrs. Cole led her to a less crowded part of the hall. "From within the Congress. My grandfather was a Loyalist during the Revolution. He was employed by the British Quartermaster General, and so was not fighting his brothers and cousins on the patriot side. And he remained in England while tempers cooled following the hostilities. That is how we were able to hold on to our lands in the valley, and were not banished to Canada. With England rumored to be stepping into the war now, on the side of cotton, old suspicions are rearing up again."

"Generations old," Tess realized.

"Exactly so. What else can I do to prove our loyalty? I have given the power of our forge, I have given them my only child for the duration of this terrible war. Ryder feels deeply responsible for his company and for the wounded in their suffering, does he not? His actions, however rash, all flow from this devotion to them. Not from insubordination, not from wildness!"

"Who's been saying he's wild?" Tess thought of his defense of Nurse Truscutt against that shifty congressman's son Breede, and Lieutenant Anderson writing, always writing what they did and said on the steamship.

"Tom, look! Madame d'Youville has returned inside the hall without him. Where did he go?"

Tess sighed hard. "Maybe he followed the smell of that five stack apple cake into the back room. Shall we try there?"

The widow laughed as she took Tess's arm. "The other officers have that French horror surrounded now! Yes, let's find him before she frees herself!"

Neither Ryder nor the apple cake were in the back room. Tess and Mrs. Cole found him at the hospital. He patiently offered portions of the cake to the soldier who'd lost his sight and half his face to the battle at Shiloh.

"Take it on the tip of your tongue. That's the way. Now, breathe it in," he urged quietly.

"Cinnamon," the soldier whispered.

"Good. What else?"

"Cloves."

"Excellent."

"And…rosewater, sir."

"Rosewater?"

"Ladies. Can't you smell them? That you, Mrs. Cole?"

"You've found us out, Private Nolan, as my companion and I have caught my son in the act of being useful."

"The doc here's your boy? Well, do tell. He's a credit to you, Ma'am."

She sent Ryder a disapproving look. "He's provided a few debits as well."

"And another sweet-smelling lady's come to keep you company amongst all us abandoned-for-the-night men?"

"Lady?"

"Beside you, Ma'am. I'm catching her scent too."

Ryder snorted. "That young lady is my staff sergeant and a crack shot with a rifle and pistol both, Private Nolan. And he's armed with his ceremonial sword at present. I suggest you alter your impression of him immediately."

Nolan turned his head in Tess's direction. "Beg pardon, sir."

Tess leaned over him. "Finish your cake, soldier. Mrs. Cole and I have pilfered a pie for you to try next."

Chapter Twenty-two

Tess watched Ryder in what had become a familiar position on mail day: slouched across the Mound City hospital's back porch landing, almost as absorbed as he became during an operation. She could sneak looks at him then. Brief, real looks, of a woman towards a man. Tess breathed in the dried lavender scent of her own packet, the herb that Sarah Waterford kept in little pouches in her drawers. "Why do you suppose she won't send us an image, Tom? Do not give me that look, you know who! Your sister."

Tess shrugged. "Been living with Quakers. They're not big on images."

He grunted, went back to his reading. Laughing. Over something she'd written. She tried to figure which part of the letter amused him. His head shot up again.

"You don't suppose your sister has become one?"

"One what?"

"A Quaker!"

"Oh. No, I doubt that, sir."

"Why not? I mean, if she has taken refuge with this couple, who are so good to her, perhaps she will come under their influence. Does she write urging you to giving up the fight, Tom? About coming home?"

"She understands what I signed on for, sir."

"And she approves? With her whole heart?"

"What is eating at you?"

"We ought to send her a *carte de viste* of us. An image. To ease her mind about us since the extended furloughs have been canceled. It is strange, is it not? When I knew we could get home, the desire to see Ashokan again was not so overwhelming as it is now. And after I recovered from my anger about my mother's trip here, I… well, was so glad to see her."

"It's right that you two are on better terms. And that you tolerate her service."

"Sometimes, when she is standing in the doorway of our ward, I imagine it's my room, at home."

"You ought to tell her that, sir."

"I cannot do that. She might think…"

"What? That you missed her company?"

"Well, yes."

"That's not such a terrible thing."

"It is if she feels my resolve weaken."

"Resolve, sir?"

"To show them, back home. That we are real Americans. I have to do that, Tom. For her. For the future of our family. Even if only our name remains in memory. It will be American." He smiled brightly, like a flash of sunlight. "She is a good nurse, is she not?"

"She's gotten you through a few scrapes, I hear." *Tell me about the French woman.* Tess's thoughts assaulted him like cannon fire. *Ryder, why did you smile, dance, speak with her? And did you do anything else before Madame d'Youville took her abrupt leave of this place?*

But he changed the subject. "Tom, do you ever imagine being home?"

"Not home," Tess realized. Would he ever speak of his reunion with the woman he freely told his Diana about? "But in the woods, sometimes." How little she thought of her father, her brothers, even whether or not Mr. Strong survived his burns.

"What times?" Ryder prompted.

"Spring. Sapping time."

"Extraordinary! Your sister mentions how the maple sap ran into April this year. How her protectors, the Waterfords, got a full sixty three gallons." He motioned to her own packet from the mail wagon. It contained one letter from Sarah Waterford. And three from him, carefully wrapped fresh and forwarded.

"Did Tess tell you about the sap too, then?"

"She told me."

"I wonder what she would think of the Ashokan foundry, the forge? She would not grow faint at the sight of fire and power, not our Tess!"

"She ain't 'our' Tess! She doesn't belong to anyone but herself. Don't you forget that!" What was wrong with her? Shouting at him like that? And him! He should be calling her up for yelling at an officer, not looking at her with those wounded eyes.

"Tom. I did not mean to offend. I apologize."

"Oh, hang your apologies."

She took a few steps down to the next landing. He did not follow, but stood, and walked back inside. Good. Being peeved at him would give her breathing room to sort through the conflicting emotions that he'd sent spinning again. This reverence in which he held her sister made her grind her teeth. *Self. Not sister, self. No, no, not self, either. Tess. Give her a name.*

Good. Tess breathed easier. Now, think. What was eating at her? Questions she didn't know how to ask, one man to another, about a woman, an old lover, who was not that old and was so very beautiful and graceful, and worldly, and charming. Did he kiss Madame D'Youville before she sailed back up the river and away from the smell of death? Did he lay with her? Why did the Frenchwoman leave so quickly? Would he ever welcome her into his home in Ashokan? The way Diana would never be welcome?

It was almost time for her monthly flow, the worst time to be having such thoughts. Tess hadn't found a quiet place along the riverbank to get out of her clothes and bathe. But she would. And she would feel better then. Breathe. Longer, deeper. She concentrated on the dense black beauty of his handwriting.

Your brother is incessant in his efforts to relieve the wounded, and none could be more faithful in the discharge

Ryder pitched his hat down the stairs. It hit her shoulder, then landed neatly in her lap. Just the spot he'd landed, years ago, on the morning of the panther. Tess looked up where the sun caught the whitened scar that the cat had left him that day. She had known him long enough for the scar to go white, long enough to apprentice beside him and share his bed and write him long letters about the rise of the moon over the Hudson. Enough to know she would love him all her life. And he didn't know her at all, only the brother she'd concocted, and a nameless whore he met in the dark.

"Come on!" he called, appearing again in the doorway. "Mr. Brady's what's-in-it-wagon's in town. The photographer of the great crowned heads of Europe is at our service, set up in a lot on Division Street!"

"How'd that come to pass?" she asked, hoping he didn't hear the nervousness in her voice.

"How? Because this is America, and we serve the cause of the preservation of the Union! Wear your full uniform now, as you did at the ball. I want Tess to see you in your dress blues, your red sash."

"You go. I'll stand by here."

"But, Tom—"

"I don't have money for such things."

"I will pay for it. Four *carte de viste* images are produced at once—one for my mother, one for Tess, and one for each of us to keep on our persons."

"Ain't finished reading my mail," she tried.

"Think of the delight you will cause when Tess has your likeness packed in your next missive to her."

"She already knows what I look like."

Ryder advanced down the stairs. Tess avoided his eyes.

"Why Tom, what's the matter? Why, you have never been photographed, have you? Our sure shot is not afraid, is he?" Tess heard both teasing and challenge in his voice.

"Not… if you'll stand with me," she breathed out.

* * *

The tent waiting room was filled with soldiers, most of them officers. Tess regretted coming. Not just because this had never been done to her. Because photographs don't lie. What if she was found out by a keen-eyed picture-maker? Her mind eased as she saw how quickly the line of freshly cleaned and polished soldiers was emptying into the make-shift, daylight studio. There wouldn't be time to take much notice of her.

When it was their turn, the photographers Mr. Landy and Mr. Gardner introduced themselves cordially. Tess picked up familiar scents—-ether, grain alcohol, iron sulfate, something they had in common with Ryder and herself. Mr. Landy led them before a painted cloth hung in the branches of a tree—it showed a blissful woodland glade that was supposed to represent their posting to Tennessee and the Western wilderness front of the war. There was also a beat-up plaster column, representing the triumph of the republic. Mr. Landy was placing it at Ryder's side when the two men were hurriedly summoned by a third, a handsome bearded man with his sleeves rolled up.

"I believe that was M. B. Brady himself, Tom," Ryder whispered.

Tess felt herself shrink back as she stared at the glaring glass eye, surrounded by a lacquered wood box and its curtain of dense black. Ryder's hand laid a comforting hold of her shoulder.

"It does not hurt, I promise!" He laughed. "The *carte de visite* portraits are made in the wet-plate process. We

162

will only have to stay motionless for a few seconds for a good result."

The famous Mr. Brady, master photographer, came to them. Tess saw how magnified the lenses of the spectacles before those intelligent eyes were, and lost some of her fear. It was sad that a photographer had such weak eyes, but good for her remaining male in his sight.

"Gentlemen." He reached out a hand. Ryder took it. "Now I know you have been waiting, but might I beg your indulgence a short while longer?"

Tess saw a rustle at the curtain behind the photographer.

"Rank has its privileges," Ryder replied, stepping back.

"Good of you, Captain—?"

"Cole," Ryder supplied. "And Tom Boyde, my sergeant-at-arms."

The curtain was whisked back by a pugnacious man in a full beard, three stars on his shoulders, and a smoking cigar between his fingers.

"Cole and Boyde, of the Third New York Volunteers?"

Tess saluted, then punched Ryder's back until he did the same. "Yes. Sir. General Grant. Sir." Ryder's stance straightened as the general's slouch grew more relaxed.

"Your company distinguished itself at Shiloh."

"That is good of you to say, sir."

"A statement of fact, Captain. We almost met on the night of April sixth. I stationed myself under a tree in that torrential rain. I thought to come inside your cabin, but decided the chance of encountering the enemy's fire was more endurable than that place you toiled."

"We were all happy to see the hospital ship, sir," Tess said quietly, touched by the general's haunted eyes.

He smiled kindly. "We both know the value of holding the command of rivers, do we not gentlemen? I believe the Third is composed of Hudson Highland boys? Chained the Hudson to secure it from the British in the War for Independence, did you not?" Ryder winced, maybe thinking of his Loyalist grandfather who was probably buying silver ware and fancy crockery in London at the time. Tess took up the response. "Well, not us personally, sir," she said, which caused their commanding officer to laugh. The sound of it was almost as good as when Ryder laughed.

He took a drag of his cigar. "Well, though Memphis has fallen, Lee is now commander of the Army of Northern Virginia. But we'll have your seasoned company's efforts joined with ours. We need the likes of you serving our wounded on the field of battle while civilian medical teams remain here."

"We're returned to our company, sir?" Tess asked, forgetting her nervousness.

"Yes, Sergeant. Mr. Brady, please accommodate these gentlemen before me. They have farewells to make with the peerless, hard-scrubbing mother of Dr. Cole."

When Tess looked upon their four *carte de visite* photographs ever after, she saw the happy anticipation in their eyes—eyes that found their focus on the man who blended his cigar smoke into the acrid chemicals, as he watched their session.

Photographs didn't lie. And being reassigned to the Third New York, she realized, was going home. She and Ryder were matched, like brothers, by that light in their eyes. The photograph fastened to the stiff board somehow shone with their happiness. And Tess would send one of her copies to the Waterfords, who would keep it safe, forever.

Chapter Twenty-three

"Try again, Tom," Davy urged. "Me and Joe will cover you."

"Please," Joe approved, "I'm about to go crazy with this."

That's what the man in the tree already was, Tess decided. Crazy. Ignoring their flag, their armbands, their duties among the dead and wounded. Mad. Like a rabid dog that needed to be shot.

Ryder held his canteen to the wounded soldier's lips. He was just being Ryder, but this time it infuriated her. The rest of their team had obeyed his order to dig in close to the ground, but he had not. Did he know what danger he was in by lifting his head? How impossible it was for her to protect him? Worse than in the wheat before Bull Run. No cover on this open field, except for the bodies of the dead.

And no help in sight.

The battle had advanced. The rebel sniper in the lone oak had been left behind. With a breech loading rifle, from how fast he was reloading, Tess concluded. The sniper went on picking off the wounded, silencing cries for help with deadly accuracy. He was out of their Starr pistols' ranges. Twenty yards closer, he'd be a dead man. But Ryder's gifts were useless here.

She was the best shot. She had to get closer. "Captain," she called, "I'll circle around."

"You will never make it," he informed her calmly. So. He was paying attention to more than the wounded after all. The man beneath his ministrations turned his head toward Tess. "My rifle's ready. There, see?" His bloodied finger indicated just as a shot knocked Ryder's canteen out of his hands and into the soldier. An agonized cry, and he was still. Tess spotted a glint, through the hazy smoke, in the leaves of the oak. Their only chance. Tess lunged for the rifle, stood, aimed, and fired. Something like a bee sting caught her side. Ryder kicked her feet out from under her with a guttural curse. Then, silence.

They looked to the tree. First the firearm, then the man dropped to the ground. A cheer rose up from the killing ground. From the wounded and from her comrades.

Tess rolled to her side, felt Ryder's steady hand turning her head.

"Tom. Look at me. Are you hit?"

"Hit?" she asked, her voice sounding vague to her.

Joe appeared, out of breath. "Sure he hit, Doc! Dead on, between the eyes. Tom, you're the surest shot on either side of the Mississippi!" He yanked her to her feet, whacked her back. Why did men do that to each other, Tess wondered, pushing him away, wiping the powder burn at her cheek, blinking.

Don't cry, a dead giveaway! She heard her own jumbled thoughts protest as the boys gathered around her. *Don't cry. Don't faint.* But the bee sting was worse, stitching up her side as she tried to walk. Stop cheering. She didn't sign up to kill, not even mad dogs out of trees. She wanted to get away from them all. Ryder caught her arm. *Ryder. Safe.* And the most dangerous of them all, of course. A wave of sudden, helpless laughter took her over. Tess sank to her knees and vomited. She was dimly aware of dust kicked up by horses' hooves. Their rescue. Late, this time. Ryder held a water-soaked handkerchief to her brow. The bee sting burned. No, she realized. Not a bee sting. A wound. Would Ryder smell the fresh blood among the carnage around them? There was no choice, she thought, struggling up to her feet. If she didn't lean on him, she would fall.

"Tom," he assured her quietly, as she held onto his waistcoat breathed in the cotton weave of his shirt. "There was nothing else you could do." A shadow passed over them. Ryder's hold on her strengthened.

"The lad's first blood?" a deep voice demanded.

"Yes, sir," Ryder answered for her.

"Are you well, son?"

Tess nodded, still not daring to raise her eyes to the man.

"I think he is, sir," Ryder spoke up for her again.

"Have this soldier in my tent at first light, Captain."

* * *

Someone had already closed the sniper's eyes before Tess got to the oak. She didn't want him to look like a man, but he did. A brown-haired man in the butternut uniform. There was a Bible and an unfinished letter home in his haversack, just as she had in hers. She didn't read the letter. But she stared hard at the glass plate daguerreotype of a woman in a plaid dress and a little girl on her lap.

Joe and Davy stood by her, leaning on their shovels, ready to help with the digging. She wanted to do it all herself, but her side felt like it was on fire, so she allowed them.

At camp, waves of weakness swayed her stance twice while she attended the wounded. Ryder dismissed her early, but it was still past midnight before she found enough privacy by the river to see to her own wound. The sniper's bullet had passed through her side, leaving two holes, gritted with dirt and fibers. She opened them with her scalpel, flushed away the blood with alcohol, then bound her side in clean linen.

If she stayed outside among the cooking and wood burning scents, Tess figured Ryder wouldn't smell the wound, the dressing. She returned to her company, eased herself to the ground, stared into the camp fire's flames and prayed. Let the officer who found her vomiting not make her leave the service. Let things be as they were. But she knew the world was different now. She had taken a human life. Tess did not even know who she was praying to. Surely God was not in this place.

Ryder's silver flask touched her shoulder. "Doctor's orders," he said softly. When had his eyes gotten that beautiful? Or was it a trick of the half moon, or the firelight? She looked away.

"Shall I spoon a dose into you?" he persisted.

Tess took the gleaming silver container ciphered with his initials, twisted open the cap, then threw a swallow down her throat. After the burn, she could breathe more deeply, at least.

"There, good," Ryder approved. "Do you want company?"

"No."

He sat beside her all the same. "Talk to me, Tom."

"I didn't mean to disgrace you in front of the field officer, sir."

"You did not disgrace anyone."

"You don't think he'll throw me out of the service, then?"

"What for?"

"I… you know. Got sick. When on duty."

"Tom. Soldiers don't get thrown out of this army for protecting the wounded and their fellows from a madman."

"Is that what he was? Mad?" She did not like the desperation in her voice. But Ryder didn't seem to mind it. He smiled in that sad way that broke her heart.

"It is the only explanation my limited capacities can devise. He was slaughtering the wounded of his own side as well as ours. And Davy said he left behind an arsenal in that tree. He might have finished us all off."

"I didn't mean to kill him, Ryder. Only to make him stop."

"Your secret's safe with me, sure shot. Have another swallow. Then your cot is waiting."

"I think I'll stay out here tonight, sir. If it's all the same to you."

"It is not all the same to me, Sergeant. I do not like the look of you. What would your sister think of me?" He felt her head with the palm of his hand. "You are not fevered. Oh, very well, have your stars."

Tess kept her burning eyes on the fire as he walked away. But she felt so bereft that she let the tears come once he departed. She thought herself safe. She didn't count on his return with his own bed tic slung over his shoulder. Mortified, she buried her face in her arms, but he still did not leave.

"Aw, Tom," he breathed out, dropping the downy comfort around her shoulders, then setting his oilcloth and sleeping mat under them.

"Don't fuss," she heard herself murmur with a shocking slur in her voice.

"I am not fussing," he insisted. "Go to sleep now."

The last thing she remembered was his arm around her shoulders before she leaned against the hard plane of his side.

* * *

"I believe that you saved many lives yesterday, Sergeant," Colonel George Sharpe observed. Tess recognized the deep voice, but this was her first sight of him. She looked down at her hands again.

"The shot was a lucky one, I think, sir. And I was given a wounded man's rifle."

"Oh? Good of the fellow to think through his own distress. I must have a word with him."

"He's dead, sir." Even though he was not one of their own regiment, Ryder was writing one of his beautiful letters to the soldier's kin even now. Making him the hero of his last moments.

"It must be very wearing on you, the constant care of the wounded and dying," Sharpe changed tack.

"It's not constant, Colonel. Just as the battles are not." She was contradicting him. Would this be the end of the man's patience? She glanced up. With his clear, compassionate eyes, his bald head and that patience, he reminded Tess more of an army chaplain than the commander of the 120th New York.

"Your company is one of Lincoln's original ninety day volunteers, are you not?" he asked now.

"We are, sir."

"I have heard good reports of your loyalty to your comrades and Captain Cole."

Who would have told him that? Why wasn't he looking after his own regiment instead of spying on hers? What did he want?

"There is need in this war for men with abilities such as yours."

Why would any of her abilities be of any interest to him?

"Your marksmanship is lost at your current post behind the battle lines, Sergeant."

"But I'm good with the wounded, Colonel. Captain Cole has made me assistant surgeon. The work I'm doing has value."

"Of that I have no doubt. But, your … protective marksmanship skills are not usually in high demand once the battle has been concluded and the wounded moved on. You might take short leaves, go on specified missions at those times, if you sought quicker promotion than your medical duties afford."

Tess felt cold. Would she be separated from the Third? "I'm not interested in promotion, sir."

"I understand your reluctance, Sergeant Boyde. I feel the same way about the 120th. I prefer the command of my regiment to higher positions in the line. But I have abilities that take me away from time to time on other duties. To perform those duties I need couriers, scouts that are good on horseback. Men who can fire an accurate rifle. And, forgive me for saying so, Sergeant Boyde, but there is a…ah, delicacy about your features that might lend itself to another purpose. Disguise.”

“I don’t understand you, Colonel Sharpe.”

“Some sensitive and timely duties are well left to the hands of ah—persons of the fairer sex, who are much less likely to be searched behind enemy lines.”

“Duties left to women?”

“Not real women, of course! What kind of man would I be to put a lady at such risk? But a soldier of already proven fortitude might be trained to take on such a disguise. I’m asking if you might see yourself as such a soldier along this borderland, Sergeant Boyde. From time to time.”

“I never thought about such things, sir.”

“No, of course not. These duties are against any man’s forthright, honest nature!” He lowered his head, wiped his hand across his jaw, before facing her again. “But they are crucial to our success. I am asking you to think about them now. Will you do that, Sergeant?”

Tess thought about visiting Ryder when he was in the field, in the dark, in skirts and veil. As Diana. Could she work that in with these new duties? She thought of the wound in her side, about Ryder’s disregard for his own safety. They had been in the field for years now. How much longer would they last in this endless war? Would she ever again taste his mouth, feel his deep yearnings through the night? Stop it. This man was talking about spying. Did she have the sand for that?

“I will think about it, yes, sir.”

“Good. Thank you. Your regiment is being returned to the Capitol for some well-deserved rest. Think about it there.”

Chapter Twenty-four

Washington D.C.

The skirts dragged long all around. Tess had dressed too fast and had forgotten the hoops. But she couldn't go back up to the dressing room, as Ryder was already pounding at the front door. She barely had time to dim the gaslight hanging over the transom.

Ryder thrust the fragrant bouquet of lilacs into her arms. Those strong hands lifted, then pressed her against the stairs, stealing her breath even as she felt his face against her throat, his tongue flicking out at the pulse beat there. Like a man on fire with love, he kissed her deeply, intensely. His belt was chaffing the wound in her side, making it hurt, back behind the joy of his touch and those deep kisses.

Tess coursed her fingers through his hair, knocking his hat off his head. How many times did she dream of him coming to her like this? No, she was not that good a dreamer. She felt a burst that made the spring-scented darkness hazy. A cry came from her throat, unbidden. She reached beyond his coat and waistcoat and found his braces. She anchored herself there, and rested against the pounding of his heart. She had never crested so fast, so intensely.

"Diana," he said. "When I heard of all the sickness at the hospital, that three nurses were among the dead, all I could think was to please God not find our house draped in black."

She tried to kiss away the terror in his voice.

He took his familiar hold of the curve of her face. "You are well?"

She nodded, lying. She was getting so good at her small lies to this man.

"Tom said you would be. He knew. You wrote to him, and not to me?" He lifted his head. "Was he even here before me?"

She stiffened, there in his arms.

"Never mind, your friendship is not my affair, you are quite right to be peeved. Listen. Might we go upstairs?"

She nodded against his chest, feeling herself blush, before he lifted her off her feet.

"Down! Too heavy," she squeaked at his ear.

He laughed. "You are not too anything. Except clothed."

She hid her face in his shoulder as he laughed again, climbing the stairs.

He kicked open the bedroom door. Would she ever be able to tell him how she'd split herself up in order to have him whole? Stay here, she admonished herself. Stay now, between these papered blue walls, on this featherbed, with his hands artfully baring the skin of her limbs for his tongue to conquer.

Her own impatient hands released his misbuttoned waistcoat, another surprise. He'd been worried enough to not dress himself properly.

"Diana, what is this?"

Was he there already? *Think. Speak.* She was going to meet him in her widow's weeds, in the downstairs parlor, and write it all out for him as they sat together, sedately. She hadn't planned on his impatience, his zealous assault. *Speak. Tell him.* He was panting hard, mad with anger or worry or both.

"D—dressing."

"I know it is dressing, damn it! What is underneath?"

"Burn."

"A burn?"

She nodded.

"You burned yourself? How?"

She curled away from him, pulling the bed sheets around her.

"Diana, stop this nonsense. Let me look at it."

"No!" That voice. Of a terrified child. Was it hers? What was wrong with her? Now she was crying. Loudly. With hiccoughs. He would think her mad. And maybe she was.

"God. Dear God, please. Stop. Diana, you are breaking my heart."

The ridiculous hiccoughs subsided.

"We had a rough time of it ourselves, this time out, the men and I, in the field. Did Tom tell you?"

He reached out, held her face in his hand. She nodded slowly.

"I do not mean to bully you, truly." He drew a deep, pained breath. "May I hold your hand?"

She released one of her iron grips at the sheets. He took her fingers in his comforting physician's hold. His other hand took her face, ready for one of their one-sided conversations.

"Thank you. Now, may I ask you some questions regarding your injury, to ease my own mind?"

She nodded against his palm.

"Did you receive it at the hospital?"

She shook her head.

"Here, then. Did it occur within this month?"

A nod.

"Within the last two weeks?"

Another nod.

"Let's see. On the fifth day of the month?"

She shook her head.

"The fourth, then?"

That was it.

"Ah. Just when we were having troubles of our own on the warfront. Now, you tended it immediately, of course?"

All she needed to do was hesitate.

"Diana," he admonished quietly, "I need the truth. Did you tend to it within minutes? No? An hour then, surely? Good God, within the day?"

Tess finally nodded, throwing in a sniff to try to ease his mounting temper.

"Stop that!" he halted her manipulation, his anger spiking. "What is so important about completing a pie or some household task that makes you women so neglectful of yourselves?"

Tess bit back retorts about his own sins of self-neglect. Ryder brought their joined hands to his lips, and kissed into the fleshy part of her palm. "Forgive me," he whispered, with no excuse attached this time. Her free hand finally released the sheet to touch his temple. She heard his intake of breath. Perhaps all hope was not lost for this night, if she could just get him over his damned doctoring business.

"Did you poltice it?" he asked.

Tess sighed. She nodded yes.

"Any swelling?"

She shook her head.

"Breaks in the skin?"

No.

"Redness of any kind?"

No.

"Did you run a fever?"

No.

"Will you marry me?"

She felt herself freeze.

"Uh, sorry," he said like a bashful schoolboy, "that one slipped out." An awkward laugh. "Badly placed, too, was it not? With all those rapid-fire 'no's' coming out of you."

Marry? She'd lit up the last man who tried to marry her. This time she'd be the one burnt...out of the friendship Tom had with Ryder, with Davy and Joe and the boys, out of the army altogether. And she'd be punished besides, she was sure, for her lie. She would be burnt out of this house, out of Ryder's bed, too, once he learned who she really was. Scorched by marriage, just like her bright-minded mama was.

So why did she feel frozen now, thinking about it? She could not pull her hand from Ryder's, could not raise the sheet past her breasts. Images came unbidden, there in the darkness—of her mama's hiding, cocooning them both in the woods, in her books, away from the men.

Ryder breathed against her smallest finger, then drew it into his mouth, his tongue gliding along its contours. Different. He was so different from other men. *Would marriage to him be different, Mama?* Warming. She was thawing. The next finger, the next, making her blood heat. He spoke the name he'd given her on the morning of the panther as he moved, touching her so lightly only the tiny hairs between their skin felt him. Then came the soft, warm, long pulls of his tongue, making her breasts, free of their binding, round, whole, womanly again. Here, in this bed, she was a woman. Not a killer. A woman named Diana, who spoke very little, but whose veins were now singing.

"Good girl, my girl, my best girl, that's the way," he whispered after she peaked again. She whickered softly at his ear, making him laugh. Diana could do that. Diana lived here. Diana had not killed a man. Diana could play love games, pretending to be his horse, the one lost to the panther.

She drew herself higher on the bolster, pulled the shirt off over his head, then, in that quiet, intimate moment between them, traced the white line beneath his heart.

"Now we are both scarred," he said sadly. "I wish I could have protected you. Listen, are you washing the wound with—"

She snorted indignantly.

"All right, then! Refuse my help! Damnation! Hellfire and damnation!"

The space opened between them. A cold space.

He found his voice again. "You are getting as hard on me as Tom, Diana, and I must confess, I find it—" Her arms circled his bare middle as she pressed her face against the tension in his shoulder.

"I find it most—" he tried again.

She brought her hand lower. He breathed out. "If you think these artful distractions are going to deter me from—oh, my sweet love, I never taught you that!"

She giggled as he hardened there against the strokes of her hand. She didn't think she had any of those sounds left inside her. Perhaps she didn't, but Diana, schooled by the finest Madame in Washington, did.

Ryder shifted, gently placing her beneath him. "You are healing. Do not move any more, not even for my pleasure. Let me please you." He lowered his lips to her ear. "Will you do that, or shall I tie those artful hands to the bolster to make sure?"

Her breath stopped. She felt a delicious breeze there, against the sheen of moisture between her breasts. Could he hear how fast her heart was pounding? His hand cupped her jaw.

"Diana?" he demanded. "Will you be still?"

She nodded, reaching her hands above her head, bound by her promise.

He pulled down all the bedcovers before he began. His warm touch between her legs went deeper, searching out what he soon stroked, sending her into mindless spirals. He captured her mouth each time she peaked, swallowing her moans of pleasure until they came out of him transformed deeper, and guttural.

Her struggle to obey his wishes by keeping herself motionless was a source of curious delight. Even as he mounted her, even as his taut muscles went slick with each long, smooth glide inside her, he avoided touching her bandaged wound.

The bedpost's silk tassels shimmered. The featherbed gave under their weight and beneath it, the horsehair mattress kept it steady. Tess heard the soft creak of the wood board underneath that, sighing as they reached their fulfillment together.

Ryder eased himself from her with the grace of their panther. No throbbing from her wound, only from the deeply satisfied place where he had been.

She tasted a tiny fleck of mint leaf when he bent down to kiss her. Released from her promise, she reached up, lost both her hands in the waves of his hair. And then, by the flickering fire's light, she noticed the first strands of silver among the dense blackness. And suddenly, all his worries about her life, her health reversed, and invaded. Silver. While three years shy of thirty. The war had put it there. This endless war. Aging them. Some day he would die. Some day she wouldn't be there to protect him, and he would die.

"Oh, Ryder," she whispered.

"What is it, love?" He took her face in his hand for her response. "No, I am sorry, that was the wrong sort of question. You cannot answer yea or nay. Let me think of a better way to phrase it. Are you in pain?"

Tess shook her head, pushing his hands away. He maintained their distance, but rasps of frustration burst from his throat. She poked her head under his arm and slid in against his heart. He pulled up the bedcovers around them. "The woman whose husband made this scar. Do you remember me telling you about that?"

Her breath caught in her throat. She nodded.

"I saw her. While on duty in Tennessee. I believe she had designs on me again. Imagine that."

She growled low, not having to imagine.

He laughed quietly. "When I first laid eyes on her again, I thought only of the pain she caused me. And then I thought of you, Diana. I realized that her lessons in eliciting a woman's pleasure, well, they … might have contributed to our mutual joy. The pain dissolved. I said the first thing that came into my mind, I thanked her for those lessons. And then I saw, in her eyes, defeat. She would pursue me no longer, when she knew of you. Imagine that, my huntress."

Tess nuzzled closer within his embrace, knowing that Madame D'Youville's wiles were not defeated by Diana the very jealous Huntress, but by Ryder Cole's kindness.

He kissed her temple. "Let me hold you. Sleep. This once. Stay."

She let her eyelids descend.

* * *

Ryder had to see her injury closely, clearly, to ease his mind. It would not be a betrayal of her trust. He would keep the light away from her face and focus it on the wound. And she would remain sleeping, and so never know. As a doctor, he reasoned, he had an obligation to her, no matter how stubbornly she refused his ministrations. So why were his hands shaking as he used a paper spill to carry the light from the hearth fire to the candle?

He had frightened her, with his blunt proposal of marriage. From where had that come? Proposing to a woman he would not recognize on the street in the light of day. One who'd shared his bed for all of, how many? Two dozen times? One whose spoken words he could count on two hands. His whore. No, she was never his whore, even at the beginning. But a fallen woman, because of him, because of his fear and desperation.

And her own choice. He didn't hold a knife to her throat that first time, damn it.

His woman, then. Is that who she was? No, that was not correct either. He had no claim on her. She had made sure of that, forming an alliance with Tom, not even giving Ryder her name, but allowing him to name her—an illusion of intimacy, of possession. An illusion only, for he feared it was becoming the other way around. Diana was beginning to possess him.

179

Oh God, he realized suddenly, he'd hurt her. On the stair landing, he remembered her gasp as he crushed her like an idiotic, love-struck boy. He must attend her now, to see if he had done any damage.

He raised the candle to her side.

Beautiful. Creamy white, untouched by the sun. He had never seen her skin so clearly. He had even begun to wonder if she was mulatto. Why else did she hide under veils, in the darkness? Damnation. The first clear sight of the curve of her hip was making him hard. Her doctor, not her lover. Not now. Concentrate. He brought the candle higher, looking for the bandage. She shifted, murmuring. He wanted to see her face. So badly. Doctor, not lover, he reminded his quickening pulse. She shifted again. Her braid slipped over her back. What color was it? He raised the light higher. A curious mix of chestnut and copper and umber. Beautiful. He would remember that hair.

There. The bandage. Good. No swelling to distort its contours. How had she burned herself? At the stove? With an iron? He peeled back the dressing.

Two wounds, which did not look like they were caused from burns at all, Ryder thought with a shock. They were entrance and exit wounds. His Diana. His beautiful Diana. She had been shot.

Suddenly, her hand appeared in his line of sight. It opened, startled, tense. Then a wail, more frightening to him than the Rebel Yell of the battlefield.

She shoved him off the bed and to the floor. The candle's wax burned his hand, making him gasp out in pain, before the room was plunged again into darkness as his lover disappeared, leaving him only the echo of her indignant shriek.

Ryder scrambled to his feet, following. Too late. The adjoining dressing room door slammed shut and he heard the metallic shift of the lock even before he reached for the knob. He twisted it anyway. Damnation. How dare she lock a door on him in his own house? And was she weeping? He pounded, demanding, admonishing, then imploring. None of it produced results.

He must have stayed there, ranting like a madman he realized later, long after she'd dressed and escaped down the back stairs.

***

All the crockery of the house's small kitchen rattled as Ryder entered from the front stairway and flung himself around its confines. Tess placed the iron pot on the stove calmly, and tried not to smile out her relief. He had not seen her face. He wasn't connecting his Diana with the visiting go-between in a lover's quarrel: Tom.

Ryder stopped suddenly, raking his black mane off his brow as he caught something in the air besides the fresh ground coffee beans Tess was hoping would cover her scent.

"Here! Diana's been here, in this room. With you."

"Yes."

"Where is she now? Tom, this unfortunate thing happened between us—"

Unfortunate, was it? "Sit down, sir. Coffee's almost ready."

"She has told you, then? She was down here with you while I was propped up against that damned door, begging her forgiveness?"

"Let me look at your hand."

He glanced briefly at the burn. "It is nothing. Tom—"

"Doctors make the worst patients."

"Diana had a wound, in her side. She would not allow me to see it. I had to—"

"That was disrespectful, Ryder. You're not her doctor."

"I'm not? Well, who the hell is?"

"Me."

"You?"

"Yes. You broke her trust."

"I did not intend—"

"Road to hell is paved with good intentions."

"Tom, you are not listening to my side of it!"

"You're right there. I'm not in a listening kind of mood. But she's in an even worse temper, so I'd leave her be a spell, if I were you."

"Women! Damn them all! Where is she?"

"Here."

"She is not! I cannot hear her up there!"

"Maybe because you're making so much noise your own self."

"You are a terrible liar!"

"No I'm not. I'm a terrible truth-teller."

"What in hell does that mean? Don't you go all mysterious on me now! Where is the damned key to that dressing room?"

Tess touched her hand to her vest pocket protectively. There, that worked. His shoulders slumped.

"She's all right up there?"

"Sure, sir. Don't fret."

"She does not care much for me, does she, Tom?"

Tess turned away, busying herself with pouring their coffee. "Now, sir, how can you think that?"

"I asked her to marry me."

"Why did you do that, Ryder?"

"Because… I think because I was so glad she was alive. It must mean I love her. It must mean I cannot live without her. When I saw the bandage, something happened. Something snapped inside me, Tom. She must be beautiful, perfect. No wounds here, in this house. This is a haven. No wounds. Perfection. What am I saying? You must think me a fool."

"No, sir."

"Why did the notion of marrying me make her cold? What happened to cause that wound? It was like a gunshot wound, not a burn, not any kind of burn I've ever seen."

"We're used to seeing gun shots, Captain. Burns go straight through flesh, too."

"It was well dressed. Did you dress it, Tom?"

"I did, sir."

"Well, she does have some sense, then. Tom, what if a child should come of our liaison?"

Tess willed her fingers still around the steaming cup. Blue and white, from China. Like his mother's Nanking porcelain at home, only cheaper made.

"None will. She's careful."

"She would tell me, would she not, Tom? She would tell me so I could provide for them both?"

"None will!" she heard herself shout. "Now, listen to me, Ryder Cole. You think this woman's got no life except for your part? You think she has no other cares because you bought a fine house and clothes? You don't own her!"

"I know that, Tom."

"So leave off that talk of marriage and children!"

"But... don't all women want marriage and children? Is that not why she won't let me see her? Because she's ashamed of what she...allows between us? Because she wants another chance at respectability?"

"So, you offered marriage just so you could get a look at her face?"

"No! No, of course not! Did I?"

"Ryder, she's poor, like me. Poor women can't afford rich people's notions of morality. She ain't ashamed of anything she does with you, understand? Maybe she wants something else for herself, after the war. Maybe she's... got plans! Did you ever think of that?"

"Well, no."

"Start to!"

He was, she could tell by the pain in his eyes, the hush in his voice when he finally spoke. "Did she tell you these plans?"

Lord, now what was she doing? She looked away from his trusting eyes and took a deeper breath.

"No, sir."

"Well, I would make myself understand them, honor her wishes. It is the least I can do. I must tell her this, Tom, or she'll leave me now, I know it."

"I'll tell her for you."

"You will do nothing of the sort. What you'll do is gain me entrance into that locked dressing room upstairs. She came down the back stairs, talked to you, then returned when she heard me descending the main stairway? Is that it? I caused all this distress, and now she's alone up there, angry. Weeping, I heard her weeping. You know how fond of the girl I am, Tom. Please. Use your key. Gain me entry."

Tess felt her mouth go dry. *Damn you, Ryder.* What did the dressing room look like? Clothes strewn about. Not a trace of her uniform: she had every piece of it on, didn't she? Yes, except its blue coat, there on the chair. Stall. He must not connect them. "She was crying because she hurt your hand. She didn't mean to. Don't dare show yourself to her without me treating your hand."

Ryder's mouth formed a sneer. "I thought I left my mother at the train station."

"Don't you go grousing about that lady in my presence, Ryder Cole!"

"No dressing," he commanded as Tess reached into his black bag. "The salve will suffice. It's only a wax burn, for the love of heaven."

Between his squirming and complaints she'd only won herself time. She couldn't think of another excuse to keep him from climbing the back stairs to the dressing room.

"Damnation!" he exploded anew when Tess unlocked the door. He rushed into the bedroom, circling its confines then rocking back on his heels. "How did she do that? Dress, slip through the bedroom, then out the front stairs without a creak in the floorboards?"

"You were making such a ruckus in the kitchen I doubt we'd of heard a regiment go down the front stairs," Tess offered.

He didn't smile. "Tom. She's out on the streets of this city after dark again. Where is that girl's sense? Where do you suppose… Madame Lanier's. She must be there. Let's go."

Tess still had her mouth open as he threw her blue coat at her.

* * *

"Why, Sergeant Boyde! Always a pleasure to have you back in the bosom of our household, sir. Arabella's been pining something fearsome for your company."

Madame Lanier's voice went cold as she regarded Tess's companion. She nodded curtly. "Captain Cole."

"I have to see her, Madame."

"Why who, sir?"

"Please. We fear she has taken refuge here, after an altercation between us that I seek to make right. Kindly tell her to show herself immediately."

She sighed. "I dare say mending fences between you two will try even my resources soundly. Why do we not allow Arabella to entertain your stalwart assistant surgeon while you tell me all about this altercation, yes? Then we will see if the lady in question wishes your company."

* * *

The warm water sluicing down Tess's back felt like heaven. Even the circular digs of Arabella's scrub brush were welcome.

"Look, backwoods gal, he's not the first man offered marriage to a whore in the heat of passion."

"He's not?"

"Lord no! They use us for practice, is all! Before they get home to their sweet shy young things, you know? Why, I've gotten more offers than I can count on fingers and toes."

185

"But Ryder, he's so serious."

"Stop fretting! They don't think too hard when they're with us, not with their heads, anyway. Get him drunk. He won't remember his offer after the second whiskey. Lord, I wish that wound of yours would allow a full tub. Head back now. Close your eyes."

Arabella ran a pearl handled brush through Tess's wet hair.

"When we heard you made it through that fearsome fighting off Tennessee, we made you presents—filled vials of your lilac scent. They'll fit in a stocking, or inside a boot. That way if he sneaks on you again up at your house, they'll help a quick change over. Our little tricks will make you feel as daring as a spy, Madame Lanier says!"

Tess took one small vile and brought it to her temple, closing her eyes.

"Why, ain't you pleased?" Arabella asked.

"Sure. And grateful. But I already got too many secrets. Arabella, this time out, I killed a man."

The brush stopped stroking through her scalp.

"The one that plugged your side there?"

"That one."

"Well. I'm surely glad he didn't get another chance to shoot at you."

Tess felt a comforting hold at the crown of her head. Like her mother's when she was sick. Arabella's lips almost touched her cheek. "Listen. My name's Ruth. Just plain old Ruth. My real name."

"Mine's Tess."

"Happy to make your acquaintance." Ruth resumed her work with the brush. "You got to kill men, Tess. You're a soldier."

"It's hard."

"Sure it is. Hard and unnatural, war."

"Yes."

"You ain't going to let that stand between you and the captain, are you? It's real polite, the way he talks about you. He treats you nice, too, over there at your little nest?

He didn't turn mean on you once he set you up in housekeeping, did he?"

"Oh, no! We're having the best time, mostly."

"Well, that's fine. Don't you worry. You two came to
the right place. Madame Lanier will listen to his worries,
then send him back to you with a good, clean apology for
sparking this row. You going to be able to go on a picnic
with us girls, before you're off again?"

"I'd like that."

"Good. Because we'd sore like to hear your stories on
your travels to Tennessee. And without hurting your feelings, Tess, your grooming's become a tad in need of refreshment since you left our regular company."

Book 4

April 1863

Chapter Twenty-five

April, 1863, Union Station, Washington D.C.

A misting of April rain cleared some of the perpetual swampy miasma of Washington City as they said their farewells. So many of them mustering out hailed from their Hudson Valley Highlands that the Third New York Volunteers was folding in with the One Hundred Sixteenth. The last two handshakes were the hardest. Davy Flanders and Joe Hartness looked like boys again, there with the rest of their musical band at the train station. Except for their eyes, which had seen things that no one should have to see. Their eyes were much older than the rest of them.

Ryder shook Davy's hand as Joe spoke. "You know we would've signed on again, sir, if the needs at home weren't so great."

Ryder smiled sadly. "I asked you to be ninety day volunteers. That was your full obligation. Mr. Krebs assures my mother that your jobs wait for you, once you get the crop in on your farms."

"Thank you, sir."

"Thank my mother. Visit her if you can, will you?"

"Sure. We all will, sir And should we look in on your sister, Tom?"

"No. She's too shy."

"Well, we won't go bargin' in. How about we write her first, just like the captain does, through you?"

Tess shrugged. "If you like."

She could easily politely decline, through the Waterfords' kindness.

When would that train whistle blow? It was the wrong time of her woman's cycle. Tess felt tears threatening.

Joe pulled her aside. "Tom, you ain't thinking you made a mistake are you, staying in?"

"No. 'Course not."

"Good. Good then. Hey." He shoved her shoulder. "All our mamas thank you for teachin' us how to scrub behind the ears."

"See that you remember."

"Aw, what's the use? Only girls ever talked to us were the ones you introduced us to, all polite."

"Well, you got stories to tell them now."

"Hey, we do at that."

Davy raised his voice. He must have been elected by the band to speak for all of them. "We're going home able-bodied. We know how lucky we are in that, sirs. We didn't understand at first, not being so bright-minded about your scheme at the beginning."

Ryder snorted. "How bright-minded was I to think you were musicians?" He sobered after their shared laughter. "Please tender our regards to your families, gentlemen. And tell them I take a measureless pride in the accomplishments of the Third New York Volunteers."

The whistle blew, warning of the train's departure, at last.

Tess watched all of their men help limbless soldiers onto the train. Davy and Joe were the most attentive.

"Those two will never get a seat themselves," Tess fretted.

"Habits," Ryder said softly.

"Training," she disagreed, but was as proud of them as she suspected Ryder was.

Once the train pulled away, they left Union Station and walked along the Mall. No companies were drilling. The day seemed as gray as the buildings around them.

"Tom," Ryder broke their silence. "I would like you to take the surgeon's exam."

"Exam, sir?"

"Yes. You already know more than any sawbones of my acquaintance, of course. So why not have the certificate—something you can take home, to help you get your new start?"

"I'm sure I couldn't pass it, sir."

"And what makes you so certain?"

"I'm not educated."

"Of course you are! Who taught me to enjoy Mr. Poe and Dickens? Come Tom, where was your schoolroom?"

"I never went to school."

"Who taught you to read and write, do sums, keep accounts?"

"My mother."

"Your mother? Extraordinary! Where did she learn?"

"She never said, sir."

"Well. Perhaps you would have some difficulty on the general questions. The ones on history, geography and the like. Why these subjects are part of the medical examination baffles me. How does knowing the fine points of the reign of the Plantagenets help you treat typhoid fevers and pneumonia? Listen, I can help prepare you for that part of the examination," he continued, his voice rising in his excitement. Ryder Cole had given himself a distraction from losing all of his men but her, Tess thought. "Let's start now, with the rise and fall of the Roman Empire, shall we?"

Chapter Twenty-six

May, 1863, Chancellorsville, Virginia

A wounded man's thin, forlorn whistle call made Tess stop at a place she usually hurried past—the tent where they put the hopeless cases, the head and gut wounded. There the medical corps made the patients comfortable if they could spare the morphine, then left them in each other's company. It was not a good return on their service, but at times like this when they were overcome with casualties, Tess had come to understand it as necessary.

The lonely whistle sounded again, among the groans and prayers. She felt a sharp pang of memory, of home. Of her brother Andrew. It slowed her step. Her brothers were not supposed to be here, at war. But with the new conscription laws in place, and being of age, and poor, how could they not?

Once more, the whistle. Tess slowed her step, then lifted the tent flap and walked inside. She was needed elsewhere. But he looked so frightened. His eyes were shut tight, like when their father was coming to beat him. She touched his forehead. Slowly, he opened his eyes.

"Hey. You're lookin' well, Tess."

She glanced behind her.

"Old Man Strong. He said the Devil himself lit up his beard that night. You were in cahoots, being a New England-bred witch woman, like Mama. And that fire-spewin' devil carried you back to Hell with him. But Laban and me, we knew you'd do all right. Once you made up your mind to go. We did all right too. After we got away from Pa. I made it to corporal."

"I see that."

"Laban got himself killed at Fredericksburg. Were you there?"

"No. Missed that one."

"Well, we did just fine before that. Army's a whole lot better than home. That the way of it for you?"

"That's been the way of it."

"We didn't do right by you, Tess, you know? When Pa wanted to sell you off. We didn't do right on account of he didn't whack you around as much as he done us. That was the excuse we gave each other. That one and another. Which I am now ashamed to tell you."

She touched his arm. "Hush now. You don't have to tell me."

"But I do. Laban's dead. How will you know if'n I don't tell you? It's this. That damned storekeeper was a mean cuss. But we told ourselves that you was an uppity woman. Needed some man to trim you back. Weren't true. We just didn't have the sand to stand up to Pa. You was a good gal. Even if you shot at that fellow back home in the woods, you must of had reason."

"I didn't shoot him."

"Well, even if you'd of. Jeeze Almighty, I'm hurtin' Tess. Got anything to help with it?"

"No. I'm sorry—"

"Tom!" The call sounded from outside the tent before Captain Cole pulled the canvas flap aside/ He was wearing his darkest, most disapproving scowl. "I have three surgeries backed up waiting for you! What in hell are you doing in here?"

Tess wiped her grimy cheeks quickly with the backs of her hands.

"Sorry, sir." She turned, tried to rise. But Andrew held onto her sleeve.

"It's him. The widow's boy. The doctor. You run off to the war with his crew, Tess?"

Ryder came closer. "Who is this man?" he demanded.

"My brother, sir."

"Brother? You never said you had a—"

"Two. I had two. The other killed at Fredericksburg. Laban, the older. I just learned it from this one, Captain. This here's… this here's—"

"*Shhhh,*" he soothed. "It's all right."

Tess's cheeks burned with shame that grew deeper when she realized the cause. She wanted Ryder gone, out of the tent. She was more worried about preserving her place in the corps than seeing her last brother out of his life.

Ryder knelt, drew the dressings of the wound back gently. "Your Christian name, soldier?"

"Andrew, sir." He coughed, and the doctor's apron had a new smear of bright red blood there, over his heart. "Corporal in the New York—"

"Andrew," Ryder calmed the frenzied eyes with the compassionate power of his voice. "Would you like some morphine?"

"I would indeed, sir."

Ryder sprinkled the drug into her brother's wound, then laid his hand on Andrew's forehead. "Better?"

"Oh, by half, sir. So, you two getting along all right?"

Ryder smiled. "We are indeed."

"I guess my sister, she weren't lying then!"

"Lying?"

"That she didn't shoot you, that time, way back?"

"Shoot me?"

"Sure. Along with that panther. The one you didn't have sense enough to track proper, said she!"

Ryder's voice took on an otherworldly cast. "I have never met your sister."

"Are you daft, doc? Who do you think's there beside you?"

"I beg your—"

Andrew laughed, his eyes glassy. "Maybe you should of shot him, Tess, or let that wild cat have him. Seems like a blamed fool to me!"

"Hush up, Andrew."

"Still, he'll look after you better than that damned shopkeeper, I figure. And you'll live in a fine house. And you love him, don't you?"

Tess felt Ryder shove her shoulder.

"I do, yes."

"He sure makes a dyin' man feel a sight better. So I guess it's all right by me, then. You have yourselves a time, hear, you two? After the war?"

"We will, yes," Ryder said quietly.

"Wish we'd of left home with you, Tess. Bet you're a right fine nurse. Wouldn't have any licorice, would you?"

"I'm clean out."

"Oh, that's all right."

Andrew's eyes left hers and steadied on Ryder's. He drew in a weak shallow breath, but still managed to sound piqued. "And what's *your* Christian name, kin? I'm missing a brother."

The eyes stilled before Ryder answered. Tess had seen enough of the dead to know that her brother had joined them. She lowered the lids over sightless eyes. She felt Ryder squeeze her shoulder.

"I have to go, Tom."

"Yes, sir. Coming."

"But—"

"I'm ready now. Honest. I appreciate what you done— did…for my brother, Captain. And in waiting for me."

"He thought you were Tess."

"Yes, sir."

"He needed to make something right with her, so he saw her in you. Does that make sense?"

"Yes. Happened before. I've been these boys' mamas and brothers, papas and sweethearts. For their good-byes."

"And so you understand?"

"I'm ignorant, but I ain't stupid, Ryder."

"I have never thought you either. But I have been both. Tess is Diana, the first Diana, there in the woods. You stood up for her against your father and brothers. And you both escaped them."

"Yes, sir. We owed your mama for the panther skin. It got us out and away. We both started new, fresh."

He frowned. "That debt is paid."

"No. I need to bring you home to your mama. Safe."

"Tom, look at me. The debt is paid."

"You're no good at business. Your mama was wise to let you study your healing."

"When were you going to tell me? That your sister was the woman who came that morning? Who shot the panther? Who helped me with Moutamin? And brothers. You had brothers. Tom, do I know you at all?"

"No," she whispered.

He traced the curve of her face with those eyes, gray here in the tent of the dying, almost without color at all, so far from the green leaves of that other spring.

"Forgive me. I do not account for your shock, your grief. This is all so... extraordinary."

That word. Tess ground her teeth together. If he started on about the bonded kinship of twins again, she thought she might shoot him after all. But he didn't. He walked at her side, without speaking, but with his arm around her shoulders, all the way back to the operating tent.

Book 5

April, 1864

Chapter Twenty-seven

***April, 1864—Winter Quarters, Army of the Potomac,
Spotsylvania County, Virginia***

The familiar sounds of the men's singing, snores, and card playing rose up around their campfires. The Spring Campaign of 1864 was in the air all around them. Ryder spread out the map. Soon a crowd of four of their comrades formed around them. Tess looked over the terrain depicted.

"Isn't this the same place we were last year, Captain?"

"Close by."

Corporal Elgin looked closer. "You two served at Chancellorsville, sir?"

"We did."

"I been reading about this countryside of Virginia since my brother signed up before me! Now I'm here. They say it will be different this time. No leaving the left flank hanging in the air to cut to pieces, now that Grant's in charge."

"Grant?" Casey, who looked too young to be in the army, said. "We're under Meade."

"Aw, everybody knows Grant's the one giving orders."

"I didn't."

"You're a bugler…that don't qualify as anybody."

"Quit your squawking!" Elgin demanded. "I want to hear what our veterans think! General Grant will keep us marching, won't he, Captain? We'll take Richmond and finish off Bobby Lee now!"

Tess watched Ryder heave a sigh before facing their gathering audience. "That is not our business, gentlemen. Our business is to keep our heads down and serve the wounded."

Once each had proclaimed his ideas on the coming advance and how soon Richmond would be taken, they began to fade back into the darkness.

Ryder stared out beyond the campfires. "Our own Musketeers. I miss them."

Tess smiled. "You got plenty of patience for these new ones."

Ryder's eyes looked troubled as he regarded the map again. "General Grant won't let Lee pull us in there."

"In where, sir?"

He tapped a green area of the map where no roads, towns or even houses were drawn. "Where our artillery cannot reach them. In those tangled woods, see? It will be another kind of war in there. The kind that General Burgoyne faced during our Revolution. Remember when we discussed the Battle of Saratoga?"

"When the British and Hessians trudged through the wilderness of Northern New York?"

"Just so." Ryder didn't smile, nod, as he usually did when she remembered one of the history lessons he taught her for the surgeon's exam. He still looked worried. "Grant is no Gentleman Johnnie Burgoyne, ignorant of the trap of a wilderness. He will not allow Lee to pull us in there," he said again.

Chapter Twenty-eight

May, 1864, Battle of the Wilderness

Ryder ran into the wheels of a Parrott gun cannon, its iron still warm. Stuck. He knew their artillery pieces would be stuck in this wilderness, why didn't General Grant? Where was Tom? Tom could always find him when he was lost.

"Cold."

Ryder leaned over the downed man in the smoking woods of battle. The uniform was scorched and riddled with holes. The face barely looked human. For the first time in his life as a physician, Ryder Cole wanted to run from a patient. To find Tom and the new battery of their new regiment. To ease his terror, the clutch at his insides. This man had to be dead. A trick of sound over distances was the voice, surely.

Then it came again. "So cold."

Ryder forced himself down to his knees.

"Surgeon?"

Sense of smell, the last to go. The man must have caught the scent of his medicines. "Yes."

"Why is it so dark?"

Sight already gone, then? "A storm is coming. We will get you out of here soon, soldier. Tom!" Ryder called over his shoulder, not for this man, but for himself. His stomach heaved.

The hand caught his sleeve. "Stay. Please. It's so cold."

"I'm here," he answered, ashamed. The soldier had heard it, his desperation to be away. Ryder pulled off his own coat, blanketed the downed man with it. "Better?"

"Much better. Smells different, inside your coat, doctor. Like lilacs. Spring."

"Does it? That's from my girl, Diana. It is her scent. I held her there, against my heart, the last time we said goodbye."

"Now, there's a picture."

Quiet. Ryder' listened for breathing, checked his neck for a pulse. The man was finally dead. His own insides stopped convulsing. Why was it easier to look upon him now? Ryder wondered again if the dying man sensed his revulsion. It did not matter. Diana had come to his rescue, with her scent. Think about it later. Other men needed him. Get up, move on. Take back his coat from the man's death grip, he commanded himself, because his bag still contained a few supplies: bandaging, some laudanum. He had to reach more of the wounded. To get to the ones who might be saved. To comfort the ones who would die here.

The smoke and the fire in the thick brush of the wilderness battleground conspired against direction, breathing, sanity. Soon it would rain, making things worse. The cries rose all around. *Keep crying*, Ryder thought. *I will find you.*

"Now!" he heard a voice command.

Ryder thought, too late, of his Starr repeater, in the coat still clutched between a dead man's hands. He saw a blur of gray, a rifle's butt, a flash of white before he fell onto the dead man.

"We get us one, Gris?"

"Sure did. And, look—a right fine firearm in this here coat."

Tom would have thought of the Starr sooner, in the coat, now absorbing the blood from his head wound. Was he shot? No, hit. Hit so hard his ears were still ringing. Tom would not be in this fix now, Ryder thought.

"Hey, surgeon. Get up."

He struggled to open his eyes.

"On your feet, man!"

But he could barely get propped on his elbow. Wet, down the side of his face, pooling in his collar. The lanky figures standing over him blurred in the waves of heat.

"Damnation. He's bleeding like a pig, Gris! Didn't tell you to split his skull! The fire's coming closer. Quint, carry him."

"That beef-fed Yankee? I'd sooner—"

"Bag him, and his kit! That's an order. Cap'n Banks needs help now."

They might have asked for his help, Ryder thought, and saved his head. Prisoner. With a head wound, perhaps a skull fracture. Not good. Well. Nothing he could do. Tom was in charge now. Everything would be all right. Tom was a good man, would be a better physician than he was, someday, if he could just get him understanding that confusing line of French kings for the examination. Did he remember to talk to his mother about helping Tom find a position after the war? Yes, in his last letter home. Would it reach her, he wondered as he fell over the biggest man's shoulder, and the poisoned, smoky world of the wilderness battlefield went black.

* * *

"Set him down."

Voices, becoming more distinct as consciousness returned. That voice with no name attached yet. Not Gris or Quint, but older, calmer, issuing orders to Gris, the one who'd hit him, and Quint, bigger, shoulders like a treefellow, who now carried him. Names. Remember them.

200

Ryder had to concentrate, even on opening his eyes. Another man. A slight figure in grey appeared: quiet, with red hair, staring at him curiously, then looking away. Here. In this dark, cold place. They had taken his firearm, but not his coat. Perhaps the dead soldier had too strong a grip.

Ryder heard birds, after a rain. He was wet and cold, he realized as Quint set him down, and the rest sat around him, opening their canteens. How much time had passed? How far had they moved? He had no strength. It terrified him, to be without strength, among his enemies.

"What's the matter with you, Yank?" That voice belonged to Gris.

Ryder turned. "Con—Concus—" he couldn't form the word. "You hit me too hard," he managed to growl out.

"No, I didn't. This here is too hard."

The blow knocked him over, to the amusement of the others. His insides became a traitor, evacuating. Vomiting. *Stay conscious. Don't choke. Head higher.* What if they wrote that to his mother? What if they told her how he died, choking on his own vomit? Someone fisted his hair, yanked him up.

"Hellfire. Clean him, before the captain sees what we done."

The red-haired one brought cold water. Washing one blood-crusted eye open, shocking his breathing back. *In, out. Better.* He could breathe. He could see. And they needed him. For their captain, there, under the tree, in the fading daylight. Groaning. Wounded.

Focus. Focus on his patient's wound. Ryder got to his feet. He wiped his mouth with the back of his hand and saw new, bright red blood. Cut lip, that's all. Not internal bleeding. Do not become panicked.

"My bag?" he whispered.

"There. That's better." A sergeant, with faded stripes on his sleeve, spoke. He cocked his head. "We were about ready to leave you to the crows, surgeon, and make do with your kit."

Ryder cast his hand forward for the grip of the supply bag's strap, but his wrist was intercepted, yanked behind his back.

"I cannot help your captain without my hands," he informed the most dangerous one, Gris.

"He dies, you'll follow him down, you understand?"

"Yes."

Surely not his own voice. So calm. As if he were saying yes to a train conductor bringing him up the Hudson, home to his mother on summer holiday from Columbia. No. Stay here, stay now, a grown man, a doctor, with obligations.

Gris gave up his bag. Ryder was barely able to maintain its weight as he approached the man under the tree. Their leader.

This was a renegade outfit of Confederates, he judged from both their ways and the inclusion of salvaged Union looted trousers stripped of identification added to their ragged clothing. What state? No flag in sight. No insignia apparent. Their wounded leader's hat had an ostrich plume in it. He wore his light hair long. Name? Had they called him by name? Ryder searched his addled head. Banks. That was it, Banks.

Captain Banks's groomed, curling mustache twitched with his effort to hold in his pain. He wore the best boots of his pack of men, the youngest of whom had his feet wrapped in rags. Perhaps he was from the Carolinas, where it all began. Well. He was not a hot-headed Secessionist now, but gravely wounded. He accepted an offer of laudanum without protest. Ryder cleared away the remnants of his blue silk vest. He cleaned the wound.

"Remember," Sergeant Quint said, as Ryder reached for a scalpel. Where was the other, the more dangerous one, Gris? There, outside their circle, his head turned, looking green. Good to know, to remember, this weakness at the sight of an open wound. Ryder dipped the scalpel in alcohol. Calm. Stay calm. Even with a pounding head and badly-focusing eye, he was the best they had.

Infection to cut away, then find the bullet. "Hold him down," he issued the gruff command. They obeyed. Captain Banks, his eyes glossy with laudanum, bolted as Ryder dug deeper. His men kept him steady. *Don't nick an artery, or we'll both be finished*, Ryder thought.

* * *

Tess still felt his hand at her shoulder, still heard his last words to her, echoing. "Get them out, Tom. I'll be following directly."

But he hadn't followed, so now she was on a battlefield long after her usefulness had ended. There was no one else to be pulled out, no one to be comforted. Tess's eyes stung from the smoke all around. She continued sifting through the remnants of the dead, the ones not consumed by the fires. Now it was a place for the units of gravediggers, mostly free Negroes. Had she spoken to all of them? Over the ridge of smoldering trees came a tall man with a gaunt face and large, forever grieving eyes. A bulging, battered canvas bag was slung over his shoulder.

"You be the doctor's man," he said quietly, a statement. "Come looking?"

"I am, sir."

The black man flinched slightly at her last word. His gruff voice softened. "Go on back to your regiment, young one."

She shook her head. "I have to find him."

"The fires didn't get to him. That be the best I can do for you." He squinted harder at her coat sleeve and its stripes. "Sergeant."

The man wasn't saying something. Something that was in those eyes.

"I have to find him," Tess repeated.

"He be under the earth now. Buried him myself."

203

"What did he look like? The man you buried?"

"Listen to me now. It better this way."

"I'm a surgeon's assistant. I've seen all manner of wounds, of—"

"Not to your captain, your friend, you ain't."

"Describe him!" she ordered.

The gravedigger sighed hard. "Can't rightly. Not much of a face left. Cannon blast. You hear what I saying?"

Tess heard it, felt it, ripping at her insides. She staggered back, before the man steadied her shoulder with his big hand. "Listen. You know his folk? Can I trust you with what I got off him?"

"What? What did you get?"

"His coat. With the fancy card picture of you two inside. That be what gives me patience with you, truth to tell. That and your captain give a remedy to my brother George, to ease his trots, back in Washington. We shared it, me and George. Worked good. Wouldn't take no fee neither. Spoke to him like he was white, George never stopped saying."

"Ryder talks to everyone the same," she said.

"You promise me you get the coat to the doctor's kin and I give it to you."

He reached into his leather sack, drew out the familiar blue officer's coat, its brass buttons blackened with soot, but the embossed eagles, the "M.S." on the epaulets coming through the grime. Ryder's coat.

Tess crushed the coat in her arms, and breathed its scent of blood and lilacs. Darkness beckoned, threatened to overcome her.

But the gravedigger's hand was at her elbow, steady. "Found it draped over him. Like a blanket. Like he was keeping hisself warm. There's a good picture for your mind's eye, young one. Not a body else would pay George nor me no mind when we was sick, 'cepting your doctor. A good man. Now, without this here coat as proof, they'll report him missin' instead of dead, you hear? I lose me this job if they find out what I done."

"It will be safe with me."

"Not safe. It needs returning. Your captain, he got hisself a wife?"

"No."

"His mama, his sister, then, gets this. Blood kin. You hear?"

"His kin, yes," she agreed.

"I got to be crazy as a loon," the gravedigger whispered, finally releasing his hold on the coat.

Chapter Twenty-nine

Ryder's patient was out of immediate danger. His captors finally allowed him a short, guarded walk to the creek side to clean his instruments and his own wound. He felt the deep crease going through the scar the panther had given him. It had swelled his right eye almost closed. Without stitches it would cause another, uglier scar. It didn't matter. Diana would not care.

His small tasks exhausted him. Still, not a time for sleep. If he went to sleep, he might die. He knew about concussions. Still, without the rush of energy that came with the operation, he found himself leaning back against the trunk of a tulip poplar and drifting, layering another reality over his own predicament. A reality of speculation, Tom clutching his coat. Blood. The blood would worry him. Poor Tom. Don't. Head wounds bleed more, you know that. Nothing you can do for me. So much work. See to the men.

The Confederate irregular's kicks brought him back. They were helping him stay awake, the kicks and taunts from Gris, while the youngest one, still a boy, watched. Later the others dragged their captain toward Ryder in a crudely constructed travois.

"Are my men treating you poorly, sir?" Banks asked in a polite Southern manner that made Ryder's skin crawl.

"Nothing less than I expected."

"Your contempt does you no service."

"It was not meant as contempt, Captain Banks. Only understanding."

"Understanding? Of what, sir?"

"Your band's status outside of the regular army of the Confederacy. That army would not hold a member of the medical services prisoner, or abuse his person."

"I would hardly expect you to understand the regrettable excesses of true loyalty. You are not a proper soldier."

"I am a soldier. Captain Ryder Cole. New York Infantry. You are obliged to—"

"Where were you trained, surgeon?"

"Columbia." Ryder struggled to fetch the rest through his pounding head. "Columbia College of Medicine."

"Ah. You are a physician as well as surgeon then, doctor. Columbia. On the island of Manhattan, is it not?"

"Yes."

"I visited New York City on several occasions in the company of a merchant seaman uncle."

"In the rice trade?"

"Indigo, sir. But your ear is good to find the Carolinas in my speech. Have you chanced to visit my country?"

"I have not had that pleasure."

"Pity. We could discuss, perhaps contrast our homelands. I regret to admit that I found your blatantly commerce-driven city barbarous."

"I live upriver."

"Ah. The mighty Hudson glorified in the art of painters Cole and Church. The country of Mr. Irving and Mr. Cooper and the Leatherstocking series of pioneer and Indian tales. That suits your compassionate nature better than that crass metropolis. There may even be a touch of the Mr. Cooper's Mohican savage in your bloodline, I think, from times gone by in those hills."

Ryder felt pressure inside his head. A memory there, behind the pain. A memory of teasing. When? Just after his father's death. Teasing about the density of blackness in his hair. From distant cousins pointing to the portrait of his long ago grandmother with the same hair, with the copper cast to her skin. His mother's back went straight with indignation when he asked her about the teasing, but Great

Aunt Letty soothed, assured him. Nonsense. She was a Frenchwoman, a Huguenot, that grandmother. They are a darker people. And the limner artist was low on his lighter pigments, no doubt. But the portrait was relegated to the attic. He must search it out, if he ever got home again, Ryder decided now.

The Carolina captain who'd touched that memory was speaking again. "Now, where I come from, we believe one drop of tainted dye spoils the vat."

Ryder Cole's indignation flared. He was no longer a child, at the mercy of cruel teasing. "Is that your rationalization for my continued captivity?" he demanded. "Are you turning me less than human, Captain Banks? Have I become a red Indian, as easy to abuse as one of your slaves?"

A twitch of the mustache. "Why, Dr. Cole, do you not enjoy our company? My health is tied to yours, sir, so I would be more willing to negotiate scruples were I you."

Ryder's mind clouded in a haze of Diana's touch at his face, remembering how he had thought her a mulatto. She would not care about tainted bloodlines. Not his Diana. He felt a kick at his side.

"Damn Yankee! Cap'n's speaking to you!"

"Now, Corporal Quint, the good doctor claims equality with my rank, though he presents nothing to prove himself. He's but a coatless gentleman recently caught stealing a remarkable repeating weapon from a dead man. Is that any way for a sensitive Northern gentleman to behave? A gentleman who will not even buy a cotton shirt unless it's woven by so-called free labor? Filthy Irish immigrants working for pennies a day, no doubt."

Had these men looked at the labels of his clothes as they carried him here, Ryder wondered, indignant.

"Perhaps they are saving those pennies to provide for families, buy farms in a free state, as free as all our United States will be," Ryder countered.

Quint, whose punishments were not as deadly as the ones from Gris, jabbed him hard.

Captain Banks held up his hand. "Now, now, we must behave better toward our well-bred guest," he reminded his man like an indulgent parent.

"Ain't he sassin' you, sir?"

"No, corporal. We are engaging in civilized debate."

"Sorry, sir. 'Twixt that awful sound of Yankee chatter and the what of his talk, can't rightly tell."

"Have Private Townsend look through the black bag and make up a head plaster for our guest."

"Aw, don't bother, sir! He's just lazy."

"I don't believe so. And if he survives your crude discipline, he could prove useful before we turn him in or shoot him. And I find him most entertaining besides, this child of the forest in his abolitionist cotton finery." Captain Banks turned his attention back to Ryder. "Now. How was your tainted family's fortune made, sir?"

Ryder struggled past his head's pain. Had he said too much? They would not force a ransom from his mother, by God. He drew in a painful breath. "My name is Captain Ryder Cole. I am in the medical corps presently attached to the New York 116th Infantry. You are honor-bound to release me."

"Ah, now you are becoming dull, sir."

Ryder's muscles tensed for another blow. But he did not feel a kick or jab this time.

They left him with only Townsend, the young one with the feral eyes, who wrapped his head with strips ripped from the hem of his cotton night shirt. They were going to allow him to sleep. That would cure or finish him, Ryder thought, before he closed his eyes and lost himself in the imagined scent of lilacs and remembered springs.

* * *

Tess packed Ryder's coat in her bag before she made her way back to her own encampment. She found only remnants of their new regiment. A dozen were missing.

Were the twelve together, protecting each other as they made their way out of that hell? The men straggled into the hospital camp one by one, the ninth with the story of how the remaining three unaccounted-for had died while being nursed by Zouaves of a Brooklyn regiment. Her new comrades continued slamming her shoulder, saying they knew Ryder would turn up. No one was allowed to shoot the surgeons, after all. How long before they gave up searching? She looked around the sick tent crowded with the burned and wounded. How dare he leave her now, when there was so much to be done?

A surgeon from the 43rd relieved her early, gave her the best place to lie down—a two man tent with cots inside. Temporary. She was not a surgeon. They would bring one in soon. Then she would have to work under him.

If she stayed.

For the first time since her enlistment, Tess thought of desertion. It would be an easy thing, turning back into a woman. She could return to Washington, to the house he'd rented for her, cocooning herself there, like the grieving widow he'd set her up to be. He'd courted both their fates toward disaster, doing that.

These were night fears, Tess told herself, not grief. She had not seen him dead. But what was she supposed to do, return to the battlefield's graves? Dig up the one of a man with a face seared off by cannon fire? They were all unmarked, the graves. She doubted the gravedigger would remember the spot. She tried to rest her mind, to sleep, drifting in the dark, behind the cries of the suffering men.

She heard Ryder's voice. Clearly. As she'd heard it many times before, calling. Tom. Diana. Names he knew her by, stolen names, not her own. She bolted up, staring, wide-eyed, at the mud-splattered walls of the tent. She pulled out his coat, held it close. Why would he be calling her in that way, as if he needed fresh bandaging, or a length of catgut thread, if he was dead?

"I hear you," Tess whispered into the fine wool fibers. She inhaled a cold, dark, sickness through the blood stain.

His blood, she was sure. Stop it. Get up. Light a lamp. She sat on the side of the bed. Ryder was a neat man, she must treat the coat better. The tent was private, no one on the other cot, no one to disturb. She tended to the coat, brushed it down, polished the brass buttons' eagles back to a high shine.

Then she reached into the deep inside pocket. Her fingers found a letter. She brought it into the light of the lamp. It was not in an envelope, but folded in the old way, then sealed all beautiful with blue wax. There was a bee on the imprint seal, like the ones his mother had in the old Dutch skeps on Belle Haven, there on the Hudson. He did not seal his letter with his family crest, or the state of New York's symbols. A bee. It made her smile. How was her man so humble and so arrogant at the same time?

She turned the letter over, leaving a smudge of red clay dirt from her thumb——the first mark on it. In his bold, deliberate hand, in dense black ink, the letter was addressed to his mother.

Of course. She was his heir, if he died for the cause in this world turned upside down, where mothers inherit from sons. "Ryder," Tess whispered. "Don't make me deliver this."

Think. The coat was draped over him, the gravedigger said. She pulled it over her and placed his image into her mind, trying to escape the terror of the cannon blast. He'd been caught unawares, more than likely, while he was hovering over a wounded man. Another scent dominated, suddenly, in the coat's silk lining. Tobacco. Tess turned the light up higher, examined the lining more carefully. An imprint was there, of a tenacious grip. Not Ryder's grip. He did not use tobacco in any form. And she had been so shocked by the blood stains that she'd failed to realize something else. His fancy Colt Starr repeater was missing.

Cannon blast was the cause of the death? How then was Ryder's coat intact? It wasn't blown off him, not if he was in it. He was not wearing it, Tess decided. Ryder Cole gave a patient his coat, a man with tobacco stained fingers. The gravedigger buried that man.

Relief washed over Tess, leaving her light-headed.

"Where are you, Ryder?" she asked.

He didn't answer.

Well, he had better things to attend to, Tess reasoned. Like staying alive without his coat.

* * *

Ryder woke, unexpectedly refreshed and clear-headed, thinking that they must not send the letter he'd written to his mother. She had asked nothing of him except to keep himself and Tom safe. *War is not a safe place, Mother.* But she knew that, even before she served the wounded after Shiloh. She knew. That's why her eyes were so wounded, there at the Ashokan train station long ago.

"Want some hard tack?" the quiet one, who had rags wrapped feet, the one who never hit him, who had made his head plaster, asked.

"No," Ryder said without thinking, before checking his own insolence. Unwise. He could not live on insolence. He tried to ignore the gnawing of his stomach.

"Go on, take it. Slow like, feel for the bugs with your tongue and teeth. Unless you like the taste of bugs."

Ryder opened his hand, took the offering. "What is your name?" he asked quietly.

"Alex Townsend. But they call me Weasel. I was who they used to beat, before you."

"You must advise me, then. Towards advancement from my replacement position."

"Eat up. Don't talk so much. And bide your time."

Townsend crept away from his side then, in just the slippery, broken- backed manner of a weasel. Ryder had never thought fondly on the animal until now. He concentrated on finding enough saliva to break down the tasteless hard tack in his mouth when two others replaced Alex Townsend. They'd done something while he was sleeping

212

so soundly, Ryder realized. Something that now made his skin crawl.

"Where are my clothes?"

"Why, what do you mean?" Gris asked.

"You blind, Yank? You got clothes on." Quint took up the humiliation.

"And you was pretty near born in them, from the stench."

The coarse fabric felt like sand, chafing his skin. And they hadn't bothered to shake out the vermin.

"Best get used to those togs," Quint advised. "In these hills, you'd be shot on sight in your clean Billy Blue."

The clothes would itch him into the madness he felt threatening since they'd first cracked his skull. Was he going mad? Give it a test, his mind, his memory. Balboa discovered the Pacific Ocean in 1513. His Cammann's Binaural Stethoscope was made where? *In Boston.* When? *1860.* He decided that he would write a letter to its manufacturers. *Their names. Think.* Find them, there, in his head. Codman and Shurtleff. *That's right.* Now, a letter, written in his mind, praising its ease of use. Expressing hope that it might become a standard for physicians, in listening. *Listening for what? Be specific. For congestion of*—Ryder felt pressure suddenly, and a wave of pain. Inside his head. Blackening his sight. Or was he closing his eyes in terror? *Fight it.* The letter to Boston. *Continue. Listening for? For congestion of the lungs. Defects of the heart.*

"You awake, Yank?"

A shove, one hard enough to kill one of the organisms living between flesh and the first layer of brutal homespun, Ryder decided. *Your mind is sound,* he told himself. *You have no control over the pressure inside your skull. Accept it. Accept the pain. Focus on your work here.* Ryder lifted his throbbing head, feeling the healing warmth of the sun. He got to his feet. "May I check your captain's condition?"

"Hey, them's better manners. Cap'n's this way. Good we got you out of your uniform. Pretty soon you'll be whistling *Dixie*."

"It is a good song. With an unfortunate narrowed purpose at present."

Quint stopped suddenly. "What in hell does that mean?"

Gris, the dangerous one, came at Ryder, smiling. Why was he smiling? Ryder felt a slam at his jaw that spiked the pain in his head higher. He let his shoulder take the brunt of the landing, like when he fell off his horses.

Townsend helped Ryder back to his feet. "Damnation, talk plainer!" he pleaded under his breath.

He was not speaking plainly? Ryder leaned on Weasel, just enough to make the horizon steady again. Perhaps he should not talk at all, he decided.

They approached Captain Banks, who now wore Ryder's cotton shirt. Ryder looked into glassy eyes. What would Tom think of the mood shifts of this man, made even more unpredictable by the laudanum he had likely helped himself to?

"Why doctor," the wounded man said, "how homespun becomes you. Poor Witchel did not fill out his clothes nearly so well."

"And it is my hope that free woven cotton sits softly against your injuries, sir," Ryder countered, wishing poor Witchel had visited the river to bathe more often. "May I examine the wound?"

"You may, sir."

Ryder noticed the hole in the loose weave of the wound's bandaging. He was not the only one plagued with itching. Captain Banks' wound had gone on to its next uncomfortable stage of healing. He eyed the bandaging Private Townsend held out as replacement.

"Was this boiled?" Ryder asked.

"Yep."

"For how long?"

"How long?"

Ryder faced the captain. "I should like that duty, if you please," he requested quietly. "It is important to keep the wound clean."

Quint and Gris laughed. "Let's make him our washer-woman for us all Cap'n," Gris proposed. "Weasel's poor at it."

Chapter Thirty

Washington D.C.

Colonel Streight rounded his desk, offering his hand. Tess took it, felt warmth and compassion in the grip.

"I am very happy to see you alive after the Wilderness campaign, Sergeant. And grieved by the news of—"

"I believe Captain Cole lives, sir," Tess warned him against offering condolences.

"Ah." Stopped cold, checking her eyes for sanity. *Careful. Steady*, she told herself.

He spoke again, more sternly. "You understand I cannot spare men to search?"

"Yes, sir. I'm only asking that my captain be kept on the missing list for the present. I do not believe I offer false hope to his mother."

Tess watched his eyes consider. She had only one card left.

"He is a widow's only child, sir."

"I'm quite aware of that, thank you, Sergeant!"

Anger. She had overplayed her hand.

"I beg your pardon," he apologized, reminding her of Ryder doing the same thing when he didn't have to, with men beneath his rank. "It has been a long, trying day," he continued. "Tom, you're asking me to give Olivia Cole many more of them. Days of seeing her son's face in every stranger's for years to come. Instead of a clean break, now."

"There's nothing clean about this war."

216

"No." He drew his hand across his chin before he spoke again. "I know your friend by reputation, son. Ryder Cole did not desert."

"No sir, I'm sure you're right about that. I'm thinking he's been captured."

"They would have paroled him by now."

"He might be sick, or injured, and can't tell them he's a doctor. Or maybe they need him so badly they're keeping him to tend their own. That's possible?"

"Possible, yes. All right. I'll give him three months on the missing roster. Then I will bring conclusive evidence to his mother, whether it is found or not. Do you take my meaning?"

"I do, sir. Thank you."

"Now. Might I be allowed to address the reason for our meeting?"

"Well sure, sir."

"Thank you. We're finally catching up with the South's command of surveillance and gathering information. But there has been an execution of one of our operatives behind enemy lines. You have agreed to consider some unconventional forms of service. This post will require the manner of disguise upon which we have spoken in the past. And I'm afraid it will take you far afield from the care of the wounded, Thomas."

"I have seen the effects of violence, sir. And I have some first-hand knowledge of it in action."

"But deceit is a stranger to you. Can you become another convincingly? Can you lie that boldly for the cause, Sergeant?"

* * *

Near Swift Creek Lake, Virginia

Ryder and the small band of irregulars were traveling along a river. Such a precious little knowledge he had gath-

217

ered of their location. Still in Virginia, he thought. *Watch the sun. Navigate. Southeast. Yes.* They were heading toward Petersburg, perhaps. The boiling water he used to clean the bandaging could be used as a weapon, Ryder knew. But the idea of scalding a man, even one of these men, was contrary to every instinct he possessed. *Think harder. Plan.* If only he was not so distracted by his headaches, by the painful rawness of his hands. Small cuts were opening now that Banks's men donated their harsh soap and filthy laundry to him whenever he boiled the bandaging. Ryder remembered changing his underwear daily at home, and how Agnes would place dried lavender from his mother's herb garden between the layers of fresh linens in his drawer. Agnes, the daughter of Sill whom he barely remembered, who had been his grandfather's slave. Did Agnes's hands look, feel as his did now? He would have noticed, wouldn't he? *Stop it.* Asking himself questions he couldn't answer, thinking about home.

"You connivin' ain't you?" Quint, his current keeper, accused as he fell behind the others. "You always dawdle when you think too hard."

"I am trying to find the plant."

"What plant?"

"Larkspur."

"What for?"

"Your captain's wound."

"How do we know you ain't trying to make him worse?"

"I am a doctor. I do not seek to make people feel worse."

"Don't you then? A fancy doctor made my mama scream bloody blue murder 'fore she died!"

"I am very sorry to hear that."

"An' you'd of cured her, that right?"

"I don't know that I could have."

"Damnation. Quit talking like that. It's getting hard enough to watch Gris have at you."

"It speaks well for you, that it is hard," Ryder said quietly as he stooped, shook the dirt from a root. Was he gaining another advocate?

"You use any remedy on your own self first, Captain says, on account you're a crafty damned Yankee. And these here plants can be used to kill."

Yes, Ryder thought. He would use the acidic larkspur in his pack to kill his own body lice as well as treat wounds. Tom had taught him that, gleaned from his sister Tess, who was Diana. Not his Diana, in their rooms in Washington, but the woman who'd shot the panther and Moutamin. But the two Dianas were fusing in his mind. He could not help it. It was too hard, thinking about leaving them both insufficiently provided for. Would his mother understand his debt to them? Would she keep them from want as he'd asked of her in his will? His will was a document that could have been incinerated, along with his coat, in the sweeping fire overtaking that battlefield. What a mess he'd made of everything. He had nothing now, except the memory of Diana's arms around him and the words of Tess's letters with its smells, sights, sounds of home. And recipes. He and Tom often used Tess's plants when he ran out of opium pills. They acted as sleeping potions for wound-weary patients. Perhaps there was a less lethal way than scalding water to aid in his own escape.

"Step lively," Quint complained. "Chiggers are eating me alive!"

"Poke root."

"What?"

"We'll find poke root to help your itching."

"Truth to tell? That's a cure?"

"Truth to tell."

"You makin' fun of me, Yankee?"

"Not at all. My girl, she comes from hill country, too. The Big Woods, we call it, back home, stretches into Connecticut. She's a wonder with plants. And a much better shot than I."

"Oh, don't start talking to me of sweethearts now, damn your eyes! It will never sit right with me when Gris kills you."

* * *

Union encampment outside Washington

Tess looked at her comrades' shining, scrubbed faces through her disguise's spectacles. She saw no trace of recognition before they turned to inspect the goods of her tradesman's cart. This was the final examination of her new position, in a new army.

One of her soldiers saluted Colonel Streight, standing beside her. "You brought us an angel, sir!" Another dropped coins into Tess's palm. "Your prices are a notch more fair than Stanley's, Mrs. Flynn."

"Are they now? That must be your reward for writing home daily, young one."

"But, I ain't written since—"

"Ah, then ye will, now that ye have purchased yer ink and writing papers! The blessed postmaster says no stamp a'tall is required for the letters of our brave fighting lads, ye know that, surely?"

"I do, Ma'am. It's my new resolution, I promise you, to write home more regular. Thank you, Ma'am."

The last of her comrades tipped his hat to her as if she were the Queen of the May and not a large Irish woman in a wide straw hat.

Tess was grateful she had spent enough time in the lilting Maud O'Neil's company to affect this disguise, and so complete the remaining test the Secret Service had demanded: fooling members of her own company.

Once the men walked on with their treasures, she looked to her two commanding officers. Major Yandell smiled his encouragement. But Colonel Streight looked worried.

220

"'Angel,' did you hear?" he grumbled low. "And I believe that rascal Sullivan was flirting with you besides, Sergeant. Your disguise is still too young." The punctual Major Yandell's smile faded as he opened his gold pocket watch. "Is there time to give you more years?"

Tess folded the flap of her wagon's canvas down. "The spectacles and my new size make me unbecoming enough, I think, sirs. The men treated me respectfully aged, it seems to me. Like an auntie."

Streight grunted. "Your own men. Who are exceptionally well-mannered. And clean. How do they remain so clean?"

"Captain Cole and I badgered them on that point sir, just as we did the Third Volunteers."

Major Yandell shook his head. "You are needed here, Thomas. How am I going to get along without you?"

"This first is a simple, limited mission. We should both stop fussing," his fellow officer assured Yandell, but looked almost as worried as he faced Tess. "Have you got your knife at the ready beneath those skirts, son?"

"'Mrs. Flynn,' if you please, sir. And my weapon is in place, yes."

Colonel Streight took her hand, patted it, for appearances, for her men, even from a distance, were surely wondering the nature of their prolonged conversation with an Irish tradeswoman. "Tom. Stay alert. And get back to us soon."

* * *

Outside Fort Corbet, Virginia

The first view Tess saw with the dawning light was a work party of black men led by a slave driver in civilian clothing. Behind them rode six soldiers in gray and their officer. Tess squinted, still unused to her clear glass lenses.

221

A lieutenant. She felt her hands grow cold as he signaled her cart to halt.

He removed his hat. "Where are you heading, good lady?"

Tess nodded, smiling to show the tooth she'd blackened. "So kind of ye to be asking, sir! I'm to trade my sundries and some little fancy provisions among the lads of Fort Corbet. In support of me ancient widowed mother."

"Without a man about your stores?"

"Ah, now. What need have I for a man when such as you will be stopping to inquire of my health and happiness? The saints preserve the gallantry of Southern gentlemen!"

He grinned. "Allow me to accompany you to the camp."

"With the greatest of pleasure, sir."

Tess tried mightily not to look annoyed when the officer transferred his horse to a subordinate, climbed into the cart beside her, and took the reins from her hand.

"You have your papers to gain entrance to Fort Corbet, of course."

"Whist, but I travel nowhere without my papers, though 'tis kind of you to be asking."

"And," his voice lowered in volume, "have you any quantity of coffee? Real coffee?"

"I do indeed, sir. And the purest refinement of cane sugar besides. I would be most obliged if you would avail yourself of a pound of each for the trouble of your protection this fine morning. And perhaps your good lady might have use of a little package of my needles and thread?"

He looked astonished. Was she offering too much? "Why, that would be most—" His eye was distracted suddenly by the appearance of a small Negro man in a red shirt and pack, tramping out of the woods beyond the road. The lieutenant reined in the horse.

"Who do you belong to, and why are you not at work?" he demanded of the man.

"Don't belong to nobody, sir. I be free and always was. I be going up yonder to help out at my sister's."

The officer turned to the big civilian. "Take this black rascal and have him join your others. If he fails to keep up, give him twenty lashes to impress upon his mind that there are no free niggers here while there's a damned Yankee left in Virginia."

There was a long whip in the civilian's belt. Tess watched the small man's face for signs of indignation, but found only resignation as he was led away.

"That vagabond is precisely why you must be on your guard with your goods, woman," the Confederate officer said, before he clicked her horse forward.

Tess realized she had gone from amusing to troublesome.

"I am Mrs. Flynn, and so grateful for this advice from a gallant captain."

"Lieutenant, Mrs. Flynn. Lieutenant Aldridge of the 20th Alabama Volunteers."

"Oh aye, just so! Are not my old eyes foolish? Or do they see into the future and a new rise in rank for you in my mistake, sir? Ah, when we reach the fort, you'd allow me a look at your hand to see if your palm speaks in this direction."

He smiled broadly now.

Tess breathed more easily that she had guessed correctly. The tattered silk of his vest and the partridge feather in his hat signified some whimsy. He was not a religious man who might be scandalized by fortune telling.

"That would be a most pleasant diversion, Mrs. Flynn. Would you allow me to present both your goods and talents at officers' quarters?"

"Ach, and doesn't the day grow ever brighter for me, sir?"

Chapter Thirty-one

Fort Corbet, Virginia

Once within the confines of the fort, Tess was grateful when Lieutenant Aldridge rescued her from the growing crowd of soldiers waiting for their turn at a palm reading. He offered exactly what she needed: a tour of the camp and its fortifications.

She walked on the officer's arm, memorizing the number of rifled cannons, both three and a half inch and four and a half inch, as well as thirty-two pounders, forty-two pounders, Columbiads, Dahlgrens, mortars, and siege howitzers. She would write the numbers and sketch the outer works when she returned. She did not miss the sham log-cannons. Colonel Streight had told her to count those too. From the outside, they made this fort look much better defended than it was.

"You are not so charmingly loquacious with me as you were with the men, Mrs. Flynn."

Loquacious. One of the words she'd not gleaned from Mama. No, Ryder had drilled that one into her, for her medical examination. Meant chatty. This Alabama lieutenant wanted chatty, not quietly counting cannons. She patted her escort's arm. "Ah, truth to tell, sir, gazing into the infinite is a bone-wearying gift! But could I do less for the brave and handsome lads quartered here?"

"And you were as generous in deed as in word. How can you charge them so little? Why, you have barely earned enough to feed your cart's horse."

She hadn't? Why didn't she find out more about how much Southern script was worth? "It's a failing, surely, to charge so little," she tried, feeling the sweat run down her back and absorb into the corset. "But sure how could I turn down any offer when I see their dear faces?"

That was not a lie. Tess had lost most notion of what side she was on when she took the script and pennies from beardless boys, listened to their questions while studying into their mud-encrusted palms. Their questions were not about battle outcome, states' rights, or even slavery. They were the same as her own comrades across the line pondered: "Will I get a letter this week?" "Will my sweetheart wait for me?" and "Will I live to see home again?"

Lieutenant Aldridge drew her hand deeper into the crook of his arm. Tess even liked this courtly man, in spite of his failings and against her own wishes. His pace slowed. "Dear lady. Your picturesque pronouncements of the future, while never directly stated, left each soldier with the gracious last gift in Pandora's box. Hope."

A too-young laugh escaped her. Did it startle him? Tess patted his arm in what she hoped was an elderly matron's way. "Why, Lieutenant, don't ye have a grace with the words yer own self! Ye make me feel all of twenty-three again!"

A civilian whose back was turned to her stood before a group of soldiers. A rope in the man's grip was attached to a beautiful white mare. She knew that horse. Tess felt her heart's hammer. Her fingers twitched in a desire to smooth the animal's brambled mane, to soothe the dread encircling her own heart. *Remain still. Listen.* Because there was nowhere to run.

"Well boys," the civilian boasted, "my ears picked up that a high ranking Yankee officer was going to visit their picket line at precisely nine of the clock. I hastened to inform our side's sharpshooters of this very punctual, pocket watch-wearing officer's appointment with his men. Shot as soon as they caught the glint of that gold watch in the sun!

How I enjoy a damned Yankee's regular habits! And so you see before you my gain of his splendid horse in the confusion that followed!"

Tess froze in her rage. She thought of the encouraging smile of Major Yandell and the brightness of his gold pocket watch. She thought of the affection Yandell had for his horse and for her men. This man had killed him, as sure as he'd pulled the trigger himself.

"I beg your pardon, Mrs. Flynn," her escort said, pulling Tess further aside, "that was not meant for your ears."

Yes, away, Tess thought. She must get away from this man.

But he turned. Hobson, their weekly visitor through the winter at camp. He was the one who gifted officers with writing paper and newspapers. But to the lower-ranked soldiers his goods were poor, his prices high. She and Ryder had chased him and his brightly colored wagon away from their men more than once. There was good reason for Ryder's distrust, Tess realized now, as she saw the peddler cart in the distance.

Hobson's tightly wound, wiry frame looked different on this side of the picket line. Even his accent drawled out toward Southern proportions. His whole being was relaxed, self-satisfied. But sharp eyes, sharp on either side of the army lines, narrowed in scrutiny.

Stay calm, Tess told herself. Hobson had seen Tom. Not her, not this freckled Irish auntie. *Breathe. Breathe easy.*

"This is my territory, woman," he informed her, showing off those small, almost filed-down teeth, set in a cold smile.

Tess found her voice. "I would not think of imposing, good sir. Might ye agree to have me provide the lads only with what ye lack in the way of merchandise?"

Lieutenant Aldridge stepped between them. "Nonsense! Don't allow him to bully you, Mrs. Flynn. Hobson, I know of your value to the cause, but Mrs. Flynn has brought such cheer to our men that I insist——"

"This misshapen matron may have charmed you, Lieutenant, but her blarney won't work with me," Hobson claimed. He began to circle her. "Something is not quite right."

Tess laughed, big and low-pitched this time. "Not right, is it? Well, have they not been saying that about the Irish for a good thousand years now?"

Lieutenant Aldridge patted her hand. "Your scrutiny of this lady does you no service as a gentleman, sir!" he proclaimed.

"Too young about the eyes for an auntie matron, I think," Hobson continued, ignoring the lieutenant's anger. His long finger pulsed at his lip. "It will come to me," he said, "for I never forget a slight. And this is not the first time this meddlesome creature has slighted me."

Tess felt the lieutenant's hand press hers "Mrs. Flynn is under my protection," he maintained.

"And I warn you sir, that 'Mrs. Flynn' might slice you sideways as much as look at you." Hobson leveled his glance at Tess. "Your clearance papers," he demanded. "I believe they deserve closer inspection."

* * *

Ryder bolted upright.

"What's the matter, doc?"

He heard Quint's voice through the ringing in his ears, the racing of his heart.

"N-nothing."

"Go back to sleep then."

Diana was calling for help from somewhere that did not smell of the cinnamon and vanilla and lilac of their home. Somewhere evil. *Think, Diana, you clever girl. Where's Tom? Go to Tom for help.* Ryder closed his eyes again, feeling useless to her, here, in backwoods Virginia, weighted down with iron.

The irregulars' commander was mounted back on his horse during their daily travels. But they kept Ryder in their company, trusting him with remedies, simple cures. They gave him Witchel's mount, Laddie, a good horse Ryder had grown attached to.

After two failures at escape, his mount picketed near the commander at night, and Ryder was locked into leg irons that Gris had stolen from a small blacksmith's forge. Time for another attempt to break free of them. Ryder sat up.

"I need to make water," he said to his keeper for the night. But Quint had already rolled over. On his other side Townsend yawned, sat up, found Quint's key, and removed Ryder's leg irons.

"Go on, Doc," he murmured, and rolled over again.

Townsend had never struck him, and had picked insects out of his food when his hands were too sore and his spirits too downhearted to bother. *Stop thinking that way*, Ryder chided himself as he reached the creek, still cradling the cold restraints in his arms. He took up the stone to pound at the lock of the irons. The best he could do for the man was to make his latest attempt at escape look harder than it was.

There, success. They might kill him this time, but they'd never use those irons on him again.

Ryder felt a rush of energy that came with his stolen freedom. Was it like what he saw shining from the weary faces of the runaway slaves he and his mother had hidden in their icehouse? He had not paid much attention to their faces. It was only a grand adventure to him back then, one that made his pulse race. He had never understood the runaways' perseverance until now.

Ryder longed to see his mother, to tell her of his discovery. He wanted to be Olivia Cole's indulged child again, her playmate at their dangerous game, one that could have cost them their home, their own freedom, once the Fugitive Slave Law was enacted. He moved upstream through the cold water. His feet were toughened since they'd taken his boots, which their commander now wore. People lived near water, didn't they? People of more modest means than his great-grandfather, who'd chosen a hilltop? Was there anyone in war-ravaged Virginia like his spirited mother, who might help him return to his regiment?

Ryder picked up his pace. He was altogether tougher now, he realized, except for the flare ups of that pounding in his head. One was coming on now. If he could dip his shirtsleeve in the water, press it against the pain, it would feel better. He went to his knees, sluiced the water over his neck. *There, better.* And his eyes were finding more details in the darkness. A straight path appeared though the shallow creek bed. He stood, sprinted off, bolting as if he was on Moutamin again, down the creek. *Yes.* There was strength in him yet. He breathed the night air, heavy with rain, into his lungs, used it to pump his muscles. Then some creek moss betrayed him, sent him down. *You are all right, nothing broken*, he told his racing heart. *Get up.* Baying hounds, in the distance. What had he been thinking? No one in Virginia, the jewel of the Confederacy, was going to help him. They were already sending out their hounds.

Get up. Climb a tree. No, think. They could not follow his scent through water. Perhaps they were following someone else? The wind blew hard, suddenly, and the clouds parted overhead. He shivered. Get up. Keep going. Fight the darkness.

Ryder gazed past the dividing clouds, remembering the celestial navigation globes at home, remembering a hand pointing to the stars, telling him stories of how the constellations received their names. He heard the voice again, a voice full of boundless energy, fascination, laughter. His father's voice. And there, over his head, his father's star: Polaris, pointing north.

Chapter Thirty-two

Fort Corbet, Virginia

Tess felt her hands and feet grow cold, even there, in the officer's tent, where his interrupted evening meal was steaming the air. "Leave her with me," Hobson demanded. "By the dawn's light, all will be out of her."

She heard Lieutenant Aldridge's teeth grind together. "Sir," he spoke to his commanding officer, the third man in the tent, "I must protest this affront to the lady's honor." The Confederate major looked up from his scrutiny of her forged clearance papers. He sighed hard.

"Some irregularities. Or perhaps merely out of date. These must be sent to Richmond for verification," he finally said. "If this creature is innocent, no harm will come to her. Now. Release her into Mr. Hobson's custody, lieutenant."

Lost, Tess thought. She was lost, as she'd barely begun at this business. She knew the kind of man Hobson was: cruel, greedy. And now his eyes burned with a hatred she didn't understand.

"Sure ye have done enough on my behalf, sir," Tess said quietly to the man at her side, who had, for a brief moment, reminded her of Ryder. "Have no worries, now. I will do what I must."

"See that you do, yes," he answered, looking dazed as he transferred her into the peddler's grip.

Hobson pulled her across the fort's parade ground. As they entered the large tent that grew off the side of his cart, she heard Lieutenant Aldridge outside, trying to calm the alarmed questions of the soldiers gathering. She'd been honored Auntie Soothsayer to them so recently.

How quickly reputations disintegrate in this business, Tess thought with a quick, snorting laugh. Hobson swung her around. His eyes narrowed, seemed to flicker in the smoky lamplight. "What do you find so amusing?"

"Only fortune's wheel, sir."

"You can put the biddy Irish on the shelf now. I know who you are."

"Do you? And you failed to tell your superior?"

"No one's my superior! I am a free agent."

The flecks in his eyes shone silver. The smell of his moldy merchandise and badly cleaned lamps sickened her.

"You betray both sides," she realized as she spoke the words.

He grabbed her jaw and slammed her against the side of a tent post. Black spots swam before her eyes. Tess felt the carefully applied rice powder and elderberry juice she'd used for aging herself bleed onto his hand.

He'd caught her, overcome her physically, as the storekeeper Mr. Strong had, years ago. How could this be happening again? Tess felt the pulse in her neck thrum madly against his tightening hold. She stared hard, daring him to choke the life out of her. He, a free agent, was looking for more gain. And she still had value.

He released her throat. "Whoreson Yankee," he said, wiping the smudge of her aging concoction off on his vest as if she'd contaminated him. Information, Tess told herself as she recovered her breath. Gather the details of this place. A handsome field bed, like the ones the highest ranking officers traveled with. A feather tic on top, amidst old, rotting merchandise. And him, eyes narrowed with intolerance.

"Chloroform, ether. Those are the stenches you're usually ranked with, isn't it, boy? Not matronly lavender."

Tess breathed through her terror of his size, his cruel intent, finding her direction. No more doubts about betraying a courtly man, or causing the deaths of beardless boys. She had a true opponent now.

"My usual scent is lilac," she said quietly. "I am younger than I appear, as you have perceived. But a woman, sir, trying to make her living unmolested."

The spittle surprised her, landing on her cheek. She struggled not to wipe herself free of it as he tightened his walk around her. "Perhaps you wish to be a woman, when in the company of a very upstanding surgeon in blue, who already has a very slippery widow, all set up in Washington. I know about your rival too, you see? I have a very wide net of information. And I keep good track of wealthy officers of both sides, and their secrets."

Tess felt invaded by this man and his words. She was not used to this kind of warfare. *Concentrate*, she told herself. *Listen.* What did he know? What did he want from her?

"Missing. That's what they told his mother after the Wilderness, to keep the guns of her foundry coming with all deliberate speed. But he didn't get out of those burning woods alive. Tell me the type of man Olivia Cole favors, favored friend of her dear departed. I will fill those dimensions, to bring her an account of her son's slaughter, replete with poetic dying words."

Tess wanted to kill him, for forcing the portrayal of that possibility into her mind. She felt herself closing down doors. The ones to her heart, to her mind. Making herself ready for battle.

Hobson advanced. "You may have fooled your comrade captain, but I am a man of the world. I know what you are."

"And what am I?"

"Questions. Nothing straight out of you, pretty boy. Because you're an aberration, a freak! Ah. That's a hit! The object of your affection went down at Wilderness and you have gotten into a new line of work, you filthy sodomite!"

"Sodom—?"

"Ignorant, besides?" he accused now, his eyes flaming with fury. And something else, Tess realized. Interest.

"Oh, very ignorant," she countered his rage submissively. "But I am a woman, sir. See for yourself," she invited in a steady voice, as she reached down slowly. "Look at the whiteness of my leg, and its curve, man of the world." She took up the hem of her skirt and petticoats. "Look at what lies between those legs, if you doubt my word."

"N-no."

There. She had him. "Come closer," she invited, backing towards that out-of-place luxurious bed, reaching for the weapon between skin and corset stays with her free hand, "Enjoy your captive. That's my only use to you, I fear. Come closer and tell me I don't possess the scent of a woman, Mr. Hobson."

He grabbed the hem of the petticoat she was lifting and ripped it up to her waist. It blended with the sound her knife made as it hacked a lateral line between his ear and collarbone. Deep, hard. Not like the surgical cuts that Ryder was teaching her. More like gutting a pig at home. Tess could not afford a cry, or any of his strength to be left in him.

She watched his startled look, felt his grasp of her thigh tighten. But his hold was only seconds in length before he realized his windpipe had been severed and his lifeblood pouring out.

The sounds that came from him were no longer hateful words, but harmless gurgles before he fell at her feet.

* * *

Along Swift Creek, Virginia

"Hey, now. Best join us."

Ryder looked down from his father's star, into the determined squint of a black woman dressed in the colors of the blue-black night.

233

"I cannot leave the water. My scent—"

"Them dogs had hold of a horse's scent. Got a mighty attachment to you, this horse, seems like. Come on out of the water, child."

Ryder saw the muddy skirts hiked up over her ankles, and felt exactly like what she'd called him, a hapless child. On the creek's bank she turned, pulling a small jar from the waistband of her skirt. He thought the powerful scent it contained would annihilate him before his pursuers did.

"Keep swallowin' down your displeasure, that's the way," she approved as she smeared it over his arms. "You get used to it." He saw a flash of her white teeth, and the gaps where others had been. "My own receipt," she proclaimed proudly. "How I make my contraband disappear into the night. Dogs won't want no part of you now." She surveyed his torn, threadbare clothes and form in the moon's light. "Lord, they been just as mean to you as they said."

"Said?"

"Oh, sure, that renegade crew of Capt'n Banks, they love to brag, never takin' no mind of folk fetchin' them water or food at farmhouses. But the folk lookin' for signs of the coming Jubilo, they listen good. So I heard all about their Yankee army doctor captain, stealed away from the fires of Wilderness. And me and my present set of travelers, we set our sights on fetching you up out of your slavery, Captain Cole."

"You did?"

"Jes' like you and your mama helped a few of mine in our hard travels North." The teeth, again. "Now, what you think on that, sir?"

Ryder blinked twice, before taking a closer look at the woman and her fierce smile. He finally saw the massive scarring on the right side of her face. People said that was the source of her visions. He bowed. "I am most grateful, Madame Moses."

"'Madame,' am I? Lord, we gonna have some fun with you!"

The pain came, unbidden, triggered by the smile she'd coaxed out of him. He felt the small woman's bony shoulder fit neatly under his arm, keeping him upright. She was much stronger, even, than she looked.

"Lord, Captain, you ain't well," she breathed, the mirth gone from her voice.

"It will pass. Please. Do not leave me here."

"I don't abandon no willin' souls, sir," she assured him, "though I'm known to shoot malingerers."

He eased himself from her support as his balance returned.

"You will not have to shoot me, Mrs. Tubman."

A single shot erupted. And the sounds of the dogs, closer.

Chapter Thirty-three

Fort Corbet, Virginia

Tess breathed in slowly, so the scent of her kill didn't make her retch, as she pulled off her bloodied skirts and covered Hobson's body with them.

She rifled through the trunk at the foot of his field bed, pulling out a shirt, trousers, a long coat. A button from the coat caught on a nail embedded in the trunk's splintered wood. Don't panic, Tess told herself, keep breathing, lift the button around where it was caught.

When she did, something clicked. A hidden spring caused a false bottom to open in the trunk. The space held small notebooks full of letters and corresponding numbers that made no sense to her. Code. Information, maybe important. Bring it north. To the colonel with kind eyes, who cared about her, about Ryder, about all the dead. She stashed her findings into the deep inner pockets of Hobson's cloth coat. In the dark, perhaps she would pass for him. Don't think about his scent—tobacco, whiskey, sweat, she thought as she pulled on his clothes, his coat, think about my small part in ending the war sooner. Tess pulled his wide brimmed hat low over her eyes. Think of fewer letters for Ryder to write home to grieving families. Where was he tonight?

The information she carried, and that in her head would help her to find him sooner. On her travels through the Southland she would show the photograph, the one Mr. Brady had made of them. She'd show it all over Virginia if she had to. For now, stay alert, stay alive. She brought down the smoky oil lamp from its post, lifted the chimney, and used it to begin a small fire, there in the rotten heart of the peddler's trunk.

Tess raised the flap of the tent. There were no sentries posted to guard an old woman in the custody of an able-bodied spy. She moved quietly, she knew how to do that, from stepping around her father's anger. Did he grieve the loss of her brothers? Did he ever think of her?

The horse lifted her head where she was tied to an oak tree, away from the others. Recognizing her new master from his clothes and scent, was she then? Tess realized she was still thinking in turned-around Irish. The Irish were good at hiding too, right in their talk. Maybe that was why she liked Maud O'Neil so much. That and her freedom. Tess approached the white horse, trying to stay calm, crooning softly. Signs of abuse, whip marks at the neck. "I'm not him," she whispered against the gleaming mane. "I'll never hurt you."

Voices sounded the alarm of the fire. The soldiers began running, struggling to get inside the ill-kept cart and tent. She saw Lt. Aldridge, his fine cotton shirt glowing, shouting her Irish name. *Don't hurt him,* she prayed to the fire, as she mounted the horse bareback, as she rode when a girl. She would never be that girl again, but some of her joy at the idea of its freedoms returned. It fought through her fear as she approached the gate's guards.

"Mr. Hobson," one called out, "what—?"

"They need you," she interrupted him gruffly.

"Yes, sir." She saw the light of the fire reflected in both sentries' eyes. Boys. Always eager to play with fire, even in the fourth year of a war. Tess dismounted and opened the gate herself, under the night watch scrutiny of the remaining guards along the fort's wall. She pressed her knees to the horse's flanks and aimed for the shelter of the distant tulip poplar trees.

Near Magnolia Grange, Virginia

Mrs. Tubman forged higher, leaving Ryder winded behind her. But she looked back, never losing him in her wake. "Seems we both been at this business since before you had your whiskers, Captain."

"Too long," he agreed, remembering when he first discovered his mother hiding runaways. Was he yet twelve? Yes, then, before whiskers. Touching his jawline, the beard he found there surprised him. He must shave it off at the first opportunity. Not a good example to the boys. What would Tom say? Mrs. Tubman's hand flashed out of the darkness, taking his arm.

"Not much longer, sir."

Ryder nodded, willing himself forward, higher. He did not like thinking about how changed he was since they'd hit him too hard. The concern in Mrs. Tubman's eyes belied their fierceness. He smiled. "I will follow you anywhere, Madame."

He heard her snort. It filled him with an unbounded joy. Amusing a woman. He could still do that. He was still alive. An elderberry shrub appeared ahead, with a dim light behind it. Perhaps she truly was Moses, then, and this was her burning bush.

"Well, Captain, does your 'anywhere' include this here bear's den?" she called down to him.

"Has he vacated the premises?"

"Oh, we smell powerful worse than he can stand!" Laughter infused her voice. "Good Lord." He heard her gasp, breaking the light mood between them. "Tappan."

Ryder heard a child's voice answer. "They ain't followed me, Moses. Shot, but ain't followed."

Mrs. Tubman knelt over a boy of about nine years. His eyes connected with Ryder's before he lost consciousness. Head wound. Not good. Ryder felt the boy's neck for a pulse. "Alive," he breathed out, lifting the child in his arms.

Light, not a great burden, even for him in his diminished state. "Lead on."

Ryder crouched low as they entered the small mouth of the cave. Silent, shadowed people. In the small fire's light they looked like ghosts. The boy was theirs. Had he been sent out of the cave's shelter to look for them? The thought sickened Ryder, that he might have occasioned the wound of a child. He saw accusation that confirmed his fears in the eyes of a girl wearing a blue kerchief wound about her hair.

"Do you have water?" he asked.

She looked past him, to Mrs. Tubman, before she answered. "What I been using to ease Mama."

"Fetch it," Harriet Tubman's no-nonsense voice instructed.

Ryder soaked his hands in the chipped tin basin. Army issued, the Army of the Potomac, his army. "Sit Tappan up please, against you, sir," he instructed the big man. "Call him," he urged the rest of the family. They did, in deep, loving cadences that pierced Ryder's heart. The boy's eyelids fluttered at the sound of his name.

"I found our Yankee doctor, Tappan," Mrs. Tubman crooned.

The boy smiled at Ryder, a miracle in this dark place. "Your horse be searchin' you out, sir."

"So I have heard."

"We got him, all safe."

"Good. Can you turn your head, Tappan?"

"Sure! " But his sharp gasp was followed by a female's cry. His head drooped on the big man's shoulder. His father, Ryder thought.

"If you would take a good, clamping hold of his jaw, sir, as I examine for damage?"

The man did so. Tappan made no sound, though his body flinched as Ryder placed his finger into the wound, probing for a ball, a bullet. None. His heart lightened. Then he found the ball's work: a sheared open vein.

"Have you a fine needle and thread?" he asked the two women, the shadowed mother, the smaller sister. Again the blue kerchief sister glanced at Mrs. Tubman first, received her nod, then returned with the things he needed quickly. Ryder sewed up the vein in the dim light of the fire. Harriet Tubman peered through her spectacles, surveying his work. "My, my, my," she whispered, "bleedin's all stopped."

The boy's eyes opened. "Mama?" he called.

"Here, Tappan." A woman emerged from the shadows fully now.

"You feeling poorly tonight still, Mama?" he asked.

"Feeling right well now. Swallow a little of my tea, son."

The girl holding the small crockery cup now looked for Ryder's nod of permission this time before she held it to her brother's lips. "Better?" she whispered.

"Hey now," he teased, "I must be bad off if I got you worryin', Delsey."

Their mother shook her head in a gesture Ryder recognized as akin to his own mother's amused exasperation with him. "You thank our Yankee doctor man now, son, for helpin' you back to us."

"Where was I?"

"Looking for me, I gather," Ryder said. "For which I am most grateful, young sir, having been in bondage myself."

The boy tilted his head. His eyes widened. Ryder took the opportunity to examine for pupil dilation. Down to pinpricks in the brown depths. Normal reaction to light.

"Ain't the likes of me a sir, sir," he protested, "not until the coming Jubilo."

"It's come. Our president has declared full emancipation. We have more work to do together in order to make it so, of course."

Harriet Tubman shook her head. "You gentlemen want to continue discussing your politics talk on watch outside? Womenfolk need to help your mama get her baby into the fine world you're makin'."

"Baby?" Ryder whispered.

"Yes, sir. Now if you'll—"

"This woman is laboring?"

"Her name's Mis' Broder. She be laborin' since afore your horse brought down the dogs on us all."

"But she must not do that. Not a good place, not a good time."

"Ain't like any part of this is of her choosing, Captain."

"Oh, yes, of course. I know that." Ryder didn't mean to spark her ire. These people were reminding him of what goodness was left in the world. And, he realized suddenly, what opportunity. "Mrs. Tubman. Might I stay?"

She cocked her head, frowning. "Why? This be woman's work."

"I have never witnessed a delivery."

"'Delivery,' is it? Mis' Broder, she ain't bringing in no package, Captain."

"I meant no offense. It is what we called it, at Columbia, and at the French Academy I attended." Stop it, he berated himself. *This woman is not interested in your credentials.* "I have studied the progress of labor and delivery, you see, from engravings in my textbooks. Good engravings, well rendered. And the procedure was demonstrated quite cleverly with…" *Stop. Stop, now.*

She cocked her head. "With?" she prompted.

"Models. Dolls."

"Dolls. Toy babies?"

She was good at making him feel like an idiot. He looked down at his hands. "I would be grateful, because in life the opportunity has not yet presented itself."

"You mean your own folks ain't trusted you with seein' a child in."

"Well, yes," he admitted. He was still an arrogant stripling in her eyes, he realized, unless he could convince her otherwise. "I will stay out of your way of course, unless I can be of any assistance."

Harriet Tubman looked tired. Or was she just out of patience with him? "Well," she said, "I suppose I don't have to worry about you fainting at the look of blood, anyhow. All right. Go on and ask Mis' Broder."

"Ask Mis' Broder," he repeated like a dense schoolboy. "Ask her... what?"

"If you might sit in on her birthin', Captain."

"Oh. Yes. Yes, of course. How very rude."

He heard the laboring mother's laughter echo off the stone walls. "Ain't much I could deny you, after you done so right by my boy, sir."

All the women were teasing him. Ryder felt honored by it. Even Delsey was smiling behind her hand.

Ryder heard a horse snort when Mrs. Tubman lit a candle. No, not a horse, how could he have missed seeing a horse in a cave? But there he was——Laddie, Wintchel's mount, welcoming him with a look of devotion. The horse provided him with a purpose. He could stand ready to remove the gelding when he went skittish because of the woman's screams.

But there were no screams, only whispers of instruction, suggestion, and encouragement.

Ryder soon realized it was he becoming skittish—more skittish than any horse he'd ever tamed. He felt bursting, full of questions he didn't dare voice as he observed the cadence among the women——resting, laboring, resting, in cycles. This was like no other medical condition he'd ever studied or attended. It was not sickness, he finally determined, but what it was he could not name. The dance of its progress absorbed him utterly.

Then, the cycle changed. Deep, guttural sounds came from the mother's throat, still quiet, but erupting. He watched the women smile, help Mrs. Broder sit high in her daughter's lap. Harriet Tubman folded her sleeves back, presented her waiting arms, arms covered with whitened scars. He had never before wondered at the source of her fire, her devotion. Could he turn his own sufferings into something like what this woman had?

There, in a profound silence, Mrs. Broder pushed a slippery baby into Harriet Tubman's waiting hands. The tiny boy, covered in a substance that looked like new cheese in the milk room. Life. The opposite of what Ryder had been battling for years. This was life: new, beautiful. Inexpressibly beautiful. The cave glowed with it.

"Hands clean?" the midwife asked him suddenly.

"Yes, Ma'am." He answered like who he hoped he was, her apprentice.

"Palms up, Dr. Cole."

He held out his hands. The woman called Moses placed the silent baby in them, still attached by the cord that led into his mother's body. "Turn him on his belly, sir, all gentle-like."

His brain froze, but his hands took over his thinking for him. They rotated the baby's small weight to his middle, there, in the protective hold of the palm of his hand. Under Ryder's index finger, a tiny pulsing heart. Life. This is not what he'd done to the doll model: hanging it by its feet like a hog in a smokehouse, slapping its back, until his teachers determined his efforts were hard enough for eliciting the "lusty cry of life." They were not his teachers now. Moses was. *Breathe. Listen. Trust her wisdom.* He heard gurgling, followed by small, snarling blasts of air.

"Stroke his back, sir," Mrs. Tubman said in that fine, silvery voice that she had used only with the women. *There.* He was finally inside their circle. He did as she instructed and was rewarded with more intakes of air, then small cries, more even breathing. The baby's limbs began stretching, exploring the new world outside his mother's womb.

"Extraordinary," Ryder heard his own awed whisper.

"Give him here now, sir," the midwife called, "This little one's got his first job to do."

Ryder watched as she carried the baby to his mother's breast, where he began to nuzzle, then suckle vigorously. The umbilical cord was now white and flat. Mrs. Tubman unwound lengths of thread. With them she tied off two sections of the cord before she sliced between them with her knife. He must acquire scissors for her, Ryder thought, he must make her a present of fine surgical scissors. Absurd thought. He did not even have boots on his feet.

The afterbirth emerged, and with it blood, and more blood. Too much. Hemorrhage.

Ryder felt his own blood turn cold in his veins. What to do? He didn't remember any instruction, any remedy. Panic rose, lodged in his throat.

"Keep him suckling, Ma'am," Harriet Tubman said quietly, "that's right, and you stay by your mama, Delsey," she instructed the girl, who was wiping Mrs. Broder's brow. Doctor," the midwife motioned him closer, "with me, sir."

Ryder joined her in kneading the mother's abdomen with his fists. The flaccid muscle beneath began to harden under their joint ministration. As it did, the blood gushing between Mrs. Broder's legs went down to a flow, then a trickle.

Ryder saw Mrs. Tubman's touch ease in its intensity. His own efforts followed suit. She smiled, nodded. Ryder sat back on his heels. "What we did, that stopped it?"

"Yes, sir. That, and her baby suckling. You pay me good mind, Captain."

Ryder felt more lightheaded than when he received his first and only compliment from Professor Belenger at the Paris Medical Academy. But their patient's cheeks were streaked with tears. He'd hurt her. Necessary hurt, but she had not cried out.

Mrs. Tubman took the baby from his mother. She put him in the middle of her own aproned skirt. With gentle vigor, those large hands worked the cheesy mass into his glorious rich skin color. Ryder followed the dancing movements of her fingers. Delsey handed her a winding sheet of linen that Mrs. Tubman used to wrap the baby snug. Then she placed him in Ryder's arms. "Go out to have the menfolk meet another of their own, whilst me and Delsey make our lady mother presentable for visiting."

Ryder opened his mouth, but was met with an impatient, "Scat!" and wave of her hand.

This duty was another gift from this gruff woman, he realized as he introduced the baby to his father and brother. It was a gift he could not hope to repay, even if he ended the war and brought on the Jubilo single-handedly.

Chapter Thirty-four

"I had no choice, sir, in the killing," Tess said, still at attention.

"No, indeed. We would have executed the man on the spot, Thomas, had we been the ones to find him out. Please, be at your ease."

"I am sorry I did not find him out before he signaled the marksman toward Major Yandell."

"A good man, who will be deeply missed by officers and men alike. He had every confidence in you."

Tess avoided the deep, compassionate eyes of Colonel Streight as he spoke again. "I wish I could do something more to thank you than offering a raise in your rank. But the nature of our work does not allow any public displays."

"I don't need a raise in rank, sir."

"And you have not yet learned that the army does not run based on your desires, Lieutenant?"

He was trying the name on, like Ryder did when he made her a corporal, then a sergeant. Lieutenant. The rank might get her a tent, and with it, some privacy. And a raise in pay. Those things had been important to Tess once. Money, sent up to the Waterfords, buying her independence from her father. Now she obeyed this man., her superior in the spying business. She was still subject to a world men had made. Tess looked down at her hands. Strong hands, hands that had killed two men. She'd wanted them to be healing hands, like Ryder's. What would he think of her now? Would he hate what she was becoming?

"Tom. I would like to give you some time off duty after your ordeal. But another assignment that I think you're suited for has come up."

"I'll take it."

Colonel Streight laughed uneasily. "Listen to what it is first, son. You still have some choice in this man's branch of the service."

Tess finally met his eyes. *Please, no time to think. Send me out again, behind the lines, where Ryder is.* Three unopened letters from Olivia Cole were still in her haversack. She couldn't face the words within them yet. She wasn't even half as brave as her commander thought.

* * *

On Swift Creek, Virginia

As he stooped to fill the canteen, Ryder watched Laddie dip into the stream to drink. How did he deserve this animal's loyalty, he wondered, as the massive old oak sheltered them in its shade.

"Captain Cole?"

The boy smiled, though Ryder saw it hurt his wound to do so.

"What have you got there, Tappan?"

"I wove it the night long, while you and Mrs. Tubman looked after my mama and the baby. It for you, sir."

Ryder took the boy's gift, a belt made of river grass, attached to a cavalry officer's buckle. A union officer.

"Well made. and where did you get this?" he asked, touching the brass.

"Mama once washed clothes for a Sessech soldier, who stole it off a dead Yankee. Sessech man, he say that horse stayed right alongside his master till his end, just like Laddie does with you, sir. Mama said she felt the Yankee's brave spirit when she shined up that buckle. But the Sessech man who worked her so hard, she figured he

247

weren't to have his prize no more. She was called to take it up, pass it on to me."

"Tappan," Ryder urged gently, "this is yours."

"I made that belt to go with it, to give to you, sir, for your doctorin' services to my family, and on account your uniform got stole off you. Now, your present trousers are a mite large, sir. Wouldn't want to lose them, shockin' the womenfolk."

"No. Indeed."

"I got the call too, you see? To keep you decent clothed. Go on, try it for size."

The belt was stronger than it looked, even when Ryder pulled it tight. He folded the extra homespun of his trousers over it. There was less of him lately, he realized.

"That feel better, sir?"

"It is perfect, thank you."

They finished filling the wooden canteens from the creek's flow.

"You got a fine farm up north, Mrs. Tubman says, sir."

"I do, yes."

"Why you ever leave it?"

"I did not. It goes with me."

The boy's eyes widened. Beautiful, dark eyes, like the baby's. "Why, that be what my granddaddy used to say about Africa, Captain. Didn't know white folks carry things that way. 'Specially Yankees. Old Master, he used to say Yankees were cowards who don't care 'bout nothing 'cept-ing money. They never come down to the Southland, fighting, not them Yankees. You folks proved Old Master mighty wrong on that account, sir. How large a spread is it, your farm?"

"Do you know, I have never asked the number of acres of my mother. Belle Haven is hers, really, passed on to her from her father. Our mountain is named for him."

"You and your mama own a mountain, sir?"

"Well, the people in town call it one, but I don't think it achieves the elevation required to have the name official-ly. I would suggest we petition to have it changed to hill status, but my mother likes the sound of Henderson Mountain much more than Henderson Hill, and she barely tolerates me on the premises as it is.”

The boy frowned. “Why, Mrs. Tubman, she says your mama thinks the sun rises and sets on you! She says… hold on. You joshing with me, Captain?”

“You have found me out, sir. Mrs. Tubman is quite observant, even in the midst of her missions.” He leaned closer to the boy, as if the crickets would carry tales. “You know the women. They will have their doting.”

“My mama dotes. So does Delsey, when they ain’t scoldin’ me.”

“We are hapless victims of the women, are we not?”

The boy smiled again. “I like the way you talk, sir. It a mite hard on the ears, but I like the meaning of it. It almost like we’s… well, the same.”

“We are the same, Tappan. Look. Two feet, two hands, a pumping heart. We even share an aching head, courtesy of our enemy.”

“But you have a farm up north, and a mountain.”

“And you and your fine family must honor me with a visit there, after the war.”

“Do you think this war will end, sir?”

Ryder looked into the child’s eyes and wondered if he had many memories that were not wartime ones. He stooped to one knee and took hold of the slight shoulders. “Yes,” he said quietly. “I believe it with all my heart.”

Laddie’s ears pitched forward, listening. Beyond the trees came the sound of hoofbeats. No time, Ryder decided, not for them both. The child had done enough, had already been grazed by a bullet on his behalf.

“Take our canteens, Tappan,” he said, strapping them over the boy’s slight shoulders. ‘Up into the oak. Then back to Mrs. Tubman and your family. Keep them safe.”

“But, Captain—”

“Orders,” he insisted, rising. “Now. A leg up, sir.”

He cupped his hands under the boy’s foot.

"Jesus keep you, Captain," Ryder heard as Tappan mounted the stout branch and disappeared among the leaves.

As he gathered the reins of his Laddie, Ryder counted six horsemen in gray. Real uniforms, not the hodgepodge of Banks's men. Confederate regulars. He swung over the horse's back and together they headed upstream. The soldiers shouted halting orders, but he didn't stop, not being subject to their command. They were good horsemen, on fresh mounts. But he and Laddie would get them as far away as they could from the little family in the cave.

When he heard the cracking gunfire, Ryder encouraged Laddie to run harder with a firm press of his knees. The worn-down horse amazed him with speed that ignited his hopes. Together, could they outrun their pursuers, to reach Union lines?

Another round of gunfire. A low branch cracked, fell, knocked him off the saddle, into the water. Time slowed enough for Ryder to tuck his head and brace for the landing. The cold water shocked him. Panic only set in when he couldn't find the surface.

Chapter Thirty-five

"Can't get this nag away from him, sir!"

Ryder Cole felt blasts of air at his back. Worried nickers, then the full force of Laddie's head turning him over onto solid ground.

The man switching the gelding's flanks came into focus. "Do not hurt that horse," he commanded.

Their leader stepped forward. "Our Lazarus rises. With a Yankee tongue in his head."

Ryder got to his feet, gave Laddie's neck a grateful pat. "I don't belong here," he said to the Confederate commander.

"I should say not."

"My name is Captain Ryder Cole of the 116th New York Volunteers."

"Captain, is it? You are out of uniform."

"It was stolen by a band of—."

"How convenient."

Ryder felt a rush of rage. "It was most inconvenient, sir!"

Look at them, look hard. Grey uniforms, worn butternut trousers. And their leader wearing a major's stripes. These were not the men who had broken down his health, his strength. These men were his enemies, but they were listening. *Calm yourself. Speak.*

"I was captured after the battle at Wilderness," he explained.

"Why were you not delivered as a prisoner of war? Why was your uniform stolen?"

"They needed me, a pack of men. Raiders. Irregulars. Their leader was injured and I am a doctor—"

"Now you are a doctor?"

"I am, sir."

"Then you should know that we do not hold captured doctors, here in the Confederacy. We parole them immediately, as a mark of civility."

"I was not treated with anything approaching civility."

"Yes. I'm sure there is a picturesque story that goes with your rough appearance as well. But I'm afraid my men and I are presently being detoured from an engagement. And we have no more time for stories. It is my belief that you are exactly who we were sent to look for, a slave stealer. So, you have two choices. Either direct us to the property seeking to cross enemy lines to become contrabands of war, or cling to your abduction story and be hanged forthwith, out of uniform, as a spy."

Ryder felt Laddie's head lean to his shoulder, the way Moutamin's used to when looking for a piece of maple sugar from his waistcoat pocket. He had nothing to give this mount except a rub behind the ears. As he did, he felt the creek water dripping from his hair, absorbing into his rough linsey-woolsey shirt. The air was thick with the smell of new honeysuckle. It was a fine moment. Of a fine day.

"Well," he said. "I suppose you will have to hang me."

* * *

The world kept getting more beautiful to Ryder as the corporal tied his hands behind his back. The colors of the creek bed stone glistened, as did the leaves of the tulip poplar, the oak, the graceful willow. So many shades of green. The sky was gray, so the colors intensified on their own, without being kissed by the sun. The greens grew luminous from within each leaf. Did that happen on every overcast day? Why had he never noticed before?

"It does not seem right, sir," he heard a young corporal say to his superior.

"What does not?"

"Not offering up a prayer for him, or letting him write a goodbye to his wife or mother."

"Spies take care of those things before they go into the service."

"Have you, sir?" the boy asked Ryder.

"Not being a spy, I have not. But I am grateful for your concern."

There was another scent, back behind the honeysuckle. A distant scent, coming in on the breeze. Water, sweet and delicious. Water over stone, rushing. A waterfall. What did it look like, Ryder wondered, as they helped him mount Laddie, as they led the horse to the tree limb, the rope.

Not high. His neck would probably not break. His would be a slow death, with choking as its cause. He knew exactly how it would happen. Never mind. He'd done the best he could for the men. And he'd left them Tom, his partner. Tom would keep himself alive, and take care of the women, their women—sister, mother, lover, after the war.

Up there, mounted on the horse, the scent of water-infused air was stronger, more intense. So beautiful. His parents had brought him to the falls at Niagara once. When was that? He was very young. He had clung to his father's neck, but loved the spray against his face, and his father's laughter. Why had he not laughed more, over his own life? He saw again the flecks of red in his father's silk cravat, felt his father's chin skim the top of his wet head. On the way to kissing his mother. He was the product of that kiss, their love, Ryder had known it even then. What incredible grace had touched his life. What gifts. He wished he had not been so careful with Diana, suddenly. He wished they were leaving a child behind, to keep his mother's heart from breaking.

At the major's command, the corporal leaned over, fingers faltering as he worked the two mismatched bone buttons to open the collar of the homespun shirt. Tears glistened in the boy's eyes as he cinched the knot of the heavy rope around Ryder's neck. So young, Ryder realized suddenly, without whiskers yet. "Breathe deeply," he counseled, "you'll be all right."

"Yes, sir. Thank you, sir."

"You will not talk to the prisoner, corporal. You will secure the other end of the rope!"

But Ryder hardly heard them. His father was back, handsome, smiling during a sun-drenched breakfast in the front drawing room. "Sit up straight at table, mate," he admonished. "Shipshape!"

Instinctively, Ryder obeyed. The gleam of Tappan's gift, the belt buckle, caught the young corporal's eye. He fisted back Ryder's shirt folds for a closer look.

"Major!" he called out, jubilant. "Look, there. The prisoner is wearing a Yankee soldier's buckle! He is in uniform, sir!"

The officer rode his mount forward. He grabbed the ropes end, pulling the noose tight, lifting Ryder up off the saddle. He felt the veins in his neck bulge.

"Damnation," the officer finally muttered, releasing, throwing off Ryder's balance. He slid off Laddie, his face and shoulder hitting the ground first. The horse's feet danced around the rope, coiling out from his neck like a snake. Ryder silently thanked Tappan, and the union cavalryman, and this boy who did not want to hang him.

He struggled to his knees, allowing himself a snort of self-disgust. He had not fallen off a horse so much since his father first taught him to ride.

There it was again, as the corporal removed the noose, then reached behind him to free his hands—the echo of his father's laughter in the sound of that distant waterfall.

"Leave him bound," his superior commanded the young corporal.

"But sir—"

"We shall deposit our rudely buckled Yankee on Finley Prison's doorstep." He glared at Ryder. "A place sharing the hardships of besieged Petersburg, sir. Once incarcerated long enough, you will come to wish we'd given you a quick end here."

Chapter Thirty-six

January, 1865, Washington D.C.

Tess stared across the mess tent, scanning faces. The soldiers talked, laughed, ate. A good-natured card game sparked the west corner. She knew none of the men. She had seen fewer of her comrades each time she returned to the capital city from one of Colonel Streight's missions. But this was the first time there were no faces at all—from her battery, company, or even regiment that she recognized. No one to welcome her home.

Her series of disguises of both sexes had schooled her in using a pokeberry stain to make her face look dark along a man's beard line. She no longer got questioned about age, or saw eyes narrowing in scrutiny of her manliness. And her personal habits had gone very lax. She had become one of the men Ryder used to reprimand about keeping close-shaven and proud in uniform. Well, it made for fewer people looking twice.

Tess missed the camaraderie of her first company, the Third New York. But how could she blame them for going home to loving sisters, wives, mothers? Only she and Ryder had promised each other to last the war's duration. Her hand slipped past the pistol lodged against her heart and touched Mr. Brady's *carte de viste*, his gift to her after their service at the Battle of Shiloh. Where was Ryder?

It would be futile, Tess knew, to ask if any here recognized his image. But to not even try would be to give in a little more to the despair.

After the promised three month's wait, their superiors had sent the terse message of his death home to his mother. But the last time Tess had seen the chaplain he'd said the persistent Mrs. Cole's correspondence to her son had remained so "unabated" that now a small cedar-lined chest held it. Tess understood. She'd written to him too. In the night, to keep herself from screaming. And in the day, at times like these, when the loneliness closed in. She started one, in her mind.

Wait until you see Washington now, Ryder. Hospitals clean, all as well-scrubbed as ours were, now. And the new ambulance corps is not some rag tag group of pitiful musicians you'd despair of, but a respected unit—trained, drilled, just the way you used to train us. And the women are doing a first-rate job, which wouldn't surprise you I guess, since your mama and I finally browbeat that possibility into you. You'd be so proud of them all, Ryder.

"And you, Tom," Tess heard in her head, "I am proud of you." An old voice. From their past, with no image attached to it.

No, not me, Ryder. I ain't with them anymore, you see. I've gone and used my 'special talents' as Colonel Streight calls them. I pretend to be who I'm not. And then I sneak around, gather information. And when I have to, I kill people.

"Don't you like the stew, sir?"

Tess sat higher, looked down at her plate.

"It's good."

The well-groomed black soldier in a full apron smiled. "Saved a piece of currant cake for you, one the ladies brought over, loaded up with the fruit, see? On account of you look like you done some hard riding, sir."

Tess stared down at the plate he set before her. "Thanks."

"Well, then. Eat hardy, Lieutenant."

The man drifted back to his pots and pans. A cook. *That is his job, Ryder, imagine that? Not me struggling over a campfire to make food taste decent, but a regular cook at the meals.*

Ryder didn't answer. There was no sight of him in her mind's eye. Tess was barely able to conjure up his voice. Maybe she'd caught too many men between her sights. Ryder's image was fading with each mission, each deceit, each kill. Coffee. Would another drink of coffee make the currant cake taste like something other than ashes?

As soon as she put the cup down, a pot appeared, pouring more.

"My daddy says to attend you well, sir."

A boy now, waiting on her. Son to the soldier cook in the white apron, Tess thought. Bright-eyed, too sharp, both of them. A danger in that. The possibility of seeing through her.

"See to the others," she tried her gruffest voice to get rid of him.

"But Daddy says I'm to stand by you, sir."

"Well, I say—" Hell, what was she doing, yelling at a child? "You and your daddy come up from the southland?" she asked more quietly.

"Yes, sir. My whole family did. Had a baby born on the run, too."

"Ever meet any soldiers in your travels?"

"Sure did. Plenty. Soldiers got us our jobs here in the capitol city, too. Jobs that pay enough so mama can keep our Sal with her, all the time, like white ladies and their babies."

Tess pulled out the *carte de viste* from her coat's inside pocket. "Would you look at this image? Tell me if—"

"Why, that be our captain beside you, sir!"

"Your captain?"

"Sure enough! And don't he look fine in a real uniform!"

"You know Captain Cole?"

"Know him? Why he's the one done sewed up my head, then helped my mama bring our Sal into the world."

"Sal. Who is Sal?" Tess tried to slow him down while his words became music, singing through her veins.

"That's our baby."

"Sister."

"Nope, brother, sir. Salamander."

"Born—?"

"Down in Virginia, near abouts Cannon Creek, where we crossed paths with Captain Cole, on the run from a real mean bunch."

Tess took hold of the boy's shoulders. "What's your name?"

"Tappan, sir."

"Tappan, where is Captain Cole now?"

Tears welled in the boy's eyes. Was she holding him too hard? She eased her grip, but the cry remained in his voice.

"We aimed to keep him with us, honest we did! But we, him and me, we's out gathering up some water when the Secessh soldiers come. Our captain, he shoved me up into a big old oak so's he could lead them away. I followed as best I could, but they took him away on their horses!"

"Tappan, you bothering the Lieutenant?" The cook stepped between them. "I'm sorry for the boy, sir."

"Stay. Please stay," Tess breathed out, grabbing the man's sleeve. Like a desperate woman. But his son distracted the man's sharp scrutiny.

"Lieutenant here's a friend of Captain Cole, Daddy!"

Tess met the man's deeply sorrowful eyes. "He's not dead," she told him, a command.

He smiled slowly. "Our Moses shares your belief."

"Moses?"

"Mrs. Tubman, sir. I expect you heard of that little lady!"

"I have," Tess said slowly, her voice sounding as stunned as she felt, remembering Harriet Tubman's fired-with-purpose eyes.

"Our Moses say she 'never lost a passenger before that white man with too much learning and too little sense in him joined up with us!' Now, them's her words, sir, not any of ours about the captain. She's that blazing mad at him for ruining her reputation as a conductor of folks to the North."

Tess felt Tappan lean on her shoulder, warming it. When was the last time she'd had such contact with a child? "You'll find him, won't you, sir?"

"I will. If you'll put me on his scent."

The man nodded. "A map might help us there, Lieutenant. Expect you could get us off a tad early so's we can draw you one?"

Chapter Thirty-seven

Findley Prison, Virginia

Locked in the solitary cellar, again. He was no good to anybody here.

The other prisoners had warned Ryder about not speaking up, especially when the commander was away and the mean-eyed sergeant was out for him. The sergeant's bullwhip had cut through his scarf and collar to lash the back of his neck, surprising him. Why was he still surprised by men's cruelty?

Because they were not all cruel. Since he had reset the fractured bone in Commander Witcomb's arm, Ryder had had almost mutually respectful relations with him. The commander had told Ryder of the terrible battle in Tennessee, after which all paroles had ceased, hence the prisons filling beyond capacity. Witcomb worried over the hardships of both sides, as he had a brother in a Northern prisoner-of-war camp. He was making a case in Richmond for additional supplies and medicine. Ryder wondered if the wheels of government in the South turned as slowly as his own experience had found in Washington.

He had grown used to small spaces, at least. They'd been digging the tunnel for a month. If they were not discovered, if the engineer's calculations about distance to the outside of the walls of Finley Prison were correct, and if no one betrayed them, they would make an escape, get to the Union lines, help the army find this place, this terrible, overcrowded place of dying men in desperate need. Think about that, the escape. It should happen soon. While it was cold and hard to follow their scent. Ryder had chosen the men carefully. He was confident that no matter how much the sergeant terrorized, there would be no betrayal.

He was so happy to see the men that first day, standing at attention. He'd shed tears at the sight of their faded, threadbare blue uniforms. None of them called him out for it, though he should have controlled himself better, as their new ranking officer. Ryder still felt privileged to be among them, doing what he could, which was precious little.

Cold. He pulled the sleeves of his coat down over his suddenly shaking hands. He shoved them under his arms. He had amputated more blackened toes and fingers than he liked to think about. Not his own, please God. If he lost his hands his usefulness was gone. It was one of the few terrors left, losing his hands. Breathe through it, he told himself. It was not so bad. The Solitary Cellar was underground, so the earth itself would protect him from freezing to death, from losing his fingers. Breathe, he soothed himself, like he soothed the suffering men in the camp. He must keep moving. His legs, stopped by the earthen wall. Stretch them as far as you can, use them to feel all the space. Shake off the insects drawn to your warmth, trying to inhabit your clothes, your hair. Push through the panic, the fear that the world above, as harsh as it was, would forget you.

His coat belonged to a Calvary man in an Illinois regiment, who'd died of dysentery the day he arrived. His first patient in this place bequeathed Ryder the coat.

"My Betsy made it. Dyed it in the wool, see how fast the color is? It will hold up for you, sir." It had, and Ryder treasured it. He might die by the hand of the brutal sergeant or the effects of his own pounding head, but he would die a soldier of the Union.

Ryder had seen two hundred and sixteen more patients out of their time on earth, here in this fenced, guarded town of the dying. A few were from the effects of wounds, but most were from diseases brought on by starvation, by the cold and the punishments. Ryder's still periodically aching head made memorizing their names too trying, but he struggled to keep a running total, at least. To honor those lost, to bear witness to their devastating circumstances, if he survived this place.

Ryder closed his eyes and expanded his horizons. He was a man, even here in this hole—a woman's son, another's lover, a friend of Tess, Tom's sister, who'd shot his horse and wrote him short, beautiful letters of life at home. How had they celebrated Christmas, the women? How had they seen in the new year of 1865? He remembered the sound of his mother's laughter the time he found the bean in his slice of Twelfth Night cake and claimed his kiss, not of the giggling neighbor girls at the table, but of her. When was that? Long ago, in that year of his father's death, when she'd looked so sad, even through the holidays. He remembered the feel of her soft cheek, scented with vanilla and nutmeg.

Then he remembered the last Christmas that the Third New York was together—reading aloud Tess's spare, simple report of her Quaker benefactors who didn't celebrate Christmas, but gifted her with walnuts atop her apple pie. He had read the letter as Tinknor the fiddler finally made it all the way through *Silent Night* without a single mistake.

And Ryder remembered well eating the gingerbread cake Diana had baked on their last Christmas. His tongue picked apart the molasses, the spicy ginger, the rich farm eggs components there in the dark, propped against the bolster of their bed. He felt her nervousness, her eagerness to please him with her effort. And it had pleased him, beyond measure. What a strange game they had played over the years. Had she felt his smile, there in a darkness almost as dense as this one underground? *Be well, be happy, Diana. Throw me over, give another man your gingerbread this season, but live on. Thrive. There is so much death here, my darling girl. No more conditions or arguments between us. Just live.*

It was too warm, suddenly. Ryder felt his forehead with the back of his hand. Burning. Damnation. He was ill.

Fevered. Perhaps the wound from the Sergeant's lash at his neck had become infected, despite his efforts to keep it clean. Get up. Call. Tell them. But his mouth was too dry, and his limbs would not allow him to stand.

* * *

Tess turned up the oil lamp with the broken chimney. She stared down at the man in the narrow rope bed. His miraculous health and stamina had broken down at last. "Ryder," she called.

No response.

She checked under the fresh bandaging she'd wrapped around his neck. Still inflamed, hot to the touch.

His face was leaner, more angled at the jaw shaded by a growth of beard. His hair was not the vibrant, glossy black she remembered. Even after she'd crushed the crawling vermin between her nails and sponged his scalp clean, she could not restore his hair's luster. As it dried, Tess saw that the silver that had begun at his temple was now a streak, a jagged bolt of lightning that landed behind his ear, full of its own strange, dynamic beauty. She touched it, as a woman touches her lover's hair. She could do that here, in the curtained, private room they had provided. Neither prisoners nor keepers wanted to lose their doctor. Behind his ear, her fingers found it again: a knob, a swelling. *Dangerous. Ryder. Don't leave me. Not here, not now.* The linen shirt she'd bedded him in was damp, the fever spiking. His breathing became shallow, high in his chest, fitful. She felt his forehead, beaded with sweat.

"Cold," he whispered through clenched teeth. "I am so cold."

Tess pulled the threadbare blanket over his shoulders.

"Thank you," he whispered. "See to the others now."

He had to open his eyes, she decided, before she went out of her mind.

"Ryder," she summoned.

264

There, his eyes, glassy, unfocused, as gray as their surroundings. And bleak, without hope. Tess had never seen his eyes without hope.

"See to the others," he repeated. "Give up the field here, soldier."

She pulled in a breath. "You ain't going to die. I'm here to take care of you."

A spark of recognition. "Tom?"

She smiled. "Who else would I be?"

"Tom," he said slowly, as if convincing himself.

"Yes, sir. You're back inside camp, see?"

"How? I did not betray anyone?"

"Betray? No. The commander's returned. He had you brought out of that hole. And the sergeant, he ain't going to be mean to you no more. Fell off a tower while on picket duty. Broke his neck."

"Tom. Where are the others?"

"Close. You're an officer, remember? Entitled to private quarters."

"Are they warm, the men?"

"Sure."

"Good of you to come, Tom, as long as you are part of the fever, and not really here.."

"Ryder, you quit talking like that!" No good. Her voice shaking, betraying her fear. An idea dawned in her, powerful, dangerous. Change skin. His lids were lowering again. "Ryder, listen. I brought someone else. Someone bound to help you feel better."

"Who?"

"Diana is who."

A ghost of his old smile flickered across his mouth. "This dream is getting better. If you will pardon my saying so, Tom."

"I take no offense, sir. Now, I got to turn down the light. You know how she likes it."

"Yes. The lady and I have a decidedly peculiar intimacy."

"Rest. That's the way. And wait."

Tess had brought no state secrets on this last trip beyond enemy lines. Only her uniform, hidden, until she approached the place that Tappan said the rebel horsemen had captured Ryder. She shed her skirts and became Tom there and waited to surrender. Three boys had left their picket duty to accept both surrender and her leftover current cakes before they escorted her into Finley Prison. She only wished she'd hidden some cake away for the walking skeletons who were her new comrades.

Tess broke open the small glass vial from her boot's hidden space, and spread its contents across her throat and between her breasts before she slipped naked into the bed beside Ryder Cole. She'd learned from the dying men she'd nursed that they heard until the end, that they felt her touch, and caught scents. Scent, the last to go.

But this man wasn't going anywhere.

He struggled against her touch. "Left flank. They are breaching! "

"No, love." Soft, soothing, in its higher pitch. Was that her own long lost voice? Tess wasn't sure. It had been so long since she'd heard it.

Ryder groaned, turning his head, making the wound bleed fresh red through the bandage "Turn the cannon around."

"*Shhhh*, now."

"Have we no morphine, or whiskey? I cannot stand their cries."

"Hush. Nobody's crying."

"No use at all. I am sorry. Useless." His words trailed away, incoherent and poisoned with despair.

"Ryder," she called at his ear.

He smiled. "Lilacs."

"There. Good. You've caught my scent."

"Sweet voice," he said without opening his eyes. "I love that sweet voice."

Tess bowed her head on his chest, a soft laugh escaping.

"Now this is beyond my imaginings, lady."

"Nothing is beyond them. Say we can forget all the pain, Ryder." She kissed his whitened panther's scar, his cheek.

Startled eyes sprang open. "Diana. I am ill."

"Hush now," she whispered at his temple. "We'll break this fever with one of our own. Shall we?"

"We should not—"

She laughed. "Dreams don't catch fevers."

"Are you sure?"

She mounted him, led his erection between her legs, and eased herself down. "Yes," she promised.

"Real," he gasped out. "This is real."

"As real as the moon, see it?"

He looked over her shoulder, out the frost-edged window. "Yes. Full winter moon. Beautiful. Diana's moon."

"Now come away with me, you baneful man."

He smiled. "Baneful, am I?" His hand cupped her buttocks. She felt his tongue flick out, touch her right nipple.

"Ryder," she said, astonished.

"Do I please you, Diana?" he asked shyly, like a boy.

"Oh, yes." She rocked harder, there, above him.

"It's just that. Well. You never said."

"Always," she cried, "you always did."

"Forgive—"

"Nothing!" she hissed at him in a furious whisper even as he responded to her deep inside squeezes.

"I have ruined you."

"No."

He took her hips between his hands and coursed his seed inside her.

Afterward, she held him in her arms, stroking his hair, listening to decelerating heartbeats, waiting for more of the rhythm of his sickness. Ready to ease fever or chills.

"Diana," he whispered, gliding the back of his fingers along her side. "I am the most fortunate of men."

Tess pulled away. "Don't talk nice to me." She felt tears in the creases of her eyes.

"Why not? I love you," came out of the darkness.

"Hush, now," she warned.

"I do not mind, Diana."

"Mind what?"

"Dying."

"You're not dying."

"I have written to my mother. Explaining us. You must go to her, she will welcome you, help give you a start in the life of your choosing. I promise." He reached out. "Diana?"

"I'm here," she assured him, taking his hand. "Not a burden. Only a dream, remember?"

Chapter Thirty-eight

In the dim light, the faces came into focus. Men, crowded around his bed. Breene's color was better, and the swelling around the cut on Hobson's face was going down. It was good to see them again.

"They let me out." His voice was a thin rasp.

"Of Solitary? Oh, that was a while back, sir," Hobson reported. "You been sick since. But the lieutenant knew what to do. Now you're sprung and on the road to wellness besides."

"Lieutenant?"

"Yep. Your friend, sir. New amongst us."

They parted for the man wiping his hands on a scrap of linen. Tom. No, not here. Tom didn't belong here, not this place. Only with their company in the regiment, the Third, the 116th. And bringing Diana to him in his dreams. Perhaps this was another dream. Perhaps, if he closed his eyes…

"Ryder?"

He groaned, turned his head to the wall. Those hands turned him back. Made him look into that face. Different, harder, but Tom.

"Captain, what's bothering you, sir?"

"You. Go away. Do not be here, Tom."

Tess laughed uneasily. "You think you can order things your way?"

"He not sound in the head?" Mallory asked in his always-worried voice.

"He's all right," Tess said. "I'll talk to him awhile."

"You do that, sir," Hobson urged. "Come on, Mallory, Captain don't need to look at your hang-dog face no more." Hobson drew Mallory out of sight.

Ryder shoved her ministering hand back.

"Hey. I told these fellows we were friends. You going to make a liar out of me?"

His eyes remained sullen, serious. "I did not summon you. I only dreamed. I cannot control the dreams."

"You think I asked to be here?" she demanded, then winced, because she had. "I was captured, damn it, same as you! Listen to me. I found your coat after the Wilderness. The gravedigger, he told me you were under it, dead. Already buried. I couldn't check. I had to get back to the boys. The fighting went on for days more. I couldn't go back, hear? Couldn't see for myself until they had that body in the ground."

"The gunner," Ryder remembered. "I gave him my coat."

"I know. I figured out what you done. But, back in Washington, they didn't take my side of it. Think on that, sir. Think of your mama. Now, I been doing the best I can here, while you're sick" she confided, quietly now. "But we need you. Ryder, you got to pull yourself together."

Ryder frowned. "My. So many responsibilities. I shall have to recover."

She wiped the track of red clay mud from her cheek with the back of her hand. "Quit it, Ryder," she groused. "You scared me spitless."

"You? I think not, sure shot. You are not afraid of much."

* * *

Tom forced a vile tasting concoction down his throat.

"One more swallow."

"Will it put me out of my misery?"

"It might get you home to your mama with all your teeth still in your head. Come on Ryder, it's the same brew

270

I made on encampments, except I ain't got the licorice to sweeten it up."

"The oak bark acid?"

"That's right."

"That's how you kept the scurvy from our ranks on long marches. I should have remembered. Administer some to those Connecticut boys who have been enduring this place for two years and suffer from night blindness."

"Already have. Now be a good example to us all. One more spoonful."

Ryder obeyed, earning himself a nod of satisfaction. Not a smile. This new Tom didn't smile, he realized.

"They got pines here too, so's I don't have to rob the oaks to death," his friend went on now, as he casually placed the chipped crockery bowl back on the tray with that efficient grace Ryder remembered.

"Well, I see that in your formidable company again, I will have to struggle to keep up with you."

"That ain't been the way of it, Captain."

"It most certainly has. I have had plenty of time to think about it. When I am in my proper mind. Which I am not always." He had to tell Tom his fear. But how to do it without frightening him further? "You noticed the swelling around a skull fracture when you examined my head?"

Tom's eyes scanned the pressed dirt floor. "I did, sir."

Hell, he was already worried, then. Just say it. "They hit me too hard."

"Who did, sir?"

"One in a company of irregulars, in the Wilderness battlefield. A concussion, I think. Perhaps something worse. My vision blackens periodically, my head pounds too, sometimes. Stop looking at me with those eyes now, good's come of it too."

"What good?"

"I have been remembering things from my distant past. A heightened sort of remembering, with exquisite clarity of taste, smell, even musical pitch. It is quite extraordinary.

And Tom, I have the most wonderful dreams. They have conspired to make me quite reluctant to open my eyes on the world at all!"

Damnation. Not what he meant. He'd frightened the boy again. No, not a boy any more. In their time apart, Tom had somehow become a man. A man's whose uneasy, joyless laughter unnerved him. Still, he felt compelled to finish. "You need to know Tom, in case it takes me, suddenly, the effects of that blow. There was nothing you could do, you must tell yourself that, and go on, understand?"

Tom took in an unsteady breath, but answered simply. "Yes, sir."

"Good. All right then. Help me sit higher, will you? Report on our regiment, our company. Any captured with you?"

"No, sir."

"Well, that was fortunate. How did we fare at Wilderness?"

"Regiment lost twenty-three. Of our company, three casualties. The Putnam brothers, dead."

"Good God, Tom, both of them?"

"By the same cannon blast, sir."

"Could not separate them. Did I not do everything in the world to separate them? How shall I console their family?"

"I wrote the mother and sister, sir. Not like you do, of course. Said we were real sorry and told them to chain up those younger ones if they have to, to keep them home on the farm. Samuels, the bear-baiter from Greene, he lost his leg at the knee."

"Did you perform the surgery?"

"Yes, sir. He'd only have me, when he heard you were among the missing."

"His recovery?"

"Progressing, last I heard."

"Good. We'll still travel up to those northern Catskills together to visit his bears, you'll see, Tom. Are you now company surgeon?"

"No, sir."

"Why not? You did not fail the written examination, surely! Who promoted you, without your success at the written exam?"

"Colonel Streight, sir."

"Ah, the mysterious Colonel Streight."

"Ryder, I got to tell you something now. About this time we been parted."

"Yes?" His friend remained silent. Why, Ryder wondered. Nerves? "What is it, Tom?" he prompted.

"I left the medical corps after Wilderness, sir. To do some work for Colonel Streight. It wasn't our work, sir, helping work. It was…" Another stumble, and devastation, Ryder realized, watching, listening carefully. "It was work I ain't even allowed to tell you about, Ryder. But some of it was mean work. And I, well, I don't feel worthy of your company no more."

Rumors flew around the officers' quarters that Streight was more than the head of the signal corps. He had been biding his time, waiting for their separation before ensnaring Tom into his spying network. "You did what you had to do."

"But you don't know—"

"I do not have to know. I know you, the man you are. Have I done better, filling your young life with things you should never have seen? We made a promise together, Tom, to see it through, for the Union, for something else now, the furtherance of liberty for all Americans. We both do what we have to in order to help turn the tide of this endless war."

"Do we, sir?"

The question hung between them, precarious. But something had changed in the damp, acrid air of their prison. Ryder could not name it, but it was faint with the scent of healing.

"We need you, Tom. A party of us are digging a tunnel. We are going to get out."

"We are?"

"Yes. Soon. It is still winter?"

"Oh yes. But we're well into the new year." Tess hesitated. "Of eighteen hundred and sixty-five."

Ryder laughed. "I know what year it is! What is the date?"

"The twenty-third of February, sir."

"Good. Splendid. The fighting time will be coming again. We plan to meet General Grant's army. We hear his guns, sometimes. We'll show him this camp, so we can help free the rest of us. How does that sound?"

"Real fine, sir."

A smile. At last, Ryder thought, that shy smile, then the attempt to hide the slightly snaggled teeth. He loved that gesture, Ryder realized. He loved this man. And it no longer troubled him. Because neither of them had the luxury for anything but gratitude.

"A basket of blankets, that is what we were working on procuring before my last visit to Solitary. Blankets to make into capes to hide what's left of our uniforms, when we get out. Mallory," he called his aide-de-camp, "come here. We have another tailor to help you with your patches-on-top-of-patches sewing."

Mallory appeared, bowed slightly, as he must have done a thousand times as his former master's valet. "Just so that I am covered, sirs, that's all I ask, even if it's for my box. Put me in, with my head placed toward the north, if you would, sirs."

"Our Mallory is somewhat funereal," Ryder explained to Tom.

"I noticed."

The shy smile again, prompted by that exasperating aged private in perpetual mourning. Mallory suddenly became dear to Ryder, for making Tom smile.

Chapter Thirty-nine

March, 1865, Finley Prison

Within the small circle of men in the officers' quarters, which was different from the mean huts and tents of the enlisted men only in size, Tess regarded Ryder's clean-shaven face and neatly clipped hair.

"There. Ready to be presented at any court in the world around, if I do say so, sir," Mallory pronounced as he finished his handiwork. Tess was a little jealous of Mallory and his fussing, but she agreed. Ryder's trials had left him gaunt and pale, but he looked almost like himself now, even in the Union coat with the markings of another state's cavalry.

His eyes remained more gray than green, reflecting their surroundings and the harsh winter in this place. Sometimes he'd lose his grip on his instruments, but maybe that was the cold. Tess didn't know what to do for him except to provide her shoulder to lean on so the men under his care wouldn't see him falter. His spells may have been from lack of food. He said his ration of corn cake didn't agree with him, and slipped it to her, but she suspected he was doing it to keep her better fed.

Tess realized that she would always see Ryder the way Mallory described as he brushed off the shoulders of the borrowed blue coat: ready to stand before generals or kings or God himself.

Ryder looked around their circle of twelve. "Perhaps you should not have waited for me," he said quietly.

"Not waited, sir? Why, it was providential for us, the delay," Mallory pronounced.

"Providential?"

Sullivan stepped forward. "What Mallory means is, we been regular gophers while you been recovering. We burrowed an extra three yards out, Captain."

"Well beyond the dead line," Sergeant Stockton added. We'll come up in the shadows of the trees, past the beacon light."

"And there's a dark moon, casting no light," Kenton continued.

"In a warmer month than last, sir," Sanders reasoned. "Besides, we would have left your man in this stinking place, if we'd gone without you."

Tess grunted. His man. Is that what she was?

Ryder shook his head, going down in gracious defeat against their onslaught. "Are we in agreement on proper order?"

"Diggers first, yes, sir."

"And, after we are in the open air—?"

"We scatter in twos and threes. Partners already decided amongst us, sir."

Ryder turned to Sullivan. "And if halted by an armed guard?"

"Captain, I still say we can outrun any wet-behind-the-ears boy they'll send to fetch us back. We'll be inside Grant's lines before they've raised their old muskets to their shoulders."

"That has not been my experience with Southern marksmen of any age," Ryder claimed, with that edge in his voice Tess knew well. "Now, the agreed-to requirement, if you please?"

"We stop and raise our hands in surrender, sir," Sergeant Sullivan ground out between his teeth.

Ryder nodded, looking at each of them in turn, more like a schoolmaster than an officer, but Tess knew that it was his way of command. "I will allow no man into that tunnel who will not agree to this provision. We will not scar these confederate boys' souls with our deaths by their hands."

The glow in his eyes intensified. Then, at the sound of the fiddle being tuned in the prison yard, he smiled. The monthly camp dance began. "It has been my great honor to form our mining company with you, gentlemen, no matter the result. May it yield our freedom. Take heart and Godspeed. Now. First step—the dance floor, where our jovial state will mask our midnight plans."

As they walked in among their wider gathering of prisoners in the spare community hall, Mallory offered Tess a threadbare blanket. "Your skirt, Madame," he intoned, "and your dance card."

She grew hot. Why had she agreed to this? To please Ryder, after the men decided both their officers' should lead by example tonight. They had proclaimed her female because she was a few inches shorter than he was. She always got herself into her worst troubles for Ryder. The rest had drawn lots to see who else would have to play female partners in the dance. Private Elliott, a better fiddler than Tinknor would ever be, bowed his instrument into a lively reel.

Tess fumbled with her blanket skirt.

"Let me help you there, Miss Honey Lamb," the wolfish Walker offered.

Ryder stepped between them. "I will assist my escort, Private." He took the privilege of his rank. "Lift up your coat's wings, darlin'," he instructed, causing guffaws, which he silenced with a look. "Attend your own consorts, men," he instructed with mock severity.

"It is not so bad," he assured Tess quietly, "do everything backwards and sidestep the marauding feet of your admirers."

"Easy for you to say."

"Well, that is true enough." He pulled the knotted blanket tighter. "Why, Tom, you've got a trim little waist, you will not be losing your skirts as often as the rest!"

Her blush deepened.

"Come, now. No retreat, soldier." He turned her toward him as his voice softened. "And I shall imagine your sister's face, which I may never have the pleasure of seeing in life."

She gripped his arm. "Ryder. Don't say that."

"We cross the dead line tonight. We both know the risks, Tom."

"Yes," she admitted.

"It has all turned out so differently, hasn't it?"

She gloried in the sight of his face there in the open fire's light. "You got what you wanted. You're a fine doctor, sir. And nobody will ever say your family's not American. Loyalist grandfather or not, you're American, by word and deed."

"Why, thank you, Tom. And you. Have you gotten what you wanted?"

"More. I got so much more, sir."

"My. You sound like a career man. You will be off fighting Indians next."

"Aw, quit teasing me."

He bridged his hand to her shoulder. "Tom, if we achieve success tonight, and we survive this war, please don't go where the army takes you next. Would you consider opening a practice together?"

He blinked, distracted. Tess saw the sudden pain shoot into the right side of his face. He stifled a groan.

"Captain—"

He swallowed hard. "Would you consider it? If you did not pass the last written examination, you can take it again. I will arrange for a real teacher, who remembers his history and geometry and grr..grammar better than I do."

He breathed slowly in, out. His eyes eased from beneath the suffering he would not admit to. It was passing. Mallory's grooming had fooled her. Ryder was not well. She had to get him out of this place, tonight. But for now, she nodded. "I'll consider a partnership, yes, sir."

"Good. Splendid. Let's dance."

"That's not the way you do it, Captain!" Sullivan protested, "You say, 'may I please have the honor of this dance?'"

Ryder held their joined hands a little higher and faced the men. "This—" he paused only slightly, "lady—and I know each other better than that. There is no pretense or social convention necessary between us. We have been through a war. We will love each other all our lives."

The fiddler smiled. "Well, now," he said, and changed his melody from *Lorena* to the forbidden tune, forbidden on both sides of the lines that divided countrymen—*The Girl I Left Behind Me*.

The couple who danced was the one Ryder described, by the power of his words—partners who belonged to each other, there, on a packed dirt dance floor. Tess felt his hand's warm comfort, breathed in his breath, sweet with sassafras root. He loved her. He'd said it, in front of all. Her bound breasts responded to his closeness, she felt the familiar wetness between her legs, ready, aching.

"We will be all right, Tom," he promised. "We will get through this."

And although she knew better, she believed him. She saw nothing but him, felt nothing but their gliding steps and the music of the song that was forbidden because it caused whole companies to desert. *No need to desert, Ryder Cole,* she thought at him, smiling a full, direct, woman's smile. *The girl you left behind, has been with you since the first call to arms.*

Ryder slowed their movements, stopped. They looked around at the tears on the faces of prisoners and guards alike. The wisp of melody had worked its magic.

Ryder laughed uneasily. "Well, men, is my lieutenant the only one among you brave enough to become your sweethearts for our night's revels?" he demanded.

The remaining designated females took their places with their partners. Stockton tapped Ryder's shoulder.

"My turn with your lady, sir," he said.

Tess squeezed Ryder's hand, too hard. He laughed, shaking her off. "Ah, of course. I must not monopolize the boys who can actually dance."

He took the stub of a pencil from his coat pocket and ran an extra line on the card at her wrist. "There," he said, signing his name, "we have the last dance." He leaned in toward her ear. "Until then, remember, sidestep to avoid bruised toes," he advised, winking, then said, louder, "And no flirting, mistress mine."

The laughing men did not hear the hammering steps behind them.

"Captain Cole."

Ryder turned, facing the pair of grizzled guards in their tattered butternut trousers.

"Commander Witcomb wishes to see you, sir."

"But Private Elliot only played a few bars of it, you can hear he has switched to *Camptown Races* now."

"Ain't on the subject of the tunes, sir. If you'll come with us?"

Ryder glanced toward the door of the commander's office. The prisoners approached him protectively. He waved them back. "Go on with our revels. Please. I will be back directly."

Tess felt her fingers grow numb. Ryder smiled. "Last dance. Remember," he whispered, before taking his place between the guards.

Tess heard exasperated sounds around her. "Now what?" and "They ain't done enough to the man yet?" Sergeant Stockton did not press his suit to dance, but stood beside her as they watched Ryder disappear from the hall, then behind the commander's door.

Chapter Forty

The man standing beside Commander Witcomb was familiar, but Ryder couldn't place him. His stare was filled with raw hatred. How had it come to be directed at him? Was this man a father or brother of a patient Ryder had lost? No. The look was worse than that raging, raw grief that relatives had visited upon him over the years, as the bearer of terrible news.

Suddenly Ryder caught remembered scents of the hospital in Washington City. Before him stood the senator's son, the inspector, unmanned by Nurse Truscutt. The one whose only skills were pilfering from patients' supplies and threatening women. Breene. Inspector Lieutenant Breene. He was now in the uniform of the enemy. A high ranking uniform, Ryder was sure, though he'd never been good at that, placing rank from epaulettes and stripes.

Commander Witcomb reached out. "If you'll come into the light, Captain, please."

"No need."

That voice. So reasonable, clinical. Masking all that hate.

"Then you recognize Captain Cole, sir?" Ryder heard hope, there, in Witcomb's voice.

"No. Captain Ryder Cole was a different person entirely. And you have in your hand the written proof from an unimpeachable Federal source that Cole is dead and buried."

"We all know what a tangle the weeks at Wilderness were," Witcomb tried now. "Look more carefully. This man has been ill and may be altered."

"His height has not changed. That surgeon did not reach my shoulder. Accounting for some of his belligerence toward my person, no doubt. One does not forget men like him. Or such belligerence."

Ryder raised his head higher. "It does you no credit sir, to speak so ill of the dead," he said.

"Will you come to his defense now that you have stolen his name, straggler?"

"You, sir, were the expert at stealing," he challenged, "at least when serving the Northern cause."

"I always knew what cause I served."

"Not the helpless sick and wounded, to be sure."

The prison commander stepped between them. Witcomb had papers in his hand, stretched damp under his sweating fingertips. Official papers. They looked the same on both sides of the Mason Dixon line, those official papers. What did they say?

"Captain," Witcomb asked quietly, "Who are you?"

"Who I have always claimed to be sir, and beyond which, being a prisoner of war, you may not ask me, I respectfully add."

Not enough. Ryder saw it in the prison commander's eyes. His word was not enough. Not here. Not against those papers. Fear began to invade the roots of his hair. And the man who had somehow found him was delighting in that fear, feeding off it. *Stop. Stop his access to that, at least. Breathe easy, now. Think. What to do. Call in Tom. Tom would identify him. No. Tom's word would not be taken either, not against Breene.* Protect, Ryder thought. Breene hated Tom. He'd include Tom too, in whatever offense was on those official papers. Tom must get out. Tonight. Mallory, Ryder decided. He was a good man. Mallory would make sure Tom got out.

"I will not act on this order, sir," the commander stated in his quiet, courtly drawl. "Too many irregularities."

"Such as?"

"The Wilderness campaign was a year ago. Why did the federals take so long to declare him dead?"

"That is not your concern. I have other duties to attend to, and I would hate to report that you—"

"Spare me your threats! Could I get a worse punishment than this posting?"

There it was, the commander's slow fuse, finally lit and burning true. Ryder knew Witcomb had backbone from the way he endured the resetting of that fracture.

"This order is an insult to my command. Captain Cole has helped these poor wretches remember that they are men," he continued. "And treated my own with the same diligence. Do you think I don't know what you are about? Sacrifice a leader for the purpose of terrifying the prisoners into compliance before moving them! We can hear the artillery. We all know Grant is headed for Petersburg."

"You could resign your commission," his guest suggested. "Then I'll take over your duties here and execute this man."

Execution. Ryder's mouth went dry. But there were worse things than dying. "Don't resign, sir," he urged Witcomb quietly. "Do not leave my men and yours to him."

* * *

Sergeant Mallory held the door for Tess as he left the small, whitewashed room that held Ryder. "Lieutenant," he advised, "let the captain see you standing tall now, sir." But she could hardly stand at all. Ryder noticed, and met her halfway.

When a strange guttural sound erupted from her, he took her arms. "Tom," he said quietly, "Do not fall apart on me now."

"Yes, sir," she said out of habit, not out of any hope that she could follow his orders, which were more like polite requests, even now.

He strengthened his hold on her arms. Where did he find such strength? Then he smiled that wonderful, bashful, secret smile that he mostly reserved for her. "It is a burden, surviving, one I heartily wish I could join in the bearing. But we understand these things now Tom. We understand how little we have to do with who lives, who dies."

"Sir—"

He frowned. "I never fully succeeded in melting those "sirs" between us, did I? Another failure. I have not turned out the bright hope my mother or the town of Ashokan wished me to be. I will pass that dubious mantle on to you. You must give today meaning, Tom. You must survive this place, and live long and well. Promise me you will marry, have children."

The guard beyond the door made a small sound in the back of his throat. "Almost time, Captain," he said.

All these harsh men were speaking so quietly, so respectfully, Tess thought, grabbing at details to keep herself from freezing. Rain fell outside. A cold, heavy, night rain. A winter rain. But spring was in the air. Another spring.

Ryder's breathing quickened. "Tell my mother I love her. Madame Lanier has money to provide for Diana, give her a fresh start, but you might see her off for me, will you? And thank your sister for her service to me long ago." He smiled, more absently now. "Yes, and tell Miss Theresa Boyde that I am heartily sorry never to have had the pleasure of meeting her."

"Tess. Her name's Tess." The world was crumbling, like the clay under the strangling rain outside. Ryder took her in a gruff embrace. She clutched the lapels of his borrowed blue coat. She felt him drawing her warmth, her life. "Listen," he said. "I am counting on you. To take care of the women. To tell my mother I did my best."

He pressed his lips to her forehead, as if she were a child he'd put to bed over their years together instead of a comrade. Tess grabbed his face, kissed the place above his eye where the panther had struck. She licked the whitened scar. Deep. Hard. He blinked twice, startled. She'd done it, distracted him from his own death. He stumbled. The guard stepped forward.

Her chance. She barreled into the guard's side, called for her comrades. From nowhere came the rifle butt, crashing into her head. Ryder's hand, reaching out to help, as it always did, was the last part of him she saw.

* * *

"Come on, Lieutenant. There! Keep them eyes open now so's Mallory can check you ain't gone bats on us."

Tess took Mallory's arm, sat up slowly. Stockton was on her other side. Beyond them, more tunnelers, their faces smeared with red clay. They were beyond the prison wall, the dead line, beyond the stand of trees. Still raining, but darker. Were the guards in pursuit?

"We're out?"

"Yes, sir."

"Where's Captain Cole?"

Silence. Mallory and Stockton exchanged worried looks. Mallory spoke softly. "Sir, think back. You know the captain could not come with us."

"You let them hang him?"

"It's done, sir," Mallory said. "Not by hanging, but it's done."

Firing squad? The men went out of focus. "Go on. Leave me here," she managed to command.

"We can't do that, sir," Mallory said gruffly. "We're still under his orders. Corporal Stockton, if you would, please?"

The bigger man threw her over his shoulder.

"Ready, Stockton?"

"Sure. Why, he don't weigh nothing at all. We'll keep up," Stockton assured Mallory as her world went black again.

* * *

285

Turner Farm

Tess smelled the packed clay soil, apples, and onions of a root cellar, before hearing the dull thud of artillery fire. Later. How much later was it? Mallory wiped her brow with a cool wet cloth.

"We have made bold enough to take refuge, here among the dwindling supplies of this farm, Lieutenant. Are you feeling any better, sir?"

"How was it done?" she heard a fogged version of her own voice ask.

Mallory sighed. "Out in the yard. Only Stockton got up over the wall to witness. It was hard on him, sir. Retched up so much bile—"

She raised herself to her elbow. "Get him."

"Now, have a care with yourself, sir—"

"Get him."

"All right then!" Mallory threw down the cloth, but followed her orders.

When Corporal Stockton presented himself, Tess steadied herself in the big man's sad eyes. He wiped his mouth with the back of his hand.

"Tell me," she demanded.

He swallowed. "They put him up against the flagpole, in the middle of the yard. He was a mite unsteady walking there. Maybe Witcomb poured a bottle of his fancy bourbon down his throat, I don't know. That visiting officer read out a list of crimes. Desertion, impersonating an officer, slave stealing. I guess they threw the book at him to make it stick.

"The commander made a speech of his own then, a right nice speech that thanked our captain for his service to the camp. Then he pinned a red piece of flannel to his chest, pressed the captain's back against the flagpole, told him to stay real still and it would be over soon. Well. That's all. No blindfold, no tying of his hands. Five shooters."

Stockton tried to look away. "And?" Tess prompted.

The massive shoulders fell. "Lieutenant, he'd treated every mother's son of them for the trots or worse, what else could they do?"

"Do?"

"Captain was right about them boys, they're all good marksmen, never met a Johnny Reb who weren't, damn 'em. Not a single misfire, even in the rain. But none wanted to be the one, I guess, that caused Captain's mortal coil to separate. They missed the target, but for one, who nipped his shoulder enough to send him down in the mud. I'd of done it, hit him square in the heart, so his sufferings be done with. You'd of done the same, wouldn't you? They should have asked a crack shot like you so he wouldn't have had to go like that."

"Like what?"

"When the smoke cleared, that visiting officer, the one who came with the orders, he swore a catalogue of oaths, calling them Reb boys names I wouldn't call a dog, on account of they was out of allotment of shot for the execution. He made for our captain, but the commander stopped him where he stood. "'Stay away from him,' says Witcomb, fierce as a bear. Then he tromped out alone. The marksmen, they stood guard, not letting that son of a bitch past them. The commander knelt, lifted Captain Cole up into his arms, one of which the captain fixed for him back before you came amongst us, Lieutenant. Was plum useless, that arm, before, from back second Bull Run, I think. Maybe he was thinking of that, when I saw the steel of his knife.

Stockton wiped his mouth with the back of his hand before he continued. "I was hoping the captain was passed out from the one wound, you know? But he weren't. The commander bespoke him something all quiet, and then put in the knife and, well, blood started flowing fast. God almighty, it was nigh onto forever, that flow. The ground was red and them rifle boys was all bawling like babies. Captain Cole, he didn't need to hear that, last thing. They all could have done better, cleaner by the man!"

Stockton doubled over and began dry-heaving.

Tess saw a hand working independently of herself. Tom Boyde's hand. It rubbed Stockton's back. Her voice made the clucking, soothing sounds of her long-dead mother.

Stockton raised his head. "Thanks, Lieutenant. I'll be all right. Look after yourself now. Caught a mean wallop. You're all we got left of him, sir."

Book 6

April 1865

Chapter Forty-one

MacKendrie Farm, Rowlett, Virginia

It was something like being at Madame Lanier's, the scent of lilac water, the cool cloth soothing her brow. Tess began to think she'd escaped into the past, where Ryder was alive.

"I need—"

"To lie still," the voices finished for her, coming from a two-headed woman. No. From two women, alike from their lopsided smiles down to the braids circling their ears. Then it came back. It all came back.

"Where are my men?" Tess asked.

"Gone on. Had to leave you, on account of there are some irregulars on the prowl. Armed."

"Irregulars of what side?"

"Ours." They whispered the word, together.

"Did you hide me from them?"

"We did."

"Why?"

"They was some of the same squad from two weeks back. Not going to clean up after that bunch again."

"Not about to see what we seen after, neither," one woman reminded the other.

Tess felt her gut clench. "What did you see?"

"Train," the first began. "Coming through, nearby. They said it was full of arms they was going to capture and deliver to General Lee's army. So's they could make a stand against Grant and stay fighting, after Petersburg."

"Petersburg's taken?"

They nodded. "Richmond too. But Bobby Lee gave you Yankees the slip again, make no mistake about that."

"Leave it go now, Cornelia," the brighter-eyed one counseled.

Tess waited for the sisters, they had to be sisters, to continue their story. They did, each taking a part, when the telling got too much to bear.

"Two weeks' back, when that squad of rangers first come here to the farm, we was to put our cow on the tracks to make that train stop, so they could get the gun shipment on board. We was mighty excited, ready to do our part for the cause."

"We got it to stop, all right. But it wasn't the truth they told," the second sister explained, her voice beginning to waver. "That train was full of wounded Yankees, with their one medical man. Our boys went mad, I think, seeing what they captured."

"Nothing useful, only burdens, you see?"

"They dragged all them fellows out. Well, they killed them—the train's engineer, fireman, and all the soldiers. Ran out of shot, so they bayoneted the ones still trying to crawl away."

"Captured one Yankee pistol, the one from inside the surgeon's bag. That's what they got for all that killing of men who couldn't fight back. One pistol."

"They told us to scat after our cow got the train stopped, but we didn't. We were in the crepe myrtle bushes, seeing it all, not believing our eyes."

"Hiding," Cornelia said, her eyes dulled with pain.

"They might have killed you too," Tess said quietly.

Their shoulders sagged a little in response before Cornelia took up the story. "We waited till they was gone before we came out. There was so much blood it soaked through our skirts and petticoats both. The surgeon was still alive. 'Help them,' he said when we turned him over. That was all. 'Help them.' Then he was dead, too."

The woman wiped her raw-boned hand across her mouth as her sister took a deep breath. "Well. It weren't going to happen again, not to your crew of Yankee prisoners, no more than skeletons holding each other up. You all are still the enemy, and your General Sheridan's men came through like the horsemen of the Apocalypse and burned our crops to cinders."

"But that bunch from our side, they was scalawags, see? Not fit to be called soldiers, not true soldiers."

"No," Tess agreed quietly. Suddenly the room began to spin as if someone were playing a cruel joke with the narrow bed. Had the scalawags found her men? Were they all dead, too?

"Get the bowl, Cornelia, a retch approaches."

The basin was under Tess's head before the sentence was complete. She coughed a wad of yellow-tinged bile into its depths, then, dizzy, landed back in the lap of the one who was not Cornelia. Tess took comfort in the feel of the woman's softness.

"I beg your pardon, Ma'am," she tried to soothe any offense taken, but the one who was not Cornelia just laughed, a strange sound in the small, spare, windowless room.

"Don't pitch down your voice on our account, Lieutenant. We know what you are."

The threadbare cotton blanket slipped to her waist and Tess realized she was naked under a neatly patched nightgown. It had been so long since she'd seen herself unbound she'd almost forgotten what her own breasts looked like.

"Them's nice full bosoms what saved you more than Clara and me," Cornelia explained. "We was ripping off your Yankee togs to turn you into our bed bound mule-kicked little brother when we discovered you a sister underneath all that filthy binding.”

“So did them two stragglers.” her sister took up the story, “insisting on a look, you see? They left soon’s we also told them you were raving from a mad dog’s bite, and might just bite them if’n they came closer.”

“That moved them on soon enough,” Cordelia finished. “Now, you ought take better care of yourself, even as a man.”

“She couldn’t do no better up at the prison, don’t you know?” her sister chastised.

“Well, she can do better now, with us.”

Cornelia leaned in closer. “We are the sisters MacKendrie of Rowlett, Virginia. You are safe with us.”

“But,” Tess commanded her aching voice to explain. “I was a soldier. I’ve brought down your men, too.”

“You been listening at all, Yankee? Ain’t none of us angels, girl. Maybe them wounded on that train did their share of killing, too. That’s what war is. We all know that now, don’t we? Still, they shouldn’t have been kilt like that. They deserved a chance. And that medical man, I’ll remember his eyes to my grave. Your surgeons are like ours, ain’t they? They don’t fight in battle at all?”

“No, they don’t,” Tess could barely say, as she thought of Ryder patiently flagging their makeshift hospital as the bombs exploded around him.

“Well, as your men was heading out, your sergeant, the one looks like a hound who lost his scent? He said, ‘help him,’ just like that doctor from the train. That’s a sign from God as Clara and me’s got it figured.”

Clara nodded. “You ain’t only just you to us. You’re all of them, you see? You’re our second chance. You need to let us fuss over you, girl.”

Clara MacKendrie touched Tess’s brow with the scented lavender water and smiled shyly. “You join up with your sweetheart then?”

"Yes." That is what she'd done, all those years ago. Tess had wanted more than to learn Ryder's doctoring. She'd wanted a man who could weep over the loss of his horse, and she'd been willing to take all that came with him since then.

"We had a female cousin joined the cavalry," Clara offered when her sister had turned away to empty the wash basin. "That girl sat a horse better than any man, too! Lasted six months before they found her out and sent her home. When did you join up?"

"April."

"Why, it's April again—you almost lasted a year."

"April of sixty-one," Tess corrected.

The women stared at her, wide-eyed. "Good Lord!" Clara finally proclaimed. "They got some mighty near-sighted soldiers in the Yankee army!"

Cornelia returned, wiping her hands. "That moon-eyed sergeant, he your sweetheart then?"

"No." Tess heard her voice falter. "My sweetheart, he was killed, right before we broke out of the prison camp."

"Now, that's a terrible shame. Did he know?"

Tess looked down at her hands. "No." She felt a crushing weight from the thought that she'd never told Ryder that she was both friend and lover.

"You should of told him," Clara said softly.

"Hush, Sister."

Tess felt another wave of nausea as her throat went suddenly, unbearably dry. Was all this weakness a result of the blow to her head? Was she concussed? Cornelia passed a chipped crockery cup to her sister, who held it to Tess's lips. The tea within tasted of mint and elderberries.

"Sip it now, that's the girl," Clara urged. "Maybe his people will help you."

The idea of standing before Olivia Cole, telling her how her son met his end birthed itself in her mind, and almost paralyzed Tess with intensified grief. She couldn't do it, not as a woman or a man. She'd never have the courage for it. She shook her head. "I don't need help," she whispered.

"Oh, darlin' girl, that's the man in you talkin'. Don't we all need help now and again? Maybe one of them soldier mates of yours will marry you, if'n they all admired your man. They sure seemed to admire you a powerful amount. Took the Devil's argument to convince them to leave you with us."

Tess stared down at the edging of blue forget-me-nots embroidered into the neckline of her borrowed nightgown.

"Ain't marrying any of them, or anybody," she said, a faint echo of her thoughts after her father placed the shopkeeper in her path.

"Oh, think more on that, once your loss don't weigh so heavy," Clara urged.

Her sister frowned. "She'd best think now. Life's a hard enough row to hoe, without a bastard child on your hip."

Tess's fingers crushed around the faded blue flowers of the gown as she struggled for breath. "A... what?"

"Why, what do you think we been talking about?"

"She don't know, Sister."

"'Course she knows! Don't you?"

Another wave of nausea nudged the possibility further. Not a concussion causing it. "A child?" Tess heard herself whisper again, still not believing.

"Ain't your flow stopped?" Cornelia asked.

"Yes, but it stopped before, over hard times."

"Well, ain't you seen any waist thickening? You're two or three months gone as we figure."

Tess looked down at her distended abdomen. Other prisoners had them too, from the hunger. She'd never thought about it. Did giving Ryder the gift of his Diana get a child started between them there, in the dead of winter?

Two months. Did she tell him, the sisters MacKendrie had asked her. No. How could she, when she herself didn't know? A baby was growing inside her, even as raw grief burned at her core and she wanted only to die herself.

Suddenly, without warning, Tess felt Ryder's smile. She heard him again urging her to live, to have children. The baby might have his smile. Maybe she had to live long enough to see that.

Clara and Cornelia MacKendrie nodded their heads in unison. "There, that's better. Now, if your men don't come back for you, or none of them's willing, we got us a blacksmith in town, a little lame, but good-hearted."

Chapter Forty-two

Pratt Bridge, outside Petersburg, Virginia

Ryder smelled warmth in the air around them, and green grass shoots. Spring. It had come, at long last. He felt light pressing against his eyelids. "Come on, Captain, eyes open," the soft drawl cajoled. "Don't you want to see your mama? You get to bid her goodbye, and I get my brother back. That's not such a bad trade, is it?"

Ryder understood the words, spoken slowly, as if to a child. But goodbye was for leaving home. He had done that, years ago, then suffered his mother's tears every time he had re-enlisted. For the duration. Had Richmond been taken? Was this endless war over? Piece it together. Spring. Mama. Goodbye. A final goodbye, was it a final goodbye he was to deliver? Yes. Perhaps that was it.

"It's not an even trade, after all you've done for us on both sides at the camp."

Witcomb was the speaker, Ryder finally realized. The commander of Findley Prison held him between two strong arms. "Listen sir," he continued, "there in the execution yard, he could have killed us all for our trickery, for agreeing with the riflemen that they might miss your heart, miss you all together except just enough to knock you down so I could finish you off. I did not. Instead, I cut through the bladder of pig's blood I packed inside your coat."

Yes. Ryder remembered the rip across his chest, and the blood, all the blood, gushing over his sleeve, soaking the ground while something burst back behind his eyes.

"I thought you'd passed out from the shock of what I did," Witcomb said. "But something else happened. I wish I knew what it was... perhaps a seizure, or a stroke?"

Yes. A stroke, which started in his head, from whence the pain came before. Before, when the Southern irregular had hit him too hard.

"I had to move the men out, you see, ours, and yours that were left after the escape," Witcomb continued. "Grant was coming, so I left you there, in the cellar of the guard-house, in the care of our laundress. She has done you no more harm, I trust. When the prisoner exchanges started up again, I learned you lingered. I sent word out, to your side, of your time with us, and that I was firm in the belief that you were who you claimed to be. That's what's brought me back now. Your mother is here, Captain. You are returned to her, do you understand me? In exchange for my brother, a prisoner at Elmira. They are waiting for us across the bridge. Look, sir. Please."

There, blink back the gray dawn light, Ryder commanded his eyelids. The bridge came into focus. Slowly. *Be patient with me*, he thought at the commander. They were patient, Witcomb and the tense, gruff confederates around him. And it was not a lie from the man in threadbare gray, desperate for the return of his brother. Not a lie. The brother stood there, across the stone bridge, between two men in blue. And behind them, a miracle. His mother.

"That's the way!" Witcomb called out, jubilant. You're standing all on your own, sir!"

Ryder felt a surge of energy, responding. Absurd, but there it was. He was learning much about doctoring, as a patient. From the laundress, keeping him clean, singing him lullabies in African cadences. Spooning boiled water and honey down his throat when he could again swallow. Talking to him as if he was alive. Would he ever be able to use what she had taught him? *Mama, look at you. So beautiful, so hopeful. They lied to you about me, then.*

"And you know her, don't you, sir? It is not true, what they say. She did right by you, the laundress. You understand me. You'll last a bit. Long enough to say goodbye to your mother, You'd like that, Captain?

He would.

"I'm bound to leave you here. To fetch my brother. Not an even trade, I know," he said again, in that apologetic voice. "Lean on the wall. It will help you stand. Don't fall. Your mother is watching. Don't fall."

The stones of the bridge's ledge were cold. Yes, Ryder thought, he could do this, held by the stone, by his mother's eyes. He wished he could do more. Walk to her. Talk.

But his eyes open, and standing, seemed to be enough. She reached him, spoke his name, took hold of his hand. He could not make his fingers close around hers. To go. To walk across the bridge to the other side. She did not understand how bad he was. He was going to disappoint her again.

I'm sorry, Mother. I have lost them all. And I don't know why I'm not dead, too.

"It's all right," she whispered, holding his face between her hands, as if she'd heard his thoughts. "Ryder, it's all right."

* * *

MacKendrie Farm, Rowlett, Virginia

"We got enough wood for the next two winters, will you kindly get in here for supper?"

But Tess so loved the feeling of her strength returning that she could have split another three rows to finish the cord. Her boy would be strong, like her. And kind, like Ryder. She had to do everything she could to make it so.

How many more months? Six. From February to November, 1865 would be his duration. Tess had it figured. Come bare tree season he'd come out of hiding inside her.

298

Why did human babies take so long to finish themselves up? She wanted him in her arms now.

Tess wiped her brow with the back of her sleeve, piquing Cornelia further.

"We done spared you three of our best lawn handkerchiefs, the least you could do is remember to use one!"

Tess dug into the deep pockets of her cotton homespun gown, past the fish hook and the chunk of flint she'd found by the creek bed, to the scrap of embroidered cloth.

From the kitchen window, Clara laughed. Nervously? "Oh never mind, Sister," she said. "I need us a pinch of rosemary to make this gamey fowl you brought in taste like a plump hen. Do you think you could find some, dear?"

She held out a basket that Tess retrieved. But when she passed beneath the open window Tess heard the sisters MacKendrie conniving again.

"She must know, as you been skittery as a wren in a hailstorm!"

"And I'm supposed to let her meet him all grimy and smelling of a woodpile?"

"Least she ain't been out shooting!"

"That girl's use of Daddy's rifle has kept us in more meat than we've even seen in two years, and the Baptist preacher's son is no kind of a shot himself."

"He's also a touch soft in the head."

"He's no such a thing! Well, with numbers, maybe, which will come in handy when his firstborn comes early."

"True enough."

Tess sighed, fighting the urge to turn around and give the sisters more holy hell for again trying to get her hitched up to some unsuspecting neighbor while she was not yet showing under her skirts. She had some months yet to "pass," they claimed. As long as she pulled her corset strings tight enough and kept the lights out when her new husband had his way with her.

Tess was never going to let any man have his way with her. It was hard enough getting used to being a woman again, and a loaded with a baby one at that, without the thought of giving any other man what she'd given to Ryder Cole. She didn't care if it was foolish in the sisters' eyes. She would never take the chance of giving her child the kind of father that she had. But Ryder was right when he urged Tom to carry on, to have children. When their child needed a daddy, then she would become Tom for him, that's what.

Tess passed the small headstone she'd carved over the grave of the Yankee doctor who'd been slaughtered by the rangers. She had put Tom's name and dates on the headstone, to say goodbye to that part of her. She asked the doctor's forgiveness, as she always did when passing the grave, because she imagined him with Ryder's face, too.

Tess neared the creek between dusk and evening, when the animals came to drink. Maybe she would stay all night, to discourage the preacher's son and let the sisters know that she would not stand any more of their schemes. Her pace slowed. Could she be as quiet as she used to be in skirts, and see a few of the critters native to this rolling Virginia Piedmont? She would do this with the boy, show him how to walk through the forest without a sound. No panther would ever surprise her boy. Nor would a war, not if she could help it.

This place reminded her of home, even with its gentler rising hills. Whenever she imagined being with her child, it was on Ryder's land. And sometimes Olivia Cole was there, waiting for them in the front drawing room, with tea and sugar cake and a dancing master to teach her boy the latest steps sweeping fashionable Boston or New York. A "Dance" to the River people, a "Squeeze" to the town folks, a "Jam" to the outcasts in the Big Woods, all of them waiting to welcome her boy home.

Tess shook her head. Those dreams had to go. But she was so intent on banishing them that she almost missed the sight of a small bear cub making his way creekside. Don't get between him and the mother. She already knew how she would fight to protect her own child. Best slip back, get out of the scent line. Human. That was a human scent, of greens, corn bread. The cub was a child, a ragged child, with a small woman now at his heels.

"Don't go rushing," the woman warned him. "Check the air, that's it... sniff, for animals." She stopped talking abruptly and turned, reached into her skirt pocket. A Colt dragoon appeared. Tess stepped onto the path slowly, showing her hands. Her basket creaked on her arm.

"This your land, Missus?" the small woman asked evenly. "We don't mean no harm. We need only a drink before we're on our way, by the grace of God."

"The grace of God and your courage, I think, Mrs. Tubman," Tess said quietly.

The woman's face halved with her grin. "Why, ain't you a long way from your Big Woods, Miss," she said.

* * *

Campbell Hospital, Washington City

Ryder listened to his mother's voice, quietly reading *David Copperfield.* Then came footsteps, hurried, self-important. She stopped reading, marked her place with a sifting sound. He heard her talking above him, with the Washington doctors, one after another. Her suggestions overruled, again. Finally, acquiescence. His bright, determined mother, defeated again. Then the doctors sent her away, drew the curtains around his bed, and tortured him. With another purge, another blood-letting. Where was someone with sense? Tom had the best sense. Where was Tom?

Finally, they trussed him up, left him alone. Night time. Few on duty. When the sounds of suffering around him became too much for him to bear, Ryder slowed his breathing. So little he could control, after being master of a ward like this one, once. Deep in the night, lying flat, caught in the trap of his own helplessness, he practiced the

301

breathing. Until he found the limits to his new skill. Too slowed. Dangerous, after the blood-letting. He was losing consciousness. No voice to tell them, if any were around still. Then, through the purple spots, the weary face of a nurse. Feeling his pulse, calling out to someone behind her. Then the soothing sounds of Latin, accented Irish. The ward's chaplain, performing a rite. What did the Catholics call it? Extreme Unction. A soothing, peaceful ritual. Ryder felt a faint amusement. A good Congregationalist going out in a Catholic ceremony, incense and all.

"There, now. I commend your soul to God, Captain," the chaplain said, full of forgiveness.

Ryder hoped God was like the kind-eyed chaplain.

The ward went white. Voices more hushed, then a profound silence. Broken by a shout.

"Ryder Cole, breathe!"

Hands at his shoulders, yanking him upright, his lungs filling with air. Badgering female. Nurse Truscutt. Truculent Truscutt.

"There, a good boy, an obedient boy," she claimed, even as her frown deepened. Then, in his ear. "To the bolster with you, no more flat on your back, sir. You are our hope in this place, you hear me?"

He did. But Ryder did not know how he could be anyone's hope when none lived in him. He did not want the indomitable woman to see that, so he closed his eyes. Did he only imagine Nurse Truscutt's lips at his temple, as tender as his mother's?

Where was Tom? He would have come, if he'd survived the escape. None of them had come. Had he sent his tunneling soldiers to their deaths? Ryder wanted to ask the man who visited later in the day, the one whose deep-set eyes bore into his soul, if he knew where his fellow prisoners were. The man closed Ryder's book of sonnets, removed his spectacles, and returned them to his pocket.

"I enjoy our visits," his visitor said. "And not only because you never argue with me, Captain Cole."

Ryder felt the large hand in his, and willed himself to take hold. Had he? The man smiled. "Well. There's progress, I'd say. Do that for your doctors and they might not be so dismissive of your prospects, sir."

The doctors never took his hand, Ryder wanted to tell his visitor. The doctors never talked to him, only over his head to each other. Had he ever done that with a patient? He prayed he had not.

"They say you are dying, Captain Cole. Your mother is of a different opinion. I would like you to side with her, sir, because I know what it is to lose a child. I would not wish that fate on the worst of my enemies. Now, I am given to understand that you are one of the original ninety-day volunteers," the man continued in that strange, educated, but high-pitched backwoods twang. "You have accomplished your duty well. I only wish your country had done as well by you. It has been a long ninety days, has it not? The war is ending, but the battles are not over. There is so much work ahead, son. Others will forget what this time was about. You will never forget, will you?"

Breathe, Ryder commanded himself. *In. Out. Speak. Answer.* But he could not. *Well, then. Answer with your eyes.*

His visitor smiled. A heavy thing for his deeply-lined face to do.

The familiar two coughs of impatience emanated from the two government men standing out of Ryder's sight lines. What would he say, if he could speak, Ryder wondered.

They want you off to your next appointment, sir. Best follow them. Thank you for coming.

The smile widened. "You've become very good at the sounds my supposed subordinates rule me by, Captain. Tonight's dictums are toward pleasure, I'm happy to report. An evening's theater, in the company of my wife and, due to regrets sent from your commanding officer and Mrs.

Grant, a betrothed couple of about your years. I devoutly wish you could be seated with us.”

* * *

Ryder dreamed a terrible dream that night, of horses screaming, of women weeping. When he woke, the windows were draped in mourning crepe and the little former slave wash girl who often took her rest in the empty fireplace of his corner of the ward, sat alone on a stool by his bed. Ryder saw his own fingers lost in the dense, beautiful blackness of her hair. She lifted her head, kissed his hand. Her eyes were swollen.

“Oh, sir,” she whispered, “they done it. They done kilt your friend, Father Abraham.”

Chapter Forty-three

MacKendrie Farm, Rowlett, Virginia

Tess only meant to make a quick visit to the smoke-house, to grab enough food for Mrs. Tubman and her passengers to make a small meal before they headed north. She did not expect to run into Clara, her face tear-stained, carrying a quilt-wrapped bundle.

"Thank all that's holy that I don't have to track you!" Clara proclaimed in a muted whisper.

Tess tried to back out of the smokehouse slowly. She was not going to be made to sit at table with a preacher's son marriage prospect, not with Mrs. Tubman and her charges cold and hungry in the desolate field.

But Clara grabbed her arm. "You got to go away from us, Tess," she said.

"I do?"

"Yes. We won't do it, won't follow his will, but Jedadiah is our brother, however much changed."

"Your brother?"

"Home from the war. Relieved by General Lee himself. His regiment gave the Yankees the slip again after Petersburg and Richmond, the men ready to take to the hills, fight on. But Bobby Lee commanded them to lay down their arms. When they did, the Yankees sent them home."

Home, Tess thought. If the rebels were being sent home, were her own men too? Was the war over?

"We were so happy to see him." Clara pulled her further into the hushed world of the smokehouse, still crackling with an unnamed threat. "We unburdened our recent troubles too soon to our Jedadiah." She paced the small space. "We have always relied on his good counsel, you see? We told him of the train, and of how you came to be here with us."

"He wants me away then?"

Clara stopped. "Worse. He wants you dead."

"Dead?" Tess felt the shock, the rush of energy as her hand closed around the rifle. She would take the firearm, whether Clara offered it or not. Listen. Gather information. Protect the child.

"Says you will tell of our part in… in what happened with the train," Clara continued, "and then the Yankee invaders will come, find the graves and kill us all in retribution. He is a hardened man, a different man than the one who left. Forgive us!"

Tess stared into the anguished face. "Yes, Clara, 'course. I'll go then."

"We have every hope for you. Cornelia's slipped some of her sleeping herbs into Jedadiah's food. That will serve to give you a few hours before he finds we have not done his bidding, and he takes to hunting you down."

"If we meet, I will kill him."

"I know. Listen, we had your man's coat deep in a drawer. I fetched it. Here, inside the quilt, along with some few provisions. The angels keep you, dear girl, for we cannot."

* * *

Mrs. Tubman met Tess at their appointed spot under the redbud tree. Tess held out Clara's food, and the quilt. Ryder's coat was enough for her needs.

"You need to get going, Ma'am," she said. "Their soldier brother is home."

"Oh, we travel by night anyway, remember? With a soldier home, it may be Jubilo is fast approaching, sure enough. This the end of your stay too then?"

"Yes. He'll be after me. I'll take a different way."

306

"Why? If he bent on lookin' for a lone woman, I believe he'd pass right by a huddle of black folk."

"But—"

"We can make you one of us with a hunk of charcoal easy enough."

"You got women and children in your care, Mrs. Tubman. If they were put in extra jeopardy on account of my troubles—"

"Ha! Do you disremember who you talking to, Miss? You know first hand some of the contrabands I delivered safe up the Hudson and through the Big Woods of your own home state. Now, I would hate to pull out my firearm to convince you to take refuge with us, bein' you is a woman and child both, yourself."

Tess felt that bothersome light-headedness cause her to stumble. The small woman's strong hand took her arm, and eased her down under the tree.

"It will pass," she whispered.

"Will indeed," Mrs. Tubman assured her, as she laid those strong hands against Tess's middle.

"How do you know, Ma'am?" she asked quietly.

"It's that sweet, good look about you."

Tess felt a soft fluttering, like butterfly wings beating inside her. Was that her boy?

"Alive," Mrs. Tubman said, nodding. Her soft crooning rose up into the night air.

"What are you doing?" Tess asked.

"Calling to this child's daddy. To come, collect you both."

"He's dead."

"I don't know 'bout that."

"He's dead!" Tess cried out with a strangled fierceness.

"Well. Dead ain't gone, child. Don't hurt to call."

* * *

Campbell Hospital, Washington D.C.

Ryder only felt fully alive in the night, in his dreams. He gave himself over to this one: his father, taking him sailing up the Hudson to Albany to see the skeleton of the great whale. Standing in the jaws, holding his father's hand. His own, so small. Had he ever been that small? Then his hands became large, useful again, steady, feeling the soft distended abdomen of a woman. Harriet Tubman's hands were over his. She was singing in soft, African cadences. He tried to talk, but could not. It did not matter, she understood. She nodded her approval. Was he back in the cave? Would she give him that baby to hold again? Yes.

"Greet your child, sir."

Yes. Please. Give me the child.

The child's mother was silent, out of his reach. His Diana of the woods, always out of sight.

Then he was rudely yanked away from them by the pain, the lance at his arm, more blood flowing, robbed from collapsing veins.

Stop. I have to find them again. Please. Stop.

But they did not stop, even calling his struggle against their invasions simple reflex, or another seizure. Not looking, never looking, into his eyes, even as the black, deadly darkness descended.

Then, a woman. In the bed with him. Smelling of peaches. Madame Lanier. She grinned. "There now, that's my cure," she proclaimed, kissing his temple. "You're a difficult man to sneak up on, Captain Cole. Had to get out of my usual finery. But you know what's underneath is more interesting, yes?"

She unhitched her prim nurse's apron far enough to bare the red-dyed lace of her corset top, with her generous breasts spilling over it. Ryder watched his fingers closing around the curve of her waist. So grateful for her laughing eyes, her talking to him as if he were alive.

"We have all missed our dear captain," she said quietly.

The word. He had to find it, speak it. "Diana?"

"Oh, *cherie*." She began parting and reparting his hair under her long fingers, their nails cut blunt now. "She's gone."

"Gone?"

She looked away, why? No. Not allowed. He had Diana safe, in her house, in the Capital City. A bad idea to begin with, this city, built in a swamp. Breeding malaria, cholera. Bad water, worse drainage. Killing even the President's son, before the actor killed the president. Did Washington kill his Diana too?

"Dreamed. Of her. And a child."

"Did you?" She tucked his head under her heart. "That's a good dream. You hold onto that dream, hear? And you hold onto me now, sweet boy."

"Mrs. Lanier, have you no shame? Get out of that man's bed!"

Ryder heard Madame Lanier's chuckle as her warmth slipped away. "I thought you said he could not talk? He talks to me!" she proclaimed to Truculent Truscutt.

"Why, you brazen—"

"Hush!" Ryder heard another voice, his mother's, filmy, weak. She'd been talking to the doctors after their latest torments. She always looked like this after talking with them. Spent, tired, her hope waning. "Ryder," she pleaded, stroking the salt track remnants of his tears. "Dear God, Ryder, please. Do not leave me."

He was so tired. But he must make her some words too. Words to get him away from the doctors who did not understand what was wrong with him. He did not either, but she was right in her fear. They were killing him, and that was killing the spirit of his bright, splendid mother. Belle Haven. Perhaps if they went there.

"Home?"

Had he said it? Yes, she was smiling, and demanding they pack his bags. She was taking him home.

* * *

Belle Haven, Ashokan-on-Hudson, New York

Ryder had forgotten how much he loved this old, drafty, out-of-date house, belonging to an age when men thought reason ruled. It never would again, if ever it had. But its structural balance and symmetry calmed him. They'd planted him upstairs in the East Wing, where he could see the twin sugar maples and the Hudson gleaming from the bed's four posts. The rooms had first belonged to his short-lived grandfather, whose indulgent mother had paid Duncan Phyffe's best craftsmen to carve shafts of wheat and sunbursts on all posts, to please both the sleeper and the guests who visited his chamber over long illnesses. What funny, doting people he came from.

Who was he going to dote over? They were all dead. Never mind. Watch his mother, spooning broth into him. Do something, to please her. She worked so hard.

"Pretty," he whispered.

She put down the spoon. "What is?" she asked, before leaning her ear to his lips.

"Lace. There. At your neck."

"Why, thank you, darling," she said, then began to cry. Why was she doing that? But her eyes shone with happiness, too. "Three, Ryder. That was three sentences!" she proclaimed.

Any grammarian would disagree, but he did not correct her notion. She'd gone from beautiful to glorious in her pleasure at his accomplishment. Another day, then. To breathe in, out. To please this woman, his mother, in this life bestowing place, home.

Chapter Forty-four

September 30, 1865, Auburn, New York

"There you are! Lord, you be hard to track, woman! Look at this fine headpiece. Found you some roses, and ribbons I done dyed myself with the last of the indigo. Join us now. Everybody's waitin'."

Tess stood, feeling the bothersome tightness around her middle subside as she admired the wreath between Harriet Tubman's strong hands. But she wished she could stay in the quiet graveyard a little longer. Everyone was kind to her here where the war and Mrs. Tubman had whipsawed her to, this far-flung western corner of her native state. At the small home for dying and invalid soldiers, the patients made no cruel remarks about her widening skirts and lack of wedding ring or husband to go with them. But Tess often had a deep need to be alone. As alone as she could get with the ornery baby elbowing or kicking her, sometimes a limb showing right through her belly.

What was the truly right thing to do? Harriet Tubman had told her that this marriage would be proper and holy and fair for the child. But Tess had promised herself never to live a lie again, not for any cause or any man. The grave stones and crosses had remained mute. They were not helping her decide. Neither was Ryder.

She still sensed him, felt his quiet, desperate loneliness. What did it mean? Where was he? Why wasn't he in heaven, and happy? Was God as cruel as the war had been? She could not leave him behind, not again.

"Can't do it, Ma'am," she breathed out.

Mrs. Tubman cocked her head. "You said you would honor Sergeant Ellis's last wish. Thought you was a woman of your word."

"If I could give my heart again—"

"You done give your heart without marryin' and look where it's got you!"

"Don't you badmouth this child's papa! Maybe he didn't love me back with the marrying kind of love, but we were true friends."

The small woman scanned the graves. "Our man, the one still here on this earth, child, he tryin' to be your friend. He don't want for your heart, Tess. He just needs to do somethin' fine."

Tess closed her eyes slowly, feeling the cool breeze waft through her skirts. "I been prayin' on it, Mrs. Tubman, honest, I have."

The woman's brow lowered in judgment. "And what your great God tell you? That it don't matter how respectful our man's manner? That it ain't enough to give you and your child a proper married name? Nothing matter more than his African blood? Is that what your God been tellin' you?"

Defeated. Tess shook her head. "Good Lord, Moses, hush your voice before you raise these dead so their boney fingers can plant your damned roses on my head!"

Mrs. Tubman grunted. "Wedding jitters!" she scoffed before grabbing Tess's hand, yanking her towards the living. "Now, you quit that cussin', young one! You ain't a man or in the army no more, and that's no way for a mama to set good example to her—"

A grip around her middle made Tess squeeze that rock hard hand, easing the loneliness of the pain.

"Well," Mrs. Tubman said softly when the grip was done, "I thought you was goin' on into late next month, but looks like this one wants to see the last of September."

Tess breathed easier. "You mean…it's not from eating too many of the cherries?"

Her friend laughed. "No more cherries till this day's two jobs are done, you prickly woman."

Maybe the sign she was looking for was coming from her child, Tess thought. Maybe he wanted a name before he was born, one to go with his father's given name. Ellis was a good man's name.

They walked back to the house, now festooned with the first changing leaves of autumn. Everything seemed too colorful, too beautiful to be real: the yellow-orange leaves, the blood-red roses nested in her hair, now long enough to pin up again. Tess stood beside the bed of Sergeant Ansel Ellis. He thanked her for becoming his wife in that thready voice, when she should have been thanking him for his name's protection, for the survivor's benefits of his wartime service's pension, for herself and her child.

She remembered the ceremony through the haze of her early labor as she allowed Sergeant Ellis to do his fine thing. But she felt closed in again, almost as soon as the preacher finished tying them together. Sergeant Ellis asked her to fetch him some sassafras, knowing they were clean out of his tea, knowing the tree Mrs. Tubman had brought up from Maryland was in the far, sunlit meadow. Sergeant Ellis pressed his pen knife into her hand. "Carve me just a bitty piece of that trunk, Miss Tess," he urged her gently, "and wear your coat, now." Ryder's coat. He knew it always calmed her. Tess nodded, slipped the coat off its nail, and stepped out the kitchen door.

The edge of the far meadow was in sight, but she had to stop. She found something to lean on. Something strong, the arbor post. Tess watched her knuckles whiten as she gasped, then went to her knees, to a dark place inside her, so far inside her lover's blue coat.

Too much. It was too much to bear, alone. "Ryder," she whispered. "Help me."

* * *

313

"Help me."

Ryder thought the call was part of that dream, the one of him trying to see the woman in the cave as she gave birth. Diana's voice. She'd called his name, he was sure of it, until he felt the boy's cold fingers on his arm. He opened his eyes.

"Help me. I know I've done wrong, sir, touching your things. But please, help me."

The razor's open straight edge gleamed from the carpet, along with the wooden juggling balls. Remnants of a game that went dangerous. A trail of blood led from his dressing table to Jeff, Alice Lovell's lively boy. Ryder took his outstretched hand just as the boy fell, sprawled across his bed, unconscious.

The slash in his arm spurted red, soaking through the featherbed, the horsehair mattress beneath. Ryder's fingers responded to his mind's command. He pressed hard, harder, stopping the flow. Good.

There were people in the house, Ryder heard their voices downstairs. Some sort of meeting that his mother said he did not have to worry about. Their housekeeper's clever son was supposed to keep him company. Ryder remembered feeling sorry for the twelve-year old boy in his dull task of watching a grown man sleep.

Jeff had gotten into some deadly mischief. Think. The new town doctor was coming to his mother's meeting, wasn't he? His name? *Burns.* Ryder's right hand took up the bell on its first cast for it. Olivia Cole responded to the urgency of its ring: flush, beautiful, in her white entertaining gown, tied with a purple sash. So vibrant. Everything was so vibrant suddenly.

"Ryder—oh good God!"

"Accident. The boy is hurt. Downstairs. Dr. Burns?"

"Yes, he is here."

Ryder made his mouth work faster. "Ask him to come. With bag?"

"Yes. Yes, of course," she said, following his instructions the way Tom would have, swiftly, without question. Ryder looked down at his fingers, still holding the wound closed. There was a throbbing pulse at Jeff Lovell's neck. Not too late. Please, not too late, for the boy, this clever boy.

The doctor appeared, a big full-bearded man, bright-eyed, filling the doorway. Newly-trained, Ryder could tell, the way he looked frightened by the blood.

Patience. He'd been that way once himself, a lifetime ago.

"Young Jeff was juggling. Mixing balls with … my razor, it seems. Tied an artery ligature before?"

"Not, ah, as of yet, sir."

"I will t-tell it. Thread your needle."

"Thread?"

"In your bag?"

"Yes. Yes, of course. I have closed surface wounds, Dr. Cole. Many times."

"Similar. Mother. The blinds. At the window. Open?"

Her skirts flew by in a blur. The room brightened. Then came a fleeting glance of faces, over his mother's shoulder. One of the men, a factory foreman he remembered from before the war, held Alice Lovell's shoulders. *Don't look there*, Ryder admonished himself, at her face and its mother's terror, grief. The wound. Keep his focus on the wound.

Dr. Burns's hands were steady. He listened well, followed instructions. He was not as precise, as quick as Tom, but the deep slice was closing, the blood flow stopping. The boy's eyelids fluttered open.

Ryder motioned his mother forward, but Jeff's eyes found him first.

"Captain Cole."

"Yes."

"What am I doing in your bed, sir?"

"Recovering, I trust."

"You're talking much better now, sir. I understand every word."

"Good. Thank you. Most encouraging."

The boy's eyes began to take in the larger scene: Ryder's nightclothes splattered with blood, the doctor's opened bag, the gleam of the razor. His face distorted in fear.

"You did not cut my arm off, did you, sir?"

"No, Jeff."

"They say that's what you were good at, in the war."

"And they are right."

Mrs. Lovell gently cuffed her boy's ear. "Not that I'd allow you to complain if our Captain saw fit to, you ruffian. Look at the unholy havoc you have visited upon his fine bed!"

Ryder felt a lightness in his chest that bubbled upward and turned into something approaching laughter. His mother approached. "Mrs. Lovell and Dr. Burns might carry on from here, might they not, Captain Cole?"

"Yes, Mother," he slipped into the same formal, polite tone she was using.

"Good. I will have your mechanical chair brought." She cast a quick glance back at the silent sea of faces behind her before addressing him again. "Would you kindly dress and join us at the meeting, son?"

Dress? He did not even know where his clothes were. Why wasn't she bundling him back to his silent, dark seclusion? Why were her eyes glowing? Would she help him understand what her meeting was about? Could his mouth make words properly enough that none of them shamed her? Never mind. She needed him. His mother had been bearing so much for so long. And she needed him, not only to breathe, but to live.

* * *

Auburn, New York

There, better. The breeze took the edge off the latest wave of pain. Relief descended. In the space of time between the pains Tess felt she could chop wood, pump up gallons of water, then ride a horse into town, with rings on her fingers, bells on her toes. She heard her mother's voice finish the rhyme: *And she shall have music, wherever she goes.*

Tess would teach the rhyme to her son, that kicking rascal, coming soon. Would he grow to be as devastatingly handsome as Ryder? She supposed not, as he would have to have a little of her in him, too. But not too much. Another grip at her middle. So soon? *Breathe. Bear it. Breathe.* She closed her eyes. Glaring red and purple slashed behind her lids.

"Damnation, Ryder, what'd you get me into this time?" She ground it out, laughing as the words themselves took her over the crest of this wave. With renewed energy, she finished her task. There, done.

Tess closed the knife and placed it and the piece of the sassafras trunk into Ryder's coat pocket. The trees' shadows lengthened. Was it dusk already? So silent. Were the wedding guests still dancing? She couldn't hear the music any more. She was suddenly so thirsty. She'd be able walk on to the creek, she was sure. For water, like the other animals, at dusk.

* * *

Belle Haven, Ashokan-on-Hudson, New York

"With all respect, Captain Cole, please allow me to say we did not think much of you or that miserable band of tone-deaf musicians you led off to war. But more of our boys marched home than the regiments of the four counties around us. And your bunch saved many more of our sick

317

and wounded, and lent comfort to the dying. We are most pleased to have you home."

Not enough, Ryder thought. He should have kept all their sons and brothers safe. They should hate him. Hate him, like Tom's sister probably did, as she had not answered any of his letters written in that new, uneven scrawl that was his handwriting.

His mother applied gentle pressure at his shoulder, from where she stood behind him. The town elders waited for a gracious response, not the workings of his mind, peppered with despair. Ryder thought of the words one by one, then spoke them carefully, deliberately.

"Thank you for your assistance to my mother and the foundry." Another breath. "While I have been in service."

No more words. Do not require any more of me. That other place, one of trial and birth and new life had been tugging at Ryder throughout the meeting. He had said very little. Still, they'd leaned in to hear him make small suggestions: another room on the school, a hospital fund for the county's wounded veterans, with new doctors to practice the techniques Ryder had so brutally learned under fire. And they might build homes, for the patients who wanted to stay, and for foundry workers who were now making plows instead of guns, and fencing and gates for homes at higher elevations, clear of the smoke that had circled the town for as long as Ryder remembered. His house was on a hill above it, why not theirs? He wondered if there was enough money for all the suggestions they so readily agreed to. Had the foundry made so much profit off the war?

Well, that part of it was his mother's concern. Let the elders continue to be fooled by her demure pouring of tea and gracious deference. Ryder knew Olivia Cole better now. And loved her better than that overbearing, feckless son who had left her for a war.

Olivia Cole stepped out from the shadow of his chair. "My son has had a long, trying day. And he will desire to visit his patient before he takes his rest. May I see you gentlemen to your carriages?"

* * *

After the last handshake, all of them were finally gone. The house grew quiet, at last. Jeff Lovell slept peacefully in the music room. Ryder, returned to his own rooms, in his chair, hoisted up the wide, grand staircase by the strong arms of the factory foreman, the one who had eyes for Alice Lovell. She should marry him, if he was a good man, and loved her and Jeff.

Ryder sat in the stiff-backed mechanical chair. His room looked smaller in the fading light, dappled by the shadow of the maples in high autumn color outside his windows. So beautiful. He stared around the chamber, feeling an unnamed, unfathomable fear join his habitual loneliness. He did not know what to do with it. He shoved his shaking hands under the blanket across his lap, and sent the chatting, bustling servants away.

As the shadows were lengthening, Mrs. Lovell joined him. He covered the woman's hand. "Jeff is young. Strong. He will recover," Ryder managed to breathe out.

"Yes, sir. What's troubling you?"

He bit down on his lip, not daring to look at her. Mrs. Lovell glanced around the room, her eyes narrowing the way they did when she inspected for dust. "Maybe it's the scent of blood disturbing you, sir? Let me sprinkle some rosewater—"

"Lilacs," he blurted out.

"Captain?"

"Might you make it smell of lilacs, Mrs. Lovell?"

* * *

319

The sound of the old spiritual wafted down to the creekside.

Oh Mary don't you weep don't you moan
Oh Mary don't you weep don't you moan
Pharaoh's army got drownded,
Oh Mary don't you weep.

A strange song for a wedding celebration, so different from the dancing fiddle music they'd been playing earlier. But right for what Tess was doing now. She had survived the army, the war. She could survive now, she decided, long enough to bring forth the new life inside her.

"You are tryin' my patience, Mrs. Ellis!"

Tess lifted her head. "Mrs.—?"

Harriet Tubman sniffed. "Ain't surprised you forget your own name, for how long you stayed put at the wedding party!"

"I'm sorry. I lost track of—"

"You never lost track of nothin' caught itself in your sights, I suspect!" The crackling voice softened. "Well, you had your job to do, like we had ours."

"Sergeant Ellis asked me for fresh bark for his sassafras tea. I fetched it. It's here in my pocket."

"Don't fret on it. He got everything he needed. That be why we didn't come earlier to fetch you. Our Sergeant Ellis has slipped off to his Maker."

"Oh. Oh, no. I should have been there."

"Why he sent you off fetching for his tea, you think? He was holding himself together long enough to get that 'I do' out of you. And now you got more important things to do, he told us." Mrs. Tubman gave out a click of her tongue. "It be your turn now for some fussin' over, if'n you don't mind our company?"

Another wave of pain came, fast, hard. Tess felt the cool creek-dipped cloth at her brow. She opened her eyes to the faces of Yolanda and Artemis, smiling, on either side of her distended middle.

"I'm so glad to see you," she whispered to the three women.

Mrs. Tubman's voice charged with a pleasant richness as her hands probed. "I'd say you're sowing that gladness!"

"I am?" Tess sat up higher, "Howwww?" The word wouldn't end. It kept grinding through her throat, just as the feeling behind it, to bear down, was endless. And felt wonderful. Something burst, and the ground soaked below her feet.

Mrs. Tubman laughed. "Spread the quilt if you would, Artemis, so Mrs. Ellis's coming child don't cock a little head on the stony ground in coming out!"

"Head?"

"Right here 'twixt my hands. Now, you can grab hold of Yolanda if you'd like, Mrs. Ellis."

"Mrs. Tubman, would you please use my given name!"

"I will not."

"Why not?"

"I'm working for you, as your midwife. Wouldn't be respectful. Now, one more should get the rest of this baby into the world."

"One more what?"

"Push!"

"When?"

"When you have to."

"But howwwww?" Her body answered the question this time as Harriet Tubman's experienced hands waited.

"That's right, good," she encouraged as Tess felt something wet and long and pulsing slipping out of her along with all the breath she had left.

"Well now, here she is!" her midwife proclaimed in a voice brimming with quiet excitement.

"She?" Tess gasped out. "But I was planning on a boy!"

"Don't recall the good Lord leaving that matter up to you, Mrs. Ellis."

Tess heard small gurgles. A gasp. Then silence. Dread circled her heart. "What's wrong? Why can't I hear her? Where's my baby, Mrs. Tubman?"

"Hush now, she's a mite small. And it be cool out here. She ain't breathin' regular yet. We get her snug up close and feedin', maybe she perk up a bit. Girls?"

Yolanda and Artemis deftly worked the fasteners of Tess's bodice and shift open before Mrs. Tubman laid the blue tinged baby between her breasts. "This here's your mama, child. Come on now, find her. Root," Moses urged a new charge toward the promised land.

Tess looked down at the perfect head, swirled by Ryder's black hair. So still. A voice too high, too desperate, surely not hers, came out of her then. "I ain't mad about the kicks, or that you're a girl. You're all I got in this world. Don't die. Please," she heard herself say.

The baby seemed to recognize the voice. Her head turned, and Tess saw a nose, blinking eyes, and the mouth opening, working, pulling in the night air, pulling in her scent.

Mrs. Tubman gently led Tess's nipple toward the baby's mouth. She latched on, suckled.

"Oh. Oh my. Look!" Tess proclaimed.

Yolanda and Artemis smiled and nodded, while Mrs. Tubman draped a glowing white cotton blanket around her still blue-tinged bundle. Yolanda shook out Ryder's army coat and placed it over Tess's shoulders. The song wafted in from the distance again.

Pharaoh's army got drownded
Oh Mary, don't you weep

"She'll be all right, won't she, Ma'am?" Tess pleaded.

"Now, that's not for me to say. You just stay cozy and visit with her. You push out the afterbirth, that'd be a good thing to see."

Tess felt another urge to bear down, like an echo of the tremendous force that visited to get the baby out. She obeyed this one and felt a slithery release. She leaned over, kissed the top of her daughter's head, breathed in her new-ness.

"Afterbirth looks fine," her midwife reported. "And you be firming up well."

"And my baby?"

"Well, now, Mrs. Ellis, dear. This child come in early, and got her start in a prison."

"But I did better than most, and wasn't in long." She breathed in Ryder's scent from his coat. "And her papa, he kept giving me his own ration of food. Maybe he knew, maybe deep down inside he knew he was helping his child, you think? I know he's lonesome now, I can feel it some-times. But he can't mean to take her, can he?"

"Hush, now, that line of thinkin' does nobody good," Mrs. Tubman counseled as she drew her scissors close to the curling cord. At the snip, the baby reacted, nuzzling deeper. Harriet Tubman lifted the blanket, felt the pulse at the baby's neck, but made no comment.

"She's just quiet, a quiet little soul," Tess said.

Mrs. Tubman didn't answer, but looked toward her helpers. "Best fetch me a little bowl of the creek water, Yolanda."

"Why?" Tess asked.

"To baptize her."

"Now? Here?"

"You desire that comfort, don't you?"

"No! Don't desire anything but her!"

"Easy. Let me welcome her into the Shepherd's fold for myself, then, Tess. As a favor to your old friend here, and the Christian man your husband Sergeant Ellis was. Give me her name, so God knows her," she urged.

Tess felt tears welling, but ordered them back. "I only decided what to call a boy."

"Well, name her for yourself, then."

"No." She listened for the song again, wafting in on the night air. "For my mama, long gone, and his. Lucy. Lu-cy Olivia."

"Fine names," Mrs. Tubman approved, taking the small bowl from Yolanda's hands. "I baptize you Lucy Olivia in the name of our good Lord," she proclaimed, and sprinkled tiny drops on the baby's head.

She reacted, pulling off Tess's nipple with a soft grunt. Then she blinked indignantly and let out a howl. Tess gasped as she watched the blue cast of Lucy Olivia Ellis's skin replaced by a vibrant, rosy glow.

"Now that breathin' is plenty clear!" Harriet Tubman pronounced. "And, praise be, I believe we are seein' a miracle, now that this baby is a child of God."

Tess frowned through happy tears as Lucy continued her protest, her tiny fists pounding the soft flesh of her mother's breast. "Well. Sounds more that she don't much care for the life of a Christian woman thus far," she said.

* * *

Belle Haven, Ashokan-on-Hudson, New York

"Come, take your child, sir," Harriet Tubman urged again.

But that was not what she'd said to him in the cave, was it? Ryder reached out hands that did not shake, fine surgeon's hands. The baby was not a boy this time. A tiny girl with enormous eyes captured his soul.

Shots, in the prison yard, all aimed at him. The commander, slicing him open. Not that, go away. *Where was the baby?* Ryder bolted upright, blinking, seeing his mother in the lone candle's light. She took hold of his empty arms.

"Not my blood, this time," he breathed out. "Whose blood was it, all over me?"

"Jeff's, darling. It was Jeff's blood. All gone now. He is sleeping, remember? Recovering."

Ryder's eyes darted from the candle's light to the painting of his father's ship, to her. "This place. I am not—"

"No," she soothed, climbing onto the bed, pressing him against her heart, beating at a different pace than his. "You are not there. You are home."

"Mama?"

"Yes, I am here, Ryder. You are safe. In your room, your bed, see?"

"Dark."

"It is night, that's all. Not the other places, the dark places."

He felt the insistent pounding behind the ribcage of his chest obey hers, and slow down. "Where's Tom?" he whispered.

"When you are better you will find him. You must get well first, love."

His hands, eased of their desperation, gentled, released their grip on her shawl and the fine muslin of her dressing gown. Had he hurt her?

She took his jaw in her vanilla-scented hand. He wished she would go away before he wept. But his tears won the race.

"That's right," she encouraged, matter-of-factly, as if this were standard duty of mothers of grown sons. "Wash it away, the darkness."

"I'm sorry, Mother."

"I'm not. It feels so good to hold you in my arms again. Ryder, you have lost so much, but you are a resilient man, recovering at a ferocious pace now that you are home. This is bound to happen, from time to time. Especially after the day we have had." She glanced at Alice Lovell's bottle of lilac water on his bed table. "And you will find love again."

Ryder felt an obstruction in his throat and swallowed past it. "What if I make your choice? Will that be all right, Mother?"

He heard her catch of disappointment before she answered. "Yes, of course, my darling." She'd been made a widow at the age he was now. But she'd had him.

"You have been sitting here all night," he realized.

"Yes."

"Why?"

"Because I was afraid."

"You are not afraid. Of anything," he claimed, as he used to as a boy.

She pushed his hair back from his forehead as she'd do then. "Oh, I am afraid of a great many things. But this the most: outliving you. You have survived your wild years and a great civil war besides. Still, I had to sit here, because this is the night we lost your father."

"Is it?"

"Yes. Ryder, you are now the longest-lived of the men of three generations."

"And I suppose you want me to continue plaguing the women?"

"Not forever. But I think we could bear it for another hundred years or so."

Book 7

April 1866

Chapter Forty-five

Armstrong Hospital, Ashokan-on-Hudson, New York

Ryder crawled beneath the hospital cot and stretched out his hand. The frightened animal squawked a warning. Above him, two nurses argued. He lifted his head, too fast, hitting it against the bedframe.

"There! Allowing such foolishness has now caused Dr. Cole to injure himself—"

"Now, now," he said, easing himself out. "No harm done."

Working with strong-willed women in the hospitals of Illinois and Washington had taught Ryder to tread softly around them unless the circumstances were extreme. And these circumstances were more delicate than extreme. He sat back on his haunches and looked up into his young patient's face.

"Clarissa, what is your hen's name?" he asked the child.

"Ginger, sir."

"Does Ginger have a good appetite?"

"Oh yes! It's past her feeding time, I'm sure that's why she's not behaving."

"Ah. I am ill-tempered myself when yet to be fed."

He recovered the napkin from his pocket and opened its folds to reveal the cornbread leftovers of his breakfast. "Shall I try bringing her forth by laying a trail?"

"If you would, sir."

He crawled back under the cot and streamed the crumbs until they reached his hand. As the chicken whose name matched her coloring approached, he encouraged her with soft clicks of his tongue. She allowed him to lift her from her hiding spot. And she clucked contentedly as he transferred her to his patient's waiting arms.

"It was my idea to bring Ginger, Dr. Cole," Clarissa's brother said. They were a neighboring farm family of Davy Flanders. After witnessing the girl's scalding accident, he'd convinced them to come to the hospital that many still distrusted. "Please don't blame Mother, Dr. Cole," the boy pleaded, "or throw my sister out of your hospital. She's looking so much better!"

Ryder laid a hand on the boy's shoulder. "If Ginger is part of the cure, I must detain her."

"Detain?"

"Here. In our henhouse. With a health inspection first, of course. Do I have your permission?"

Both children's eyes widened, but they nodded in agreement. Ryder took the stethoscope he'd been using to count the steady beats of the girl's heart and turned it to the ample bosom of the chicken, listening. "Hmm. Quite sound. Now, Jacob," he addressed the boy, after a quick sideways glance to the children's pale-eyed mother. "Can she earn her corn? Is she laying?"

"Oh, sometimes three eggs a day, sir! Once she's calmed down, of course."

"Of course. Would you kindly show her out back? And fashion another nest in our hen house?"

"Be right pleased to, doctor! And she'll behave for 'Lissa, you have my word on it!"

"That suffices. Now. Any objections about Ginger's visits to this ward? Ladies?"

Ryder looked up, surprised to already have the attention of all the small patients, their visitors and the four attending matrons.

Only one of the nurses was still frowning. "Well," she huffed. "This is already more a barnyard than a proper hospital. I don't know why I stay on."

"The challenge of it, Miss Truscutt," Ryder suggested, "the challenge."

He gave Clarissa a slow wink behind the matron's stiff back. The small hands covered her mouth to stifle a giggle. The burns were healing nicely there, and their flexibility seemed almost normal.

"Send Ginger around for fare-thee-wells then, Jacob," Ryder instructed.

The boy and hen visited each bedside, where Ginger accepted a fond pat or stroke with only a few indignant ruffles of her feathers.

"This is most good of you, Dr. Cole," the children's mother finally spoke.

"Not at all. It will be very good of Ginger to tolerate the overflow of affection that will doubtless—" He forgot the end of his thought as he saw the boy slip past the three people filling the sick room's doorway. Their gray clothes made him recoil, backing into Clarissa's mother, widowed by the war.

"Doubtless—?" she repeated, urging him to finish his thought. Women were so patient with his slow speech. He blinked. To clear away those people, standing in the doorway. Ghosts. No, it was the slant of light, making them appear transparent. Not ghosts, not soldiers, not the execution yard, again. Only gray clothes, on strangers, not soldiers, he sent the message to his frantically beating heart, which was not listening. He sat on the child's bed.

"Dr. Cole. Are you well, sir?" Nurse Truscutt asked, concern banishing the last vestiges of displeasure from her voice. The scent of his mother, then. She had been part of the ghost trio? Yes. Closer, her dress was now blue, a pearly blue. His mother. Home. He was home.

"Breathe, Ryder," she commanded.

He remembered to, and felt better.

"It's past two o'clock. You neglected to take dinner again?"

"He's been sharing his breakfast remains with visiting chickens besides, Ma'am," Miss Truscutt informed on him.

Olivia Cole glided her fingers through his hair, sifting out two of Ginger's errant feathers. "How very exciting," she commented dryly. "May I take him out of your way for a few moments, matron?" she spoke over his head. Ryder hated when the women did that. He felt insignificant enough.

"Of course, Mrs. Cole."

His mother rested her cheek at his forehead, an intimate gesture that surprised him, here at the hospital. "Darling," she said, indicating the two tall gray figures still standing patiently in the doorway, "These people have come to see you."

They were a man and a woman, Ryder could see them more clearly now. Both pale and white-haired, like ghosts. Or angels. With a tapestry woven carpet bag at the woman's feet. He stood.

His mother took his arm for their walk into the hospital's small receiving room, where a steaming pot of tea was already waiting.

"You are Sarah," Ryder said slowly, as the couple's plain clothes and speech began to fit. "Sarah and Asa Waterford."

"Yes," the woman answered. "We would have come sooner, on the matter of thy recent correspondence, but—"

"Is she well?" he blurted out rudely, not deserving the woman's kind-eyed response.

"She is no longer with us, doctor."

"Please." He swallowed hard. "Tell me she lives."

"Sit. Drink your tea, Ryder," his mother said softly, but with steel in her tone. He obeyed.

"We share thy hope," Sarah Waterford said.

Both Quakers observed him closely, with lingering attention to the gray in his hair, his new mustache. Ryder took a deep breath, like when he used to jump from the ledge by the falls, trusting that the water was below. How to convince them? Talk, he demanded of his freezing brain. "Over the course of the war," he began, "Tess wrote to me of your kindness to her. And all the changes of the seasons. Your crops' rotations. The way the afternoon spring light streams through your parlor windows. I took great comfort in these things."

"That was her favorite spot to sit of an afternoon's visit, yes, that corner of the parlor," Asa contributed, a warm sympathy in his voice.

When were they going to tell him where Tom's sister went? What was this test they were making him endure? Ryder took in another breath. "My mother and I thank you for the refuge you gave her while her brother and I were in service."

Sarah Waterford's breathing went uneven, nervous, Ryder thought. "Thy mutual correspondence had a place of refuge through us," she said, as if correcting him, then took a deep breath of her own. "Doctor. We thought you were both lost to the war when that correspondence ended so abruptly. And when thy letters began again ... well, the handwriting upon them was different."

Yes. Not yet ready for surgery, or able to make proper Spencerian script.

"Then we heard of thy return, and thy recovering, and the new hospital. We determined to come, after the thaw, to see thee, to look into the reflections of the soul of the man our dear friend had followed into this terrible war. And then, lately, there arrived this…well, this complication."

"Complication?"

"Another letter. From Auburn, New York. Asking us to send the money we received regularly over the course of the war, for her safekeeping."

"Tom's pay?" Ryder tried to help.

"Yes." Brother patted his sister's hand. "Tom's pay," he repeated. "Our friend writes that she has need of it, in her new circumstances."

"Which are?"

"The letter is not specific. She says she is the woman who we knew, but now goes by the name 'Mrs. Ellis.'"

"Hence our visit, sir, to a commanding officer."

"And diligent correspondent," Sarah added. "It is not something we wished to leave to the post."

"We were hoping you might make the delivery for us," her brother said.

"We would not break our trust with her, Captain Cole." Sarah Waterford spoke with an unsteady voice, but eyes that penetrated his soul. "Not for the world."

"But it seems that thee is sent to us," Asa ventured, as he put the most recent, battered letter into Ryder's hands.

Ryder read its short message, in Tess's familiar, large block hand. It filled him with questions, like Mr. Poe's detective, contemplating the Murders at the Rue Morgue. Why had she gone away? When had she married? Did she blame him for Tom's death? Was Tom dead? Did she know any more than he and his mother had found, which was no trace of him in army rolls since he'd taken the surgeon's examination? Tom had come under the influence of Colonel Streight's spying network, and disappeared from the written record. He would find that man. He'd wring the truth out of him.

Ryder suddenly remembered Tom's desperate kiss, there, at his scarred forehead, right before the firing squad took their awful aim. No. That was a dangerous place. Go away from there.

Sarah Waterford now offered up a thick envelope, pulled from her carpetbag. Asa took one more look between him and the *carte de visite* image lying on top. Of course. Tom had sent their photographic portrait to his sister. That's why her Quaker friends had been looking at him so carefully. Matching him with the *carte de visite's* image. Had the war rendered him that much different?

"This is a considerable sum of money," Sarah said quietly. "May we leave it in thy care, Captain?"

The envelope was heavy and smelled of gunpowder. Ryder struggled to make his hands move, take it. Is not this the possibility of connection that he had wanted so desperately?

"I am honored by your trust."

"Thy work here has confirmed our friend's good opinion of thee, Captain."

"But," Ryder whispered, looking between the couple and his mother and feeling, suddenly, not up to the task they had assigned to him, "How will I know if this Auburn woman is she?"

The Waterfords smiled together. "Thee will know," Sarah assured him.

Chapter Forty-six

The Seward House, Auburn, New York

Ryder paced the length and width of the fine oriental carpet, trying to rid himself of the anger that was draining him. Anger at his mother, for releasing him onto the train with her encouragement, then telegraphing ahead to the Seward household in Auburn. He was sure of it. How else had Mrs. Seward herself met him at the railroad station, with a servant who jumped to relieve him of his small bag?

His hostess had insisted that he take his noon meal with her, and then rest in her guest chambers on the first floor. He looked around its confines. His rooms, indeed the entire house brimmed full of flowers, white exotic flowers, orchids, from her greenhouse, set out everywhere in large gleaming porcelain vases.

Mrs. Seward had stood among her blooms, her eyes misting, talking about him staying longer and going on to visit the falls at Niagara. He must go there next, it was not far, a few more stops on the train. It would do him a world of good. Did she not understand he was on a duty-bound mission, not a pleasure-seeking excursion? Patience, Ryder reminded himself. The woman was the daughter-in-law of a dear friend of his mother. And that lady became as much a casualty of the war as any fallen soldier. Frances Seward's husband and three of her children were injured by the same conspirators who had killed President Lincoln. His mother's friend and her daughter Fanny had died soon after, some said of the shock of that murderous night that Ryder had dreamed of horses screaming.

Ryder shook himself to be rid of the involuntary chill. Nothing more, just a chill, He forced himself to consider the possibility that it was not pity in Janet Seward's eyes, but joy, like his mother's, that he was alive, even in a reduced condition.

Well, his mother would not win this time, he decided. He would not wait, even for the horse promised to him for the last part of his journey, if he'd only rest overnight. He had to meet with Mrs. Ellis. Not tomorrow. Now. It was still light. He had his walking stick, if his weaker side started to betray him. He took it up from the bed and slipped away when the house went quiet, setting off toward Harriet Tubman's house on his own.

But it proved further down South Street than he had thought, out where the sidewalks disappeared and the cobblestone turned into packed down dirt. Ryder stopped, leaned his back against a roadside oak. Why did he not realize that his destination was beyond a short walk? Mrs. Tubman, for all her fame, was still a Negress, and her convalescent home was for soldiers of her own race. It was carefully set aside from the white population, even in this enlightened part of his state. The canals had brought new ideas as well as goods. The railroads continued to do the same. But Ryder did not see a single Negro on the town's streets.

What had the war been for, if this was to continue, this separation of his countrymen? Ryder remembered again the new-born child Mrs. Tubman had allowed him to hold, back when his hands were still those of a doctor. That baby was not less beautiful because of his race.

Both Ryder's legs ached, now, not just his weaker side. And he was tired, that's why this mind's retreat into the past, into loathsome remnants of self-pity. And the sun was going down as a swirling mist shrouded the road. Damnation. Could he find his way back? He didn't care. He didn't care about anything, suddenly, except his need to rest, and his thirst.

Ryder heard the sound of flowing water. He left the road, awkward, stumbling as he used his hated walking stick on the uneven ground. He traveled a trodden woodland path, he realized, made by animals seeking what he was seeking: water.

When he reached the creek, he cast aside the stick and knelt, drinking from its flow. The mist was higher. He sat back on his heels, his head spinning. He hadn't eaten enough, that's all. To pique Mrs. Seward and her hovering attention. His own stubborn petulance was now doing worse damage, igniting fear of a seizure here, where he was alone.

When was he going to learn to stop fighting the women?

Breathe. Even, deep, Ryder instructed himself. He soaked his handkerchief, pressed it against his forehead. There. This was a good place, a place of life. He would be all right. Those doting women would not win, not this time. He would be able to reach his destination before dark, if he rested here. If the mist did not become a fog.

Mrs. Tubman would not turn him away, once he found her. They were friends, were they not? Or did she only tolerate him when they were fellow lawbreakers who hid runaways together, and in their miraculous war circumstances?

So much was different now, in peacetime. The whole world was going on, without him. Would even the mighty Harriet Tubman look at him the way some did, as a painful reminder of all the losses? Would the other woman, the one Ryder had come three hundred miles to see, do the same?

That woman, Mrs. Ellis. Would Tom's fearless sister hate him for not bringing her brother back? Ryder closed his eyes, chewed on the spearmint leaves Mrs. Seward had given him after their noon dinner. Women. Always feeding him, always stuffing remnants of meals in his pockets.

Ryder heard small scurrying, shifting sounds. He was not alone. It was dusk, the time the animals drank at this place. Was his scent keeping them hidden, waiting for their turn at the creek? He should move on. But perhaps, if he was very still, if the wind was right, he might catch sight of a muskrat, a beaver, even a snake. Anything alive. To inspire him. His mother was right, again. He was not ready. Not for this meeting.

Tom's sister had a different name. She had married. Why should she not? She was Tom's twin, and so how old now? Twenty-five or six. And Tom was not there to guide her, the shy woman with the bold handwriting. Her words were like Diana's arms around him, strong, comforting, so he could serve others. Ryder realized he was converging Diana and Tess. Tom stood between them, holding each of their hands. The three combined. His throat constricted. Stop. Stop it. West. He could leave. Leave now. Find the train. Use what he carried: Tom's money, to disappear into the West before his mother knew that she'd saved his life only to watch his descent into madness.

Ryder felt as helpless as the day the panther had him down beneath Moutamin's dying protection: wounded, his strength exhausted. That was on a day like this, a place like this, though at dawn, not dusk. And in April, he realized, closing his eyes, feeling the new spring's sun warming his lids, cutting through the mist. Suddenly he heard a sound he had heard then.

The click of a rifle bolt.

He turned. The dying sun was at her back, placing a burnished halo around the figure: her kilted up skirts, her strong arms, the hair escaping its bounds. The years had made her more beautiful. Above her homespun brown skirt, she was wearing his army coat.

And she was pointing her rifle at him.

Chapter Forty-seven

Slowly, in the charged silence, she raised her deadly-aimed rifle to the sky, then replaced the bolt.

Ryder thought she might disappear into the swirling mist then, but she made a very earth-bound grunt of displeasure before barreling down on him. "Mister, I near to shot you, hunkered like that by the water. What are you doing here?" she demanded.

Impossible. Stop looking at her. This woman, who handled her firearm like Tom. She was his madness, in human form. Perhaps if he did not look at her, he could find his voice, Ryder thought. He bowed his head, pulled a hand through his hair. *Think. Please, God, help me think.* But his mind had frozen.

"Well? Speak up!"

Pull out words. Any words. "I do not talk, so much. Any more," he said quietly. There. A sentence. Inane. But speech.

He felt the vibrant life heat of her hand, hovering. He caught the scent of the iron of her firearm masking another, beneath it. Lilacs. No, Ryder told his racing heart, not lilacs. He kept his head down, buried between his shoulders. Not possible. He did not realize he was shaking until she touched his shoulder.

"Easy, now, soldier. You've come to the right place," she said, her voice soft and low, full of compassion. And so familiar. "But I don't know how I'm going to fetch home supper, being we scattered all the game. But you're welcome with us, sir. You'll be safe here. As long as you don't mind being around black folk."

Sir. Said with the same tone Tom gave the word. Ryder's peripheral vision caught the cock of her head.

"Been wandering since the war's end, have you?" she asked.

His head dropped lower. *This is real. She is real. Look at her.* She offered her hand. He did not take it.

"I'm Tess," she said.

"I know."

"Do you, now?" Amusement in her voice. And kindness. It will not last. She will hate me soon, Ryder thought.

"Well, then you know I'm not always aiming to shoot patients, but only their food." He heard her place the rifle on the ground. "Come, now. Won't you take my hand?"

Ryder looked down at his own hand, drawn into a tight fist, pressing against his sternum. It would not open. He still could not find the courage to look at her. Make this real. Make her real. The money, there, in the envelope against his chest, inside his vest, his coat. That might do it. He drew in a long breath.

"I have brought what you requested. From the Waterfords."

"Oh? Well, now I'm triple glad I didn't shoot you, if you brought my pay. We need it, to keep the place running, you understand?"

Ryder nodded, watching his clenched hand finally open. She was so close. His fingers, of their own will, brushed across a brass button.

"That's my coat," he said.

He heard a sharp intake of breath. "Not yours," she growled. "This here's my coat, you hear me? Mine!"

"Of course," he agreed quickly, trying to staunch the fury in a voice that had lost its richness, its compassion.

There. She was beginning to realize who he was. She was beginning to hate him. Ryder had thought he could bear this. He was wrong.

"Forgive me, Theresa. Tess. Please, forgive me," he said.

"What for?"

"For not keeping him safe."

He heard her angry, labored breathing stop, suddenly. Then her fingers descended into his hair, closing around the strands close to his scalp, gripping tight, then yanking his head back so that he was forced to look up into her eyes. Ryder saw slow, dawning recognition. He waited for the hatred. He saw tears instead. Her other hand formed a fist against that beautiful hip's curve.

"Ryder Cole, are you still trying to take charge of everything on God's green earth?" Tom's voice, in a familiar tone of vexation, coming out of this woman. She fell to her knees beside him. Tears ran down her cheeks now.

Her shaking fingers released, then stroked his aching scalp as she spoke. "Ryder. We lost you, at the prison. Stockton saw it. He saw it!"

"They missed my heart."

"I know. But he said the commander finished you off with his knife."

"No. He sliced into an animal bladder, full of blood. Saved me. His idea. Wish he had let me in on it. Then I was in a cellar, for a long time. Something happened, in my head. A stroke. Left over, I think, from the time, after Wilderness. How do you know everything? Did Tom—?"

"I remember." Her fingers traced his features in long, strong strokes, only softening around the old white scars the panther had made, and the new mustache. Stroking his face, the way Diana used to, in the dark. "Ryder," she laughed out his name, "it's you. It's really you."

Ryder smelled salt on her cheeks, her neck. He felt a powerful surge of physical desire in response to her touch, her laughter. He wanted to taste her tears. He continued to speak, instead.

"After Grant took Petersburg, I was traded. Went home to die. But my mother would not allow it."

"Neither would you."

Her voice was now distant, otherworldly. But Ryder wanted to hear more of it. He said whatever nonsense came into his head, just to coax more words out of her, to keep those strong, healing fingers gliding along his scalp. "My hands are coming back. I will be useful again someday, maybe. We have a hospital now, in Ashokan."

"That's good." Wonder, not hate, in her fathoms-dark eyes. Wonder, unless it was a trick of the fading light. Then that peculiar laughter, through tears again. "Oh, Ryder, you got to be real. Ghosts don't look so blamed pitiful, or smell of spearmint, do they?"

"You know. You know everything. Who are you?" he asked.

Wrong. He lost her sifting fingers through his hair. And that beautiful mouth hardened as she stood, stepped back, grabbing her rifle from the ground. He watched her knuckles whiten around the barrel.

"Now listen to me. You rid yourself of that dreamy look, hear? I'm just plain Tess. Tom and Diana, they live here, inside me. But Ryder, you can't have me anymore, not without the other two. I'm done with it, you understand? Done with splitting myself up for you!"

This was worse than her hatred, Ryder despaired. She had caught his madness.

"All right," he said, feeling sick.

Now she looked like she might haul back and whack him with that rifle. Something distracted her. A red bundle, hanging in the low branches of a young maple. She'd been protecting this when she'd taken aim at him, Ryder realized. He heard small sounds from the bundle: faint, needful. A stain seeped through her bodice. Milk flowing. She released her weapon with a grunt.

"She's hungry."

"Who?" he asked, too softly, or she chose to ignore him as she retrieved the red calico sling from the branch. Ryder saw small stretching limbs emerge from the red, responding to her clucking sounds. She sat on the sloping surface of the rock and unfastened her bodice at the waist, There appeared a flurry of soft cotton. She lifted the little white capped head into its depths and had the baby suckling before a real cry had emanated. Ryder saw a small foot mold itself to her hip, then settle. The baby helped her breathe easier, it seemed. Ryder drank in the sight of the two of them.

Tom's sister had married. *You knew this. You already knew this. Give her the money. Get out.* He stood, approached them.

"Yours?" he whispered.

"Mine."

"And, your husband—"

"He was a patient here at Mrs. Tubman's, looking to do some good for us before he died, don't you go bad-mouthing him."

Ryder blinked slowly. "I would not think of it, Mrs. Ellis." Pull away. Pull out of the circle they made, the three of them. But her iron grip took hold of his hand.

"My name's Tess, Ryder Cole. Only ever Tess!"

The baby began to sputter. Tess broke the suction with her finger and sat the child upright. About six months old. Round everywhere. Radiant. *Do not look.*

"See what you done?" Tess accused him. "She's got a bubble now, from my aggravation with you!"

She. Yes. A girl. "I—fail to understand—"

"Well, you got that much right!"

She rested the fussing baby's middle across the palm of her hand and used the other hand to pat her back. The child responded with a chortle, then a belch, then a curious look at him. *Oh God.* The eyes, the color of roasted chestnuts at Christmas. Like her mother's. Look away. He stepped back.

"Ryder, get over here, she won't bite!"

His fingers ached for the feel of that soft newness. "She's beautiful," he whispered.

"Well of course she is, being yours."

He took in a startled breath. The baby responded, laughing, as if he were playing a game.

"How?" he asked.

Tess frowned. "Now, you know the answer to that." Warmth from her eyes tempered her annoyance, he thought.

"That night, in prison," he said, slowly. "It was not a dream."

"No. Not a dream. Didn't I tell you then? I never lied to you about important things, Ryder. Give me that much."

He came forward, took up her short brown braid in one hand, the curve of her face in the other. He inhaled deeply.

"Lilacs. Diana?" he whispered.

She nodded into the palm of his hand, as she'd done countless times over the course of their years together. He leaned over, kissed her softly, before he spoke the madness that was no longer madness.

"Tom. Tess. Diana."

She nodded, clucking softly again, to the child. Soft sounds, like she'd made for him, after his nightmares. Sounds of love, acceptance, of the way he saw her, or did not see her.

"Then… I am not alone?"

She pulled him down to sit beside them. "Not nearly. And we got us a young one, besides. Oh Ryder, ain't she grand?"

She faced the baby out on her lap, between them. "This here's your papa, Lucy. She's Lucy Olivia. I named her for my mama and yours. Was that all right by you?"

Ryder shook his head, astounded by this woman, by the lively, miniature being in her lap. He felt every bit as pitiful as she called him, beside their beauty.

She granted him a rueful smile. "Well, then. Looks like your mama's doing a right fine job of patching you together again," she changed her initial assessment.

Slowly, he offered his finger. Lucy grasped it. An involuntary sound erupted from him at the contact. A sound he had not made in years, it seemed. Laughter. He caught their daughter's scent, followed it to the sweet spot between her ear and neck. When his nose touched her skin, Lucy giggled. He felt himself falling into deep love.

"Take her, darlin'," Tess urged. "She's missed you something awful, too."

"Too," he repeated.

"Well, sure."

She placed the baby in his arms. "I can do this," he said, quietly determined. "I can hold her, can I not? She is small."

"She'll get bigger."

"I will get stronger."

"I guess you'd better, Papa."

He raised his head. "This is real," he said slowly. "Not madness. Real."

"Oh, yes," Tess assured him.

He glanced over at his forgotten walking cane. "Tess? I am not the man I was."

She leaned close enough for him to catch her milk scent. "Neither am I," she said softly.

He felt his smile widen, then turn into another laugh. Full of release, full of pure joy.

Lucy Olivia Ellis pulled the chain at his vest pocket, then yanked harder when she discovered her treasure reluctant to appear. He lifted the watch out, just as he remembered his father doing for his small hands. He placed the gold case in his palm, tilting it to catch the dying rays of the sun coming through the evening mist. Then he popped the latch.

Lucy's eyes almost disappeared into merry creases. The small hands clapped together. She was the most clever child in all the world, Ryder decided. He swooped past her to kiss her mother. Tess returned the kiss full bore. Her milk spurted between them, seeping through the weave of his vest. Had he done that? He pulled back suddenly, breathless, from the dew-eyed woman and her chortling baby, feeling thoroughly intoxicated. He closed his watch and spun it before Lucy's delighted eyes.

"I had.. something beyond brotherly affection for Tom. It plagued me, because I had always been a woman's man. I could not—do you remember? At Madame Lanier's? I could not feel desire, accomplish fulfillment, except with Diana, and then only always in the dark, hidden. Was it because… Tess, was I in love?"

"I made it so complicated for you. I'm sorry, Ryder."

"I did love a man. The man in you. This remains complicated. And interesting."

"Interesting?" She crossed her eyes. "A unique bond?" Her face twisted more sour still. "Extraordinary?"

"Yes. In fact, I should like to study it forever, Lieutenant, if—"

"No rank!" she protested, though her eyes were not convincing him of her displeasure. "What did I say to you? Only Tess! Only—"

Ryder brought forth the thick white envelope as their daughter began gnawing on his watch's chain.. "You desire your pay without admitting your rank?"

"I have earned my pay, as well you know it, Ryder Cole!"

He recaptured her waist before she could finish berating him. "You passed the Assistant Surgeon's examination, even if you do not know much about the reign of Henry II. Your certificate is in the envelope too."

He kissed her again. Soundly. Marking her. He lifted Lucy higher. The baby's strong legs sought their balance on his thigh. She patted his cheek. Was there ever a child as wonderful as this one? Her mother's smile widened.

So did his. Ryder was not sure he could hold so much happiness. "You will keep those skills sharp beside me at the hospital won't you, Tess?"

Her ripe mouth opened. Ryder snared it, wishing for her in uniform again, with fewer layers between them.

Then came a ruckus that sounded like an advancing army: birds scattering from trees, branches breaking underfoot.

"Enough of that," the stern voice demanded.

They turned to see Mrs. Tubman, leading a portly, out-of-breath preacher. Behind them, two young women hastily wove haloes of spring wildflowers while walking beside the servant who had taken his bag at the train station. He offered a few of Mrs. Seward's hothouse orchids to their creations—one small, one larger. And behind them, walking arm-in-arm with Olivia Cole, was Brigadier General William Seward Jr.

"This was all supposed to take place tomorrow, you baneful man!" proclaimed the last in the procession, Mrs. Seward, her small daughter and son in white satin dresses, toddling along at her skirts.

"Never mind," Olivia Cole said, laughing, her clothes dusty from the road and railway. "I have grown used to my son's surprises." She held out both hands to Tess. "But few prove as miraculous as this one."

Ryder watched the three women he loved best in the world stare at each other in wonder.

"Say you will marry him, Tess," Olivia urged.

"Mother," he summoned, "I had not yet gotten to ask—"

Olivia Cole's eyebrow shot up as she granted him only an arch view of her profile. "And I'm supposed to wait how much longer for that?" she demanded.

Harriet Tubman took up his walking stick and slashed it against the rock. Ryder fully expected water to pour forth as it had for the other Moses. She opened her mighty voice in the silence. "You all are in my neck of the woods at present!"

Everyone, everything, stopped.

"Now," she lifted the baby from Ryder's arms. "Lucy, you get yourself acquainted with your grandmother, child," she said, facilitating the transfer.

Then she returned to Ryder's side. "Your mama's right, Captain. You two can catch up plenty once Reverend Zenon makes you legal wed. I got me a respectable reputation to maintain in these parts. Yolanda, Artemis" she summoned, "plant them flowery crowns on Mrs. Ellis and Lucy. And bring me Mrs. Ellis's shotgun if you would, Yolanda. Don't want the good doctor sayin' it was our Tess held it on him in future tellings of this day."

"Mrs. Tubman, I would never—" Ryder began to protest. But she silenced him with a raise of her mighty hand. "Get a good clear look at who's now holding the weapon, sir," she proclaimed. "You see the heft of this arm? This here's the who you'll answer to if you don't do right by your womenfolk before that sun goes down."

Ryder turned to Tess then, wreathed in yellow hawkweed, white orchids and purple lilacs. One of her hands held his mother's. The other's fingers reached either for her flower-wreathed baby or her rifle, he could not tell which.

Tess rocked back suddenly, this woman who had been his friend, his lover and his balance for years. Ryder realized that he did not know what she would do. He would probably never know, one day to the next, were they to live together into the next century. But he liked the idea of it so much he prayed that, for whatever reason, she would choose him, there in that tottering moment of holy possibility.

She righted herself, threw her shoulders back as if advancing into battle, and took his outstretched hand.

The End

More by Eileen Charbonneau from BWL Publishing, Inc.

The Code Talker Chronicles
Book 1: I'll Be Seeing You
Book2: Watch Over Me

About the Author

Eileen Charbonneau is the author of the multiple award-winning Code Talker Chronicles series as well as historical novels for adults and young people. Her stories explore America through eyes seldom put front and center: her immigrants, her native peoples, her women. Eileen's books have been praised by Kirkus, Library Journal, Publishers Weekly, Booklist, The Washington Post, Boston Globe and many others, so she might be on to something. She runs a small bed and breakfast inn with her husband in the brave little state of Vermont, where the world appears on their doorstep to see the leaves go glorious every autumn. Eileen is addicted to maple creemies, period dramas and American roots music.

Seven Aprils is inspired by the lives of all the women who served in secret during the American Civil War. One was Sarah Edmonds. She first disguised herself as a man after running away from home to avoid an arranged marriage. As Franklin Thompson, she served in the Second

Michigan Volunteer Infantry as a male nurse. Later in the war, Edmonds/Thompson became a Union spy, who went disguised in both male and female personas behind enemy lines.

Many fellow storytellers and readers and fine editors at Scholastic, Macmillan, Kensington, Timeless Treasures, New Street Communications, and BWL had a hand in crafting this novel and my writing life as a writer over the years. I am profoundly grateful to them for their help over many drafts. Among them are Judith Pittman, Janet Lane Waters, Deborah Barnhart, Yolanda Sly, Eileen O'Finlan, Liz Matis, Sunny Hogg, Ed Renahan, Claire Ruane, Mary Bloxsom, Robert Crooke, Jenna Kernan, Gianna Simonne, Kathy Attalla, Nina Shengold, Juilene Osborne-McKnight, Mark Schoen, Liz Armstrong, Natalia Aponte, Victoria Lea, Susan Wallach, Charlie Rineheimer, Mitzi Flyte, Nancy Bell, Andrea Peterson, Jane Seiver, Tim Bentler-Jungr, Jennifer Probst, Susan King, Janet Evanovich, Cindy Skaggs, Mariah Stewart, Chér Coen, Judy Fitzwater, Nicole Quinn, Sarah Johnson, Minette Gunther, Andrea Sadler, Yvonne Pinney, Rosemary Morris, Bill Lockwood, Kathleen Gilles Seidel, Jonathan Kruk, Stephanie Cowell, Kathryn Anderson, Denise McInerney, Cindi Myers, Robyn Amos Pope, Laurie Treacy, Dennis Yerry, Anita Gordon, K.I. Going, Evan Pritchard, Joe Bruchac, Joanna Withey, Mary Lenaburg, Maureen Morrison, Jo-Ann Power, Pamela Manché Pearce, Dee Oliler, Wanda Shapiro, Pam Palmer, Eileen Nauman.

I have a special love and appreciation for local booksellers and libraries and all they do for authors and readers. We have great ones in Célina and crew at the Rockingham Public Library and Pat, Alan and Myles at Village Square Booksellers here in Bellows Falls, Vermont.

In memory of my sisters Marie and Kate, my brother Dave, and my dear little brother bookseller Scott Meyer, all gone too soon and too good for this world.

With grateful thanks for their love and patience to my beautiful and forever dear children, daughters Abigail and Marya and sons Lawrence and Teddy. And the man who made our family possible, Edward. As I finished this book Marya and her Brendan are adding another generation to our family. Welcome to the world, darling Desmond Baptiste.